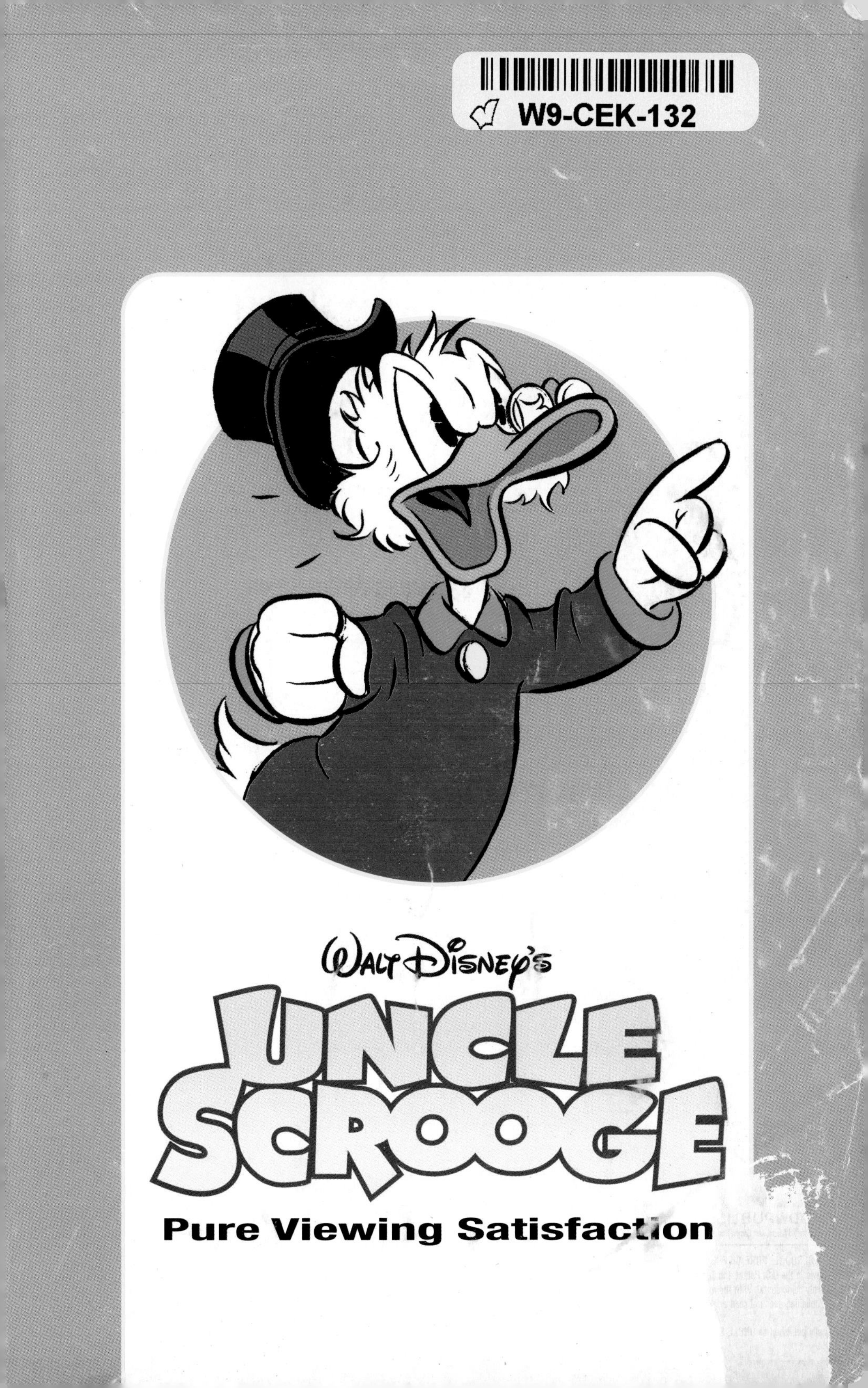

Walt Disney's

Uncle Scrooge

Pure Viewing Satisfaction

VWORN
001

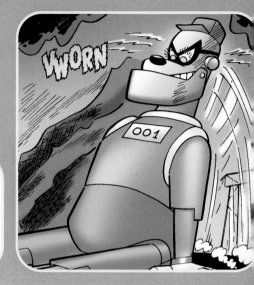

Gigabeagle: King of the Robot Robbers

Writer: Rodolfo Cimino
Artist: Romano Scarpa
Inker: Giorgio Cavazzano
Colorist: Digikore Studios
Translation & Dialogue: Jonathan H. Gray

Pure Viewing Satisfaction

Writer: Alberto Savini
Artist: Andrea Freccero
Colorist: Disney Italia with David Gerstein
Translation & Dialogue: David Gerstein

Stinker, Tailor, Scrooge and Sly

Writers: Romano Scarpa & Luca Boschi
Artist: Romano Scarpa
Inker: Sandro Del Conte
Colorist: Disney Italia with Digikore Studios
Translation: David Gerstein
Dialogue: Joe Torcivia

HANDS UP! THIS IS ROBBERY, GOODNIKS!

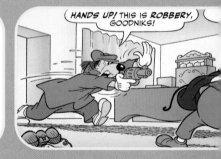

Special thanks to Curt Baker, Julie Dorris, Manny Mederos, Beatrice Osman, Roberto Santillo, Camilla Vedove, Stefano Ambrosio, Carlotta Quattrocolo, and Thomas Jensen for their invaluable assistance.

ISBN: 978-1-63140-388-0

18 17 16 15 1 2 3 4

IDW®
www.IDWPUBLISHING.com
IDW founded by Ted Adams, Alex Garner, Kris Oprisko, and Robbie Robbins

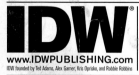

Ted Adams, CEO & Publisher
Greg Goldstein, President & COO
Robbie Robbins, EVP/Sr. Graphic Artist
Chris Ryall, Chief Creative Officer/Editor-in-Chief
Matthew Ruzicka, CPA, Chief Financial Officer
Alan Payne, VP of Sales
Dirk Wood, VP of Marketing
Lorelei Bunjes, VP of Digital Services
Jeff Webber, VP of Digital Publishing & Business Development

Facebook: **facebook.com/idwpublishing**
Twitter: **@idwpublishing**
YouTube: **youtube.com/idwpublishing**
Tumblr: **tumblr.idwpublishing.com**
Instagram: **instagram.com/idwpublishing**

Originally published as UNCLE SCROOGE issues #1–3 (Legacy #405–407).

Shiver Me Timbers

Writer: Jan Kruse
Artist: Bas Heymans
Colorist: Sanoma with Tom B. Long
Translation & Dialogue: Jonathan H. Gray

Yo!

Writer: Alberto Savini
Artist: Andrea Freccero
Colorist: Disney Italia with David Gerstein
Translation & Dialogue: David Gerstein

Meteor Rights

Writers: Frank Jonker & Paul Hoogma
Artist: Maximino Tortajada Aguilar
Inker: Comicup Studio
Colorist: Sanoma with Tom B. Long
Translation: David Gerstein
Dialogue: Joe Torcivia

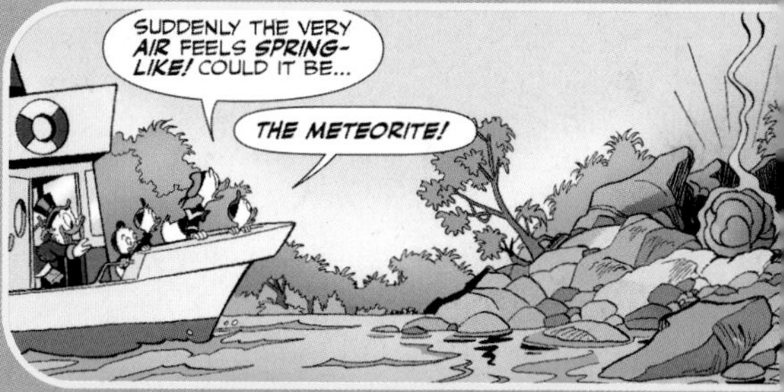
SUDDENLY THE VERY AIR FEELS SPRING-LIKE! COULD IT BE...
THE METEORITE!

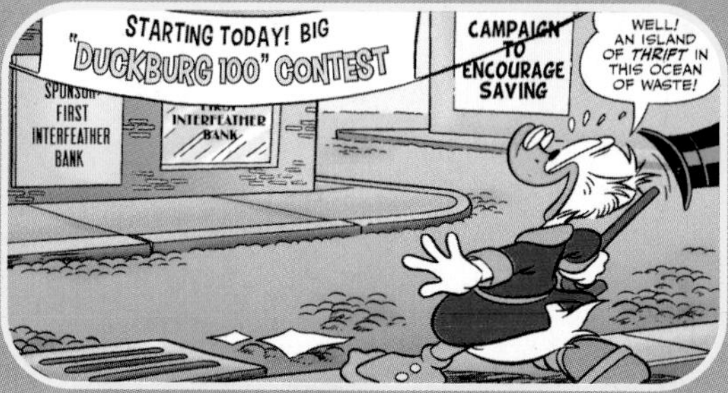
STARTING TODAY! BIG "DUCKBURG 100" CONTEST
CAMPAIGN TO ENCOURAGE SAVING
WELL! AN ISLAND OF THRIFT IN THIS OCEAN OF WASTE!
FIRST INTERFEATHER BANK
INTERFEATHER BANK

The Duckburg 100

Writer & Artist: Romano Scarpa
Inker: Rodolfo Cimino
Colorist: Disney Italia with Digikore Studios
Translation: David Gerstein
Dialogue: Joe Torcivia

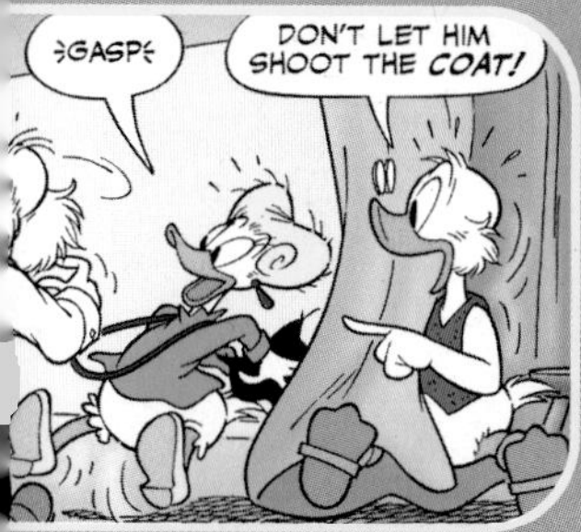
GASP
DON'T LET HIM SHOOT THE COAT!

Donald's Gabby Guest

Artist: Tony Strobl
Colorist: Digikore Studios
Translation & Dialogue: Thad Komorowski

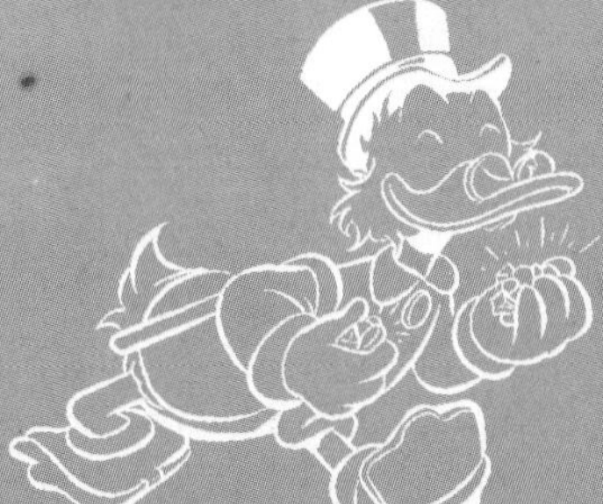

Letterer: Tom B. Long
Series Editor: Sarah Gaydos
Archival Editor: David Gerstein

Cover Artist: Derek Charm
Collection Editors: Justin Eisinger & Alonzo Simon
Collection Designer: Clyde Grapa

Disney Comics

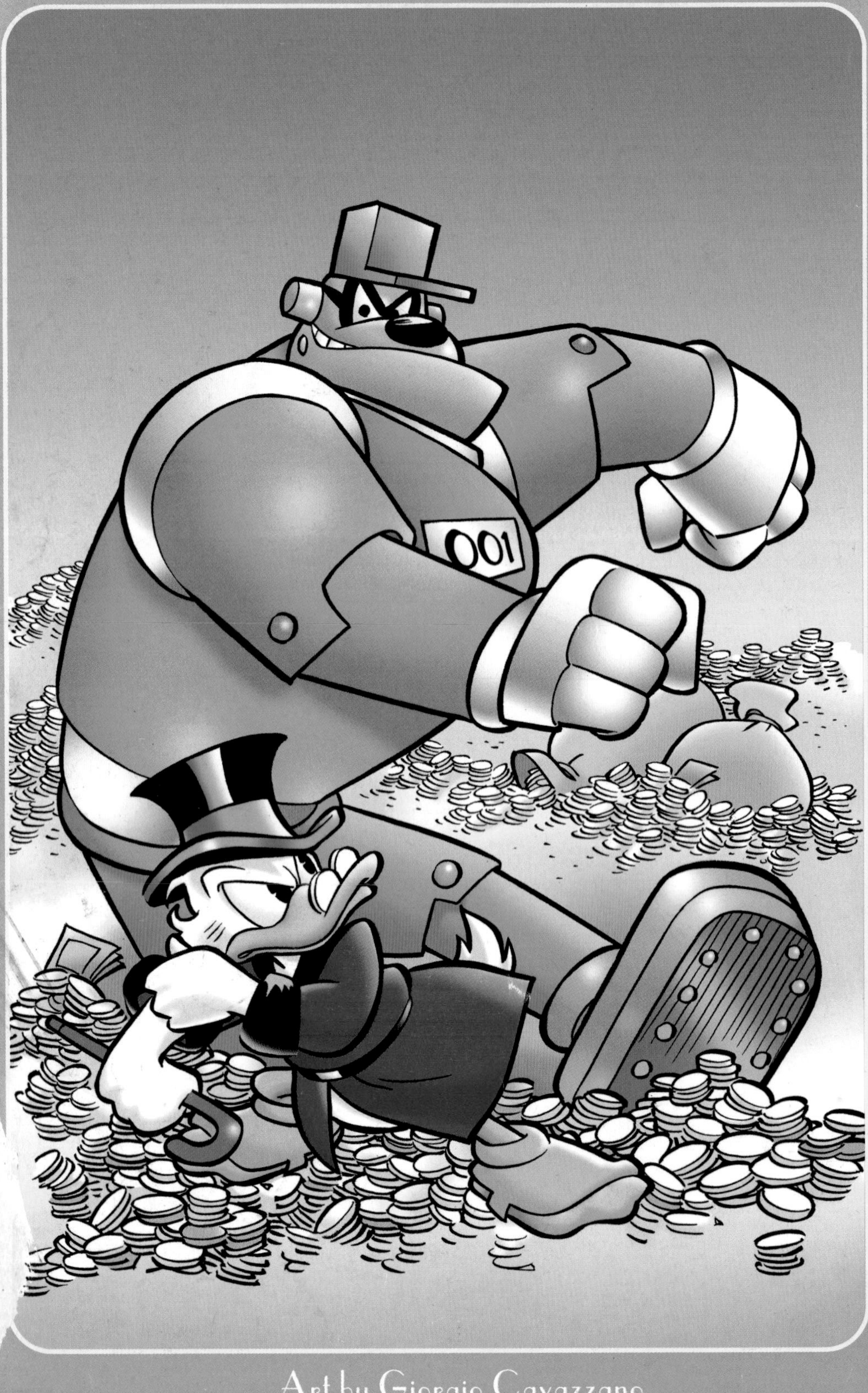
001

Art by Giorgio Cavazzano

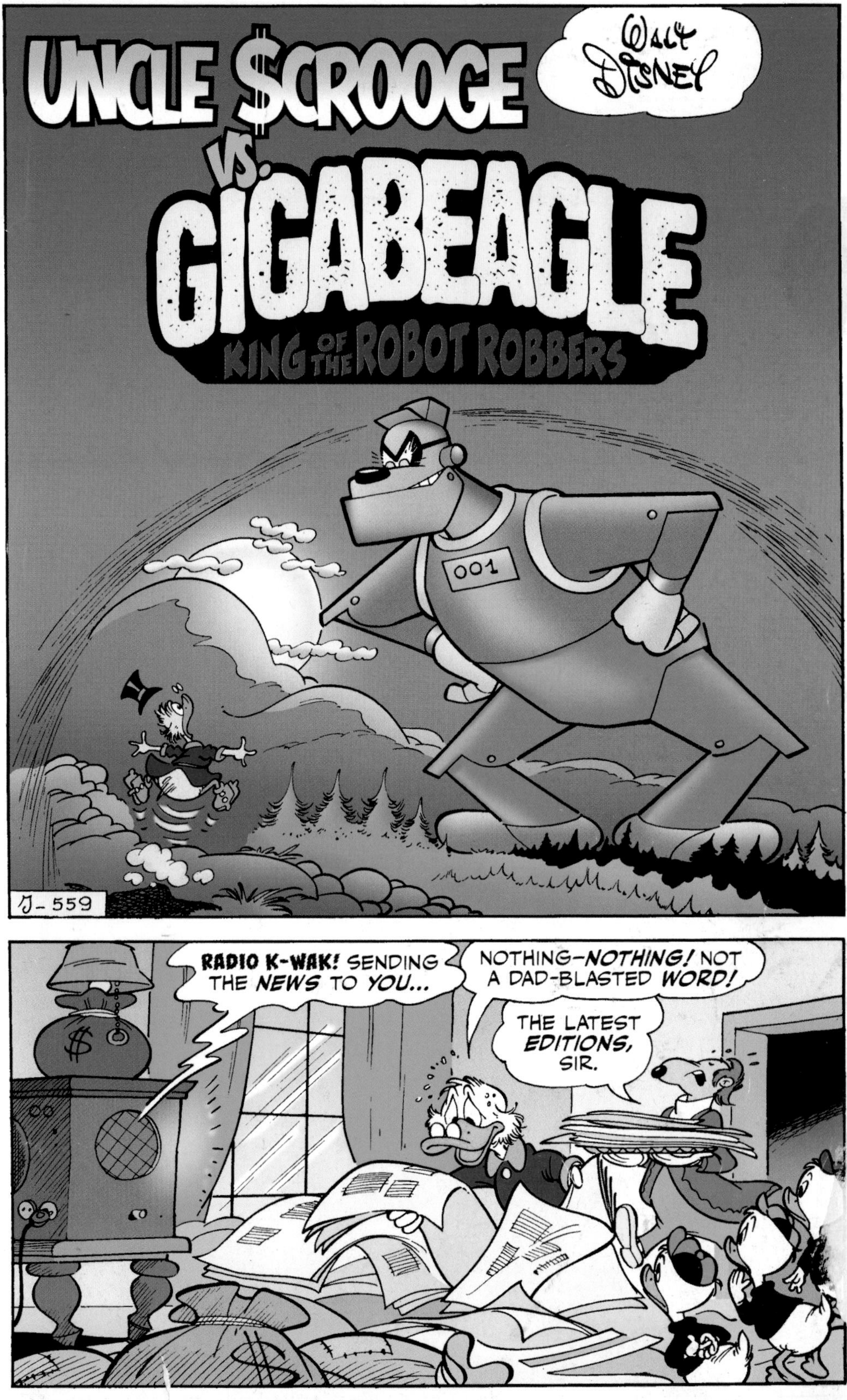

UNCLE $CROOGE
WALT DISNEY
VS. GIGABEAGLE
KING OF THE ROBOT ROBBERS
001
J-559
RADIO K-WAK! SENDING THE NEWS TO YOU...
NOTHING–NOTHING! NOT A DAD-BLASTED WORD!
THE LATEST EDITIONS, SIR.

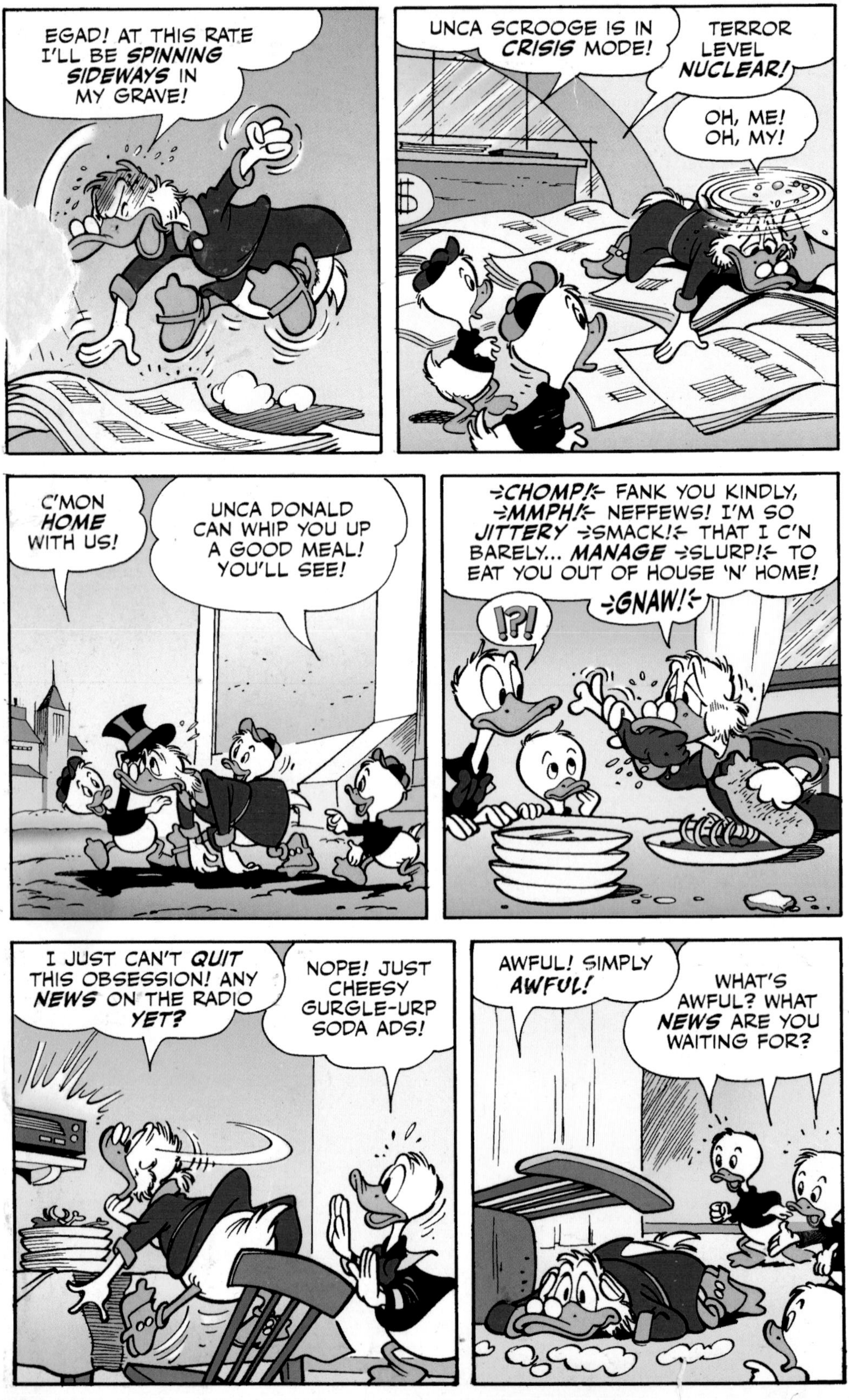
EGAD! AT THIS RATE I'LL BE SPINNING SIDEWAYS IN MY GRAVE!
UNCA SCROOGE IS IN CRISIS MODE!
TERROR LEVEL NUCLEAR!
OH, ME! OH, MY!
C'MON HOME WITH US!
UNCA DONALD CAN WHIP YOU UP A GOOD MEAL! YOU'LL SEE!
CHOMP! FANK YOU KINDLY, MMPH! NEFFEWS! I'M SO JITTERY SMACK! THAT I C'N BARELY... MANAGE SLURP! TO EAT YOU OUT OF HOUSE 'N' HOME!
GNAW!
!?!
I JUST CAN'T QUIT THIS OBSESSION! ANY NEWS ON THE RADIO YET?
NOPE! JUST CHEESY GURGLE-URP SODA ADS!
AWFUL! SIMPLY AWFUL!
WHAT'S AWFUL? WHAT NEWS ARE YOU WAITING FOR?

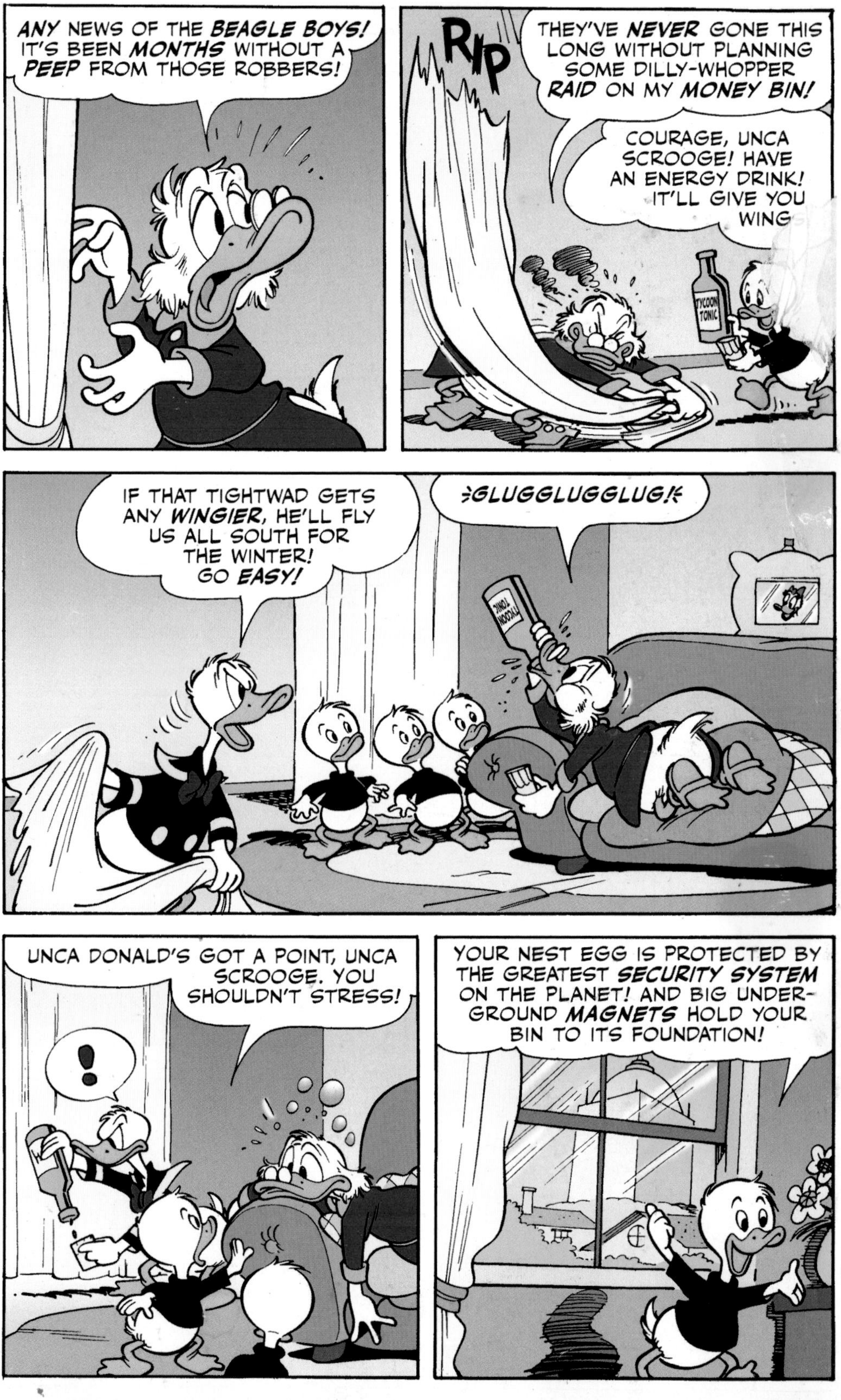
ANY NEWS OF THE BEAGLE BOYS! IT'S BEEN MONTHS WITHOUT A PEEP FROM THOSE ROBBERS!
RIP
THEY'VE NEVER GONE THIS LONG WITHOUT PLANNING SOME DILLY-WHOPPER RAID ON MY MONEY BIN!
COURAGE, UNCA SCROOGE! HAVE AN ENERGY DRINK! IT'LL GIVE YOU WINGS
TYCOON TONIC
IF THAT TIGHTWAD GETS ANY WINGIER, HE'LL FLY US ALL SOUTH FOR THE WINTER! GO EASY!
GLUGGLUGGLUG!
TYCOON TONIC
!
UNCA DONALD'S GOT A POINT, UNCA SCROOGE. YOU SHOULDN'T STRESS!
YOUR NEST EGG IS PROTECTED BY THE GREATEST SECURITY SYSTEM ON THE PLANET! AND BIG UNDER-GROUND MAGNETS HOLD YOUR BIN TO ITS FOUNDATION!

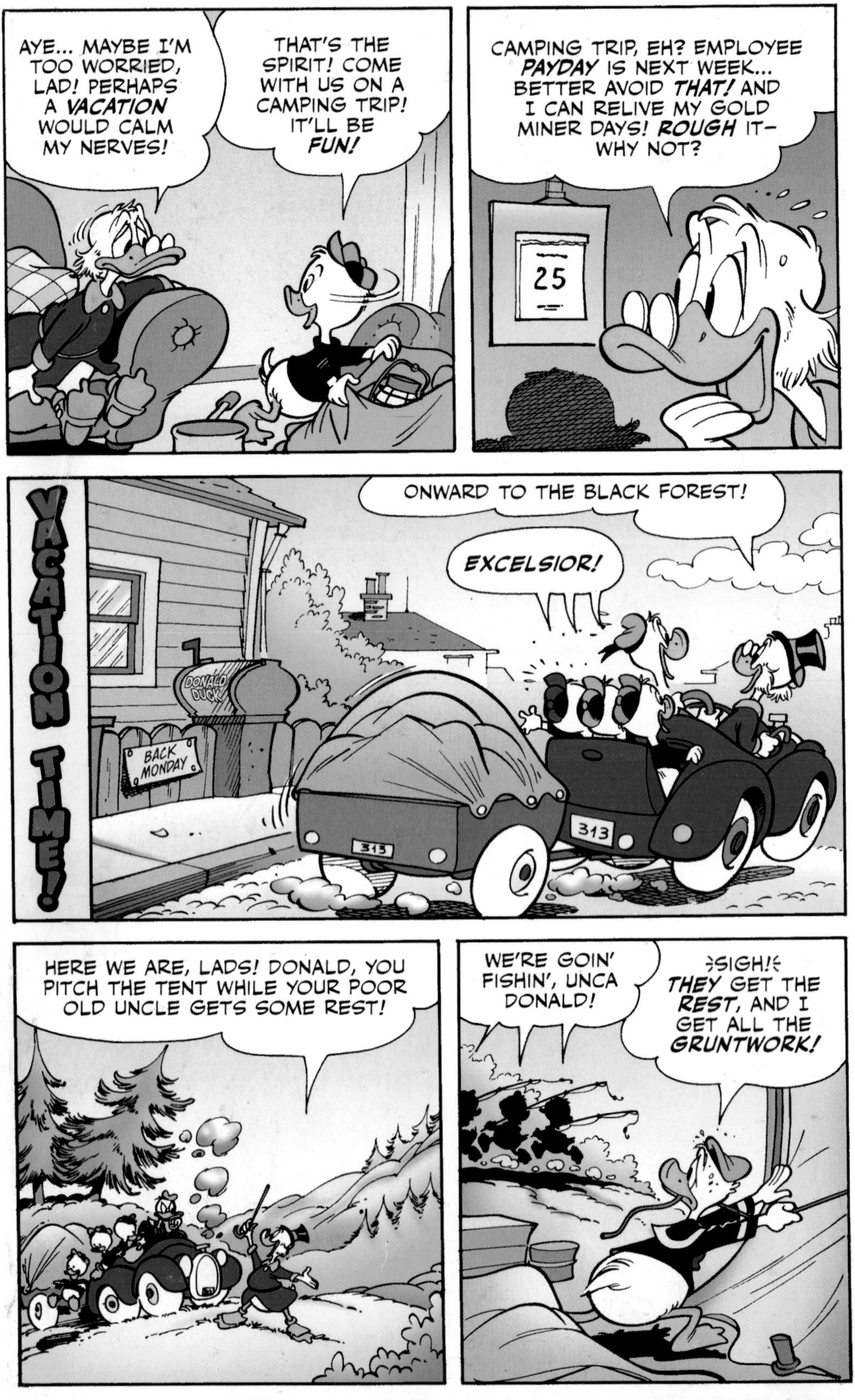
AYE... MAYBE I'M TOO WORRIED, LAD! PERHAPS A VACATION WOULD CALM MY NERVES!
THAT'S THE SPIRIT! COME WITH US ON A CAMPING TRIP! IT'LL BE FUN!
CAMPING TRIP, EH? EMPLOYEE PAYDAY IS NEXT WEEK... BETTER AVOID THAT! AND I CAN RELIVE MY GOLD MINER DAYS! ROUGH IT— WHY NOT?
25
VACATION TIME!
ONWARD TO THE BLACK FOREST!
EXCELSIOR!
DONALD DUCK
BACK MONDAY
313
313
HERE WE ARE, LADS! DONALD, YOU PITCH THE TENT WHILE YOUR POOR OLD UNCLE GETS SOME REST!
WE'RE GOIN' FISHIN', UNCA DONALD!
SIGH! THEY GET THE REST, AND I GET ALL THE GRUNTWORK!

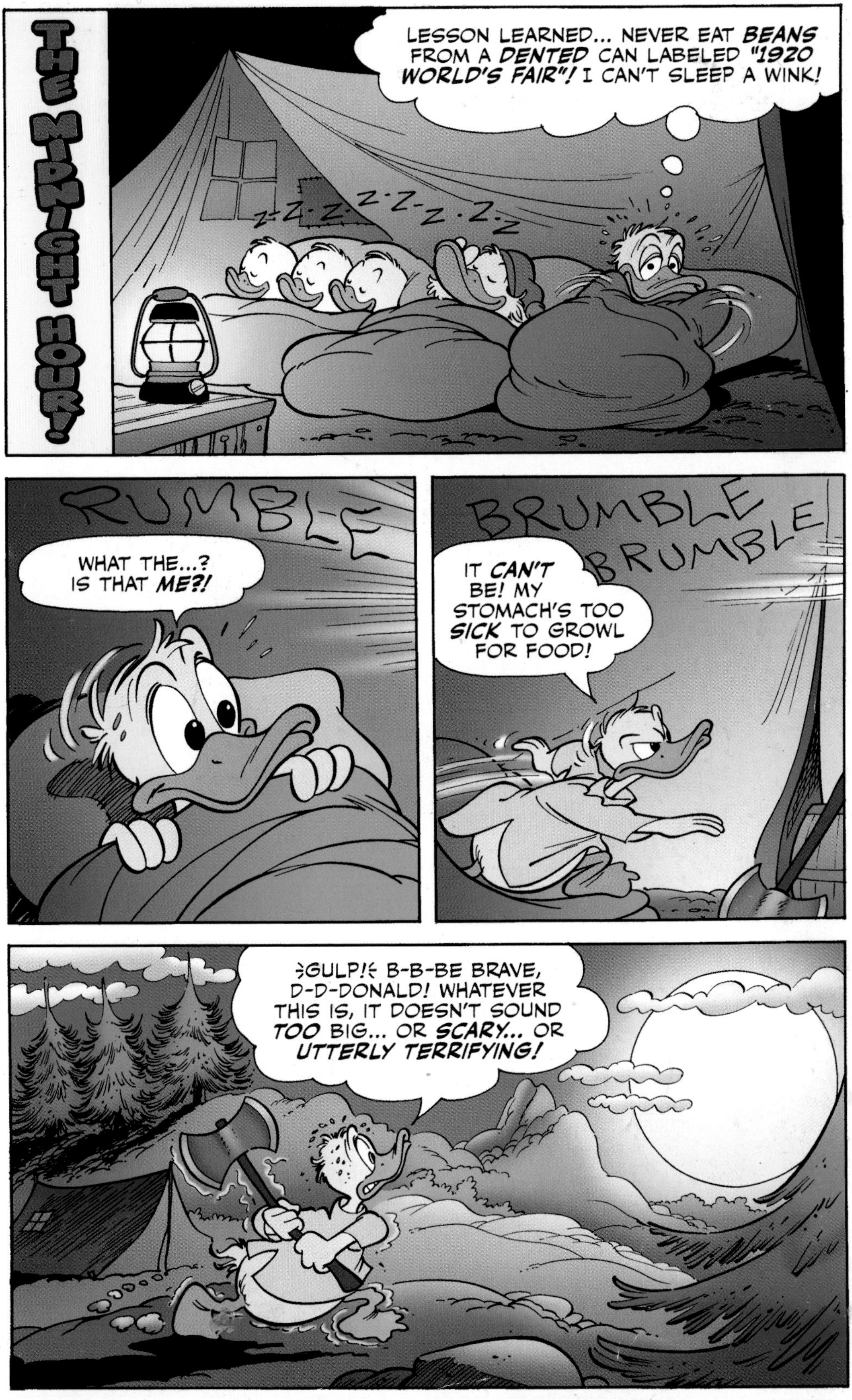
THE MIDNIGHT HOUR!
LESSON LEARNED... NEVER EAT BEANS FROM A DENTED CAN LABELED "1920 WORLD'S FAIR"! I CAN'T SLEEP A WINK!
Z-Z-Z-Z-Z-Z-Z-Z-Z
RUMBLE
WHAT THE...? IS THAT ME?!
BRUMBLE BRUMBLE
IT CAN'T BE! MY STOMACH'S TOO SICK TO GROWL FOR FOOD!
GULP! B-B-BE BRAVE, D-D-DONALD! WHATEVER THIS IS, IT DOESN'T SOUND TOO BIG... OR SCARY... OR UTTERLY TERRIFYING!

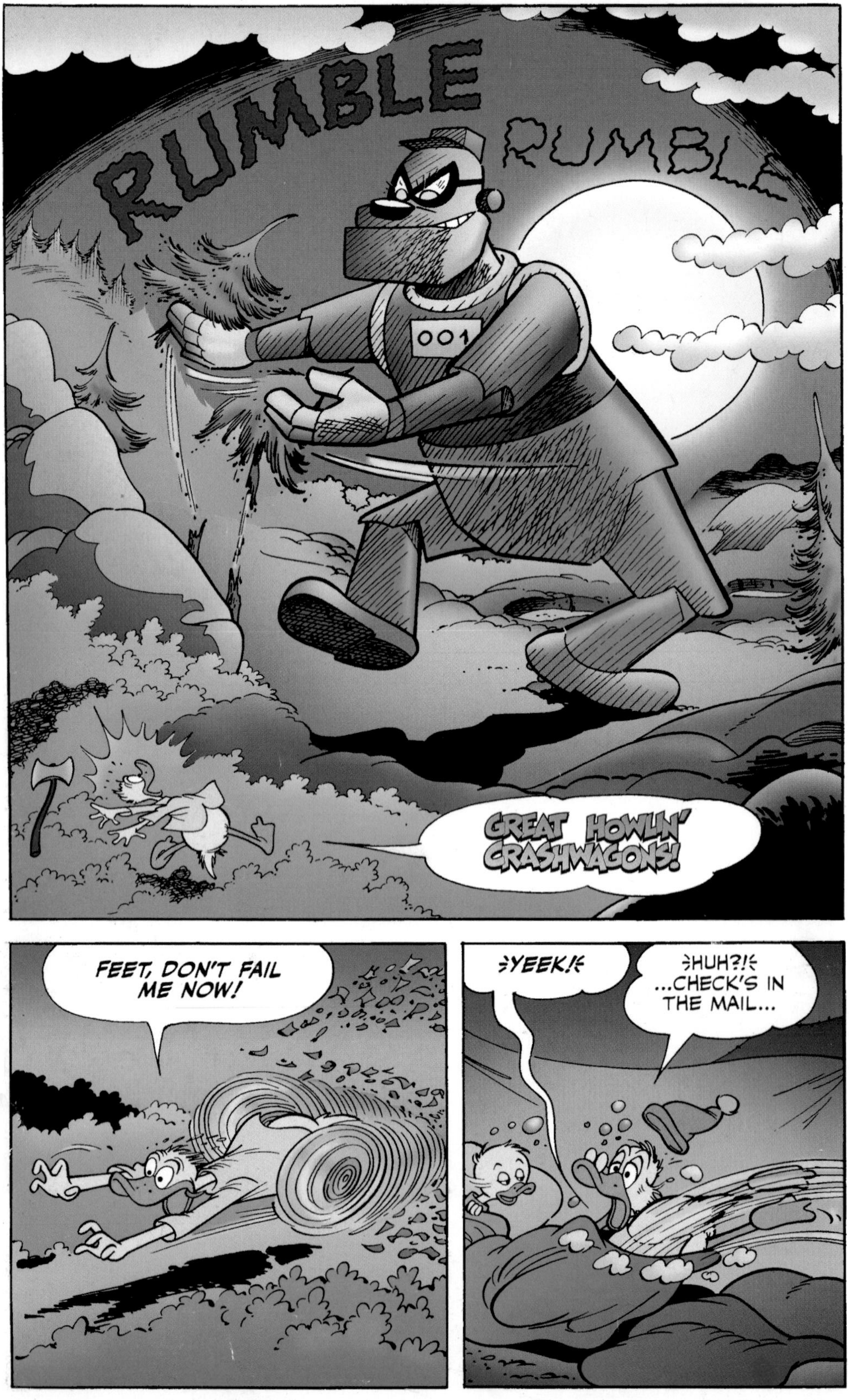
RUMBLE
RUMBLE
001
GREAT HOWLIN' CRASHWAGONS!
FEET, DON'T FAIL ME NOW!
YEEK!
HUH?! ...CHECK'S IN THE MAIL...

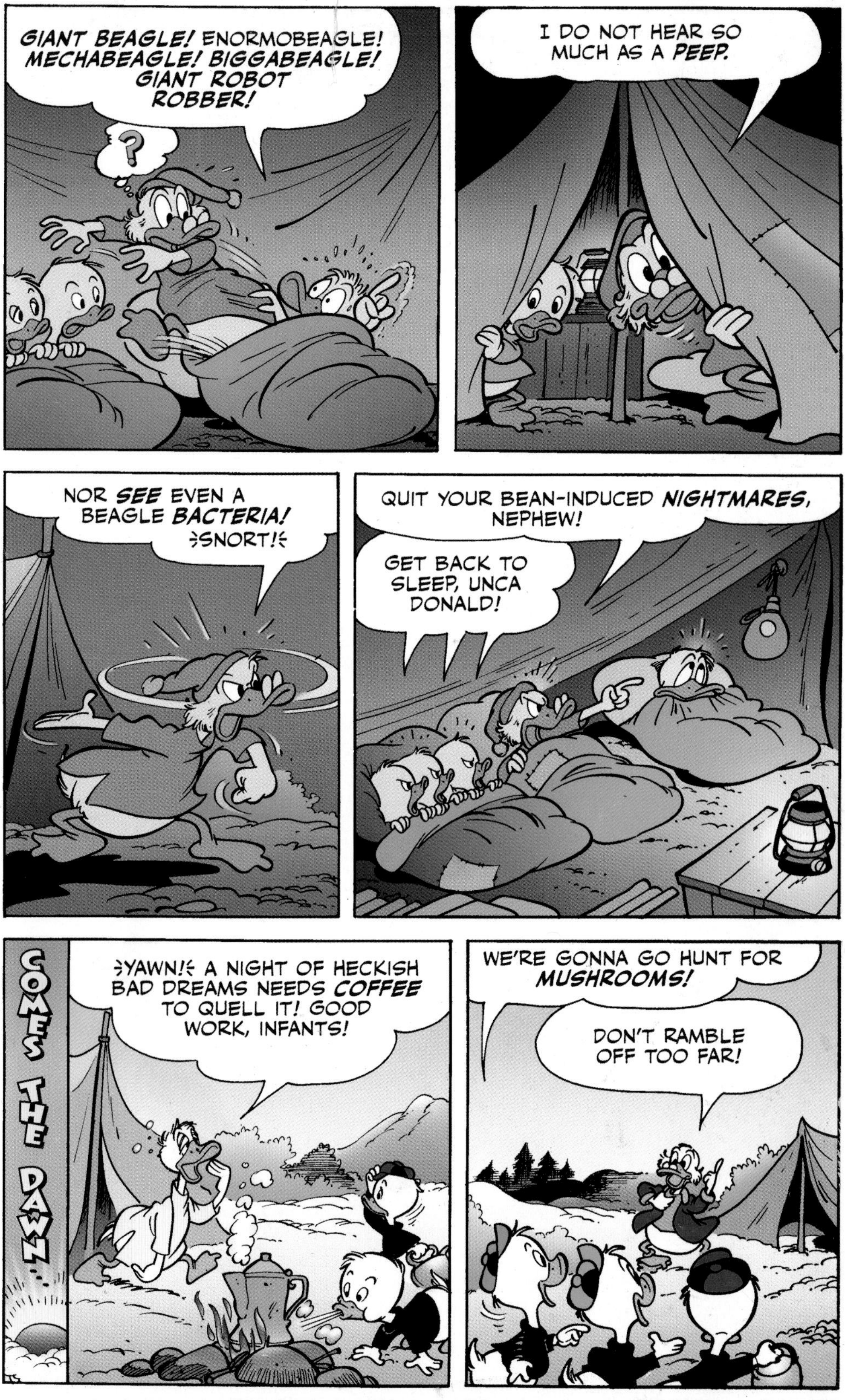
GIANT BEAGLE! ENORMOBEAGLE! MECHABEAGLE! BIGGABEAGLE! GIANT ROBOT ROBBER!
?
I DO NOT HEAR SO MUCH AS A PEEP.
NOR SEE EVEN A BEAGLE BACTERIA! SNORT!
QUIT YOUR BEAN-INDUCED NIGHTMARES, NEPHEW!
GET BACK TO SLEEP, UNCA DONALD!
COMES THE DAWN...
YAWN! A NIGHT OF HECKISH BAD DREAMS NEEDS COFFEE TO QUELL IT! GOOD WORK, INFANTS!
WE'RE GONNA GO HUNT FOR MUSHROOMS!
DON'T RAMBLE OFF TOO FAR!

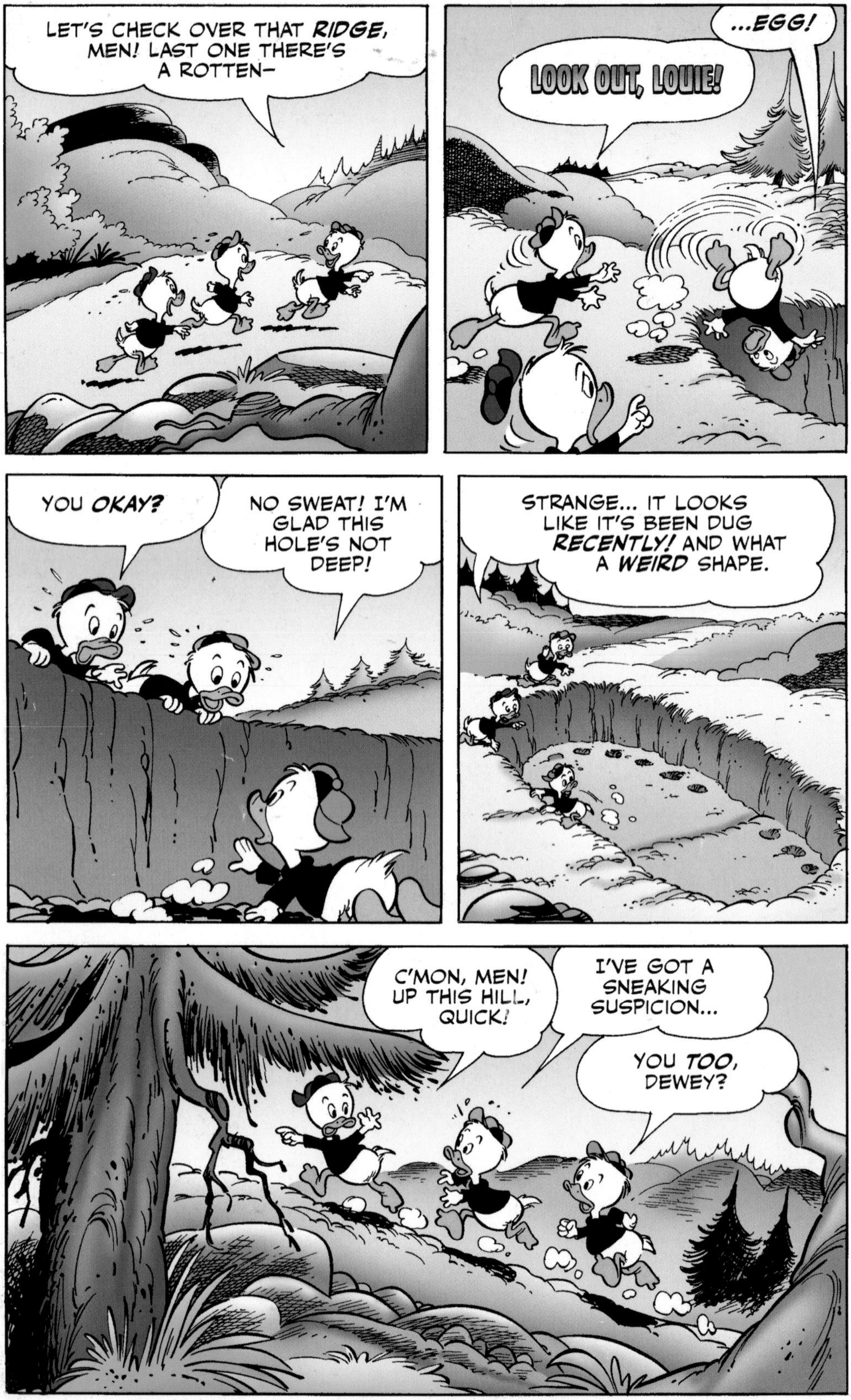
LET'S CHECK OVER THAT *RIDGE*, MEN! LAST ONE THERE'S A ROTTEN–
LOOK OUT, LOUIE!
...EGG!
YOU *OKAY?*
NO SWEAT! I'M GLAD THIS HOLE'S NOT DEEP!
STRANGE... IT LOOKS LIKE IT'S BEEN DUG *RECENTLY!* AND WHAT A *WEIRD* SHAPE.
C'MON, MEN! UP THIS HILL, QUICK!
I'VE GOT A SNEAKING SUSPICION...
YOU *TOO*, DEWEY?

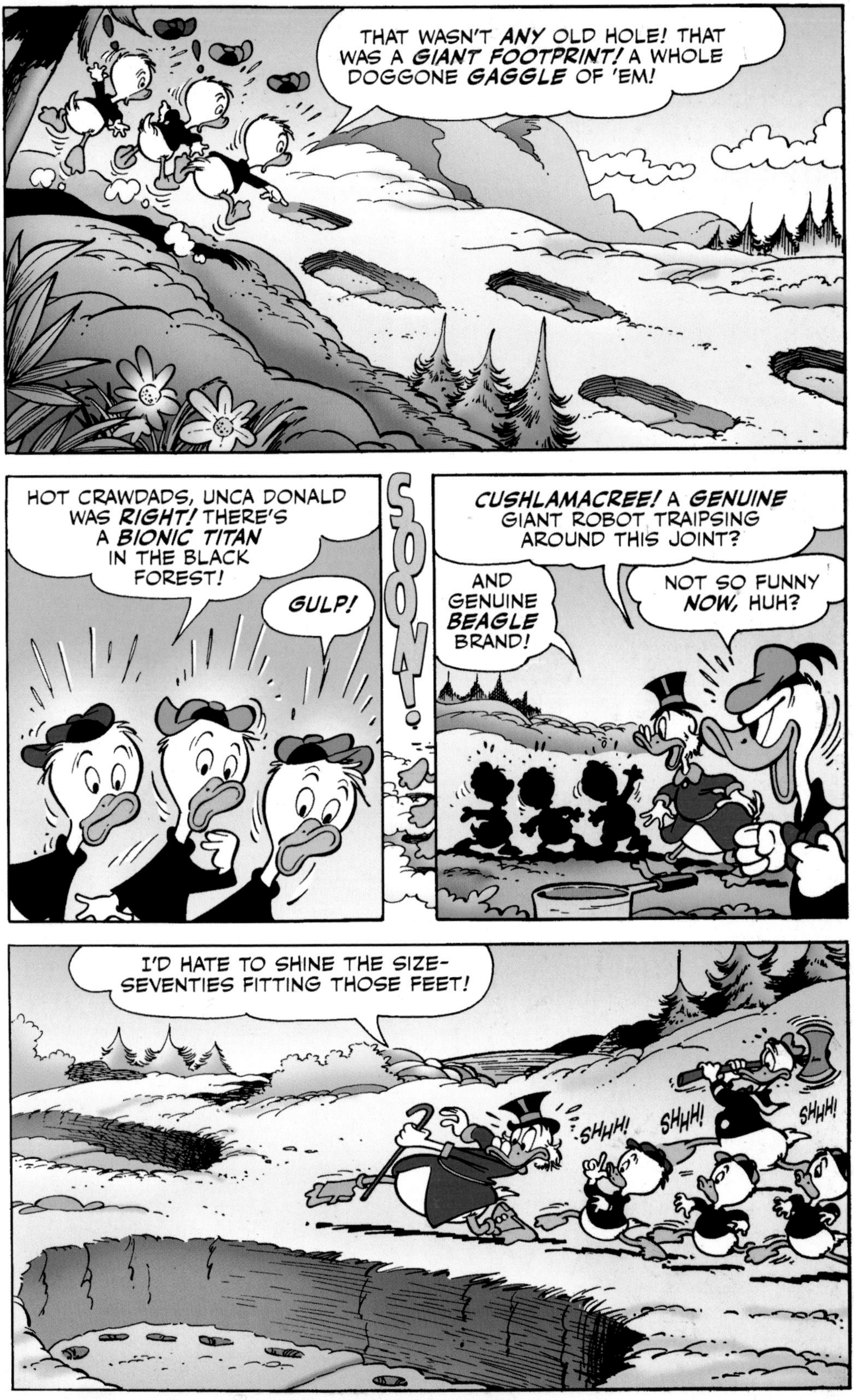
THAT WASN'T ANY OLD HOLE! THAT WAS A GIANT FOOTPRINT! A WHOLE DOGGONE GAGGLE OF 'EM!
HOT CRAWDADS, UNCA DONALD WAS RIGHT! THERE'S A BIONIC TITAN IN THE BLACK FOREST!
GULP!
SOON!
CUSHLAMACREE! A GENUINE GIANT ROBOT TRAIPSING AROUND THIS JOINT?
AND GENUINE BEAGLE BRAND!
NOT SO FUNNY NOW, HUH?
I'D HATE TO SHINE THE SIZE-SEVENTIES FITTING THOSE FEET!
SHHH!
SHHH!
SHHH!

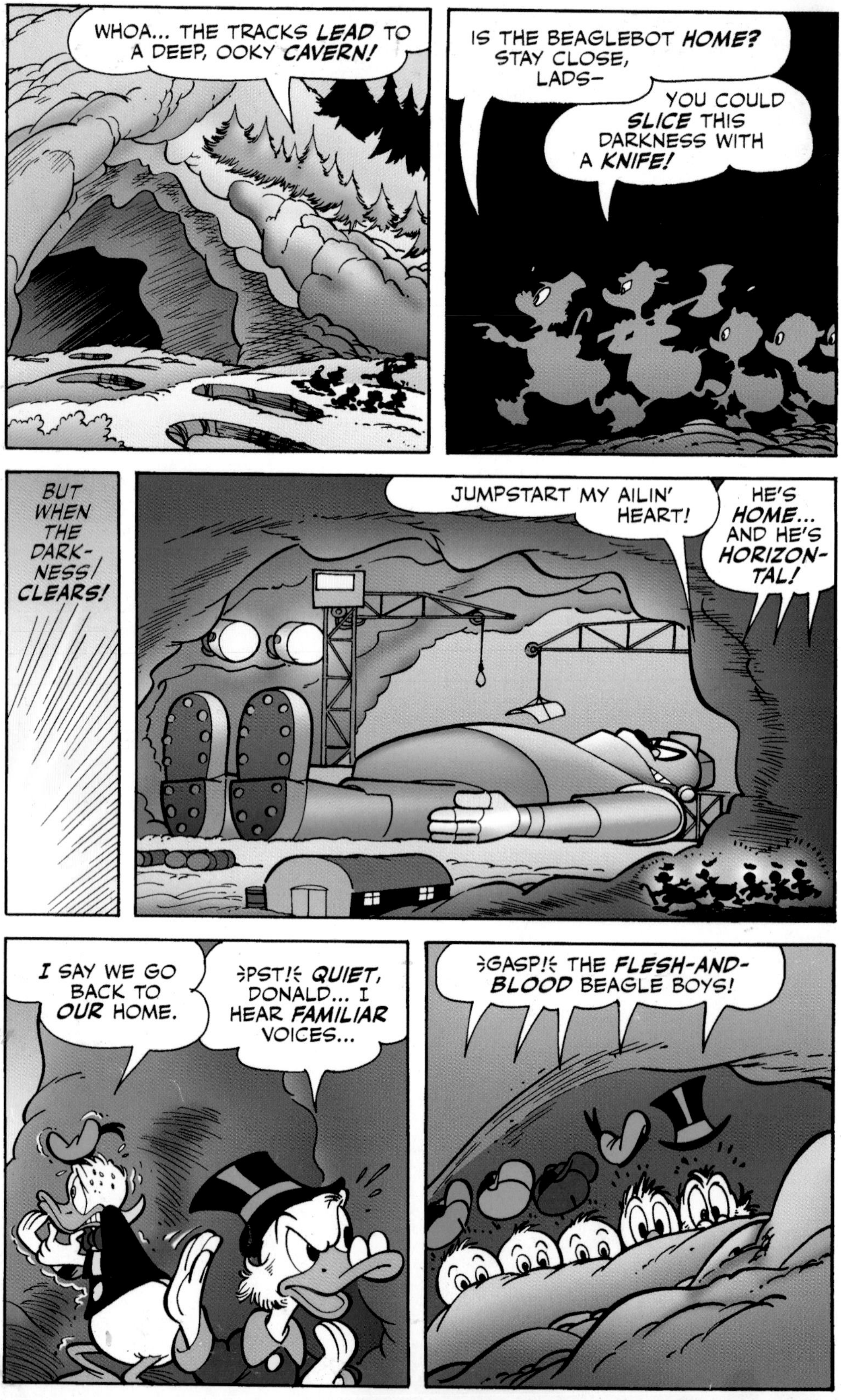

WHOA... THE TRACKS LEAD TO A DEEP, OOKY CAVERN!
IS THE BEAGLEBOT HOME? STAY CLOSE, LADS–
YOU COULD SLICE THIS DARKNESS WITH A KNIFE!
BUT WHEN THE DARK-NESS/ CLEARS!
JUMPSTART MY AILIN' HEART!
HE'S HOME... AND HE'S HORIZON-TAL!
I SAY WE GO BACK TO OUR HOME.
≻PST!≺ QUIET, DONALD... I HEAR FAMILIAR VOICES...
≻GASP!≺ THE FLESH-AND-BLOOD BEAGLE BOYS!

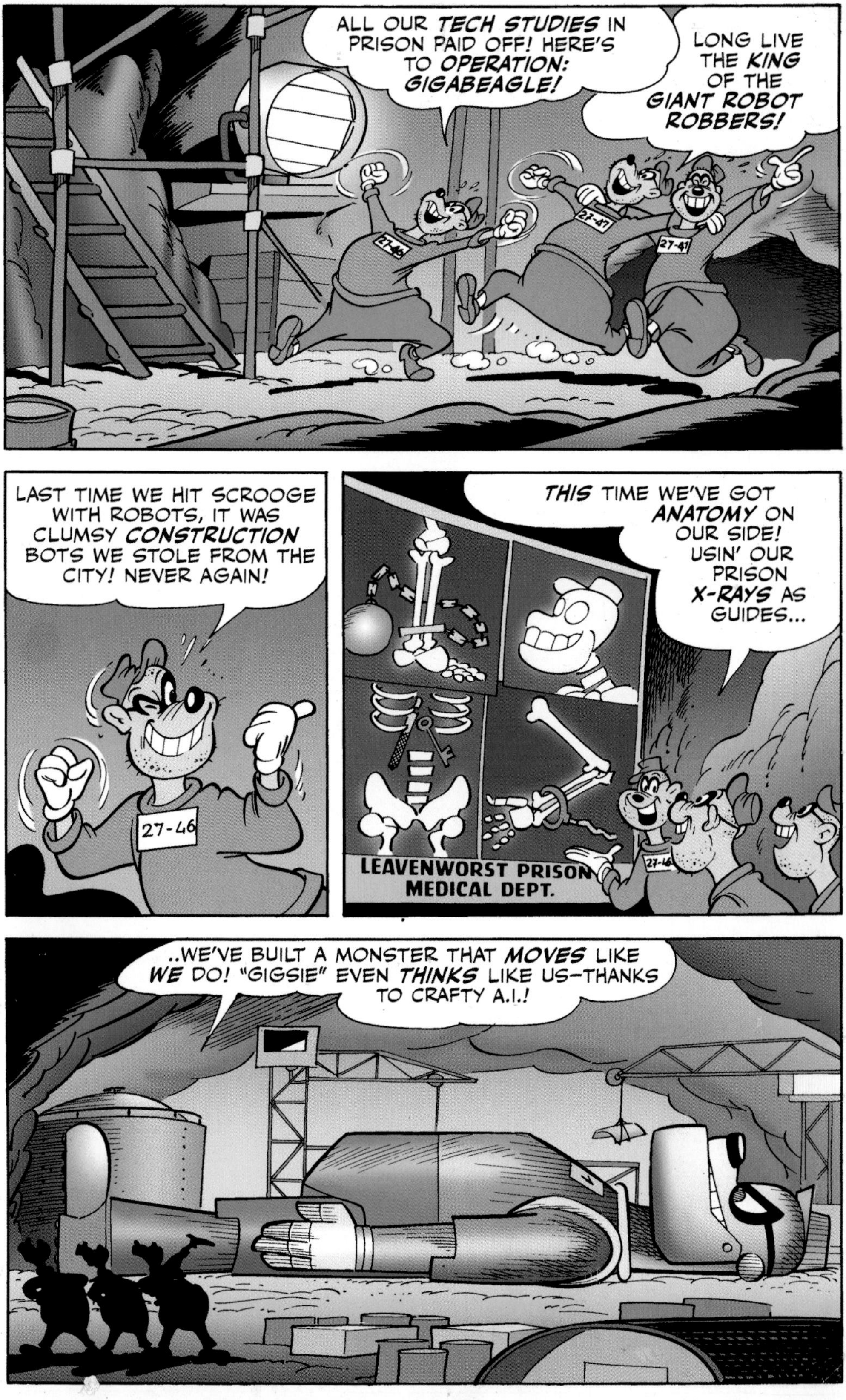
ALL OUR TECH STUDIES IN PRISON PAID OFF! HERE'S TO OPERATION: GIGABEAGLE!
LONG LIVE THE KING OF THE GIANT ROBOT ROBBERS!
27-46
27-47
27-41
LAST TIME WE HIT SCROOGE WITH ROBOTS, IT WAS CLUMSY CONSTRUCTION BOTS WE STOLE FROM THE CITY! NEVER AGAIN!
27-46
THIS TIME WE'VE GOT ANATOMY ON OUR SIDE! USIN' OUR PRISON X-RAYS AS GUIDES...
LEAVENWORST PRISON MEDICAL DEPT.
..WE'VE BUILT A MONSTER THAT MOVES LIKE WE DO! "GIGSIE" EVEN THINKS LIKE US–THANKS TO CRAFTY A.I.!

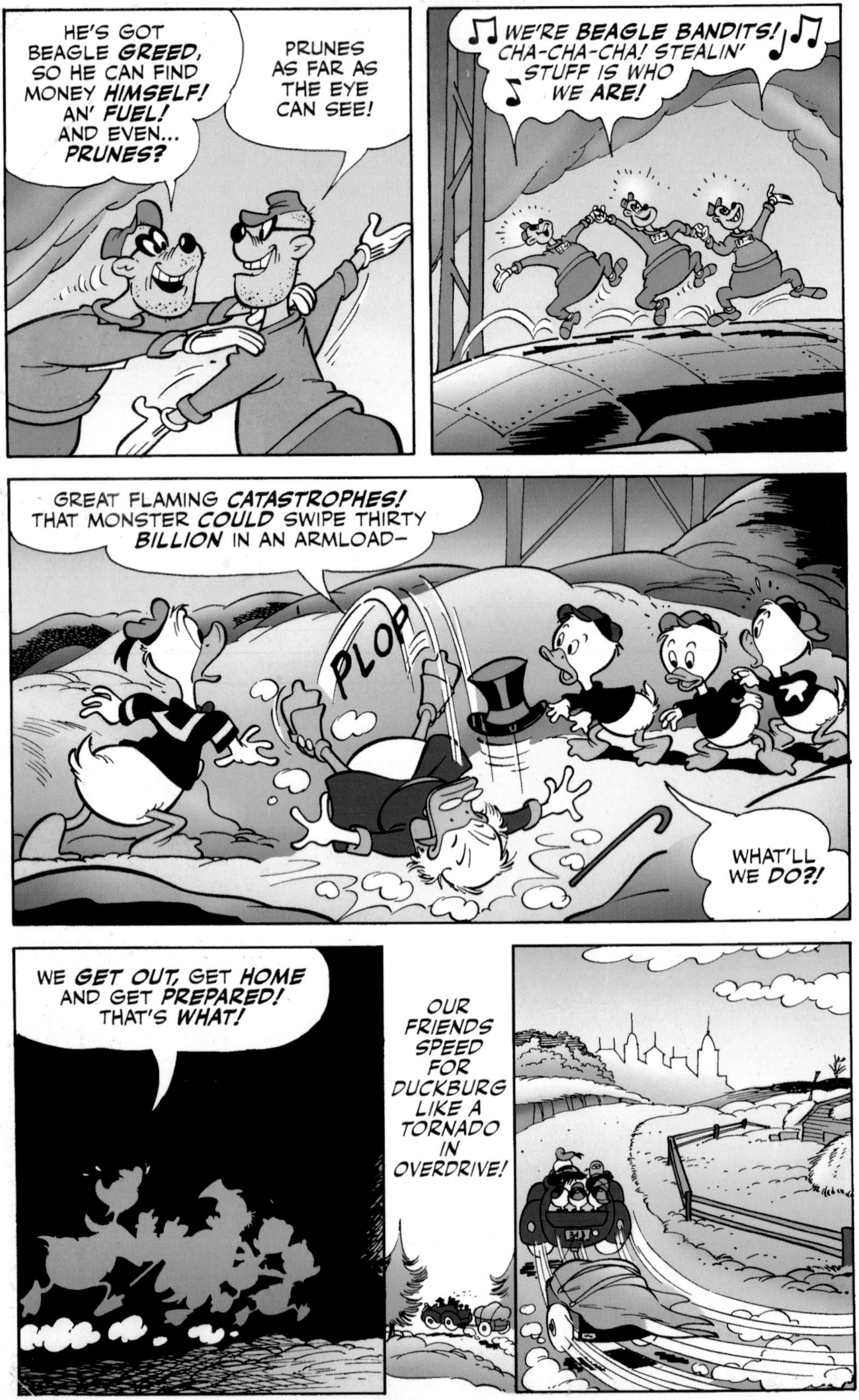
HE'S GOT BEAGLE GREED, SO HE CAN FIND MONEY HIMSELF! AN' FUEL! AND EVEN... PRUNES?
PRUNES AS FAR AS THE EYE CAN SEE!
WE'RE BEAGLE BANDITS! CHA-CHA-CHA! STEALIN' STUFF IS WHO WE ARE!
GREAT FLAMING CATASTROPHES! THAT MONSTER COULD SWIPE THIRTY BILLION IN AN ARMLOAD—
PLOP
WHAT'LL WE DO?!
WE GET OUT, GET HOME AND GET PREPARED! THAT'S WHAT!
OUR FRIENDS SPEED FOR DUCKBURG LIKE A TORNADO IN OVERDRIVE!

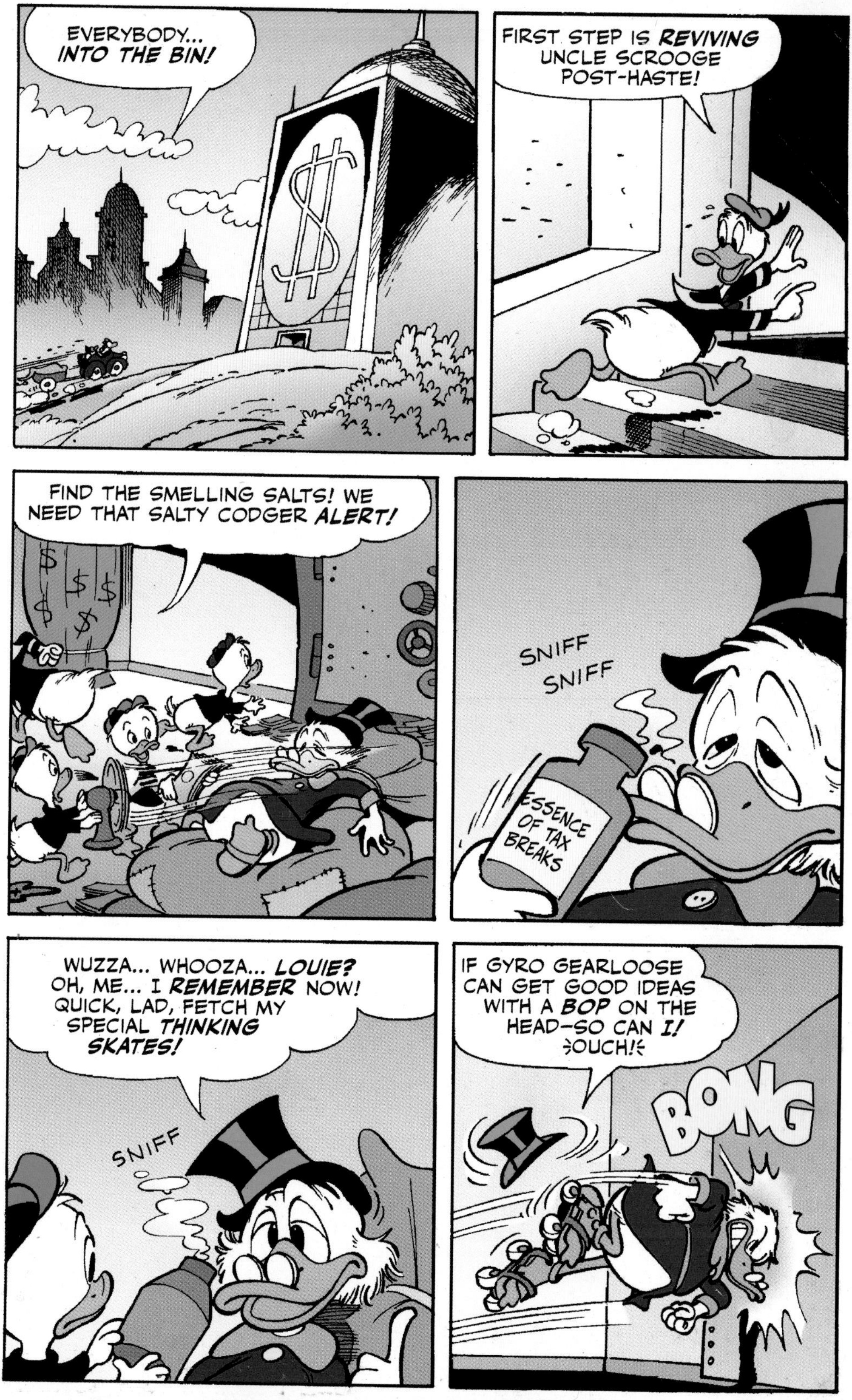
EVERYBODY... INTO THE BIN!
FIRST STEP IS REVIVING UNCLE SCROOGE POST-HASTE!
FIND THE SMELLING SALTS! WE NEED THAT SALTY CODGER ALERT!
SNIFF SNIFF
ESSENCE OF TAX BREAKS
WUZZA... WHOOZA... LOUIE? OH, ME... I REMEMBER NOW! QUICK, LAD, FETCH MY SPECIAL THINKING SKATES!
SNIFF
IF GYRO GEARLOOSE CAN GET GOOD IDEAS WITH A BOP ON THE HEAD—SO CAN I! OUCH!
BONG

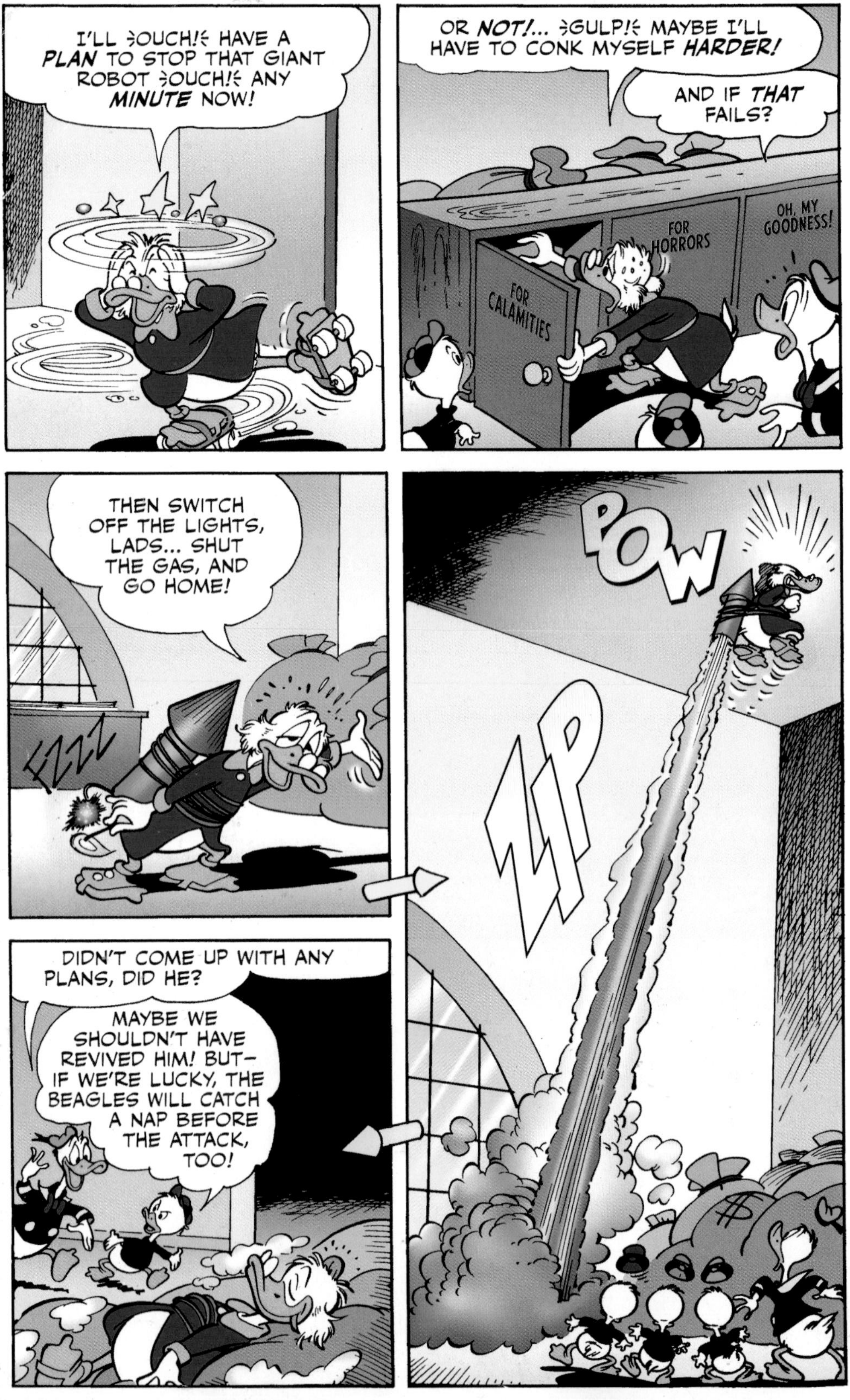
I'LL ⋟OUCH!⋞ HAVE A *PLAN* TO STOP THAT GIANT ROBOT ⋟OUCH!⋞ ANY *MINUTE* NOW!
OR *NOT!*... ⋟GULP!⋞ MAYBE I'LL HAVE TO CONK MYSELF *HARDER!*
AND IF *THAT* FAILS?
FOR CALAMITIES
FOR HORRORS
OH, MY GOODNESS!
THEN SWITCH OFF THE LIGHTS, LADS... SHUT THE GAS, AND GO HOME!
FZZZ
POW
ZIP
DIDN'T COME UP WITH ANY PLANS, DID HE?
MAYBE WE SHOULDN'T HAVE REVIVED HIM! BUT— IF WE'RE LUCKY, THE BEAGLES WILL CATCH A NAP BEFORE THE ATTACK, TOO!

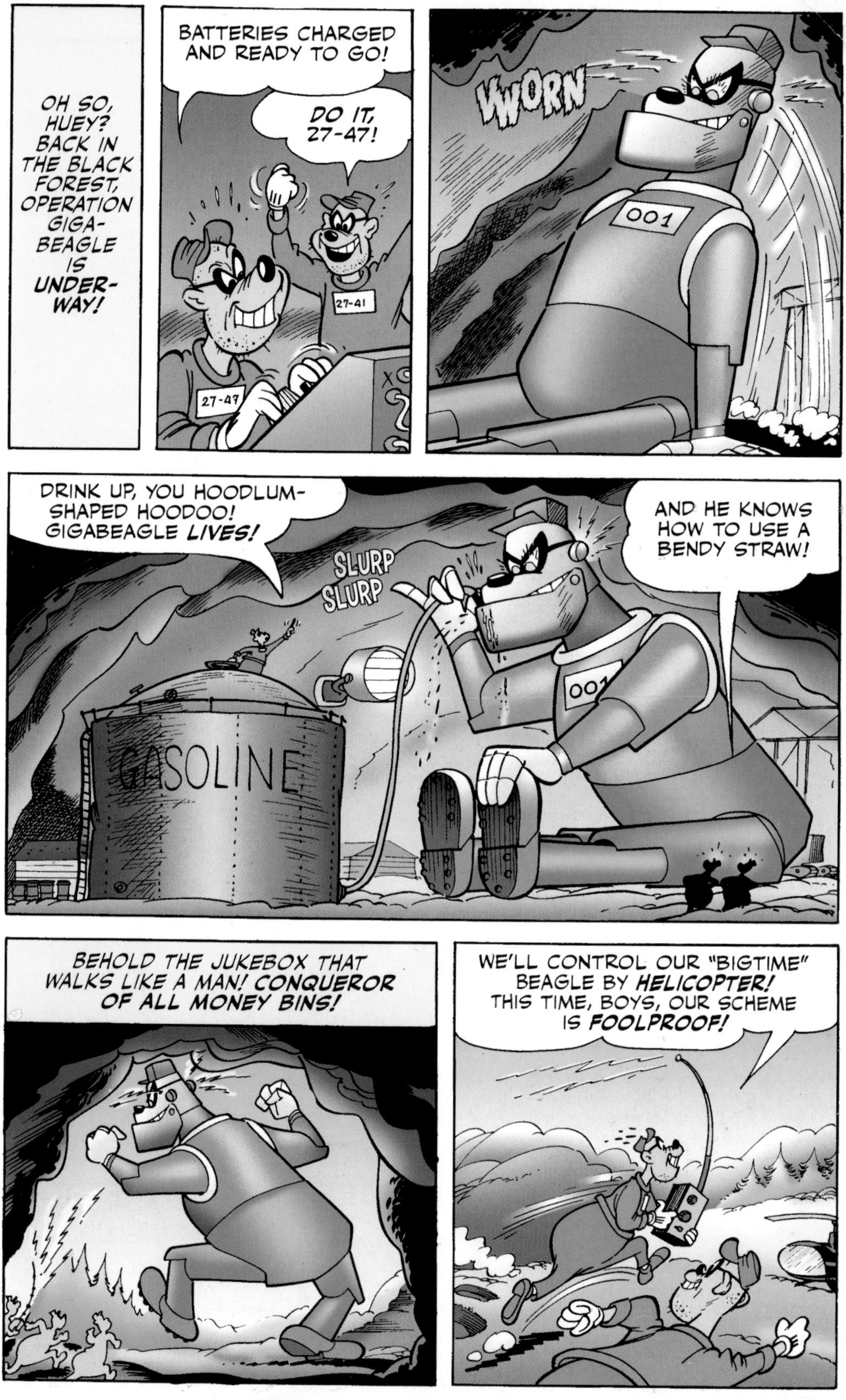
OH SO, HUEY? BACK IN THE BLACK FOREST, OPERATION GIGA-BEAGLE IS UNDER-WAY!
BATTERIES CHARGED AND READY TO GO!
DO IT, 27-47!
27-41
27-47
VWORN
001
DRINK UP, YOU HOODLUM-SHAPED HOODOO! GIGABEAGLE LIVES!
SLURP SLURP
AND HE KNOWS HOW TO USE A BENDY STRAW!
GASOLINE
001
BEHOLD THE JUKEBOX THAT WALKS LIKE A MAN! CONQUEROR OF ALL MONEY BINS!
WE'LL CONTROL OUR "BIGTIME" BEAGLE BY HELICOPTER! THIS TIME, BOYS, OUR SCHEME IS FOOLPROOF!

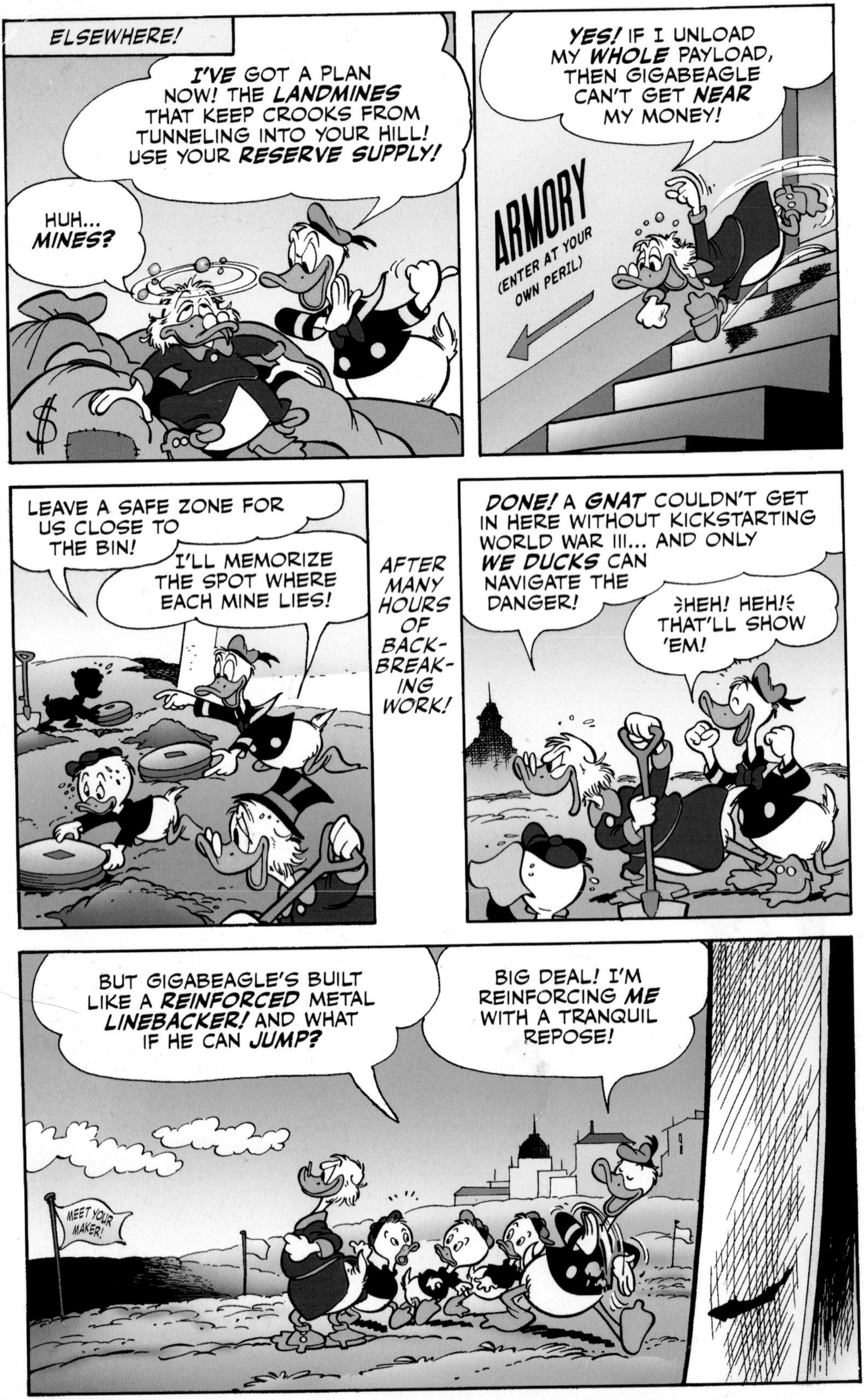
ELSEWHERE!
I'VE GOT A PLAN NOW! THE LANDMINES THAT KEEP CROOKS FROM TUNNELING INTO YOUR HILL! USE YOUR RESERVE SUPPLY!
HUH... MINES?
YES! IF I UNLOAD MY WHOLE PAYLOAD, THEN GIGABEAGLE CAN'T GET NEAR MY MONEY!
ARMORY
(ENTER AT YOUR OWN PERIL)
LEAVE A SAFE ZONE FOR US CLOSE TO THE BIN!
I'LL MEMORIZE THE SPOT WHERE EACH MINE LIES!
AFTER MANY HOURS OF BACK-BREAKING WORK!
DONE! A GNAT COULDN'T GET IN HERE WITHOUT KICKSTARTING WORLD WAR III... AND ONLY WE DUCKS CAN NAVIGATE THE DANGER!
HEH! HEH! THAT'LL SHOW 'EM!
BUT GIGABEAGLE'S BUILT LIKE A REINFORCED METAL LINEBACKER! AND WHAT IF HE CAN JUMP?
BIG DEAL! I'M REINFORCING ME WITH A TRANQUIL REPOSE!
MEET YOUR MAKER!

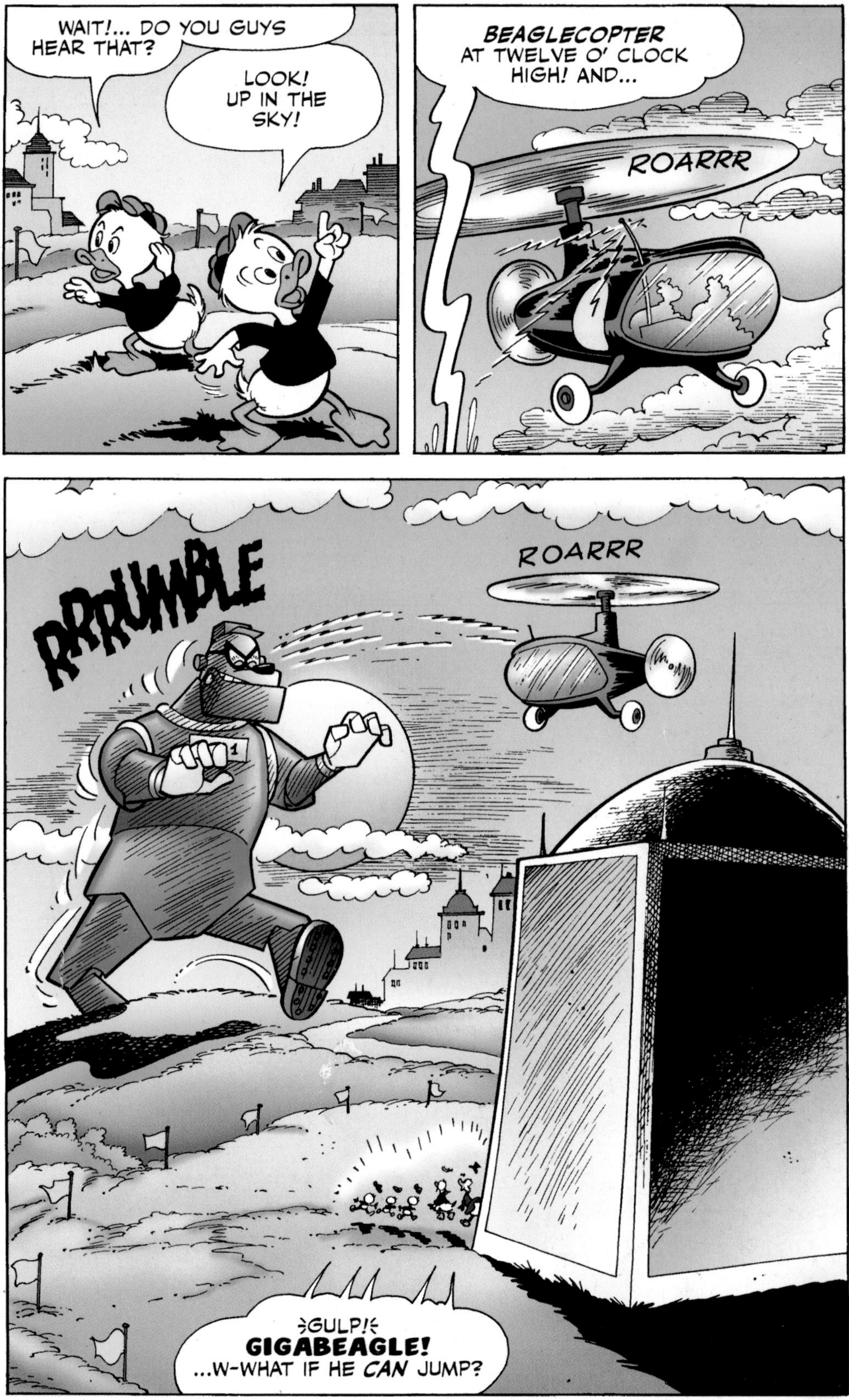
WAIT!... DO YOU GUYS HEAR THAT?
LOOK! UP IN THE SKY!
BEAGLECOPTER AT TWELVE O' CLOCK HIGH! AND...
ROARRR
RRRUMBLE
ROARRR
1
GULP!
GIGABEAGLE! ...W-WHAT IF HE CAN JUMP?

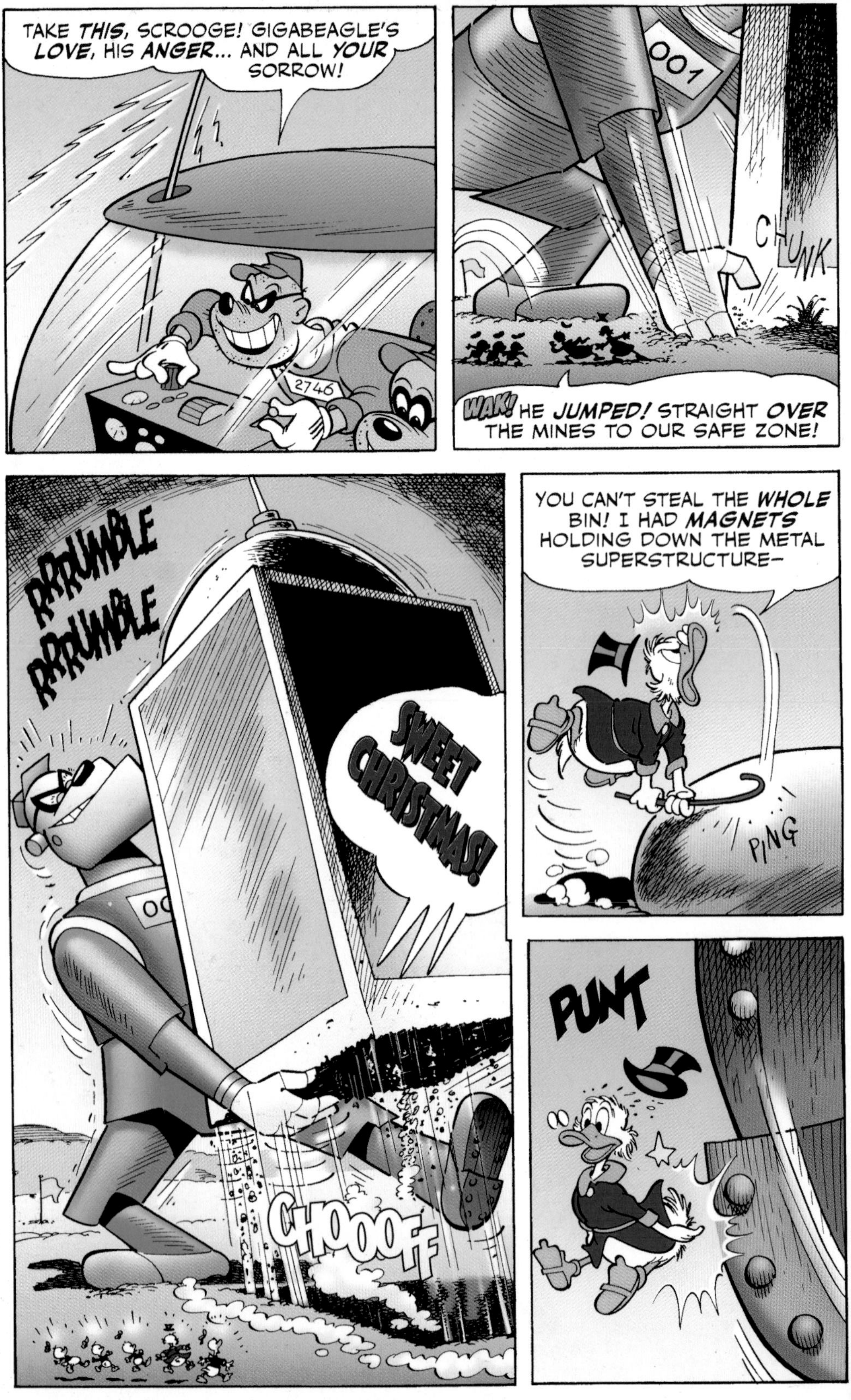
TAKE THIS, SCROOGE! GIGABEAGLE'S LOVE, HIS ANGER... AND ALL YOUR SORROW!
2746
001
CHUNK
WAK! HE JUMPED! STRAIGHT OVER THE MINES TO OUR SAFE ZONE!
RRRUMBLE RRRUMBLE
SWEET CHRISTMAS!
CHOOOFF
YOU CAN'T STEAL THE WHOLE BIN! I HAD MAGNETS HOLDING DOWN THE METAL SUPERSTRUCTURE–
PING
PUNT

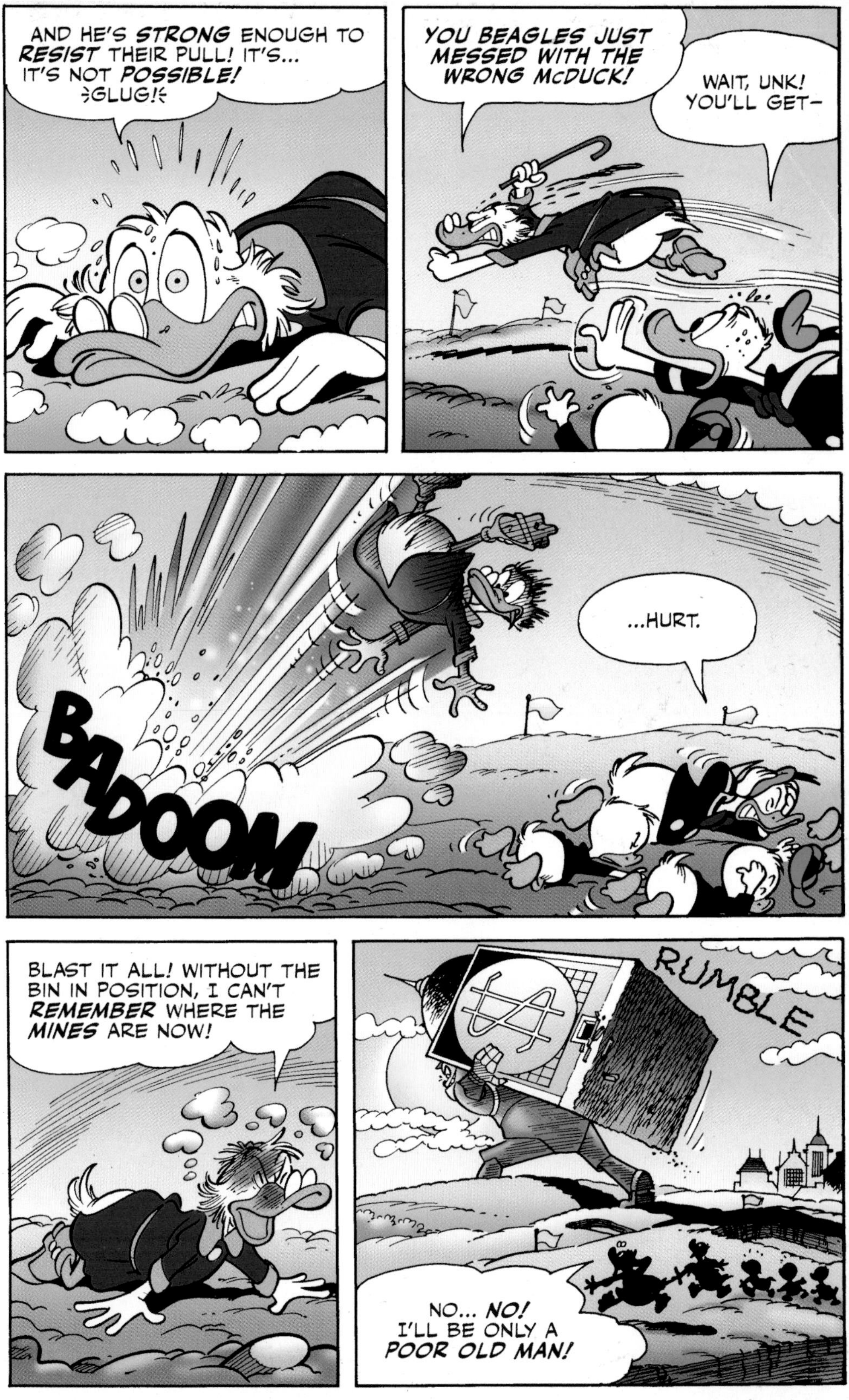
AND HE'S STRONG ENOUGH TO RESIST THEIR PULL! IT'S... IT'S NOT POSSIBLE! GLUG!
YOU BEAGLES JUST MESSED WITH THE WRONG McDUCK!
WAIT, UNK! YOU'LL GET–
...HURT.
BADOOM
BLAST IT ALL! WITHOUT THE BIN IN POSITION, I CAN'T REMEMBER WHERE THE MINES ARE NOW!
RUMBLE
NO... NO! I'LL BE ONLY A POOR OLD MAN!

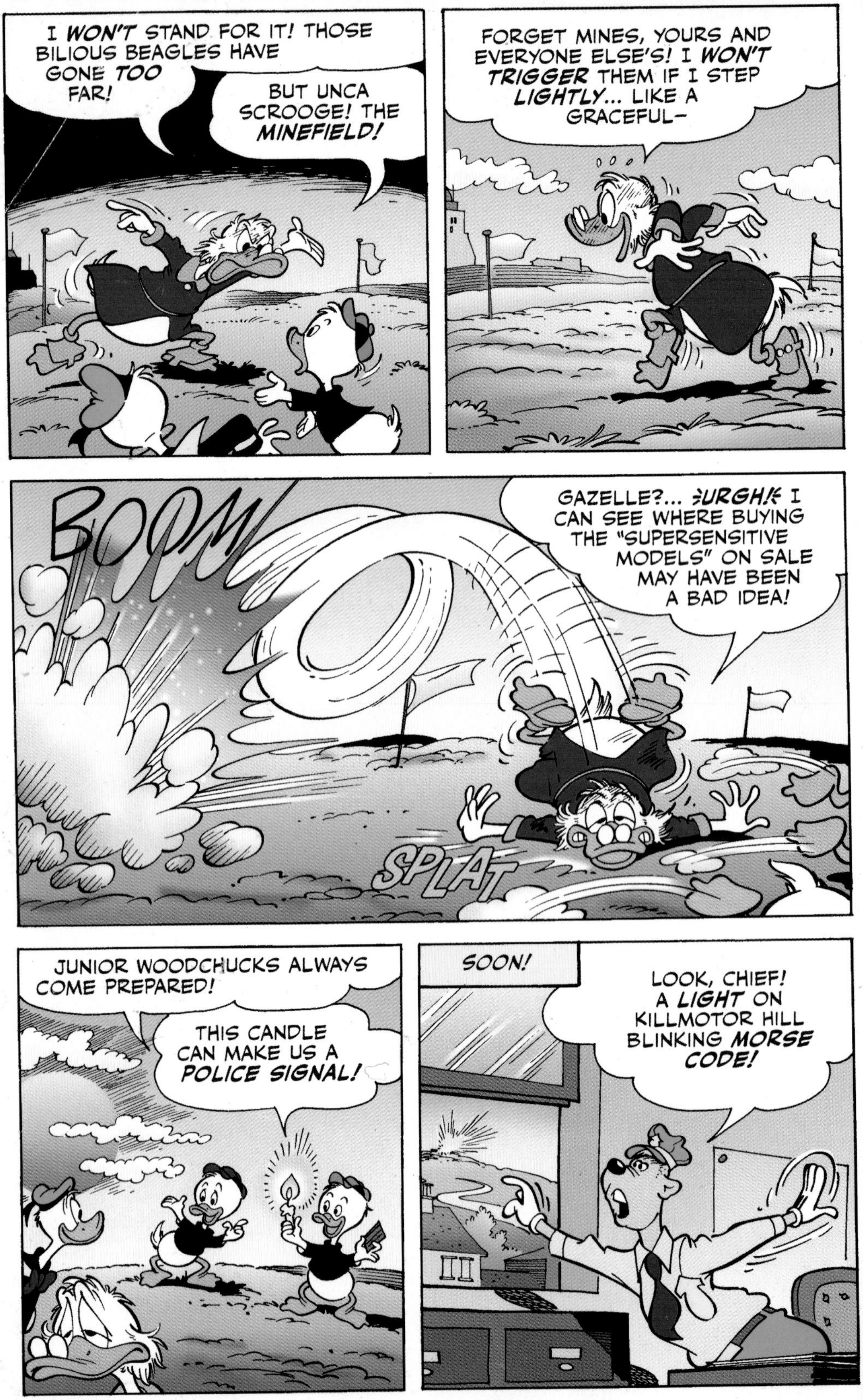
I WON'T STAND FOR IT! THOSE BILIOUS BEAGLES HAVE GONE TOO FAR!
BUT UNCA SCROOGE! THE MINEFIELD!
FORGET MINES, YOURS AND EVERYONE ELSE'S! I WON'T TRIGGER THEM IF I STEP LIGHTLY... LIKE A GRACEFUL–
BOOM
GAZELLE?... URGH! I CAN SEE WHERE BUYING THE "SUPERSENSITIVE MODELS" ON SALE MAY HAVE BEEN A BAD IDEA!
SPLAT
JUNIOR WOODCHUCKS ALWAYS COME PREPARED!
THIS CANDLE CAN MAKE US A POLICE SIGNAL!
SOON!
LOOK, CHIEF! A LIGHT ON KILLMOTOR HILL BLINKING MORSE CODE!

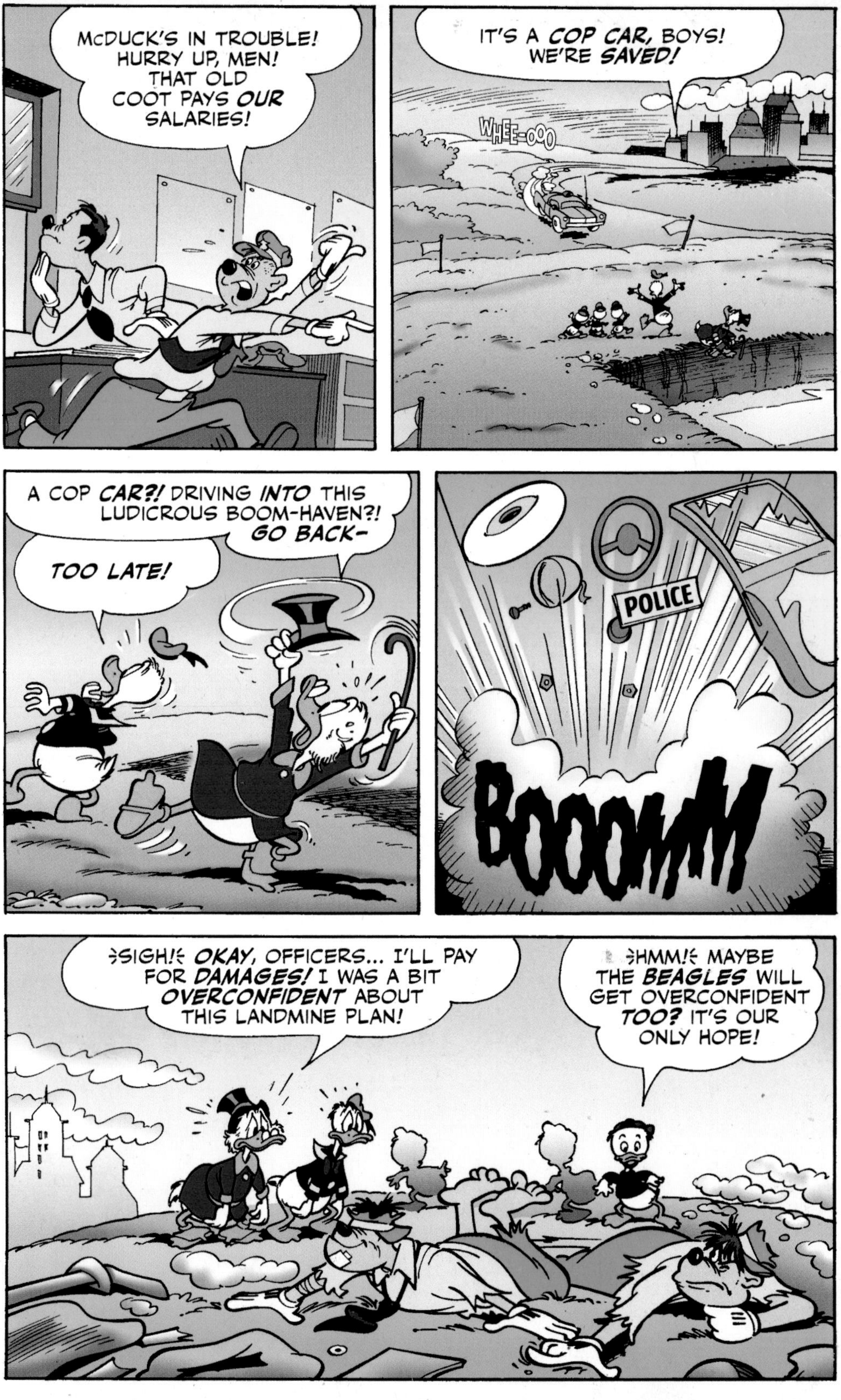
McDUCK'S IN TROUBLE! HURRY UP, MEN! THAT OLD COOT PAYS OUR SALARIES!
IT'S A COP CAR, BOYS! WE'RE SAVED!
WHEE-OOO
A COP CAR?! DRIVING INTO THIS LUDICROUS BOOM-HAVEN?! GO BACK–
TOO LATE!
POLICE
BOOOMM
⥽SIGH!⥼ OKAY, OFFICERS... I'LL PAY FOR DAMAGES! I WAS A BIT OVERCONFIDENT ABOUT THIS LANDMINE PLAN!
⥽HMM!⥼ MAYBE THE BEAGLES WILL GET OVERCONFIDENT TOO? IT'S OUR ONLY HOPE!

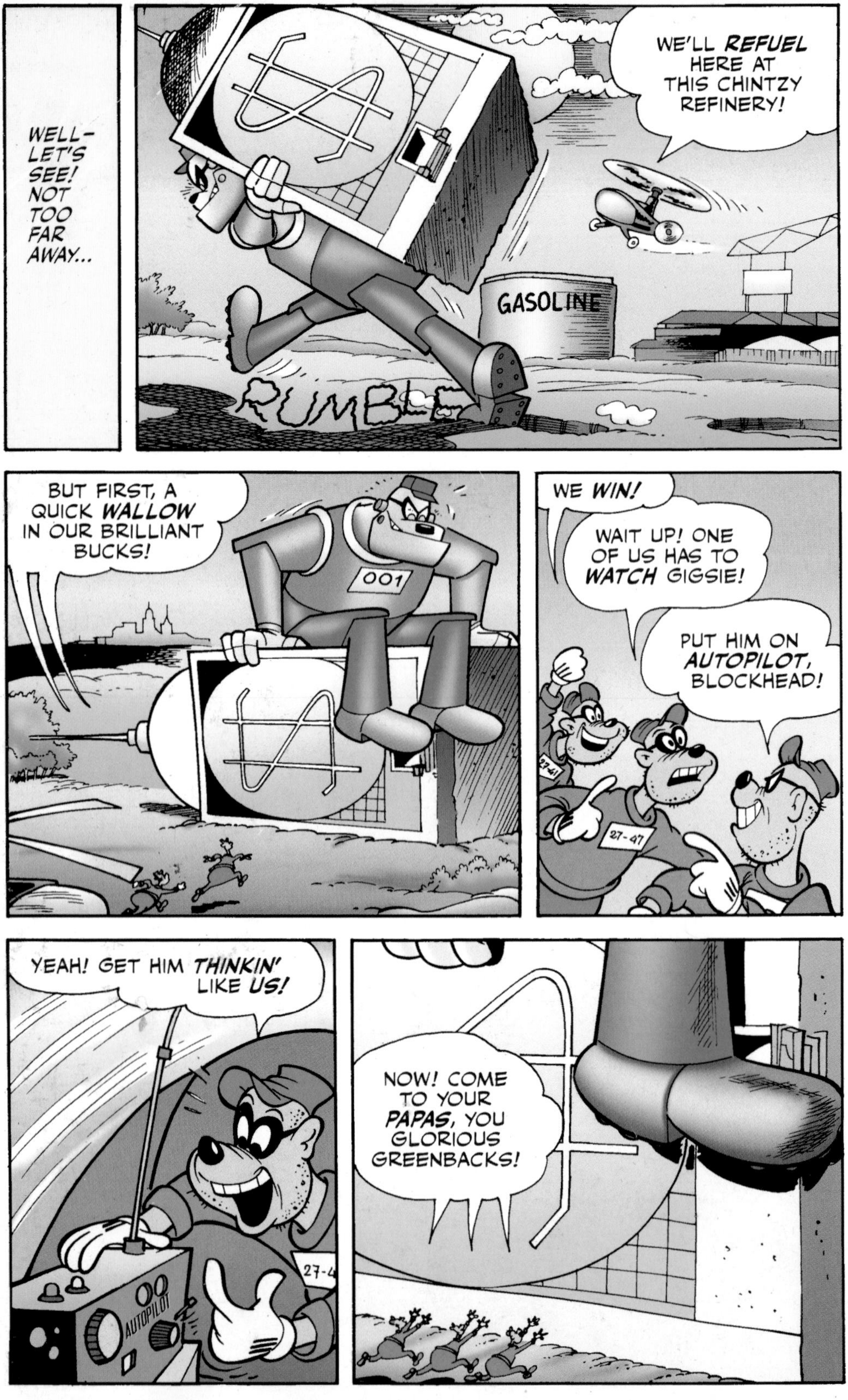
WELL-LET'S SEE! NOT TOO FAR AWAY...
WE'LL REFUEL HERE AT THIS CHINTZY REFINERY!
GASOLINE
RUMBLE
BUT FIRST, A QUICK WALLOW IN OUR BRILLIANT BUCKS!
001
WE WIN!
WAIT UP! ONE OF US HAS TO WATCH GIGSIE!
PUT HIM ON AUTOPILOT, BLOCKHEAD!
27-41
27-47
YEAH! GET HIM THINKIN' LIKE US!
AUTOPILOT
NOW! COME TO YOUR PAPAS, YOU GLORIOUS GREENBACKS!

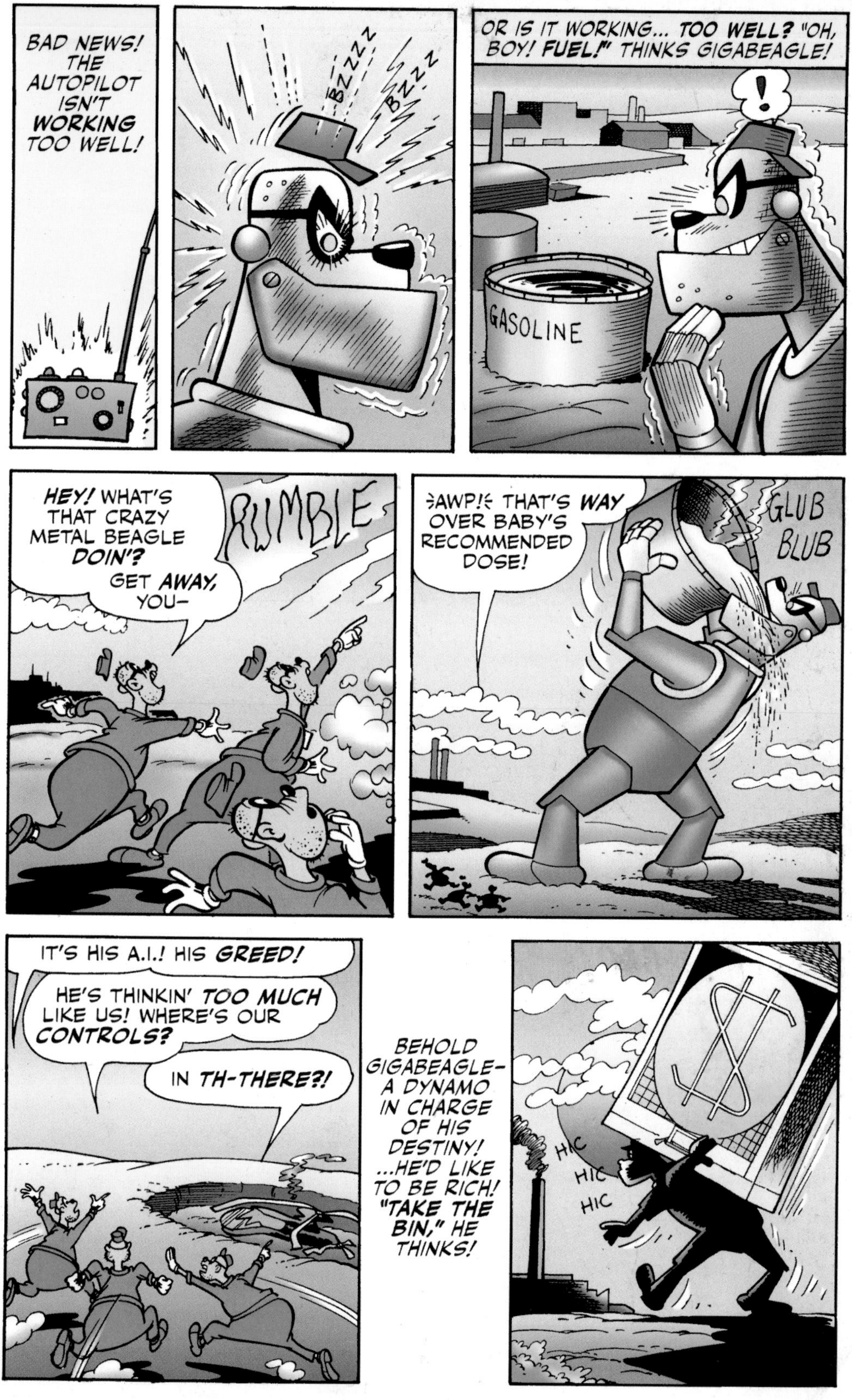
BAD NEWS! THE AUTOPILOT ISN'T WORKING TOO WELL!
BZZZZ
BZZZZ
OR IS IT WORKING... TOO WELL? "OH, BOY! FUEL!" THINKS GIGABEAGLE!
!
GASOLINE
HEY! WHAT'S THAT CRAZY METAL BEAGLE DOIN'?
GET AWAY, YOU–
RUMBLE
GAWP! THAT'S WAY OVER BABY'S RECOMMENDED DOSE!
GLUB BLUB
IT'S HIS A.I.! HIS GREED!
HE'S THINKIN' TOO MUCH LIKE US! WHERE'S OUR CONTROLS?
IN TH-THERE?!
BEHOLD GIGABEAGLE– A DYNAMO IN CHARGE OF HIS DESTINY! ...HE'D LIKE TO BE RICH! "TAKE THE BIN," HE THINKS!
HIC
HIC
HIC

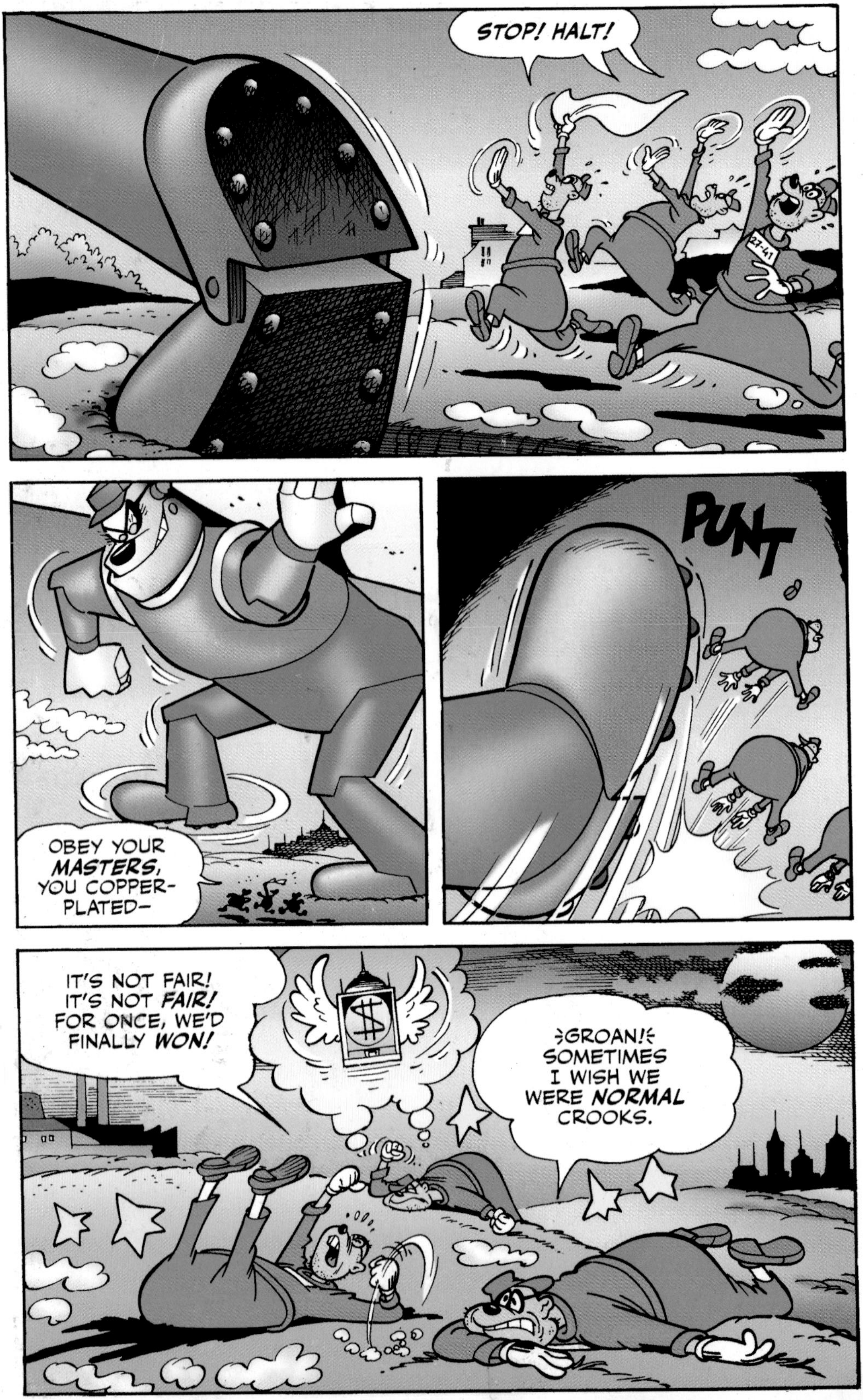
STOP! HALT!
27-41
OBEY YOUR *MASTERS,* YOU COPPER-PLATED—
PUNT
IT'S NOT FAIR! IT'S NOT *FAIR!* FOR ONCE, WE'D FINALLY *WON!*
$
⁼GROAN!⁼ SOMETIMES I WISH WE WERE *NORMAL* CROOKS.

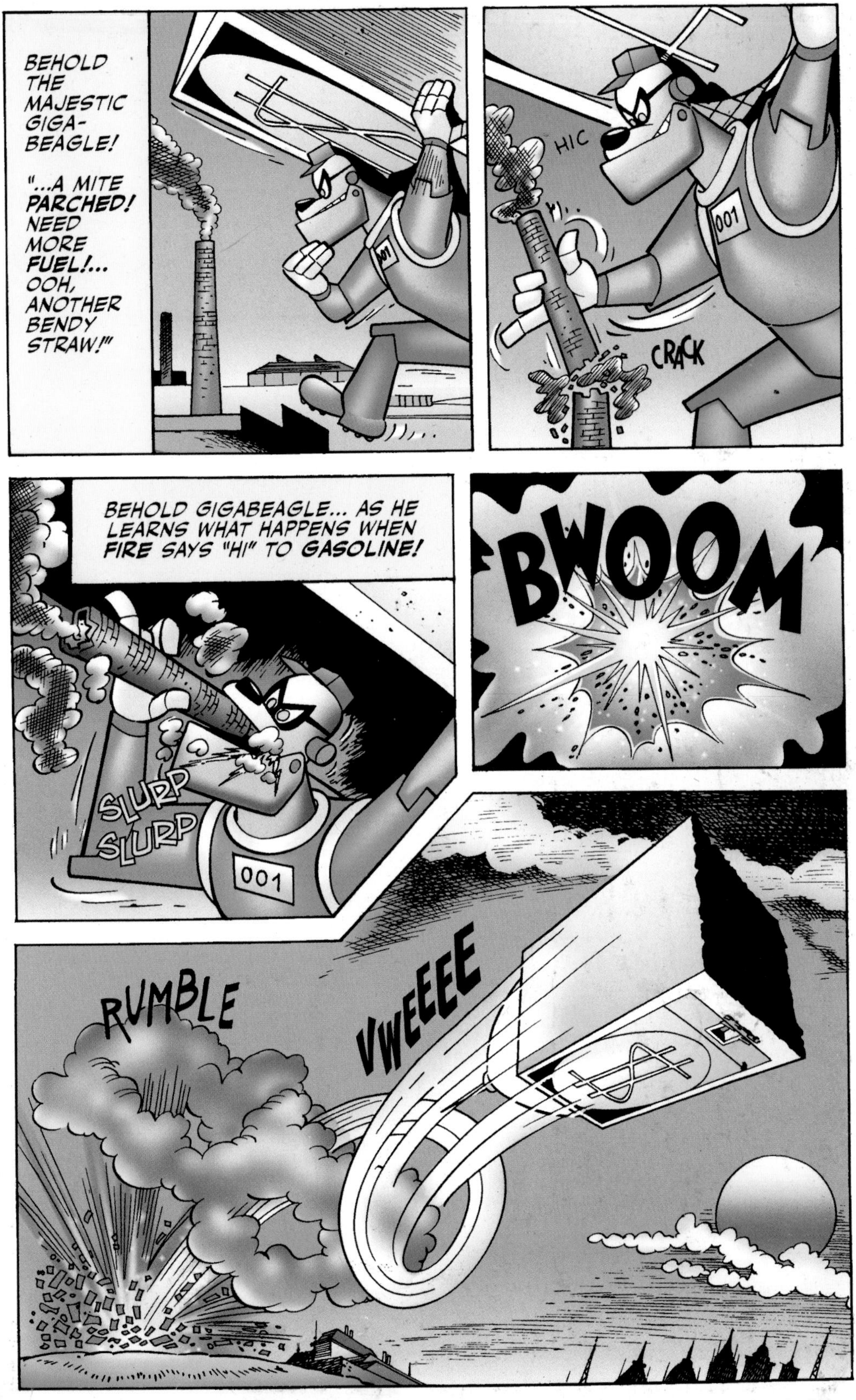

BEHOLD THE MAJESTIC GIGA-BEAGLE!
"...A MITE PARCHED! NEED MORE FUEL!... OOH, ANOTHER BENDY STRAW!"
001
HIC
001
CRACK
BEHOLD GIGABEAGLE... AS HE LEARNS WHAT HAPPENS WHEN FIRE SAYS "HI" TO GASOLINE!
SLURP
SLURP
001
BWOOM
RUMBLE
VWEEEE

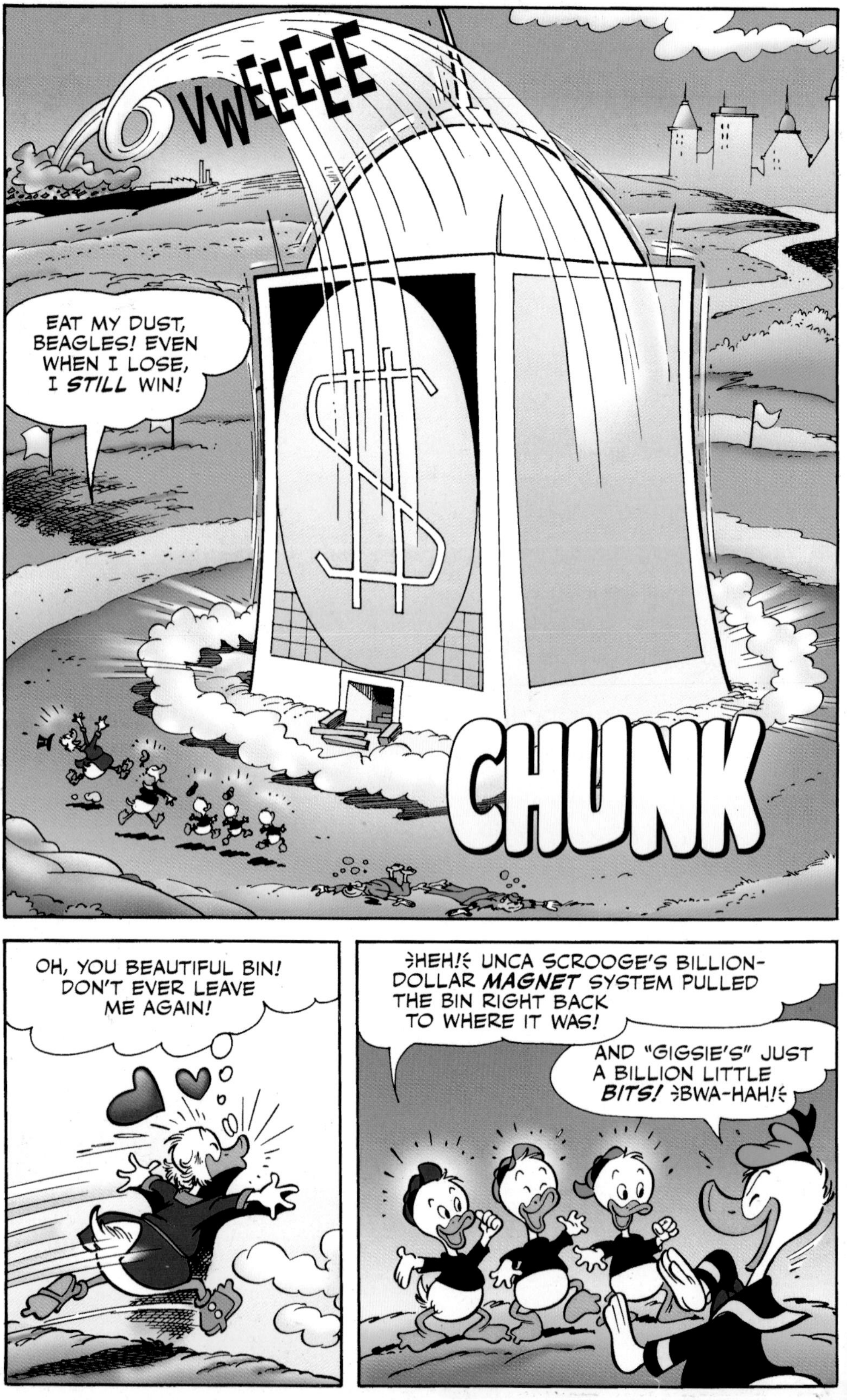
VWEEEEE
EAT MY DUST, BEAGLES! EVEN WHEN I LOSE, I STILL WIN!
CHUNK
OH, YOU BEAUTIFUL BIN! DON'T EVER LEAVE ME AGAIN!
HEH! UNCA SCROOGE'S BILLION-DOLLAR MAGNET SYSTEM PULLED THE BIN RIGHT BACK TO WHERE IT WAS!
AND "GIGSIE'S" JUST A BILLION LITTLE BITS! BWA-HAH!

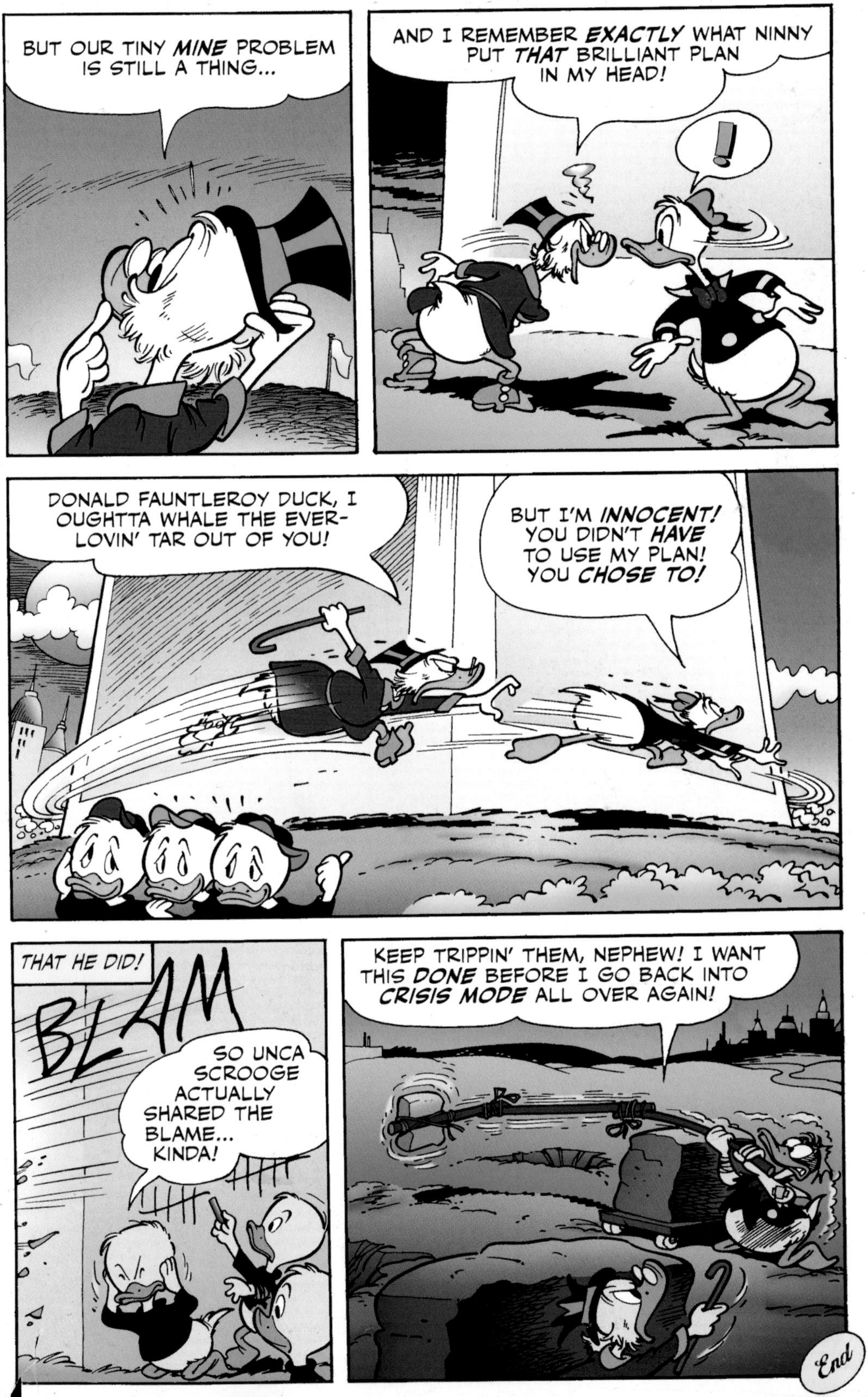
BUT OUR TINY MINE PROBLEM IS STILL A THING...
AND I REMEMBER EXACTLY WHAT NINNY PUT THAT BRILLIANT PLAN IN MY HEAD!
!
DONALD FAUNTLEROY DUCK, I OUGHTTA WHALE THE EVER-LOVIN' TAR OUT OF YOU!
BUT I'M INNOCENT! YOU DIDN'T HAVE TO USE MY PLAN! YOU CHOSE TO!
THAT HE DID!
BLAM
SO UNCA SCROOGE ACTUALLY SHARED THE BLAME... KINDA!
KEEP TRIPPIN' THEM, NEPHEW! I WANT THIS DONE BEFORE I GO BACK INTO CRISIS MODE ALL OVER AGAIN!
End

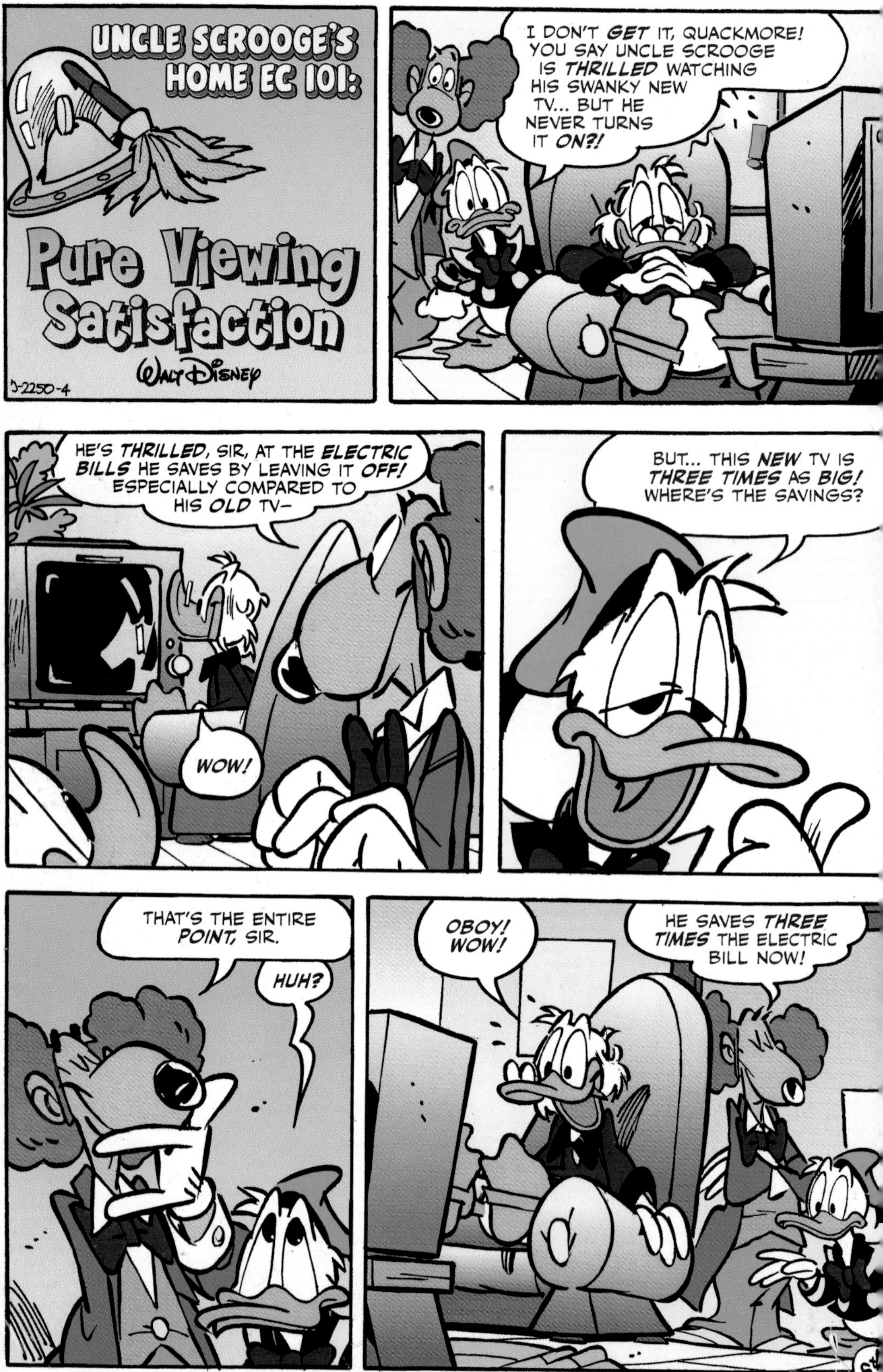
UNCLE SCROOGE'S HOME EC 101:
Pure Viewing Satisfaction
WALT DISNEY
J-2250-4
I DON'T GET IT, QUACKMORE! YOU SAY UNCLE SCROOGE IS THRILLED WATCHING HIS SWANKY NEW TV... BUT HE NEVER TURNS IT ON?!
HE'S THRILLED, SIR, AT THE ELECTRIC BILLS HE SAVES BY LEAVING IT OFF! ESPECIALLY COMPARED TO HIS OLD TV–
WOW!
BUT... THIS NEW TV IS THREE TIMES AS BIG! WHERE'S THE SAVINGS?
THAT'S THE ENTIRE POINT, SIR.
HUH?
OBOY! WOW!
HE SAVES THREE TIMES THE ELECTRIC BILL NOW!

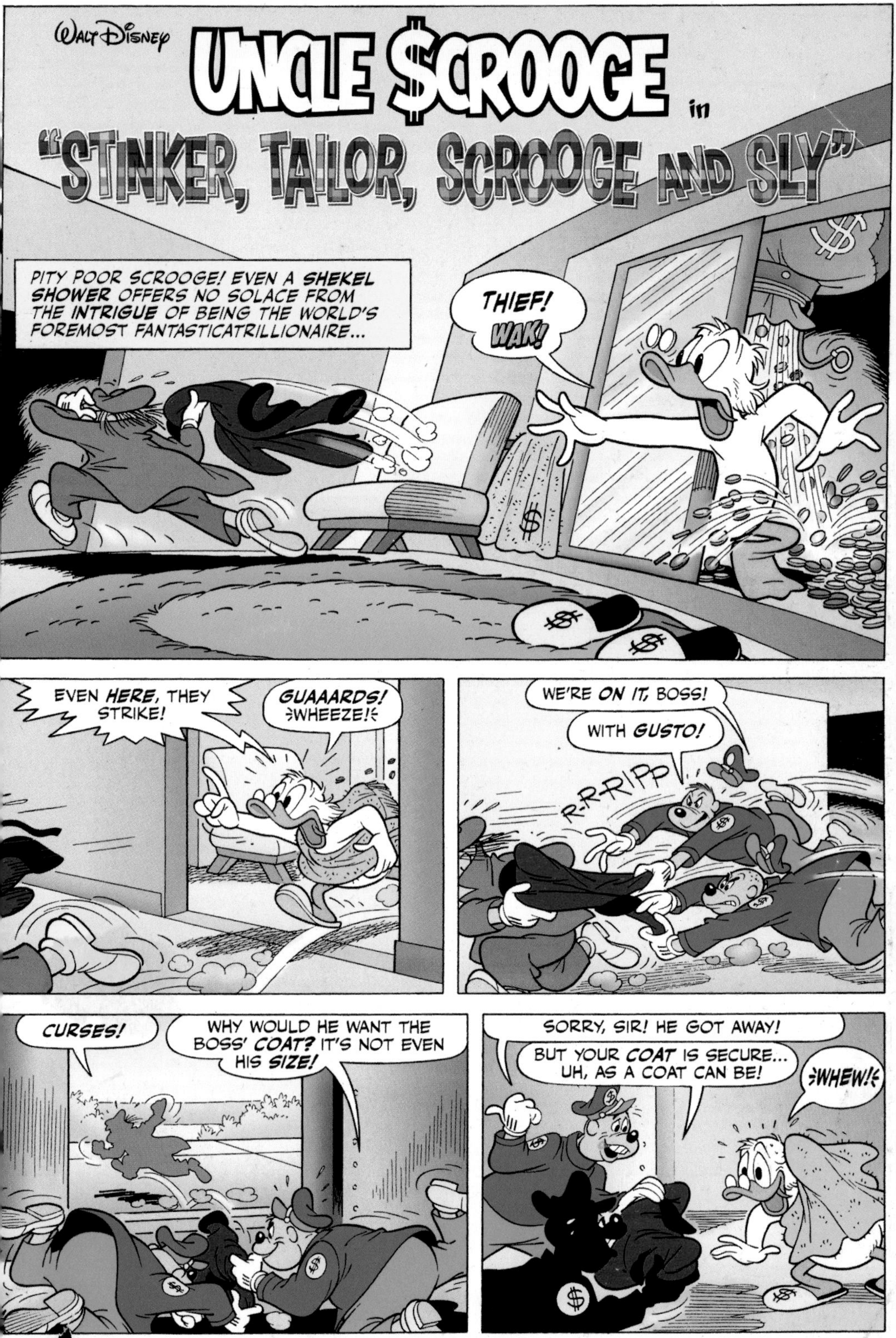

WALT DISNEY
UNCLE $CROOGE in
"STINKER, TAILOR, SCROOGE AND SLY"
PITY POOR SCROOGE! EVEN A SHEKEL SHOWER OFFERS NO SOLACE FROM THE INTRIGUE OF BEING THE WORLD'S FOREMOST FANTASTICATRILLIONAIRE...
THIEF! WAK!
EVEN HERE, THEY STRIKE!
GUAAARDS! WHEEZE!
WE'RE ON IT, BOSS!
WITH GUSTO!
R-R-RIPP
CURSES!
WHY WOULD HE WANT THE BOSS' COAT? IT'S NOT EVEN HIS SIZE!
SORRY, SIR! HE GOT AWAY!
BUT YOUR COAT IS SECURE... UH, AS A COAT CAN BE!
WHEW!

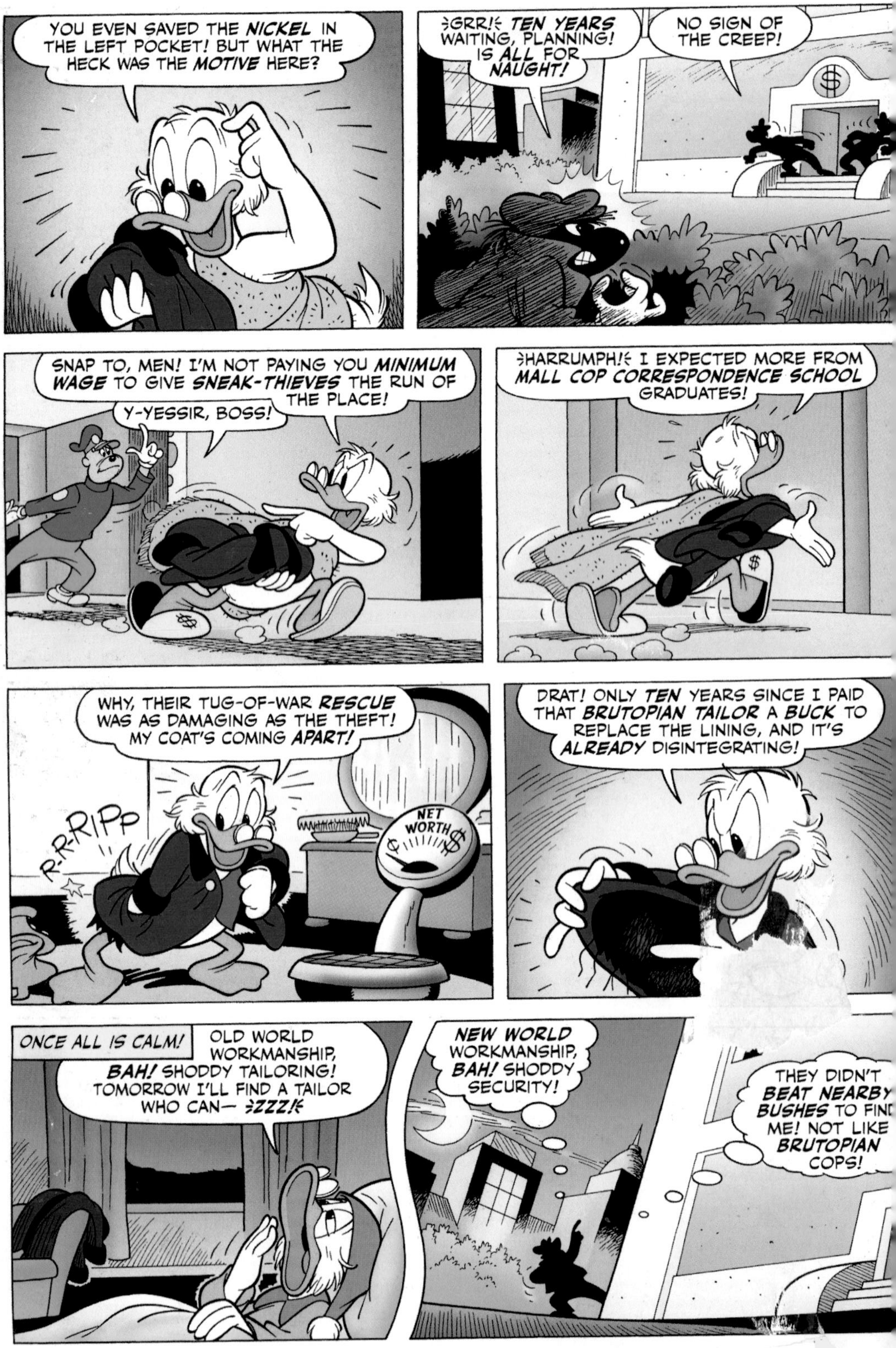
YOU EVEN SAVED THE NICKEL IN THE LEFT POCKET! BUT WHAT THE HECK WAS THE MOTIVE HERE?
GRR! TEN YEARS WAITING, PLANNING! IS ALL FOR NAUGHT!
NO SIGN OF THE CREEP!
SNAP TO, MEN! I'M NOT PAYING YOU MINIMUM WAGE TO GIVE SNEAK-THIEVES THE RUN OF THE PLACE!
Y-YESSIR, BOSS!
HARRUMPH! I EXPECTED MORE FROM MALL COP CORRESPONDENCE SCHOOL GRADUATES!
WHY, THEIR TUG-OF-WAR RESCUE WAS AS DAMAGING AS THE THEFT! MY COAT'S COMING APART!
R-R-RIPP
NET WORTH
DRAT! ONLY TEN YEARS SINCE I PAID THAT BRUTOPIAN TAILOR A BUCK TO REPLACE THE LINING, AND IT'S ALREADY DISINTEGRATING!
ONCE ALL IS CALM!
OLD WORLD WORKMANSHIP, BAH! SHODDY TAILORING! TOMORROW I'LL FIND A TAILOR WHO CAN— ZZZ!
NEW WORLD WORKMANSHIP, BAH! SHODDY SECURITY!
THEY DIDN'T BEAT NEARBY BUSHES TO FIND ME! NOT LIKE BRUTOPIAN COPS!

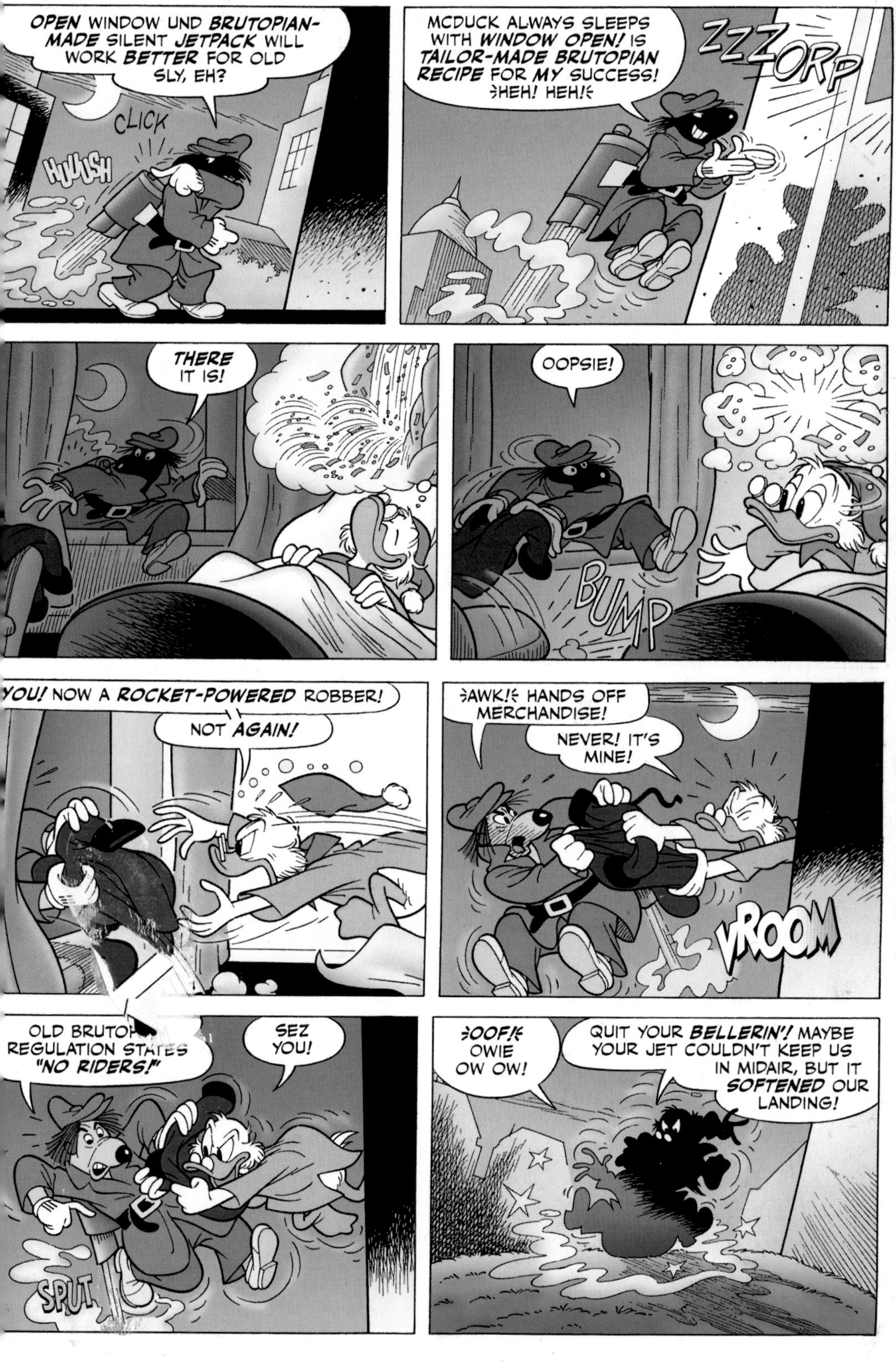
OPEN WINDOW UND BRUTOPIAN-MADE SILENT JETPACK WILL WORK BETTER FOR OLD SLY, EH?
CLICK
HUUUSH
MCDUCK ALWAYS SLEEPS WITH WINDOW OPEN! IS TAILOR-MADE BRUTOPIAN RECIPE FOR MY SUCCESS! HEH! HEH!
ZZZORP
THERE IT IS!
OOPSIE!
BUMP
YOU! NOW A ROCKET-POWERED ROBBER!
NOT AGAIN!
AWK! HANDS OFF MERCHANDISE!
NEVER! IT'S MINE!
VROOM
OLD BRUTOPIAN REGULATION STATES "NO RIDERS!"
SEZ YOU!
SPUT
OOF! OWIE OW OW!
QUIT YOUR BELLERIN'! MAYBE YOUR JET COULDN'T KEEP US IN MIDAIR, BUT IT SOFTENED OUR LANDING!

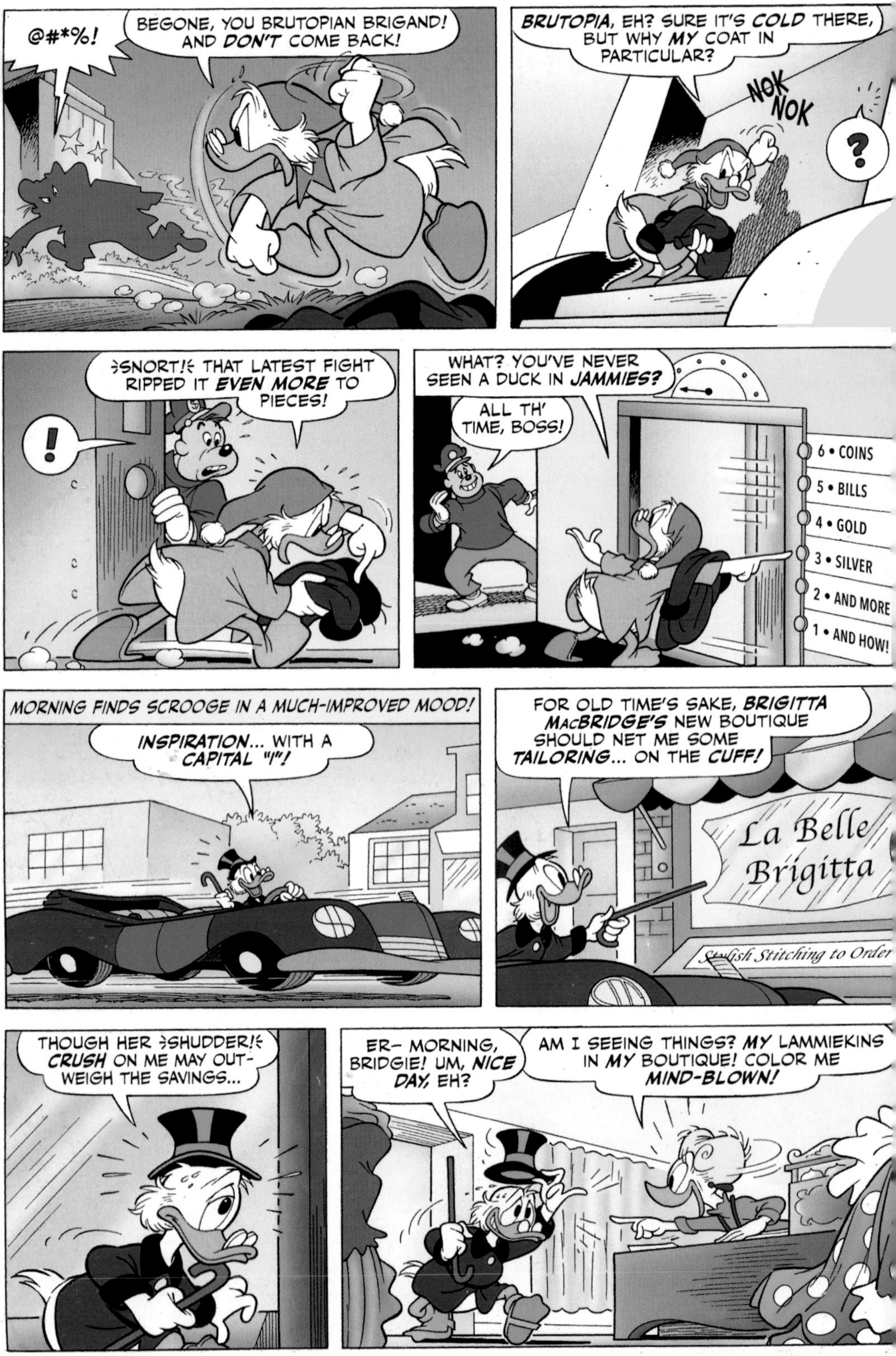
@#*%!
BEGONE, YOU BRUTOPIAN BRIGAND! AND DON'T COME BACK!
BRUTOPIA, EH? SURE IT'S COLD THERE, BUT WHY MY COAT IN PARTICULAR?
NOK NOK
?
!
SNORT! THAT LATEST FIGHT RIPPED IT EVEN MORE TO PIECES!
WHAT? YOU'VE NEVER SEEN A DUCK IN JAMMIES?
ALL TH' TIME, BOSS!
6 • COINS
5 • BILLS
4 • GOLD
3 • SILVER
2 • AND MORE
1 • AND HOW!
MORNING FINDS SCROOGE IN A MUCH-IMPROVED MOOD!
INSPIRATION... WITH A CAPITAL "I"!
FOR OLD TIME'S SAKE, BRIGITTA MACBRIDGE'S NEW BOUTIQUE SHOULD NET ME SOME TAILORING... ON THE CUFF!
La Belle Brigitta
Stylish Stitching to Order
THOUGH HER SHUDDER! CRUSH ON ME MAY OUTWEIGH THE SAVINGS...
ER– MORNING, BRIDGIE! UM, NICE DAY, EH?
AM I SEEING THINGS? MY LAMMIEKINS IN MY BOUTIQUE! COLOR ME MIND-BLOWN!

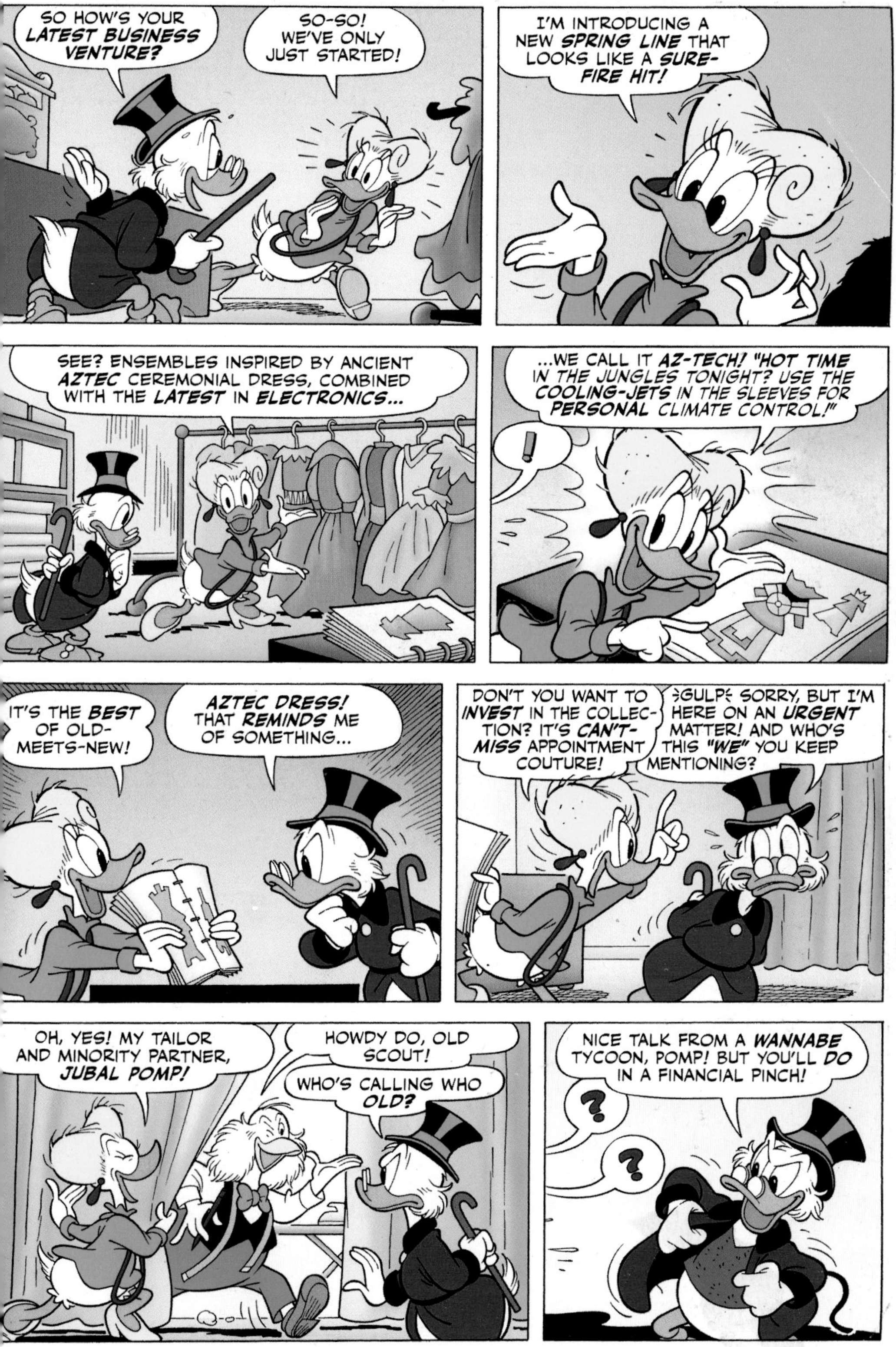
SO HOW'S YOUR LATEST BUSINESS VENTURE?
SO-SO! WE'VE ONLY JUST STARTED!
I'M INTRODUCING A NEW SPRING LINE THAT LOOKS LIKE A SURE-FIRE HIT!
SEE? ENSEMBLES INSPIRED BY ANCIENT AZTEC CEREMONIAL DRESS, COMBINED WITH THE LATEST IN ELECTRONICS...
...WE CALL IT AZ-TECH! "HOT TIME IN THE JUNGLES TONIGHT? USE THE COOLING-JETS IN THE SLEEVES FOR PERSONAL CLIMATE CONTROL!"
!
IT'S THE BEST OF OLD-MEETS-NEW!
AZTEC DRESS! THAT REMINDS ME OF SOMETHING...
DON'T YOU WANT TO INVEST IN THE COLLECTION? IT'S CAN'T-MISS APPOINTMENT COUTURE!
GULP SORRY, BUT I'M HERE ON AN URGENT MATTER! AND WHO'S THIS "WE" YOU KEEP MENTIONING?
OH, YES! MY TAILOR AND MINORITY PARTNER, JUBAL POMP!
HOWDY DO, OLD SCOUT!
WHO'S CALLING WHO OLD?
NICE TALK FROM A WANNABE TYCOON, POMP! BUT YOU'LL DO IN A FINANCIAL PINCH!
?
?

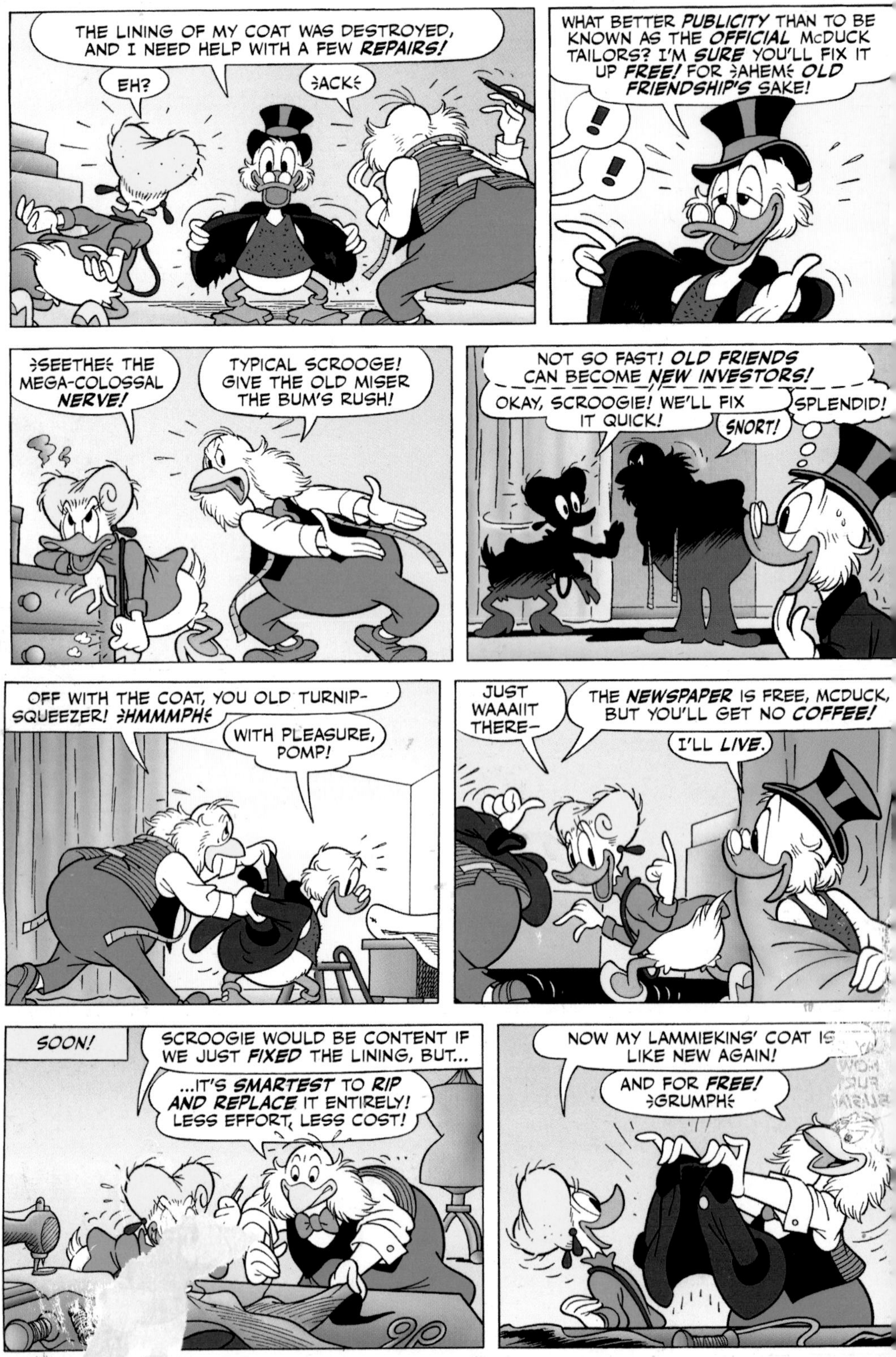
THE LINING OF MY COAT WAS DESTROYED, AND I NEED HELP WITH A FEW *REPAIRS!*
EH?
ACK
WHAT BETTER *PUBLICITY* THAN TO BE KNOWN AS THE *OFFICIAL* McDUCK TAILORS? I'M *SURE* YOU'LL FIX IT UP *FREE!* FOR AHEM *OLD FRIENDSHIP'S* SAKE!
!
!
SEETHE THE MEGA-COLOSSAL *NERVE!*
TYPICAL SCROOGE! GIVE THE OLD MISER THE BUM'S RUSH!
NOT SO FAST! *OLD FRIENDS* CAN BECOME *NEW INVESTORS!*
OKAY, SCROOGIE! WE'LL FIX IT QUICK!
SNORT!
SPLENDID!
OFF WITH THE COAT, YOU OLD TURNIP-SQUEEZER! *HMMMPH*
WITH PLEASURE, POMP!
JUST WAAAIIT THERE—
THE *NEWSPAPER* IS FREE, MCDUCK, BUT YOU'LL GET NO *COFFEE!*
I'LL *LIVE.*
SOON!
SCROOGIE WOULD BE CONTENT IF WE JUST *FIXED* THE LINING, BUT...
...IT'S *SMARTEST* TO *RIP AND REPLACE* IT ENTIRELY! LESS EFFORT, LESS COST!
NOW MY LAMMIEKINS' COAT IS LIKE NEW AGAIN!
AND FOR *FREE!* GRUMPH

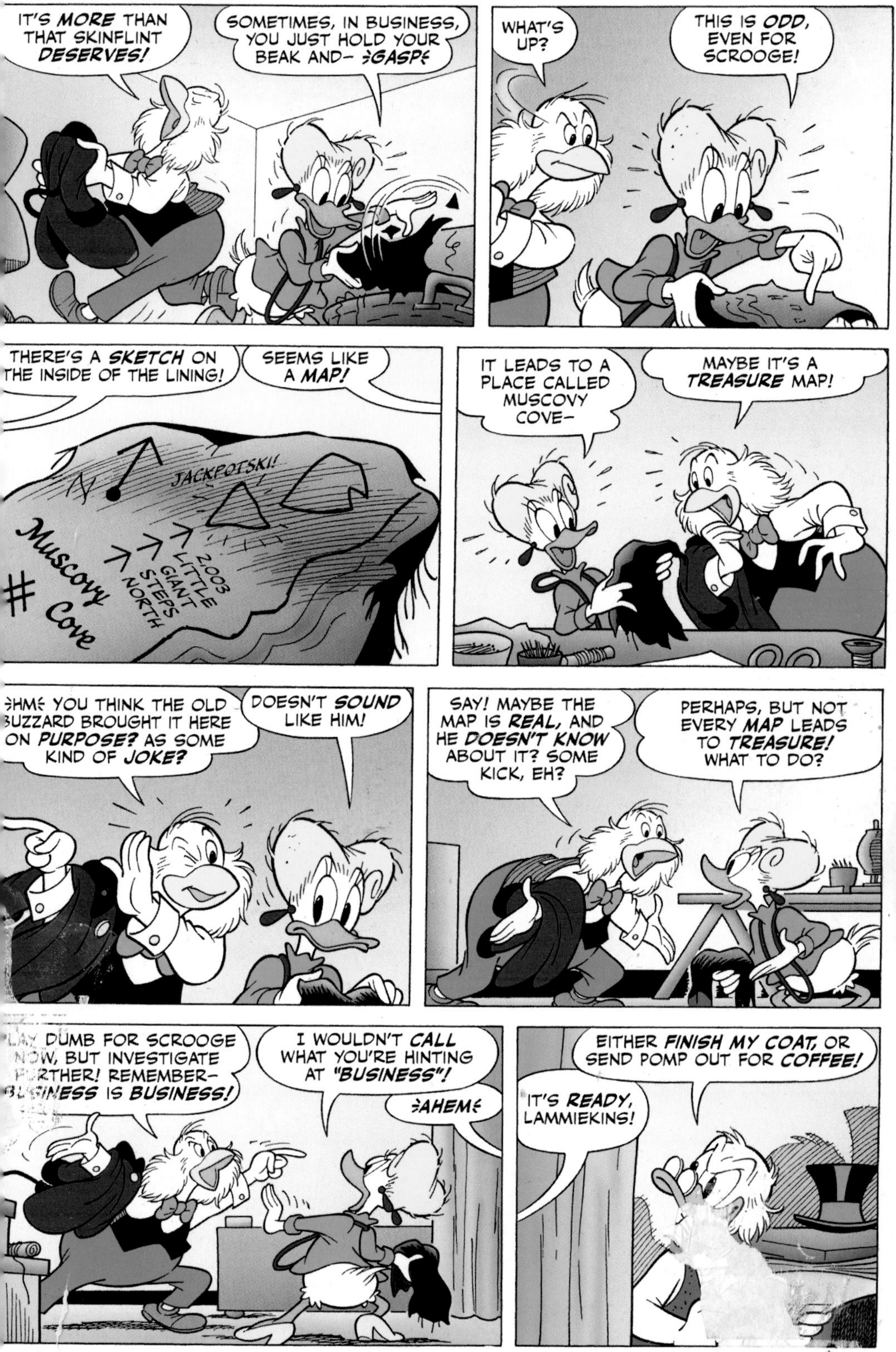

IT'S MORE THAN THAT SKINFLINT DESERVES!
SOMETIMES, IN BUSINESS, YOU JUST HOLD YOUR BEAK AND– GASP
WHAT'S UP?
THIS IS ODD, EVEN FOR SCROOGE!
THERE'S A SKETCH ON THE INSIDE OF THE LINING!
SEEMS LIKE A MAP!
JACKPOTSKI!
Muscovy Cove
2003 LITTLE GIANT STEPS NORTH
N
IT LEADS TO A PLACE CALLED MUSCOVY COVE–
MAYBE IT'S A TREASURE MAP!
HM YOU THINK THE OLD BUZZARD BROUGHT IT HERE ON PURPOSE? AS SOME KIND OF JOKE?
DOESN'T SOUND LIKE HIM!
SAY! MAYBE THE MAP IS REAL, AND HE DOESN'T KNOW ABOUT IT? SOME KICK, EH?
PERHAPS, BUT NOT EVERY MAP LEADS TO TREASURE! WHAT TO DO?
PLAY DUMB FOR SCROOGE NOW, BUT INVESTIGATE FURTHER! REMEMBER– BUSINESS IS BUSINESS!
I WOULDN'T CALL WHAT YOU'RE HINTING AT "BUSINESS"!
AHEM
EITHER FINISH MY COAT, OR SEND POMP OUT FOR COFFEE!
IT'S READY, LAMMIEKINS!

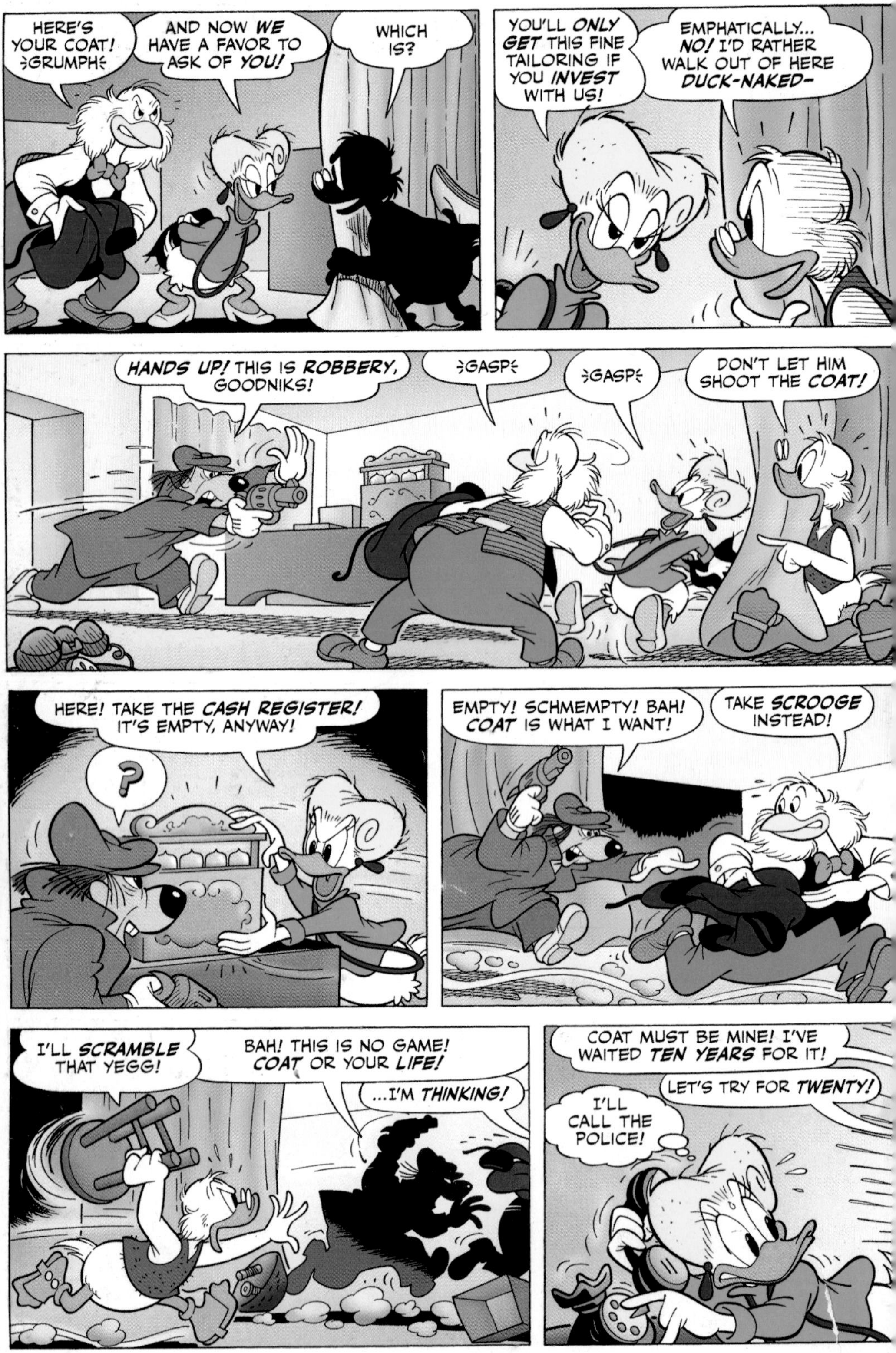
HERE'S YOUR COAT! ≻GRUMPH≺
AND NOW WE HAVE A FAVOR TO ASK OF YOU!
WHICH IS?
YOU'LL ONLY GET THIS FINE TAILORING IF YOU INVEST WITH US!
EMPHATICALLY... NO! I'D RATHER WALK OUT OF HERE DUCK-NAKED—
HANDS UP! THIS IS ROBBERY, GOODNIKS!
≻GASP≺
≻GASP≺
DON'T LET HIM SHOOT THE COAT!
HERE! TAKE THE CASH REGISTER! IT'S EMPTY, ANYWAY!
?
EMPTY! SCHMEMPTY! BAH! COAT IS WHAT I WANT!
TAKE SCROOGE INSTEAD!
I'LL SCRAMBLE THAT YEGG!
BAH! THIS IS NO GAME! COAT OR YOUR LIFE!
...I'M THINKING!
COAT MUST BE MINE! I'VE WAITED TEN YEARS FOR IT!
LET'S TRY FOR TWENTY!
I'LL CALL THE POLICE!

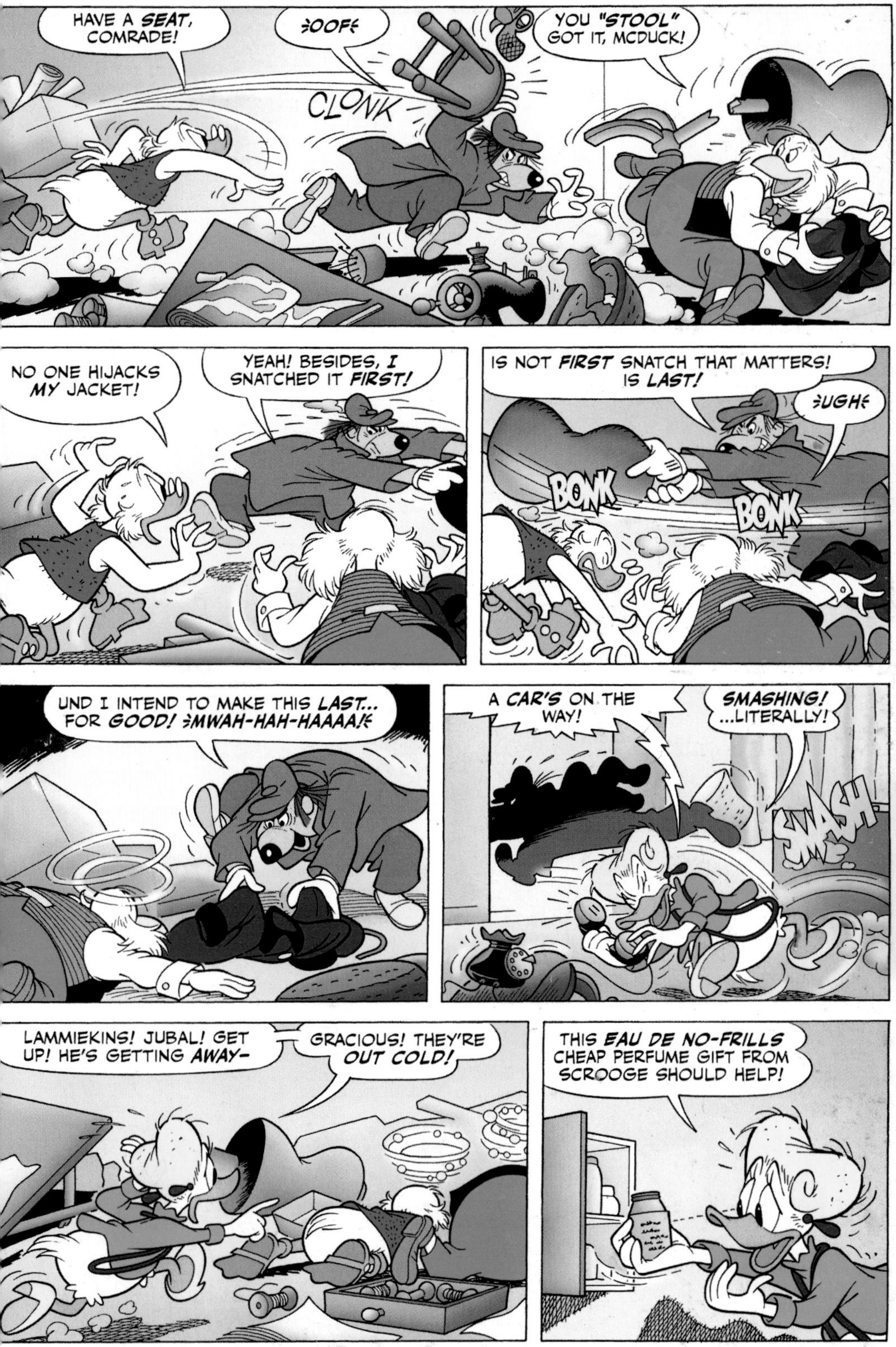
HAVE A SEAT, COMRADE!
≯OOF≮
CLONK
YOU "STOOL" GOT IT, MCDUCK!
NO ONE HIJACKS MY JACKET!
YEAH! BESIDES, I SNATCHED IT FIRST!
IS NOT FIRST SNATCH THAT MATTERS! IS LAST!
≯UGH≮
BONK
BONK
UND I INTEND TO MAKE THIS LAST... FOR GOOD! ≯MWAH-HAH-HAAAA!≮
A CAR'S ON THE WAY!
SMASHING! ...LITERALLY!
SMASH
LAMMIEKINS! JUBAL! GET UP! HE'S GETTING AWAY—
GRACIOUS! THEY'RE OUT COLD!
THIS EAU DE NO-FRILLS CHEAP PERFUME GIFT FROM SCROOGE SHOULD HELP!

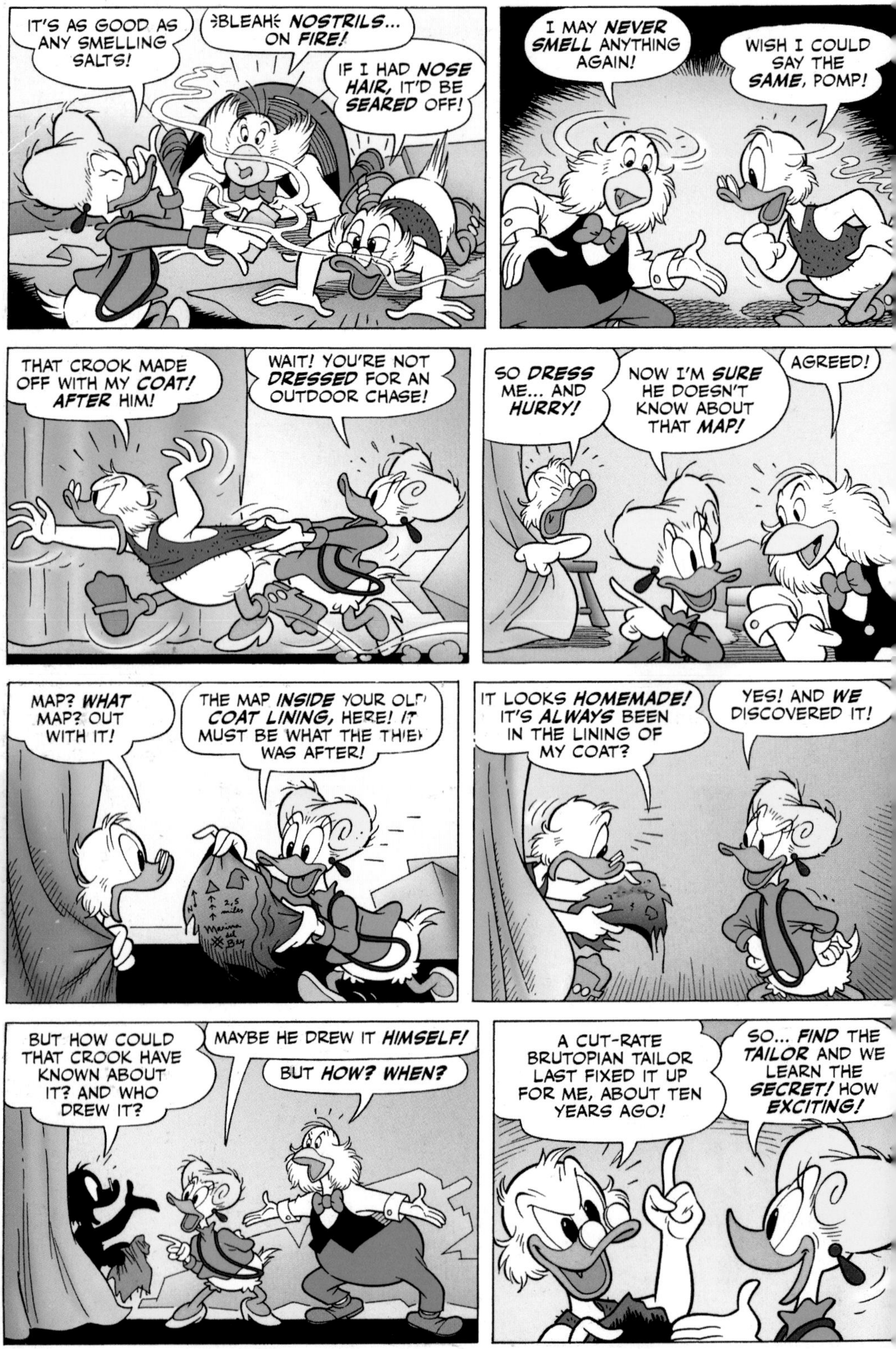
IT'S AS GOOD AS ANY SMELLING SALTS!
BLEAH! NOSTRILS... ON FIRE!
IF I HAD NOSE HAIR, IT'D BE SEARED OFF!
I MAY NEVER SMELL ANYTHING AGAIN!
WISH I COULD SAY THE SAME, POMP!
THAT CROOK MADE OFF WITH MY COAT! AFTER HIM!
WAIT! YOU'RE NOT DRESSED FOR AN OUTDOOR CHASE!
SO DRESS ME... AND HURRY!
NOW I'M SURE HE DOESN'T KNOW ABOUT THAT MAP!
AGREED!
MAP? WHAT MAP? OUT WITH IT!
THE MAP INSIDE YOUR OL COAT LINING, HERE! IT MUST BE WHAT THE THIE WAS AFTER!
IT LOOKS HOMEMADE! IT'S ALWAYS BEEN IN THE LINING OF MY COAT?
YES! AND WE DISCOVERED IT!
BUT HOW COULD THAT CROOK HAVE KNOWN ABOUT IT? AND WHO DREW IT?
MAYBE HE DREW IT HIMSELF!
BUT HOW? WHEN?
A CUT-RATE BRUTOPIAN TAILOR LAST FIXED IT UP FOR ME, ABOUT TEN YEARS AGO!
SO... FIND THE TAILOR AND WE LEARN THE SECRET! HOW EXCITING!

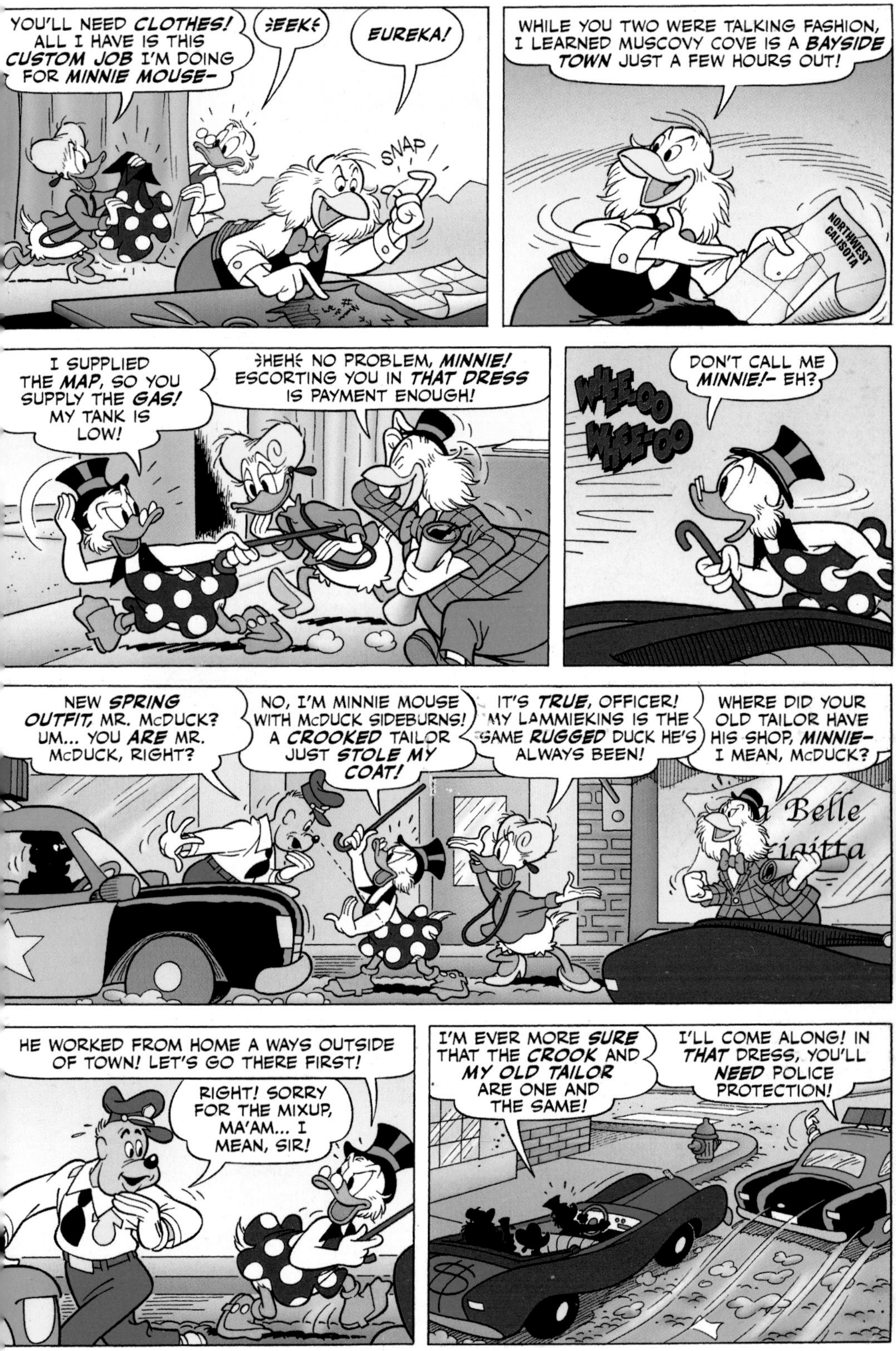

YOU'LL NEED CLOTHES! ALL I HAVE IS THIS CUSTOM JOB I'M DOING FOR MINNIE MOUSE-
EEK
EUREKA!
SNAP
WHILE YOU TWO WERE TALKING FASHION, I LEARNED MUSCOVY COVE IS A BAYSIDE TOWN JUST A FEW HOURS OUT!
NORTHWEST CALISOTA
I SUPPLIED THE MAP, SO YOU SUPPLY THE GAS! MY TANK IS LOW!
HEH NO PROBLEM, MINNIE! ESCORTING YOU IN THAT DRESS IS PAYMENT ENOUGH!
WHEE-OO WHEE-OO
DON'T CALL ME MINNIE!- EH?
NEW SPRING OUTFIT, MR. McDUCK? UM... YOU ARE MR. McDUCK, RIGHT?
NO, I'M MINNIE MOUSE WITH McDUCK SIDEBURNS! A CROOKED TAILOR JUST STOLE MY COAT!
IT'S TRUE, OFFICER! MY LAMMIEKINS IS THE SAME RUGGED DUCK HE'S ALWAYS BEEN!
WHERE DID YOUR OLD TAILOR HAVE HIS SHOP, MINNIE- I MEAN, McDUCK?
HE WORKED FROM HOME A WAYS OUTSIDE OF TOWN! LET'S GO THERE FIRST!
RIGHT! SORRY FOR THE MIXUP, MA'AM... I MEAN, SIR!
I'M EVER MORE SURE THAT THE CROOK AND MY OLD TAILOR ARE ONE AND THE SAME!
I'LL COME ALONG! IN THAT DRESS, YOU'LL NEED POLICE PROTECTION!

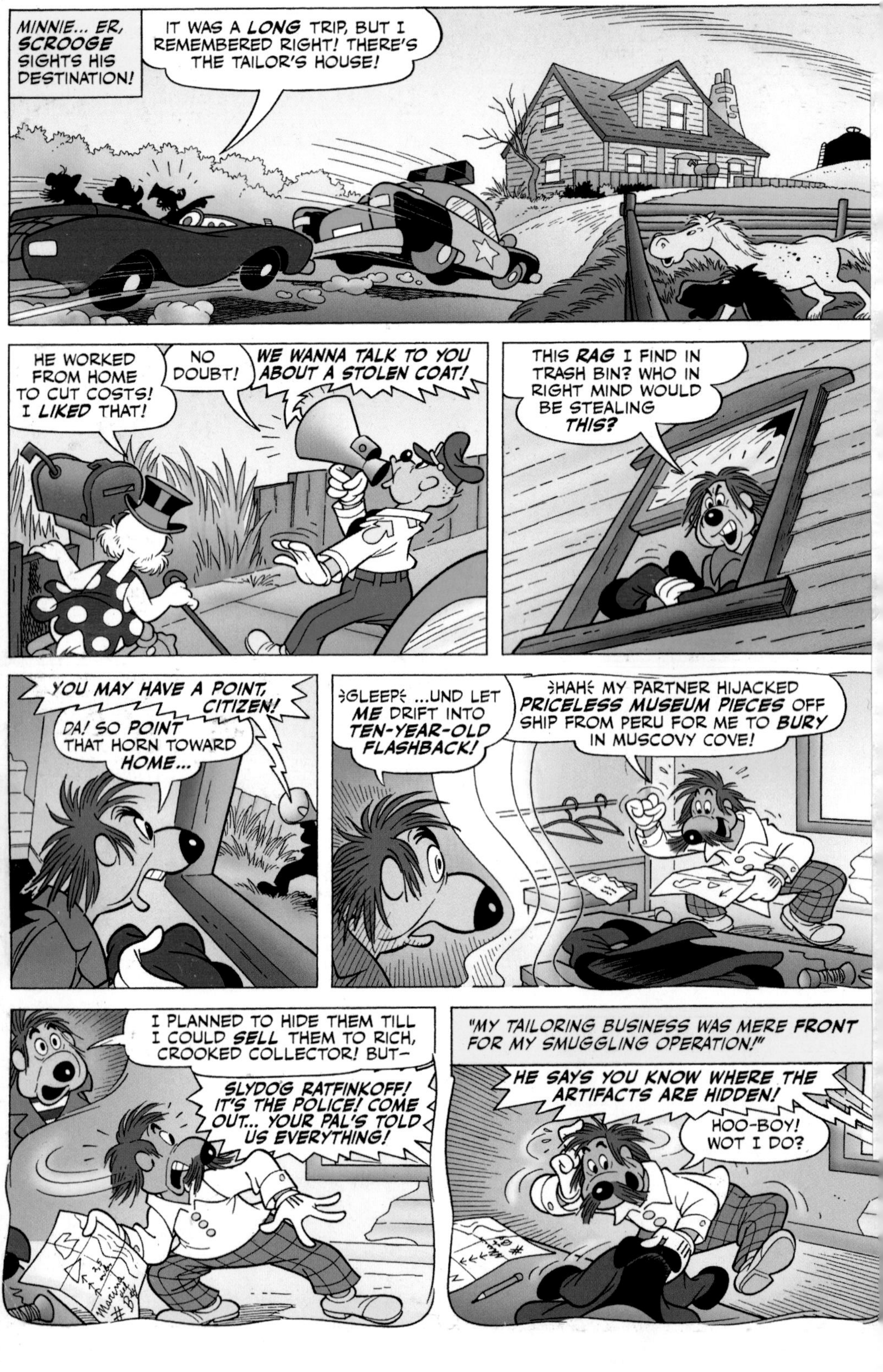
MINNIE... ER, SCROOGE SIGHTS HIS DESTINATION!
IT WAS A LONG TRIP, BUT I REMEMBERED RIGHT! THERE'S THE TAILOR'S HOUSE!
HE WORKED FROM HOME TO CUT COSTS! I LIKED THAT!
NO DOUBT!
WE WANNA TALK TO YOU ABOUT A STOLEN COAT!
THIS RAG I FIND IN TRASH BIN? WHO IN RIGHT MIND WOULD BE STEALING THIS?
YOU MAY HAVE A POINT, CITIZEN!
DA! SO POINT THAT HORN TOWARD HOME...
GLEEP ...UND LET ME DRIFT INTO TEN-YEAR-OLD FLASHBACK!
HAH MY PARTNER HIJACKED PRICELESS MUSEUM PIECES OFF SHIP FROM PERU FOR ME TO BURY IN MUSCOVY COVE!
I PLANNED TO HIDE THEM TILL I COULD SELL THEM TO RICH, CROOKED COLLECTOR! BUT—
SLYDOG RATFINKOFF! IT'S THE POLICE! COME OUT... YOUR PAL'S TOLD US EVERYTHING!
"MY TAILORING BUSINESS WAS MERE FRONT FOR MY SMUGGLING OPERATION!"
HE SAYS YOU KNOW WHERE THE ARTIFACTS ARE HIDDEN!
HOO-BOY! WOT I DO?

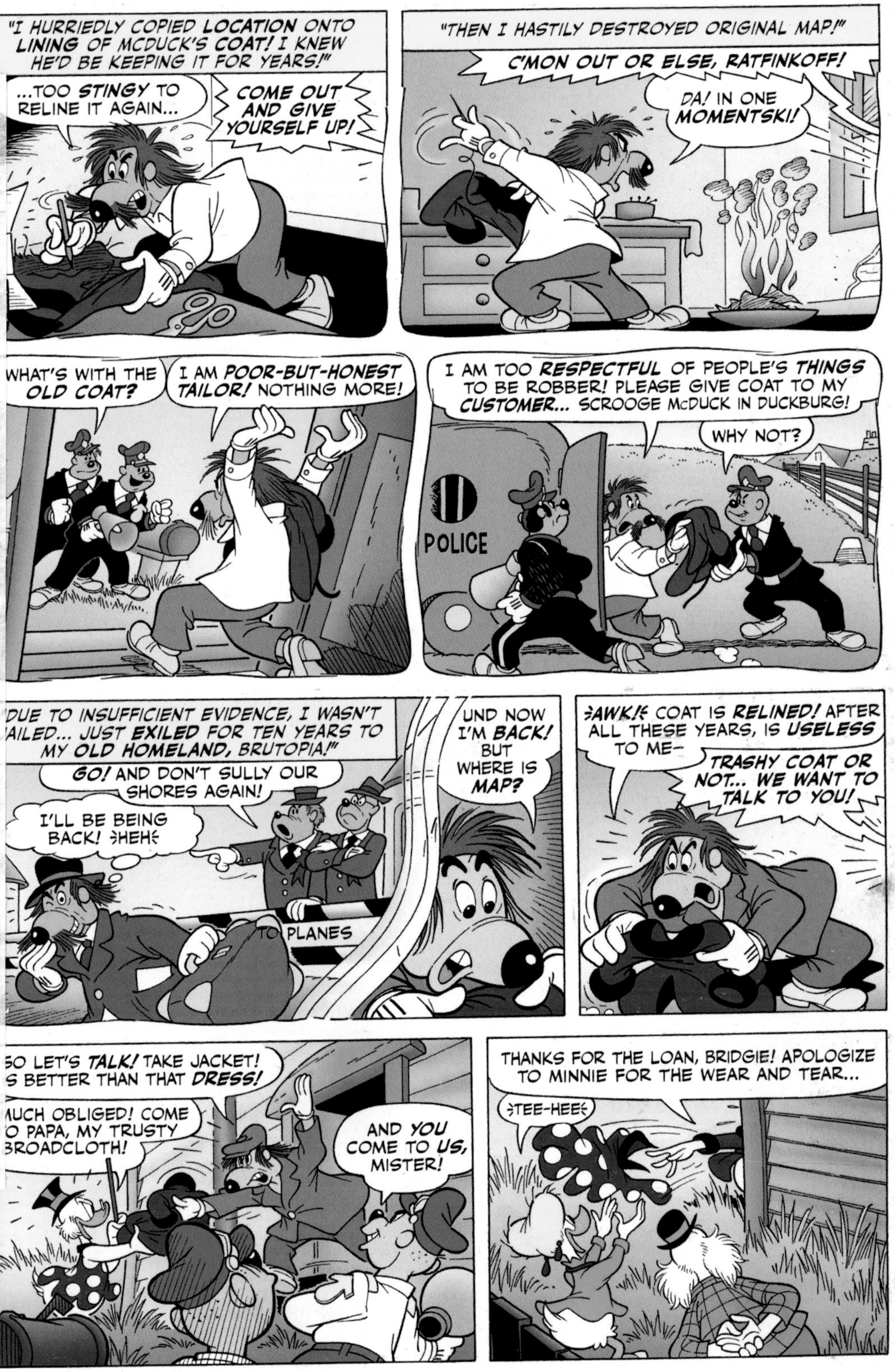
"I HURRIEDLY COPIED LOCATION ONTO LINING OF MCDUCK'S COAT! I KNEW HE'D BE KEEPING IT FOR YEARS!"
...TOO STINGY TO RELINE IT AGAIN...
COME OUT AND GIVE YOURSELF UP!
"THEN I HASTILY DESTROYED ORIGINAL MAP!"
C'MON OUT OR ELSE, RATFINKOFF!
DA! IN ONE MOMENTSKI!
WHAT'S WITH THE OLD COAT?
I AM POOR-BUT-HONEST TAILOR! NOTHING MORE!
I AM TOO RESPECTFUL OF PEOPLE'S THINGS TO BE ROBBER! PLEASE GIVE COAT TO MY CUSTOMER... SCROOGE McDUCK IN DUCKBURG!
WHY NOT?
POLICE
"DUE TO INSUFFICIENT EVIDENCE, I WASN'T JAILED... JUST EXILED FOR TEN YEARS TO MY OLD HOMELAND, BRUTOPIA!"
GO! AND DON'T SULLY OUR SHORES AGAIN!
I'LL BE BEING BACK! HEH
TO PLANES
UND NOW I'M BACK! BUT WHERE IS MAP?
AWK! COAT IS RELINED! AFTER ALL THESE YEARS, IS USELESS TO ME–
TRASHY COAT OR NOT... WE WANT TO TALK TO YOU!
SO LET'S TALK! TAKE JACKET! 'S BETTER THAN THAT DRESS!
MUCH OBLIGED! COME TO PAPA, MY TRUSTY BROADCLOTH!
AND YOU COME TO US, MISTER!
THANKS FOR THE LOAN, BRIDGIE! APOLOGIZE TO MINNIE FOR THE WEAR AND TEAR...
TEE-HEE

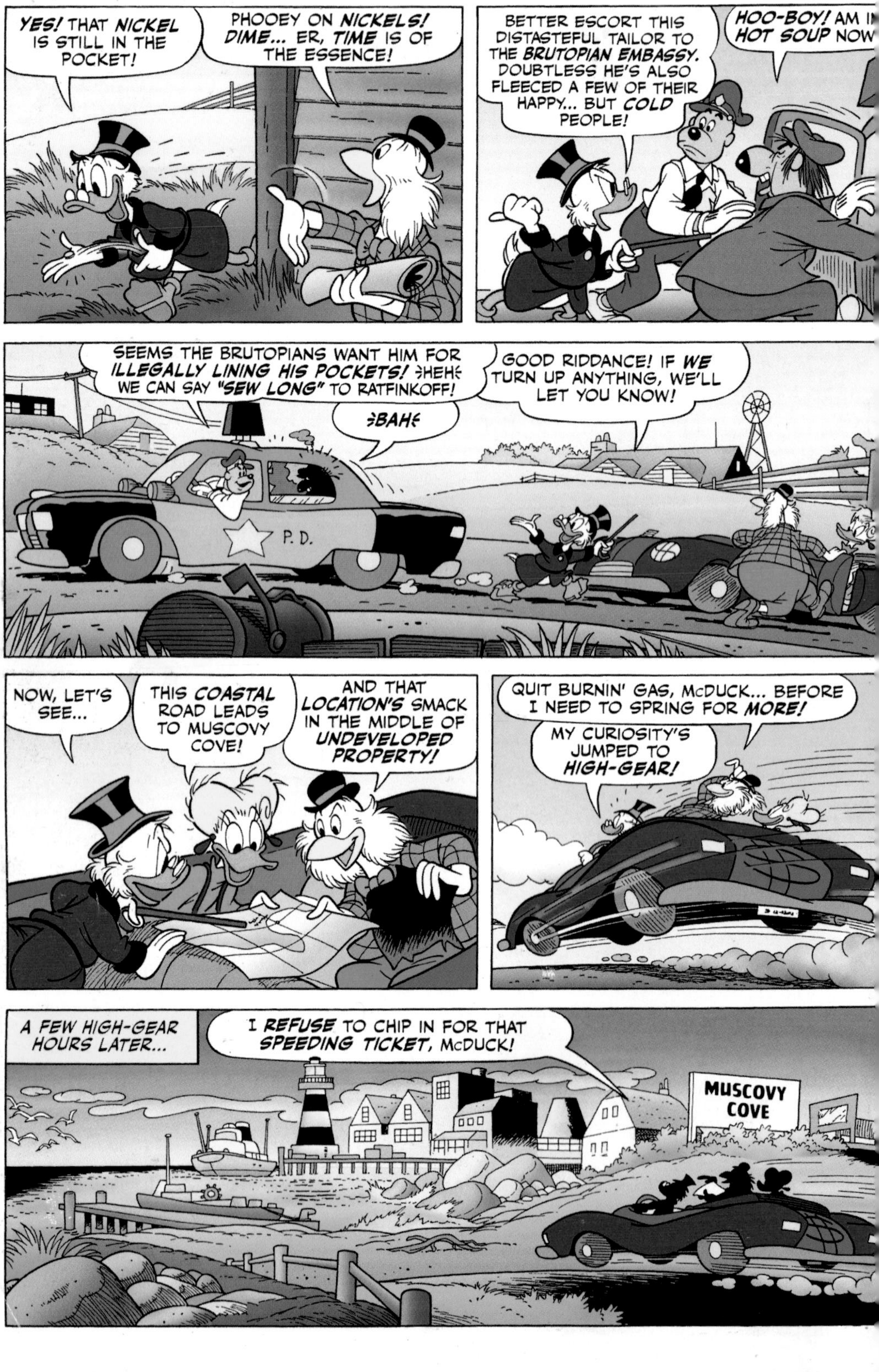
YES! THAT NICKEL IS STILL IN THE POCKET!
PHOOEY ON NICKELS! DIME... ER, TIME IS OF THE ESSENCE!
BETTER ESCORT THIS DISTASTEFUL TAILOR TO THE BRUTOPIAN EMBASSY. DOUBTLESS HE'S ALSO FLEECED A FEW OF THEIR HAPPY... BUT COLD PEOPLE!
HOO-BOY! AM I' HOT SOUP NOW
SEEMS THE BRUTOPIANS WANT HIM FOR ILLEGALLY LINING HIS POCKETS! HEH WE CAN SAY "SEW LONG" TO RATFINKOFF!
BAH
GOOD RIDDANCE! IF WE TURN UP ANYTHING, WE'LL LET YOU KNOW!
P.D.
NOW, LET'S SEE...
THIS COASTAL ROAD LEADS TO MUSCOVY COVE!
AND THAT LOCATION'S SMACK IN THE MIDDLE OF UNDEVELOPED PROPERTY!
QUIT BURNIN' GAS, McDUCK... BEFORE I NEED TO SPRING FOR MORE!
MY CURIOSITY'S JUMPED TO HIGH-GEAR!
A FEW HIGH-GEAR HOURS LATER...
I REFUSE TO CHIP IN FOR THAT SPEEDING TICKET, McDUCK!
MUSCOVY COVE

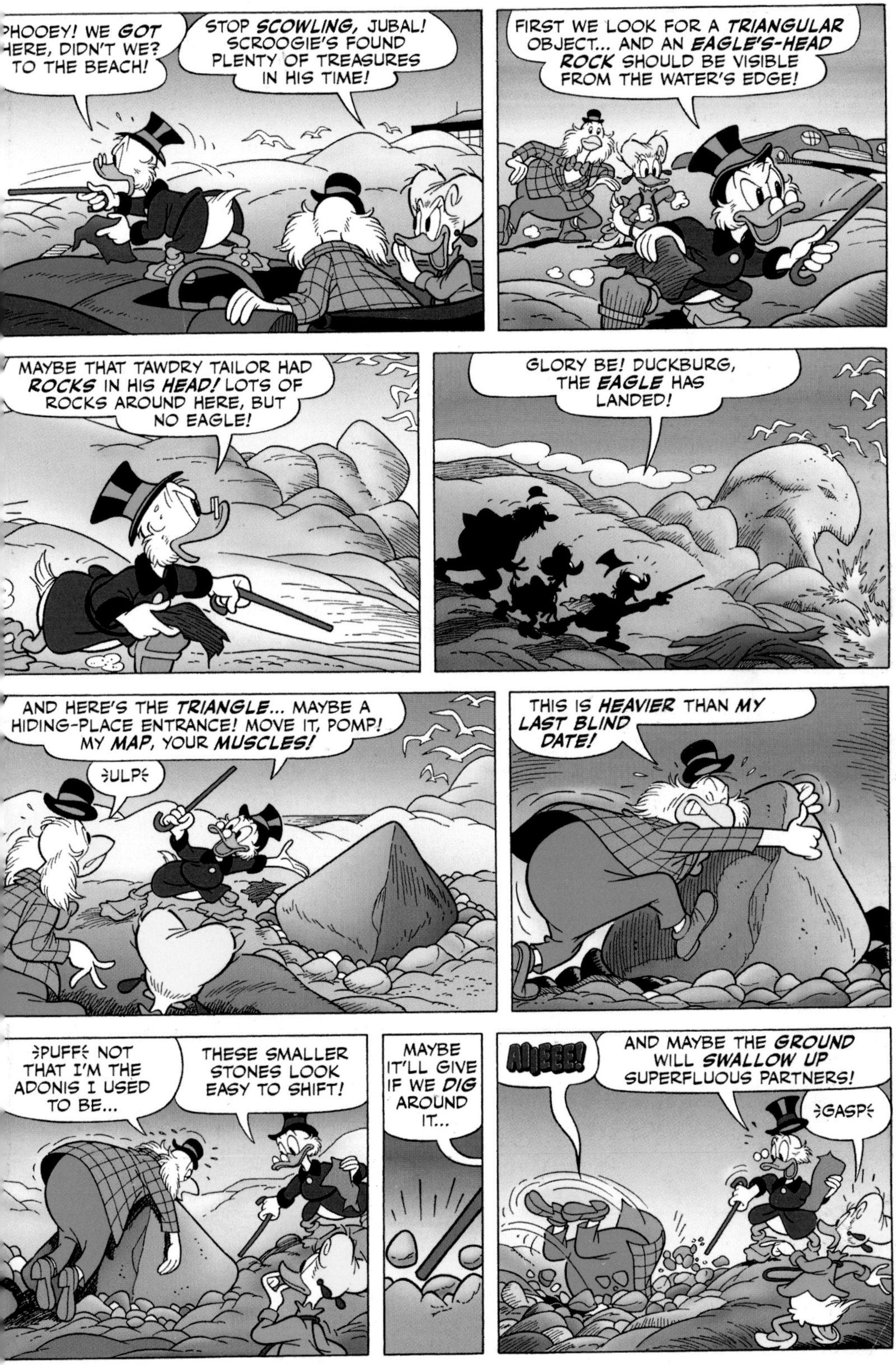
PHOOEY! WE GOT HERE, DIDN'T WE? TO THE BEACH!
STOP SCOWLING, JUBAL! SCROOGIE'S FOUND PLENTY OF TREASURES IN HIS TIME!
FIRST WE LOOK FOR A TRIANGULAR OBJECT... AND AN EAGLE'S-HEAD ROCK SHOULD BE VISIBLE FROM THE WATER'S EDGE!
MAYBE THAT TAWDRY TAILOR HAD ROCKS IN HIS HEAD! LOTS OF ROCKS AROUND HERE, BUT NO EAGLE!
GLORY BE! DUCKBURG, THE EAGLE HAS LANDED!
AND HERE'S THE TRIANGLE... MAYBE A HIDING-PLACE ENTRANCE! MOVE IT, POMP! MY MAP, YOUR MUSCLES!
ULP
THIS IS HEAVIER THAN MY LAST BLIND DATE!
PUFF NOT THAT I'M THE ADONIS I USED TO BE...
THESE SMALLER STONES LOOK EASY TO SHIFT!
MAYBE IT'LL GIVE IF WE DIG AROUND IT...
AIIEEEE!
AND MAYBE THE GROUND WILL SWALLOW UP SUPERFLUOUS PARTNERS!
GASP

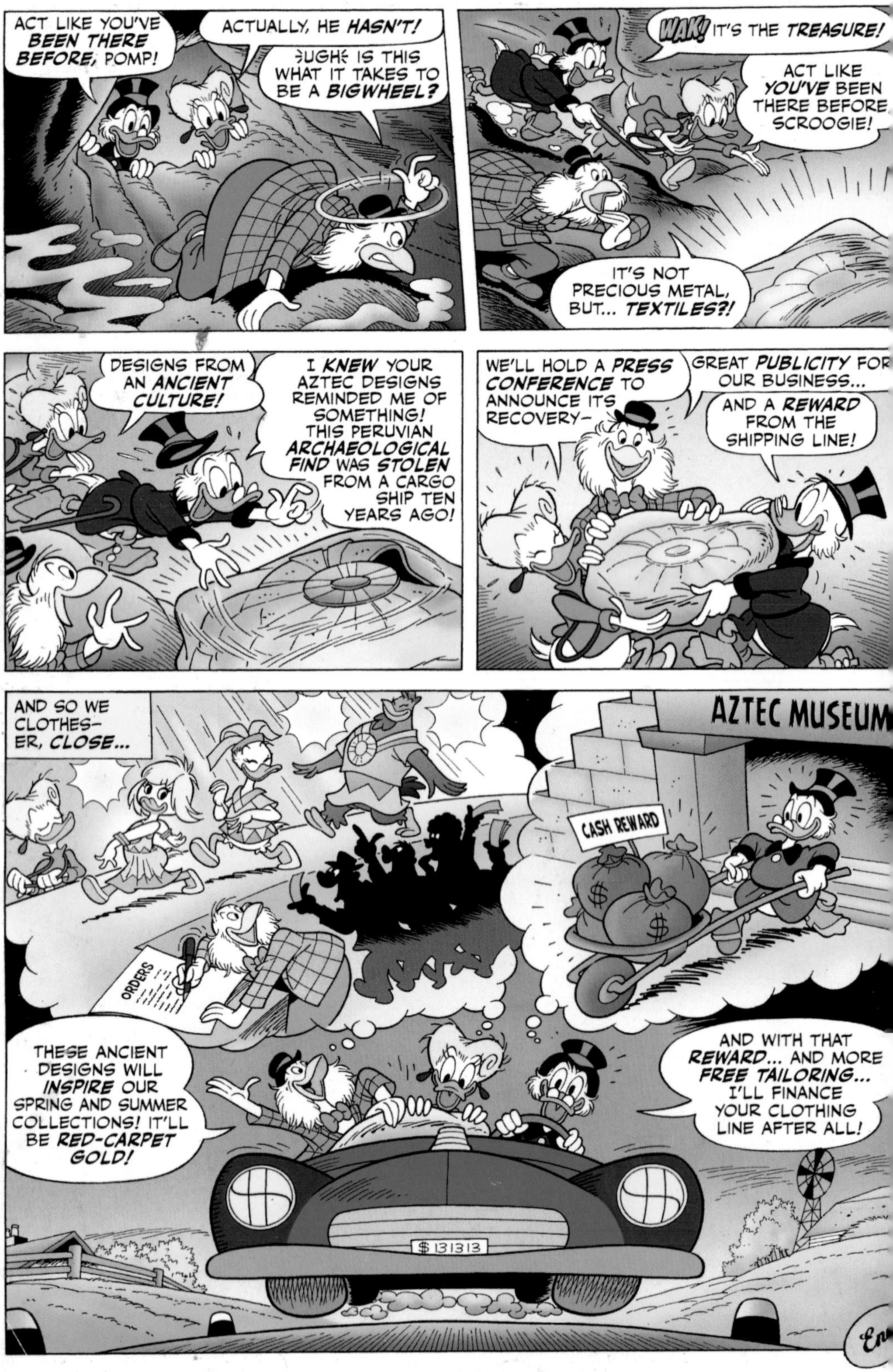
ACT LIKE YOU'VE BEEN THERE BEFORE, POMP!
ACTUALLY, HE HASN'T!
UGH IS THIS WHAT IT TAKES TO BE A BIGWHEEL?
WAK! IT'S THE TREASURE!
ACT LIKE YOU'VE BEEN THERE BEFORE SCROOGIE!
IT'S NOT PRECIOUS METAL, BUT... TEXTILES?!
DESIGNS FROM AN ANCIENT CULTURE!
I KNEW YOUR AZTEC DESIGNS REMINDED ME OF SOMETHING! THIS PERUVIAN ARCHAEOLOGICAL FIND WAS STOLEN FROM A CARGO SHIP TEN YEARS AGO!
WE'LL HOLD A PRESS CONFERENCE TO ANNOUNCE ITS RECOVERY—
GREAT PUBLICITY FOR OUR BUSINESS...
AND A REWARD FROM THE SHIPPING LINE!
AND SO WE CLOTHES— ER, CLOSE...
AZTEC MUSEUM
CASH REWARD
ORDERS
THESE ANCIENT DESIGNS WILL INSPIRE OUR SPRING AND SUMMER COLLECTIONS! IT'LL BE RED-CARPET GOLD!
AND WITH THAT REWARD... AND MORE FREE TAILORING... I'LL FINANCE YOUR CLOTHING LINE AFTER ALL!
$ 131313

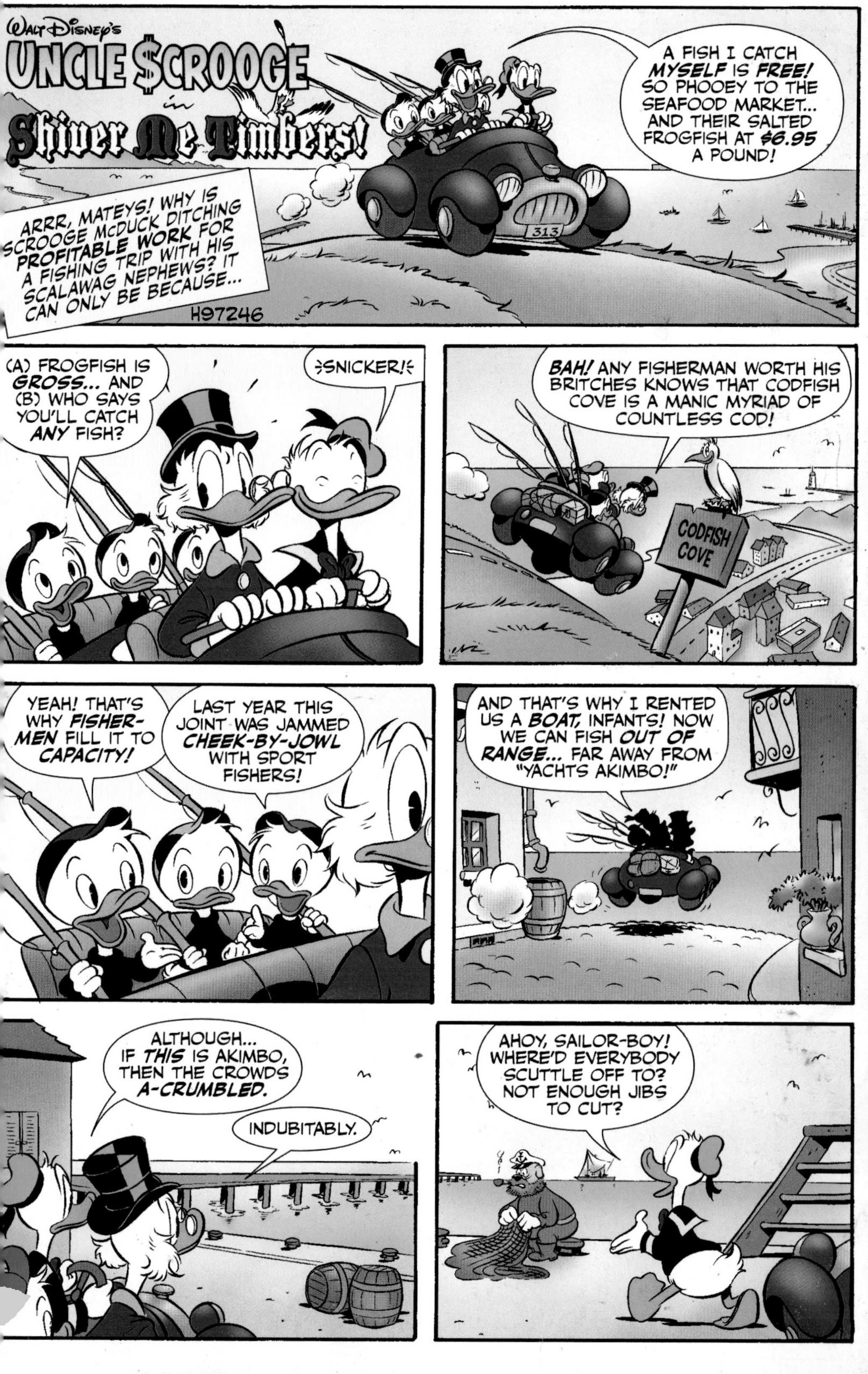
Walt Disney's
UNCLE $CROOGE
in
Shiver Me Timbers!
A FISH I CATCH MYSELF IS FREE! SO PHOOEY TO THE SEAFOOD MARKET... AND THEIR SALTED FROGFISH AT $6.95 A POUND!
ARRR, MATEYS! WHY IS SCROOGE McDUCK DITCHING PROFITABLE WORK FOR A FISHING TRIP WITH HIS SCALAWAG NEPHEWS? IT CAN ONLY BE BECAUSE...
313
H97246
(A) FROGFISH IS GROSS... AND (B) WHO SAYS YOU'LL CATCH ANY FISH?
SNICKER!
BAH! ANY FISHERMAN WORTH HIS BRITCHES KNOWS THAT CODFISH COVE IS A MANIC MYRIAD OF COUNTLESS COD!
CODFISH COVE
YEAH! THAT'S WHY FISHER-MEN FILL IT TO CAPACITY!
LAST YEAR THIS JOINT WAS JAMMED CHEEK-BY-JOWL WITH SPORT FISHERS!
AND THAT'S WHY I RENTED US A BOAT, INFANTS! NOW WE CAN FISH OUT OF RANGE... FAR AWAY FROM "YACHTS AKIMBO!"
ALTHOUGH... IF THIS IS AKIMBO, THEN THE CROWDS A-CRUMBLED.
INDUBITABLY.
AHOY, SAILOR-BOY! WHERE'D EVERYBODY SCUTTLE OFF TO? NOT ENOUGH JIBS TO CUT?

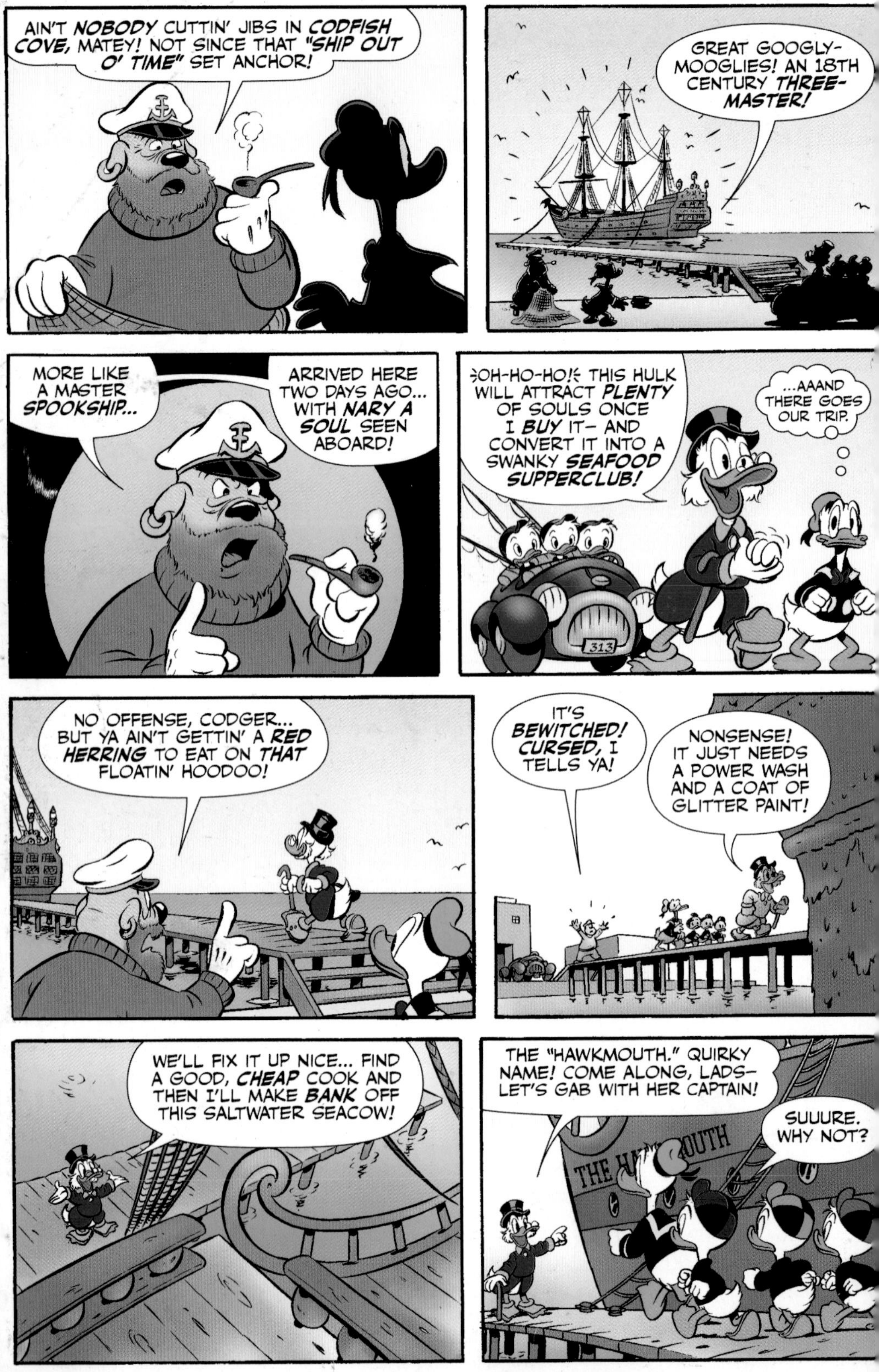
AIN'T NOBODY CUTTIN' JIBS IN CODFISH COVE, MATEY! NOT SINCE THAT "SHIP OUT O' TIME" SET ANCHOR!
GREAT GOOGLY-MOOGLIES! AN 18TH CENTURY THREE-MASTER!
MORE LIKE A MASTER SPOOKSHIP...
ARRIVED HERE TWO DAYS AGO... WITH NARY A SOUL SEEN ABOARD!
OH-HO-HO! THIS HULK WILL ATTRACT PLENTY OF SOULS ONCE I BUY IT— AND CONVERT IT INTO A SWANKY SEAFOOD SUPPERCLUB!
...AAAND THERE GOES OUR TRIP.
313
NO OFFENSE, CODGER... BUT YA AIN'T GETTIN' A RED HERRING TO EAT ON THAT FLOATIN' HOODOO!
IT'S BEWITCHED! CURSED, I TELLS YA!
NONSENSE! IT JUST NEEDS A POWER WASH AND A COAT OF GLITTER PAINT!
WE'LL FIX IT UP NICE... FIND A GOOD, CHEAP COOK AND THEN I'LL MAKE BANK OFF THIS SALTWATER SEACOW!
THE "HAWKMOUTH." QUIRKY NAME! COME ALONG, LADS— LET'S GAB WITH HER CAPTAIN!
SUUURE. WHY NOT?

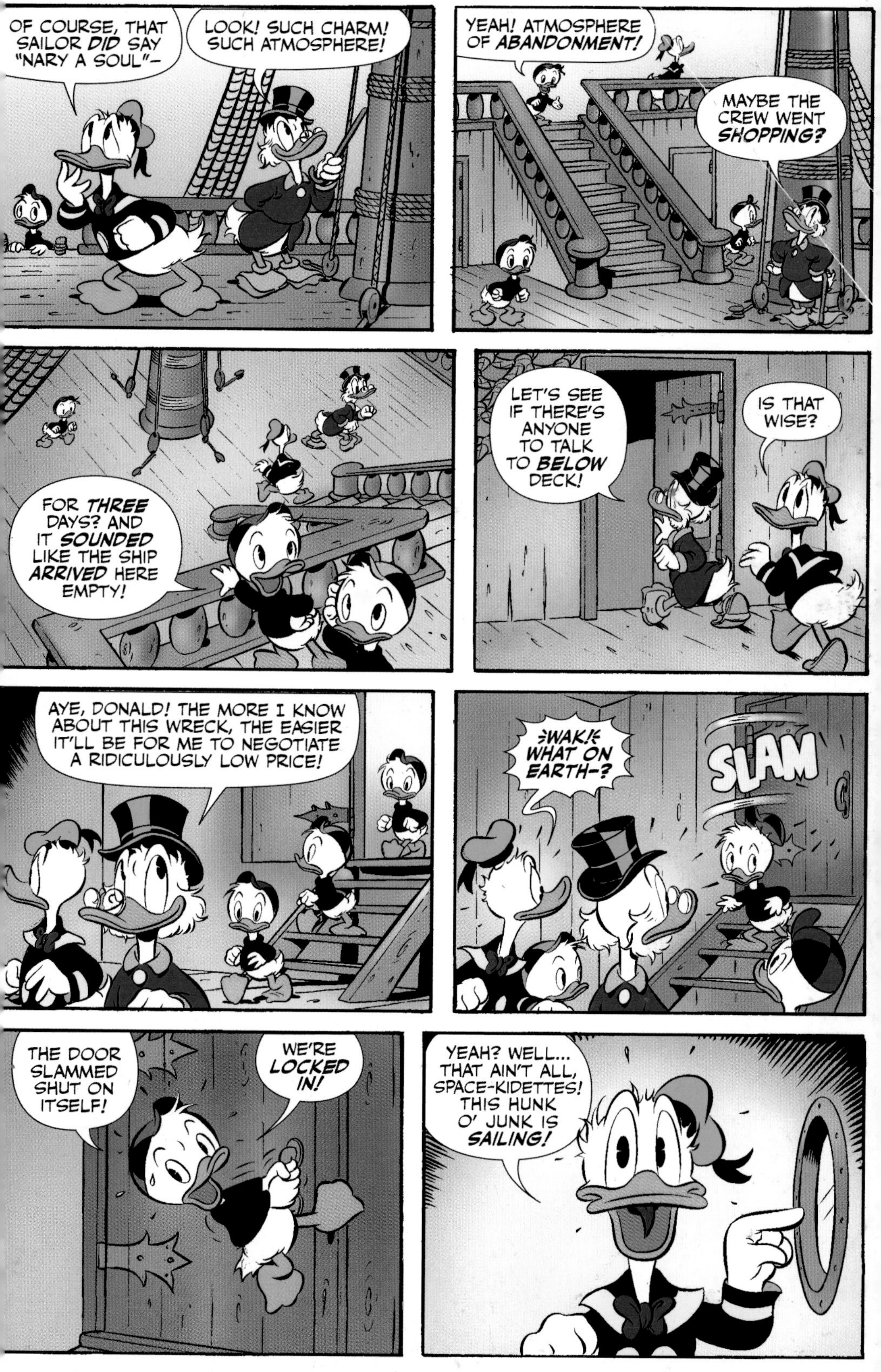
OF COURSE, THAT SAILOR DID SAY "NARY A SOUL"–
LOOK! SUCH CHARM! SUCH ATMOSPHERE!
YEAH! ATMOSPHERE OF ABANDONMENT!
MAYBE THE CREW WENT SHOPPING?
FOR THREE DAYS? AND IT SOUNDED LIKE THE SHIP ARRIVED HERE EMPTY!
LET'S SEE IF THERE'S ANYONE TO TALK TO BELOW DECK!
IS THAT WISE?
AYE, DONALD! THE MORE I KNOW ABOUT THIS WRECK, THE EASIER IT'LL BE FOR ME TO NEGOTIATE A RIDICULOUSLY LOW PRICE!
WAK! WHAT ON EARTH–?
SLAM
THE DOOR SLAMMED SHUT ON ITSELF!
WE'RE LOCKED IN!
YEAH? WELL... THAT AIN'T ALL, SPACE-KIDETTES! THIS HUNK O' JUNK IS SAILING!

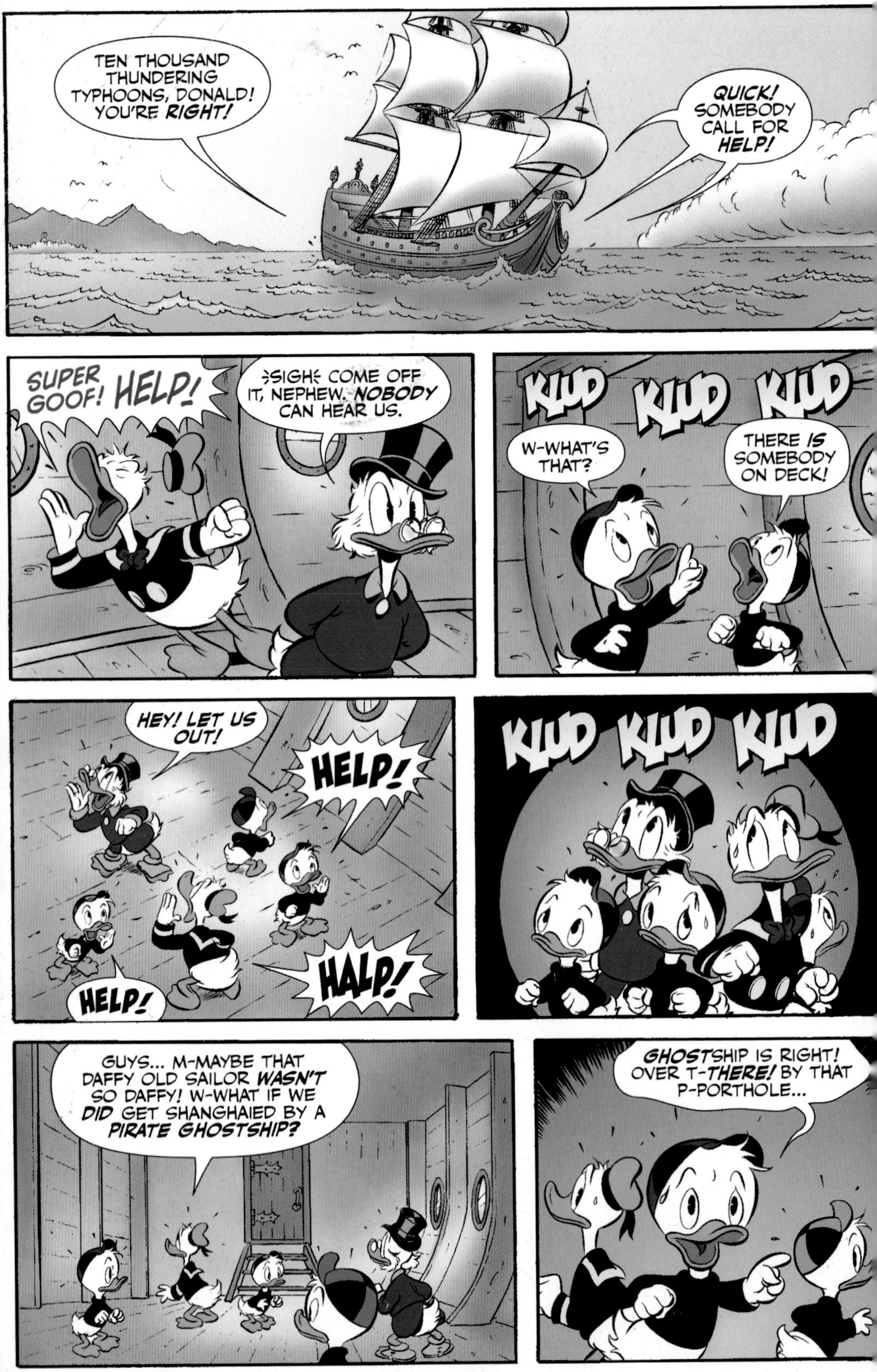
TEN THOUSAND THUNDERING TYPHOONS, DONALD! YOU'RE RIGHT!
QUICK! SOMEBODY CALL FOR HELP!
SUPER GOOF! HELP!
☆SIGH☆ COME OFF IT, NEPHEW. NOBODY CAN HEAR US.
KLUD KLUD KLUD
W-WHAT'S THAT?
THERE IS SOMEBODY ON DECK!
HEY! LET US OUT!
HELP!
HELP!
HALP!
KLUD KLUD KLUD
GUYS... M-MAYBE THAT DAFFY OLD SAILOR WASN'T SO DAFFY! W-WHAT IF WE DID GET SHANGHAIED BY A PIRATE GHOSTSHIP?
GHOSTSHIP IS RIGHT! OVER T-THERE! BY THAT P-PORTHOLE...

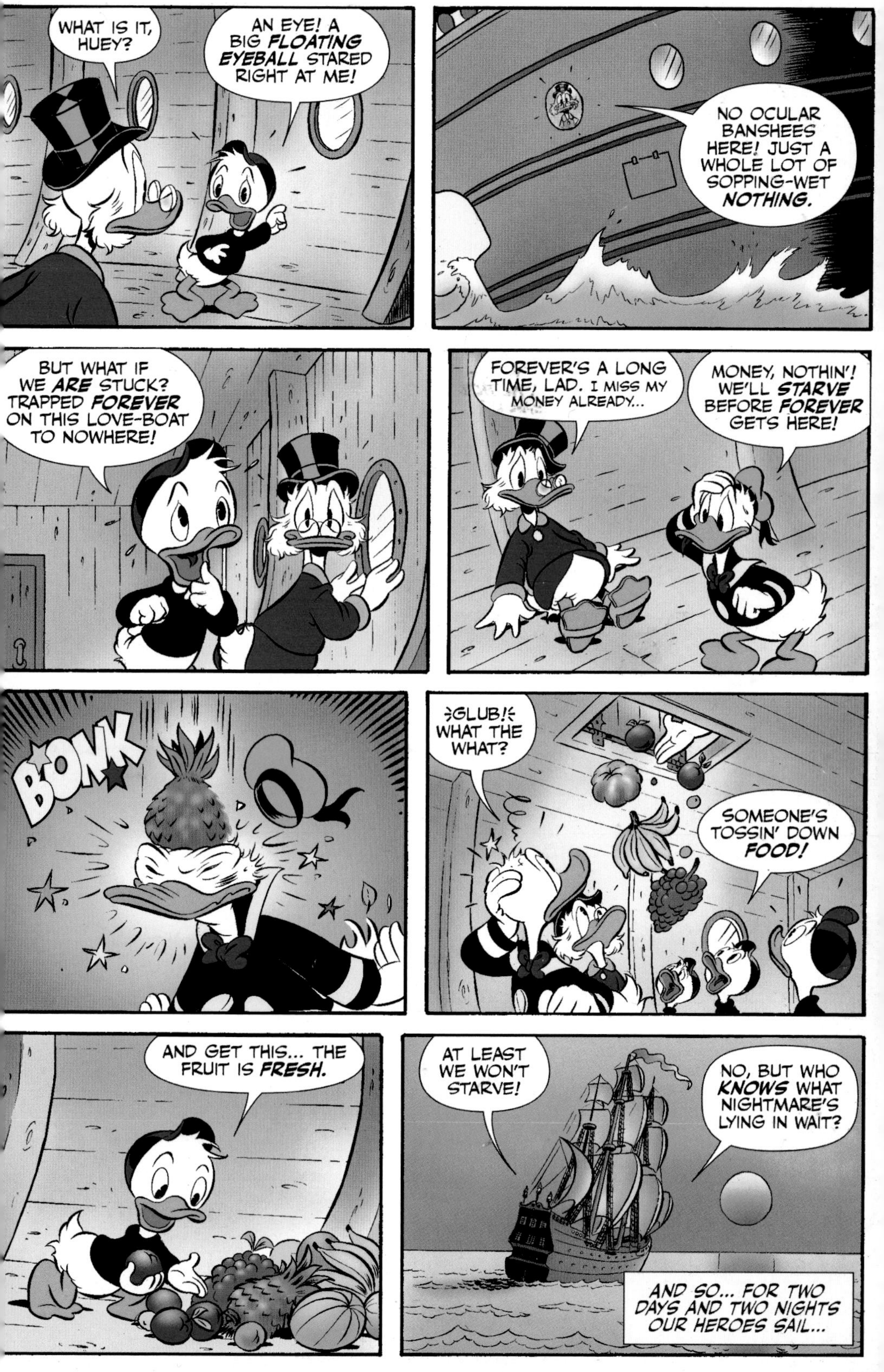
WHAT IS IT, HUEY?
AN EYE! A BIG FLOATING EYEBALL STARED RIGHT AT ME!
NO OCULAR BANSHEES HERE! JUST A WHOLE LOT OF SOPPING-WET NOTHING.
BUT WHAT IF WE ARE STUCK? TRAPPED FOREVER ON THIS LOVE-BOAT TO NOWHERE!
FOREVER'S A LONG TIME, LAD. I MISS MY MONEY ALREADY...
MONEY, NOTHIN'! WE'LL STARVE BEFORE FOREVER GETS HERE!
BONK
GLUB! WHAT THE WHAT?
SOMEONE'S TOSSIN' DOWN FOOD!
AND GET THIS... THE FRUIT IS FRESH.
AT LEAST WE WON'T STARVE!
NO, BUT WHO KNOWS WHAT NIGHTMARE'S LYING IN WAIT?
AND SO... FOR TWO DAYS AND TWO NIGHTS OUR HEROES SAIL...

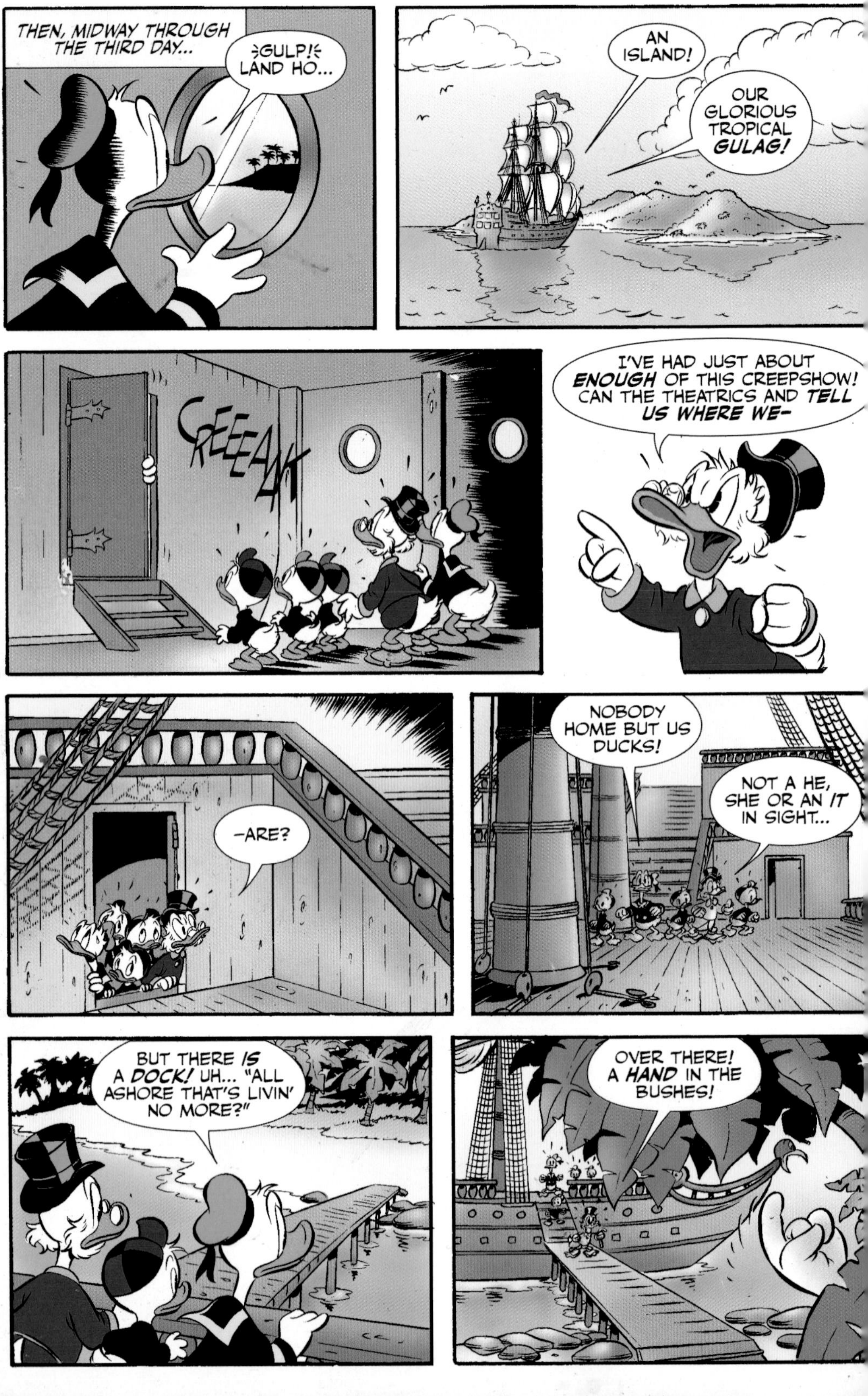
THEN, MIDWAY THROUGH THE THIRD DAY...
GULP! LAND HO...
AN ISLAND!
OUR GLORIOUS TROPICAL GULAG!
CREEEAAK
I'VE HAD JUST ABOUT ENOUGH OF THIS CREEPSHOW! CAN THE THEATRICS AND TELL US WHERE WE-
-ARE?
NOBODY HOME BUT US DUCKS!
NOT A HE, SHE OR AN IT IN SIGHT...
BUT THERE IS A DOCK! UH... "ALL ASHORE THAT'S LIVIN' NO MORE?"
OVER THERE! A HAND IN THE BUSHES!

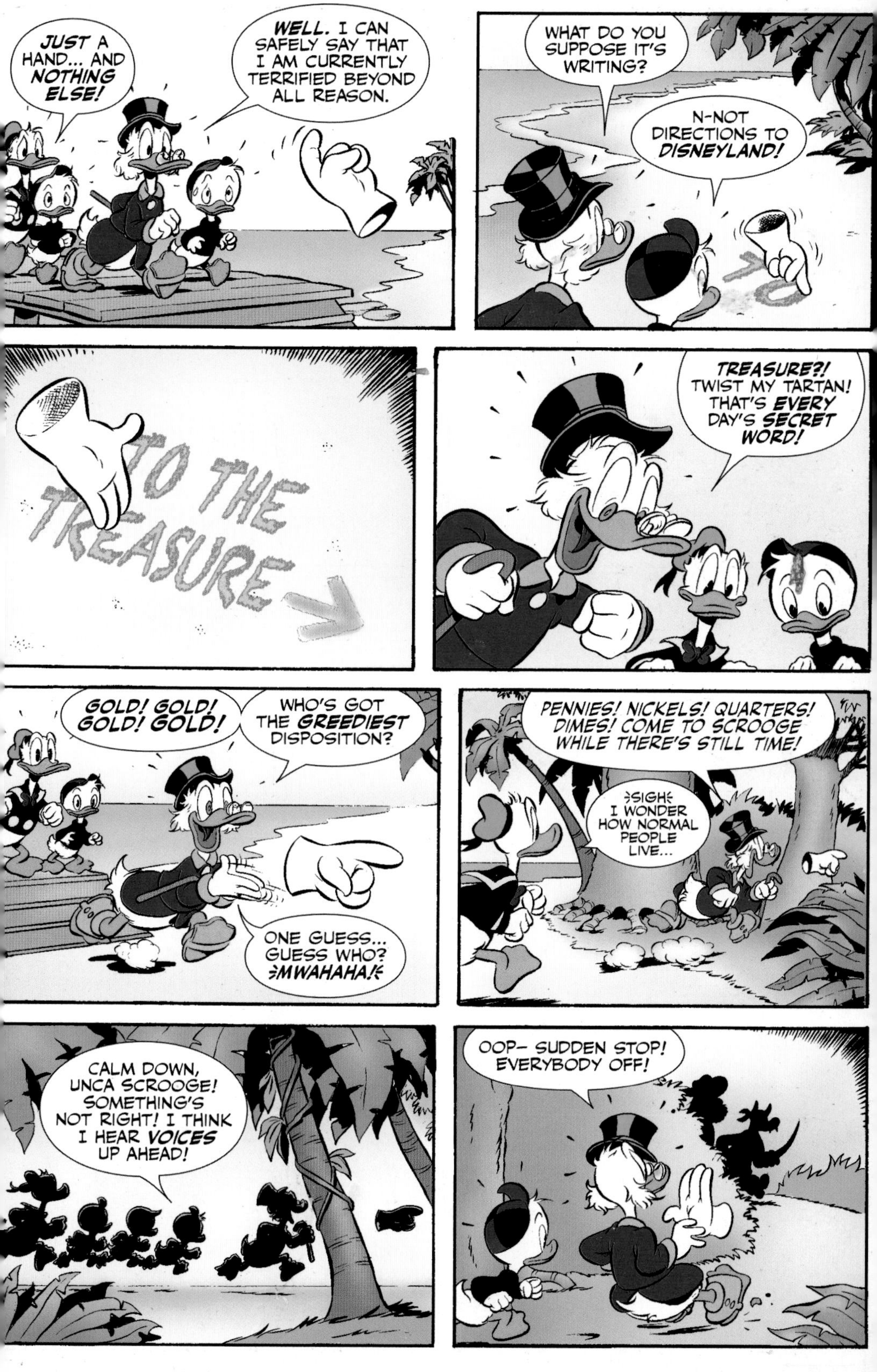
JUST A HAND... AND NOTHING ELSE!
WELL. I CAN SAFELY SAY THAT I AM CURRENTLY TERRIFIED BEYOND ALL REASON.
WHAT DO YOU SUPPOSE IT'S WRITING?
N-NOT DIRECTIONS TO DISNEYLAND!
TO THE TREASURE
TREASURE?! TWIST MY TARTAN! THAT'S EVERY DAY'S SECRET WORD!
GOLD! GOLD! GOLD! GOLD!
WHO'S GOT THE GREEDIEST DISPOSITION?
ONE GUESS... GUESS WHO? MWAHAHA!
PENNIES! NICKELS! QUARTERS! DIMES! COME TO SCROOGE WHILE THERE'S STILL TIME!
SIGH I WONDER HOW NORMAL PEOPLE LIVE...
CALM DOWN, UNCA SCROOGE! SOMETHING'S NOT RIGHT! I THINK I HEAR VOICES UP AHEAD!
OOP– SUDDEN STOP! EVERYBODY OFF!

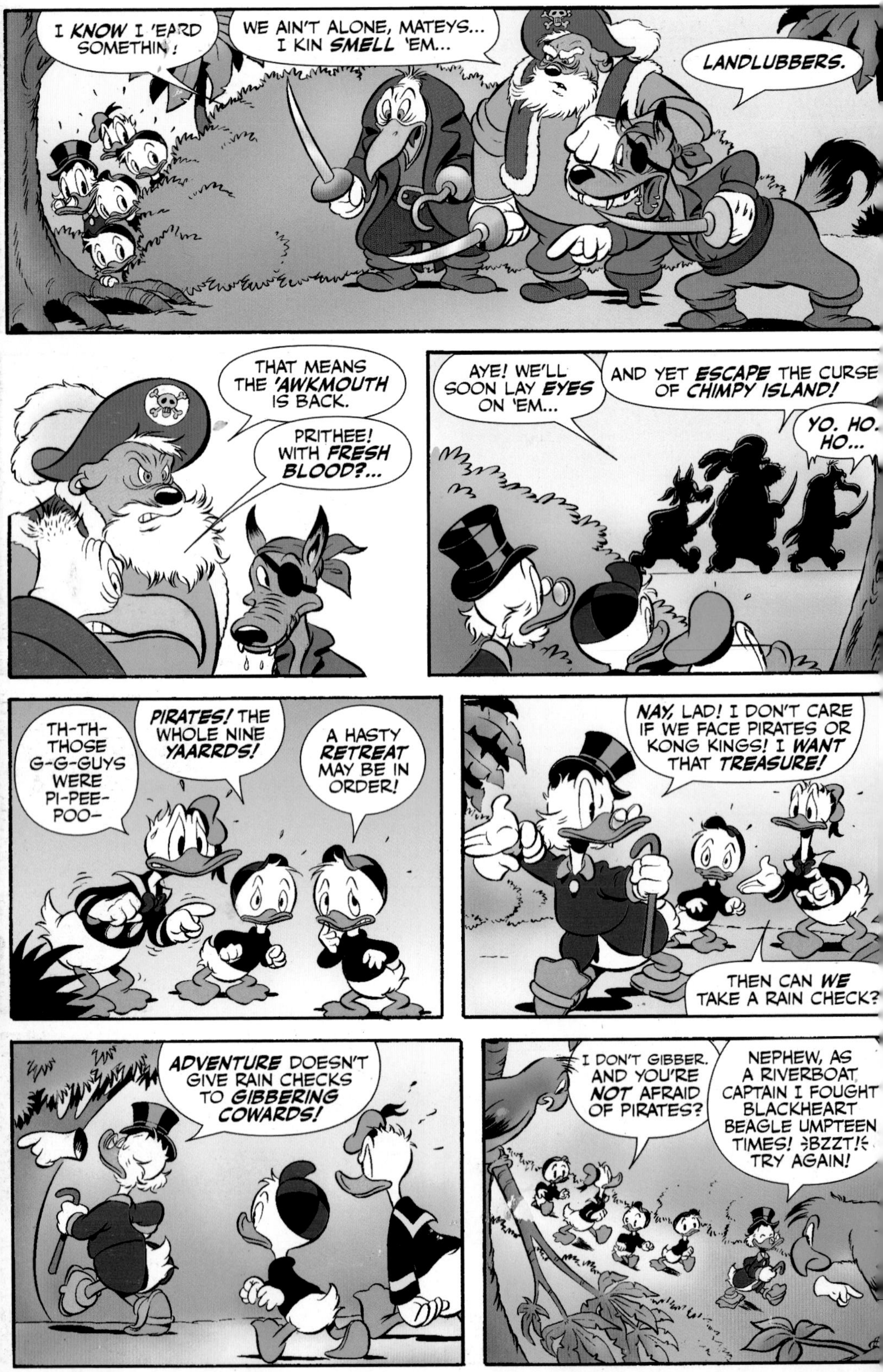
I KNOW I 'EARD SOMETHIN'!
WE AIN'T ALONE, MATEYS... I KIN SMELL 'EM...
LANDLUBBERS.
THAT MEANS THE 'AWKMOUTH IS BACK.
PRITHEE! WITH FRESH BLOOD?...
AYE! WE'LL SOON LAY EYES ON 'EM...
AND YET ESCAPE THE CURSE OF CHIMPY ISLAND!
YO. HO. HO...
TH-TH-THOSE G-G-GUYS WERE PI-PEE-POO-
PIRATES! THE WHOLE NINE YAARRDS!
A HASTY RETREAT MAY BE IN ORDER!
NAY, LAD! I DON'T CARE IF WE FACE PIRATES OR KONG KINGS! I WANT THAT TREASURE!
THEN CAN WE TAKE A RAIN CHECK?
ADVENTURE DOESN'T GIVE RAIN CHECKS TO GIBBERING COWARDS!
I DON'T GIBBER. AND YOU'RE NOT AFRAID OF PIRATES?
NEPHEW, AS A RIVERBOAT CAPTAIN I FOUGHT BLACKHEART BEAGLE UMPTEEN TIMES! ƎBZZT!Ɛ TRY AGAIN!

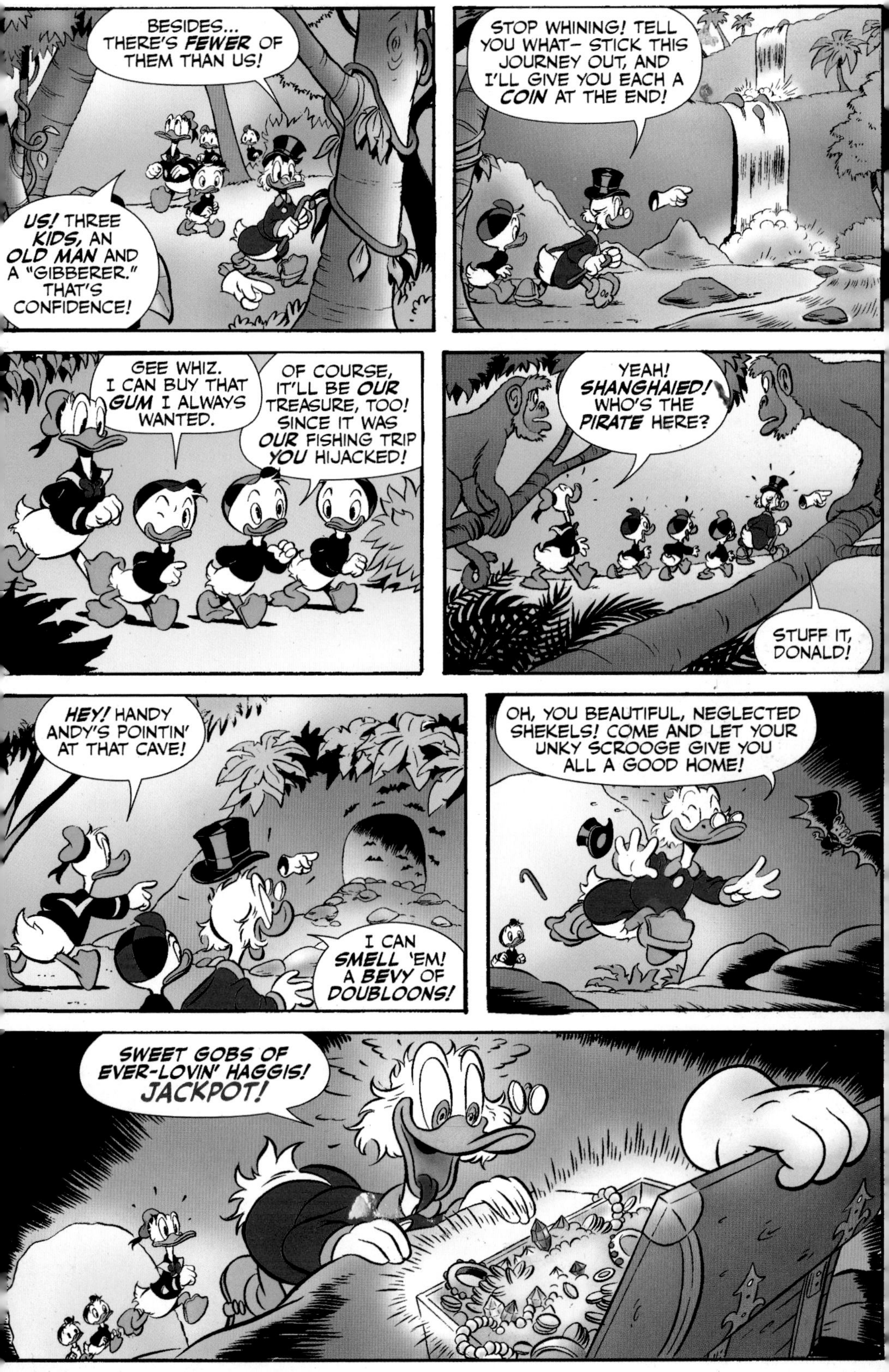
BESIDES... THERE'S FEWER OF THEM THAN US!
US! THREE KIDS, AN OLD MAN AND A "GIBBERER." THAT'S CONFIDENCE!
STOP WHINING! TELL YOU WHAT– STICK THIS JOURNEY OUT, AND I'LL GIVE YOU EACH A COIN AT THE END!
GEE WHIZ. I CAN BUY THAT GUM I ALWAYS WANTED.
OF COURSE, IT'LL BE OUR TREASURE, TOO! SINCE IT WAS OUR FISHING TRIP YOU HIJACKED!
YEAH! SHANGHAIED! WHO'S THE PIRATE HERE?
STUFF IT, DONALD!
HEY! HANDY ANDY'S POINTIN' AT THAT CAVE!
I CAN SMELL 'EM! A BEVY OF DOUBLOONS!
OH, YOU BEAUTIFUL, NEGLECTED SHEKELS! COME AND LET YOUR UNKY SCROOGE GIVE YOU ALL A GOOD HOME!
SWEET GOBS OF EVER-LOVIN' HAGGIS! JACKPOT!

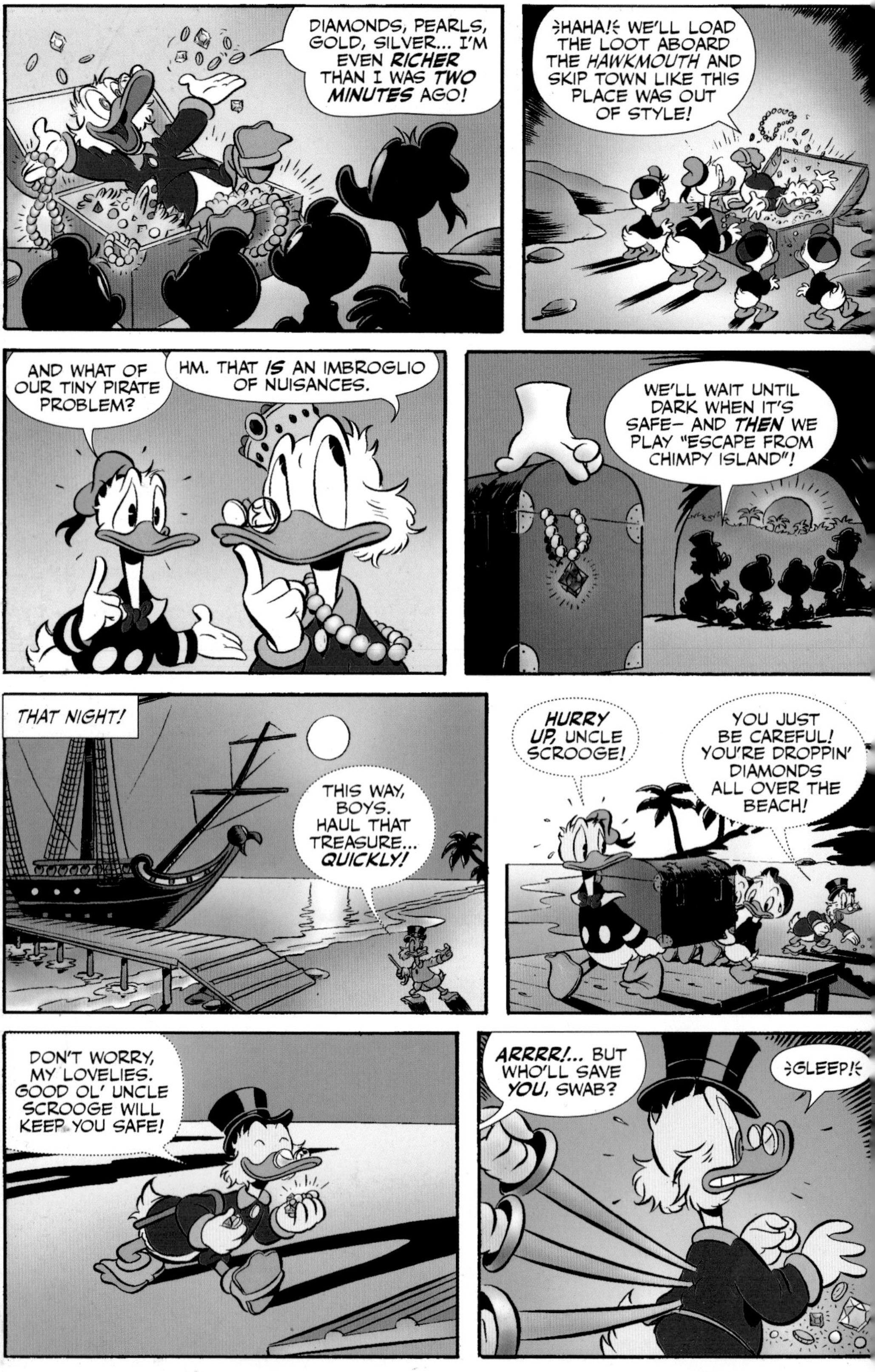
DIAMONDS, PEARLS, GOLD, SILVER... I'M EVEN RICHER THAN I WAS TWO MINUTES AGO!
HAHA! WE'LL LOAD THE LOOT ABOARD THE HAWKMOUTH AND SKIP TOWN LIKE THIS PLACE WAS OUT OF STYLE!
AND WHAT OF OUR TINY PIRATE PROBLEM?
HM. THAT IS AN IMBROGLIO OF NUISANCES.
WE'LL WAIT UNTIL DARK WHEN IT'S SAFE– AND THEN WE PLAY "ESCAPE FROM CHIMPY ISLAND"!
THAT NIGHT!
THIS WAY, BOYS. HAUL THAT TREASURE... QUICKLY!
HURRY UP, UNCLE SCROOGE!
YOU JUST BE CAREFUL! YOU'RE DROPPIN' DIAMONDS ALL OVER THE BEACH!
DON'T WORRY, MY LOVELIES. GOOD OL' UNCLE SCROOGE WILL KEEP YOU SAFE!
ARRRR!... BUT WHO'LL SAVE YOU, SWAB?
GLEEP!

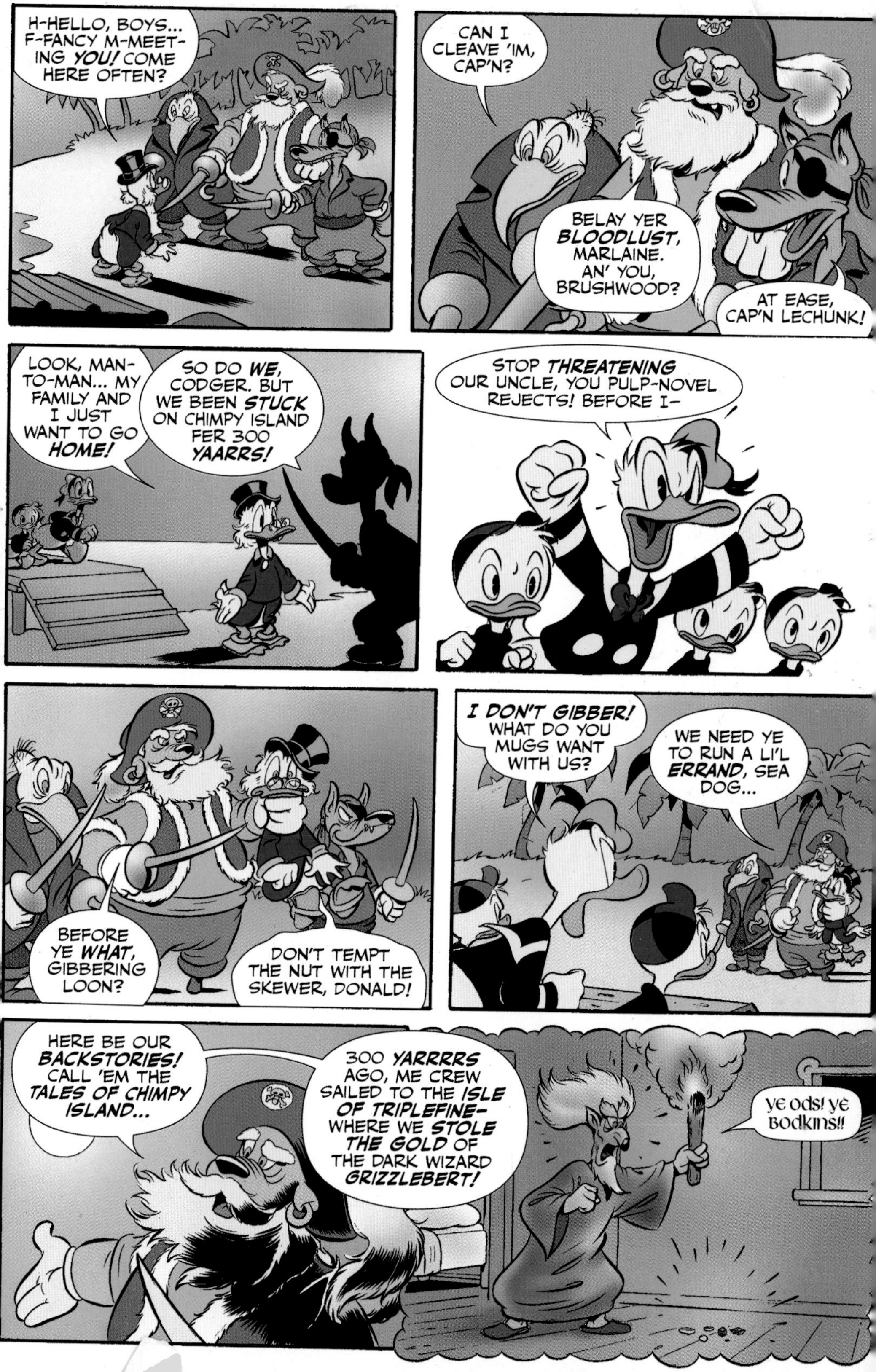

H-HELLO, BOYS... F-FANCY M-MEETING YOU! COME HERE OFTEN?
CAN I CLEAVE 'IM, CAP'N?
BELAY YER BLOODLUST, MARLAINE. AN' YOU, BRUSHWOOD?
AT EASE, CAP'N LECHUNK!
LOOK, MAN-TO-MAN... MY FAMILY AND I JUST WANT TO GO HOME!
SO DO WE, CODGER. BUT WE BEEN STUCK ON CHIMPY ISLAND FER 300 YAARRS!
STOP THREATENING OUR UNCLE, YOU PULP-NOVEL REJECTS! BEFORE I–
BEFORE YE WHAT, GIBBERING LOON?
DON'T TEMPT THE NUT WITH THE SKEWER, DONALD!
I DON'T GIBBER! WHAT DO YOU MUGS WANT WITH US?
WE NEED YE TO RUN A LI'L ERRAND, SEA DOG...
HERE BE OUR BACKSTORIES! CALL 'EM THE TALES OF CHIMPY ISLAND...
300 YARRRRS AGO, ME CREW SAILED TO THE ISLE OF TRIPLEFINE– WHERE WE STOLE THE GOLD OF THE DARK WIZARD GRIZZLEBERT!
ye ods! ye Bodkins!!

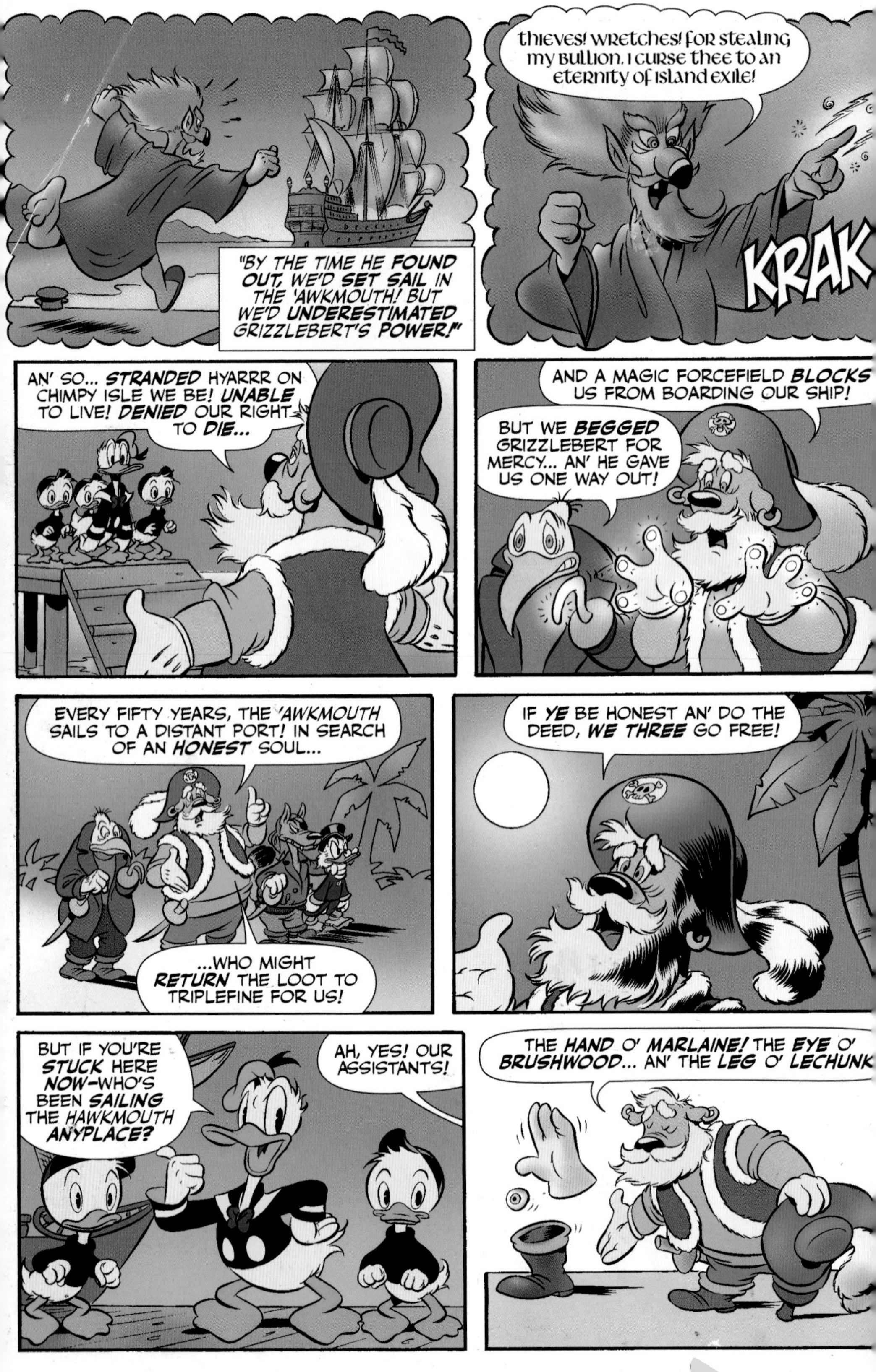
"BY THE TIME HE FOUND OUT, WE'D SET SAIL IN THE 'AWKMOUTH! BUT WE'D UNDERESTIMATED GRIZZLEBERT'S POWER!"
thieves! wretches! for stealing my Bullion, I curse thee to an eternity of island exile!
KRAK
AN' SO... STRANDED HYARRR ON CHIMPY ISLE WE BE! UNABLE TO LIVE! DENIED OUR RIGHT TO DIE...
AND A MAGIC FORCEFIELD BLOCKS US FROM BOARDING OUR SHIP!
BUT WE BEGGED GRIZZLEBERT FOR MERCY... AN' HE GAVE US ONE WAY OUT!
EVERY FIFTY YEARS, THE 'AWKMOUTH SAILS TO A DISTANT PORT! IN SEARCH OF AN HONEST SOUL...
...WHO MIGHT RETURN THE LOOT TO TRIPLEFINE FOR US!
IF YE BE HONEST AN' DO THE DEED, WE THREE GO FREE!
BUT IF YOU'RE STUCK HERE NOW—WHO'S BEEN SAILING THE HAWKMOUTH ANYPLACE?
AH, YES! OUR ASSISTANTS!
THE HAND O' MARLAINE! THE EYE O' BRUSHWOOD... AN' THE LEG O' LECHUNK

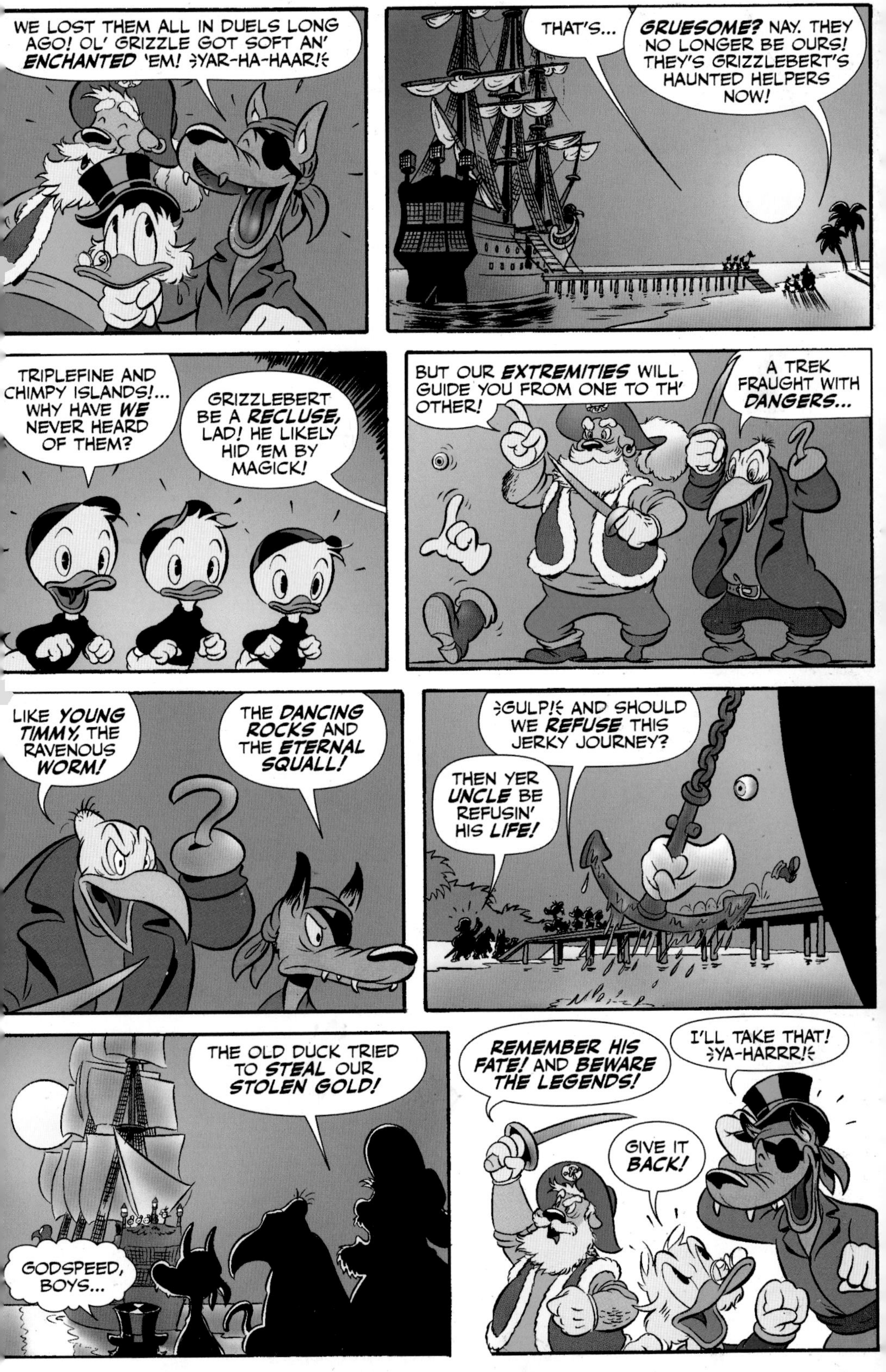

WE LOST THEM ALL IN DUELS LONG AGO! OL' GRIZZLE GOT SOFT AN' ENCHANTED 'EM! ∋YAR-HA-HAAR!∈
THAT'S...
GRUESOME? NAY. THEY NO LONGER BE OURS! THEY'S GRIZZLEBERT'S HAUNTED HELPERS NOW!
TRIPLEFINE AND CHIMPY ISLANDS!... WHY HAVE WE NEVER HEARD OF THEM?
GRIZZLEBERT BE A RECLUSE, LAD! HE LIKELY HID 'EM BY MAGICK!
BUT OUR EXTREMITIES WILL GUIDE YOU FROM ONE TO TH' OTHER!
A TREK FRAUGHT WITH DANGERS...
LIKE YOUNG TIMMY, THE RAVENOUS WORM!
THE DANCING ROCKS AND THE ETERNAL SQUALL!
∋GULP!∈ AND SHOULD WE REFUSE THIS JERKY JOURNEY?
THEN YER UNCLE BE REFUSIN' HIS LIFE!
THE OLD DUCK TRIED TO STEAL OUR STOLEN GOLD!
GODSPEED, BOYS...
REMEMBER HIS FATE! AND BEWARE THE LEGENDS!
I'LL TAKE THAT! ∋YA-HARRR!∈
GIVE IT BACK!

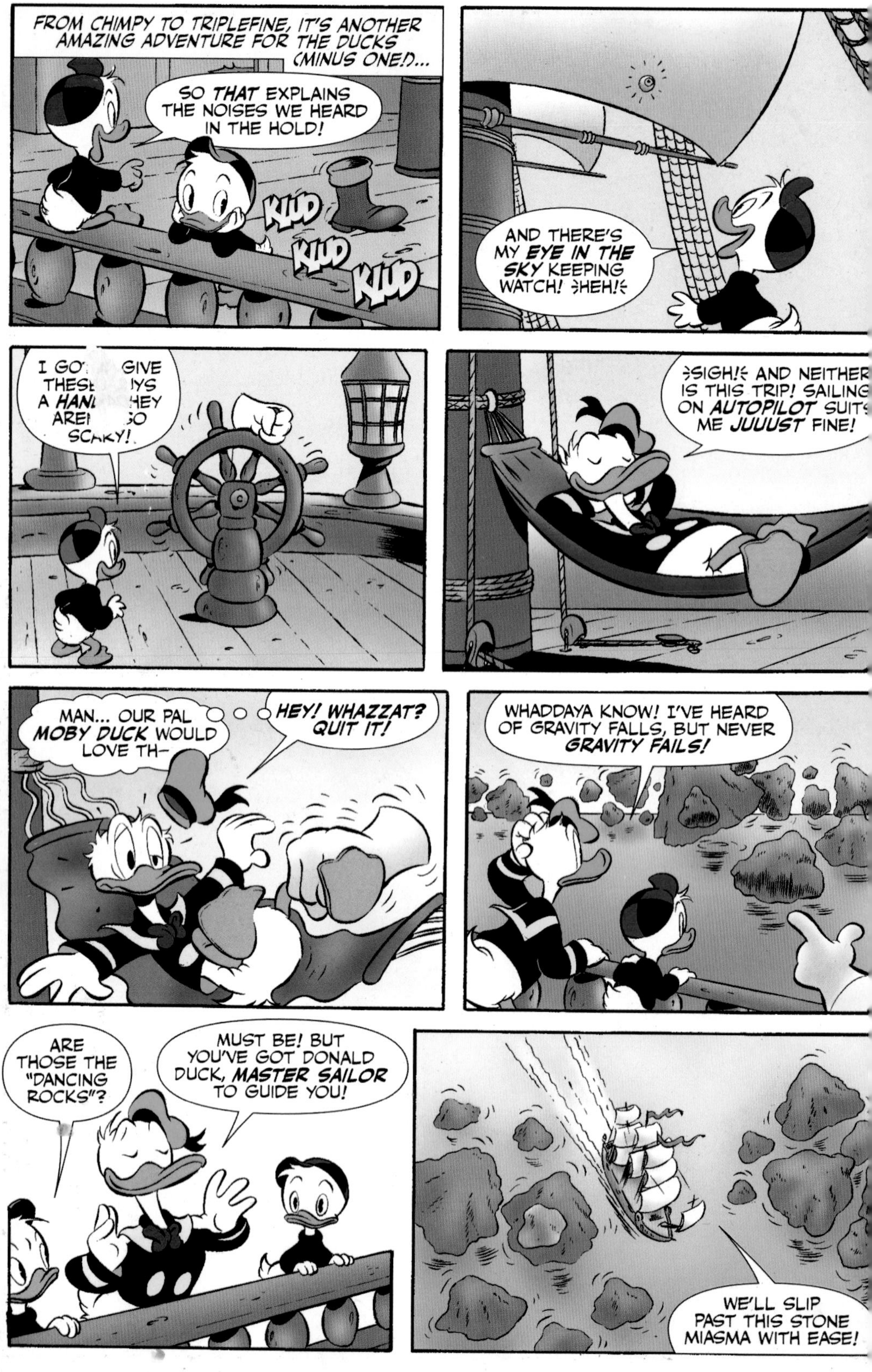
FROM CHIMPY TO TRIPLEFINE, IT'S ANOTHER AMAZING ADVENTURE FOR THE DUCKS (MINUS ONE!)...
SO THAT EXPLAINS THE NOISES WE HEARD IN THE HOLD!
KLUD KLUD KLUD
AND THERE'S MY EYE IN THE SKY KEEPING WATCH! HEH!
I GOT GIVE THESE YS A HAN HEY AREN SO SCARY!
SIGH! AND NEITHER IS THIS TRIP! SAILING ON AUTOPILOT SUIT ME JUUUST FINE!
MAN... OUR PAL MOBY DUCK WOULD LOVE TH—
HEY! WHAZZAT? QUIT IT!
WHADDAYA KNOW! I'VE HEARD OF GRAVITY FALLS, BUT NEVER GRAVITY FAILS!
ARE THOSE THE "DANCING ROCKS"?
MUST BE! BUT YOU'VE GOT DONALD DUCK, MASTER SAILOR TO GUIDE YOU!
WE'LL SLIP PAST THIS STONE MIASMA WITH EASE!

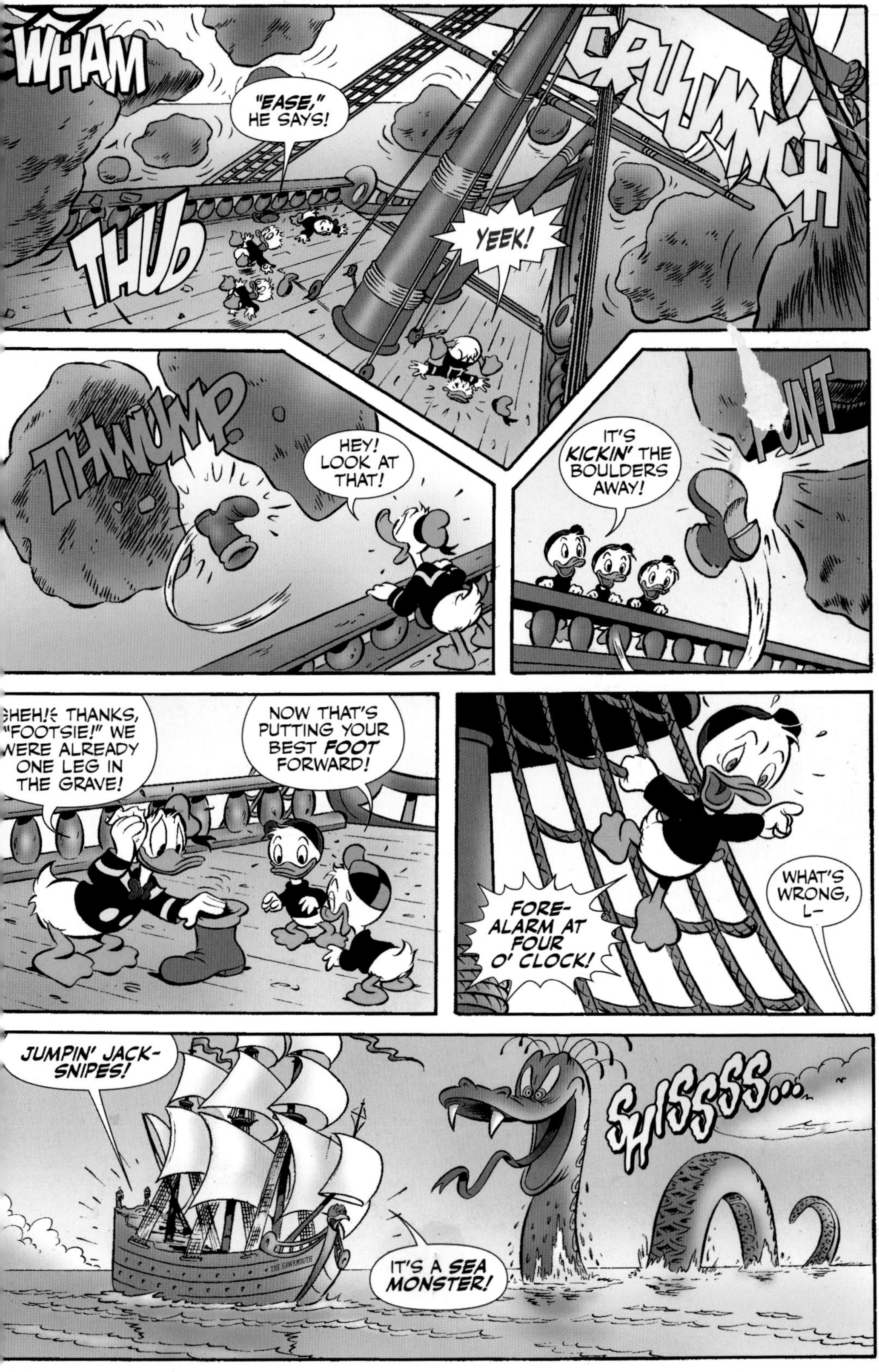
WHAM
"EASE," HE SAYS!
CRUNCH
THUD
YEEK!
THWUMP
HEY! LOOK AT THAT!
IT'S KICKIN' THE BOULDERS AWAY!
PUNT
HEH! THANKS, "FOOTSIE!" WE WERE ALREADY ONE LEG IN THE GRAVE!
NOW THAT'S PUTTING YOUR BEST FOOT FORWARD!
WHAT'S WRONG, L—
FORE-ALARM AT FOUR O' CLOCK!
JUMPIN' JACK-SNIPES!
SHISSSS...
IT'S A SEA MONSTER!

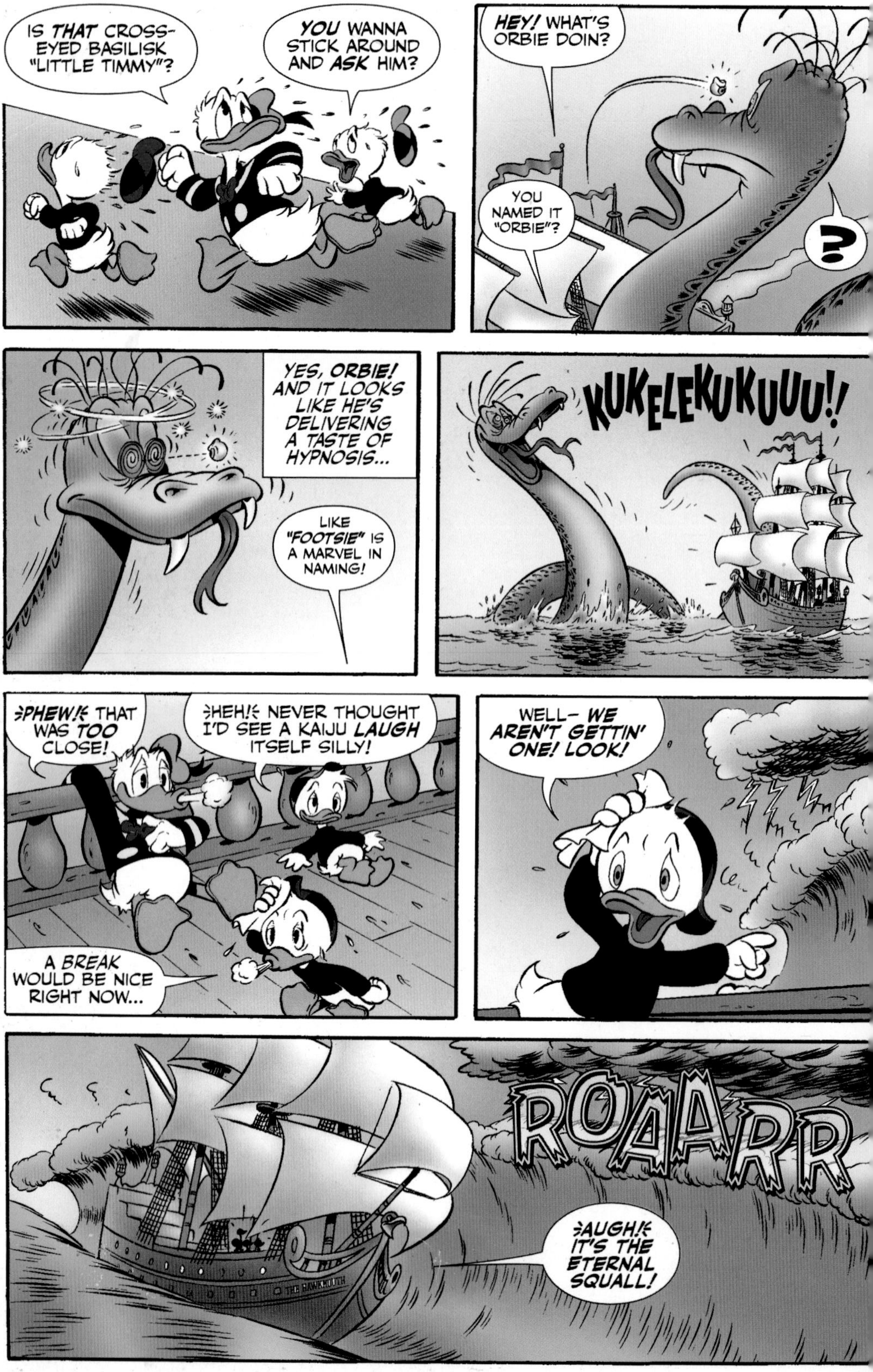
IS THAT CROSS-EYED BASILISK "LITTLE TIMMY"?
YOU WANNA STICK AROUND AND ASK HIM?
HEY! WHAT'S ORBIE DOIN?
YOU NAMED IT "ORBIE"?
?
YES, ORBIE! AND IT LOOKS LIKE HE'S DELIVERING A TASTE OF HYPNOSIS...
LIKE "FOOTSIE" IS A MARVEL IN NAMING!
KUKELEKUKUUU!!
PHEW! THAT WAS TOO CLOSE!
HEH! NEVER THOUGHT I'D SEE A KAIJU LAUGH ITSELF SILLY!
A BREAK WOULD BE NICE RIGHT NOW...
WELL- WE AREN'T GETTIN' ONE! LOOK!
ROAARR
AUGH! IT'S THE ETERNAL SQUALL!

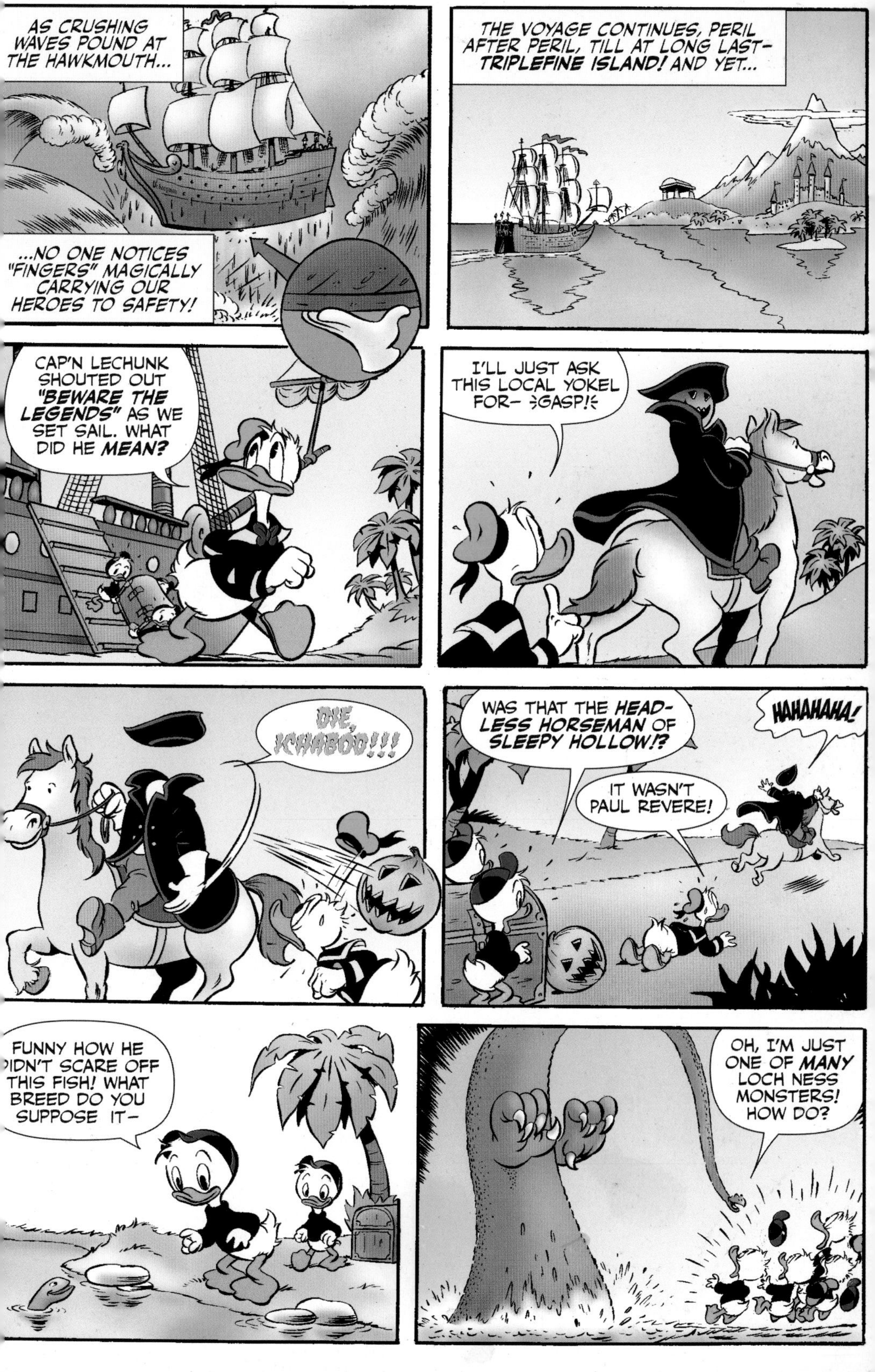
AS CRUSHING WAVES POUND AT THE HAWKMOUTH...
...NO ONE NOTICES "FINGERS" MAGICALLY CARRYING OUR HEROES TO SAFETY!
THE VOYAGE CONTINUES, PERIL AFTER PERIL, TILL AT LONG LAST- TRIPLEFINE ISLAND! AND YET...
CAP'N LECHUNK SHOUTED OUT "BEWARE THE LEGENDS" AS WE SET SAIL. WHAT DID HE MEAN?
I'LL JUST ASK THIS LOCAL YOKEL FOR- GASP!
DIE, ICHABOD!!!
WAS THAT THE HEADLESS HORSEMAN OF SLEEPY HOLLOW!?
HAHAHAHA!
IT WASN'T PAUL REVERE!
FUNNY HOW HE DIDN'T SCARE OFF THIS FISH! WHAT BREED DO YOU SUPPOSE IT-
OH, I'M JUST ONE OF MANY LOCH NESS MONSTERS! HOW DO?

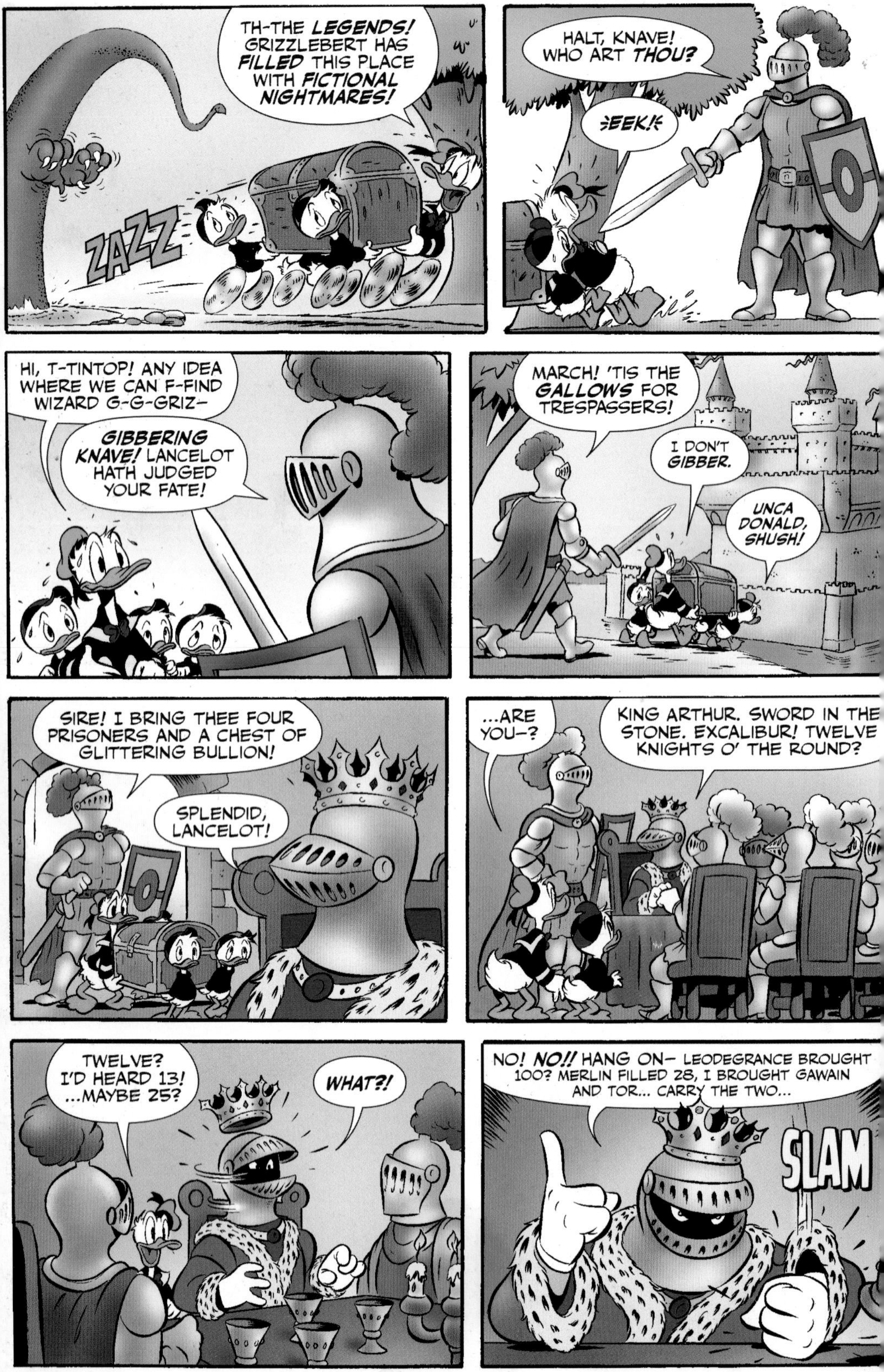

TH-THE LEGENDS! GRIZZLEBERT HAS FILLED THIS PLACE WITH FICTIONAL NIGHTMARES!
ZAZZ
HALT, KNAVE! WHO ART THOU?
EEK!
HI, T-TINTOP! ANY IDEA WHERE WE CAN F-FIND WIZARD G-G-GRIZ–
GIBBERING KNAVE! LANCELOT HATH JUDGED YOUR FATE!
MARCH! 'TIS THE GALLOWS FOR TRESPASSERS!
I DON'T GIBBER.
UNCA DONALD, SHUSH!
SIRE! I BRING THEE FOUR PRISONERS AND A CHEST OF GLITTERING BULLION!
SPLENDID, LANCELOT!
...ARE YOU–?
KING ARTHUR. SWORD IN THE STONE. EXCALIBUR! TWELVE KNIGHTS O' THE ROUND?
TWELVE? I'D HEARD 13! ...MAYBE 25?
WHAT?!
NO! NO!! HANG ON– LEODEGRANCE BROUGHT 100? MERLIN FILLED 28, I BROUGHT GAWAIN AND TOR... CARRY THE TWO...
SLAM

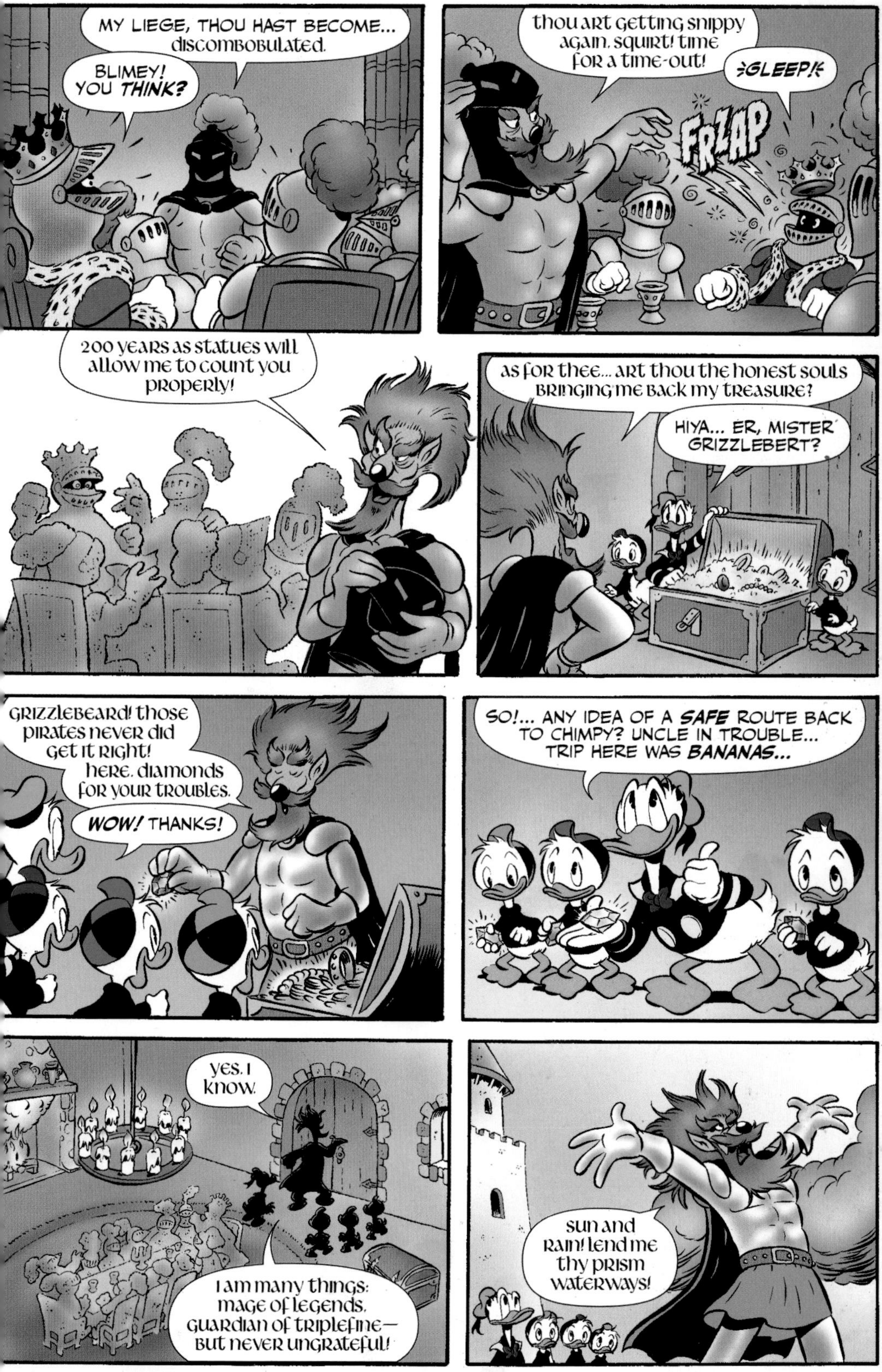

MY LIEGE, THOU HAST BECOME... discombobulated.
BLIMEY! YOU THINK?
thou art getting snippy again, squirt! time for a time-out!
GLEEP!
FRZAP
200 years as statues will allow me to count you properly!
as for thee... art thou the honest souls bringing me back my treasure?
HIYA... ER, MISTER GRIZZLEBERT?
grizzlebeard! those pirates never did get it right!
here, diamonds for your troubles.
WOW! THANKS!
SO!... ANY IDEA OF A SAFE ROUTE BACK TO CHIMPY? UNCLE IN TROUBLE... TRIP HERE WAS BANANAS...
yes, i know.
i am many things: mage of legends, guardian of triplefine— but never ungrateful!
sun and rain! lend me thy prism waterways!

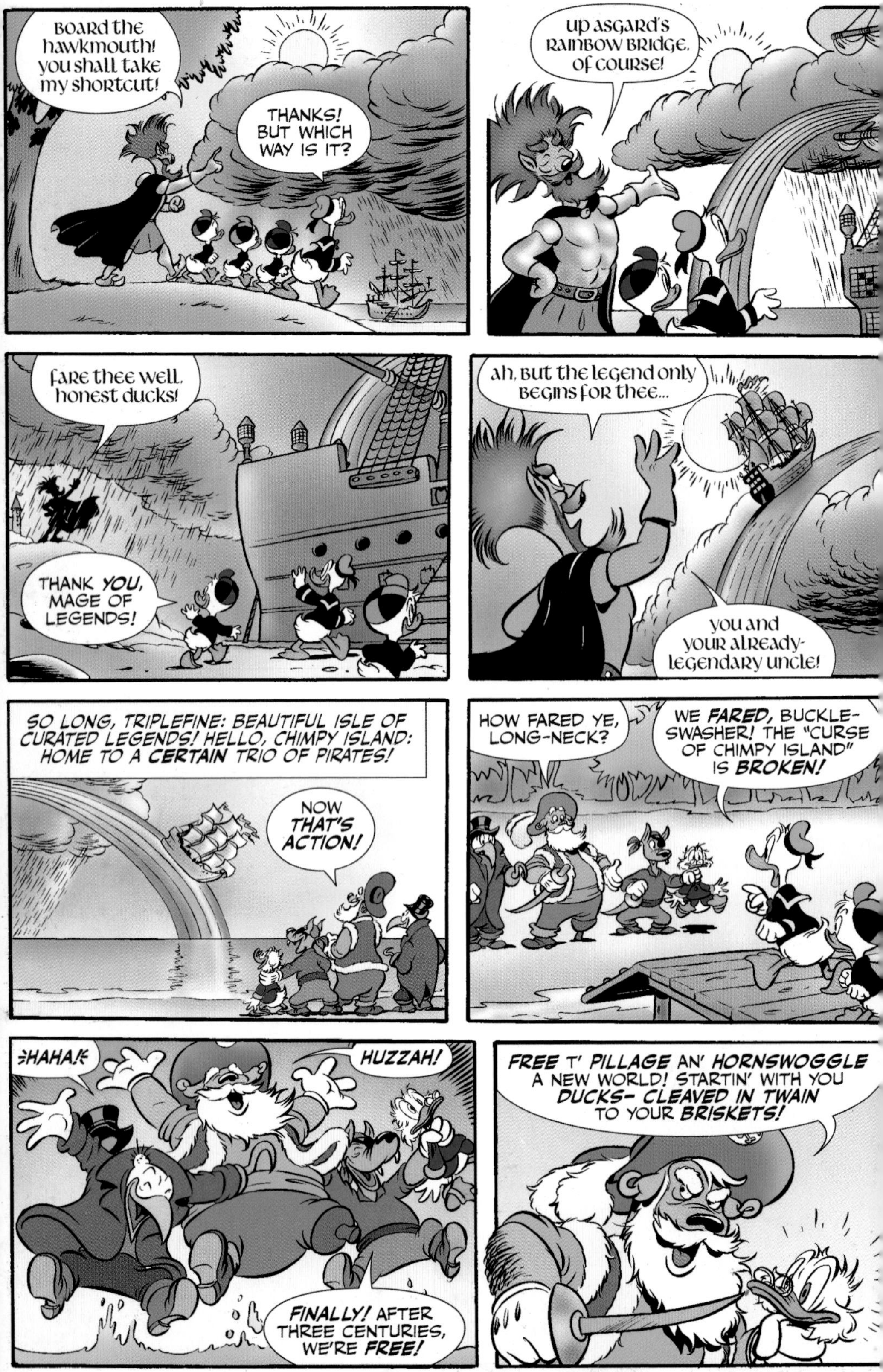
BOARD THE HAWKMOUTH! YOU SHALL TAKE MY SHORTCUT!
THANKS! BUT WHICH WAY IS IT?
UP ASGARD'S RAINBOW BRIDGE, OF COURSE!
FARE THEE WELL, HONEST DUCKS!
THANK YOU, MAGE OF LEGENDS!
AH, BUT THE LEGEND ONLY BEGINS FOR THEE...
YOU AND YOUR ALREADY-LEGENDARY UNCLE!
SO LONG, TRIPLEFINE: BEAUTIFUL ISLE OF CURATED LEGENDS! HELLO, CHIMPY ISLAND: HOME TO A CERTAIN TRIO OF PIRATES!
NOW THAT'S ACTION!
HOW FARED YE, LONG-NECK?
WE FARED, BUCKLE-SWASHER! THE "CURSE OF CHIMPY ISLAND" IS BROKEN!
HAHA!
HUZZAH!
FINALLY! AFTER THREE CENTURIES, WE'RE FREE!
FREE T' PILLAGE AN' HORNSWOGGLE A NEW WORLD! STARTIN' WITH YOU DUCKS— CLEAVED IN TWAIN TO YOUR BRISKETS!

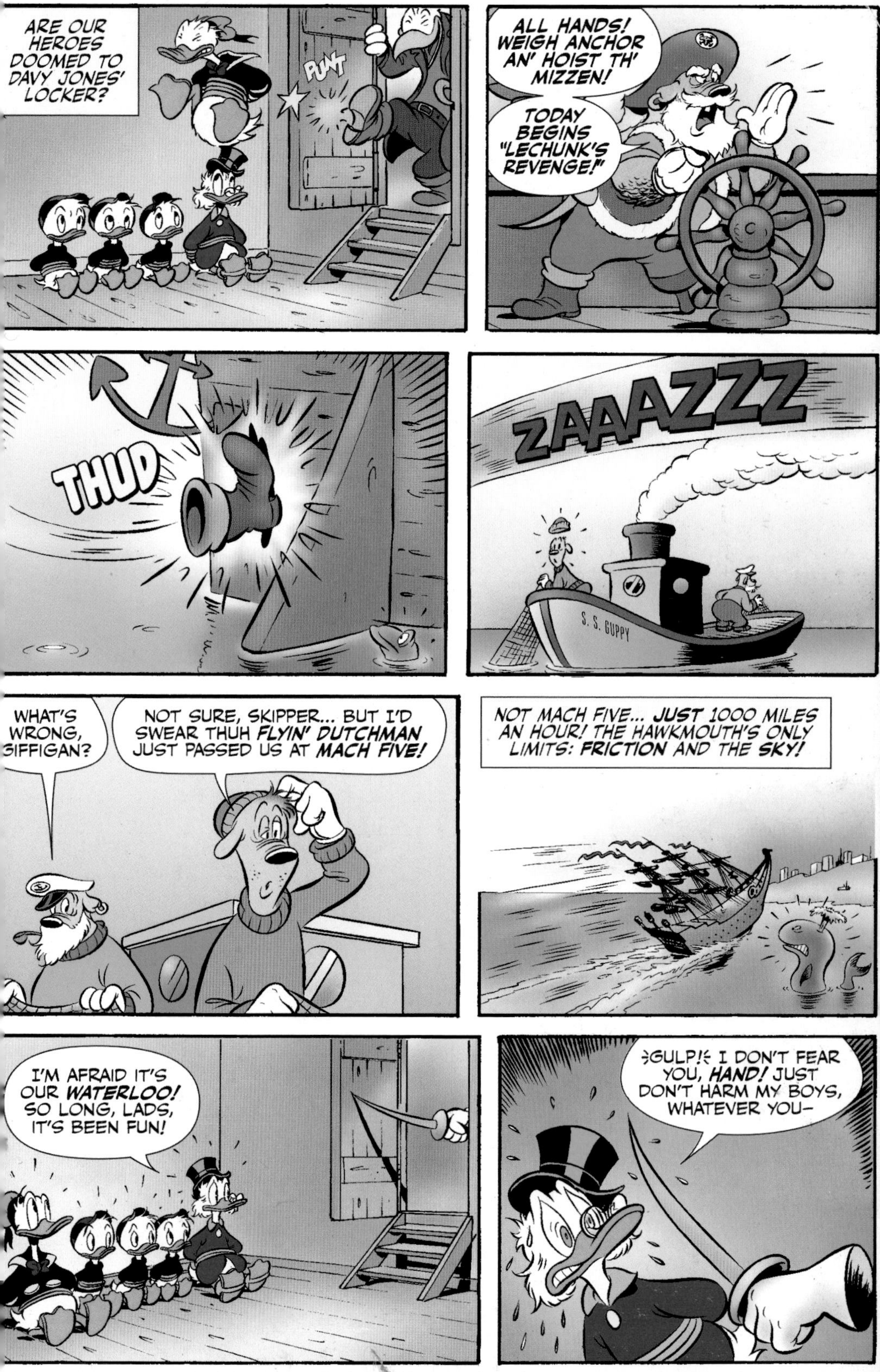
ARE OUR HEROES DOOMED TO DAVY JONES' LOCKER?
PUNT
ALL HANDS! WEIGH ANCHOR AN' HOIST TH' MIZZEN!
TODAY BEGINS "LECHUNK'S REVENGE!"
THUD
ZAAAZZZ
S. S. GUPPY
WHAT'S WRONG, GIFFIGAN?
NOT SURE, SKIPPER... BUT I'D SWEAR THUH FLYIN' DUTCHMAN JUST PASSED US AT MACH FIVE!
NOT MACH FIVE... JUST 1000 MILES AN HOUR! THE HAWKMOUTH'S ONLY LIMITS: FRICTION AND THE SKY!
I'M AFRAID IT'S OUR WATERLOO! SO LONG, LADS, IT'S BEEN FUN!
GULP! I DON'T FEAR YOU, HAND! JUST DON'T HARM MY BOYS, WHATEVER YOU–

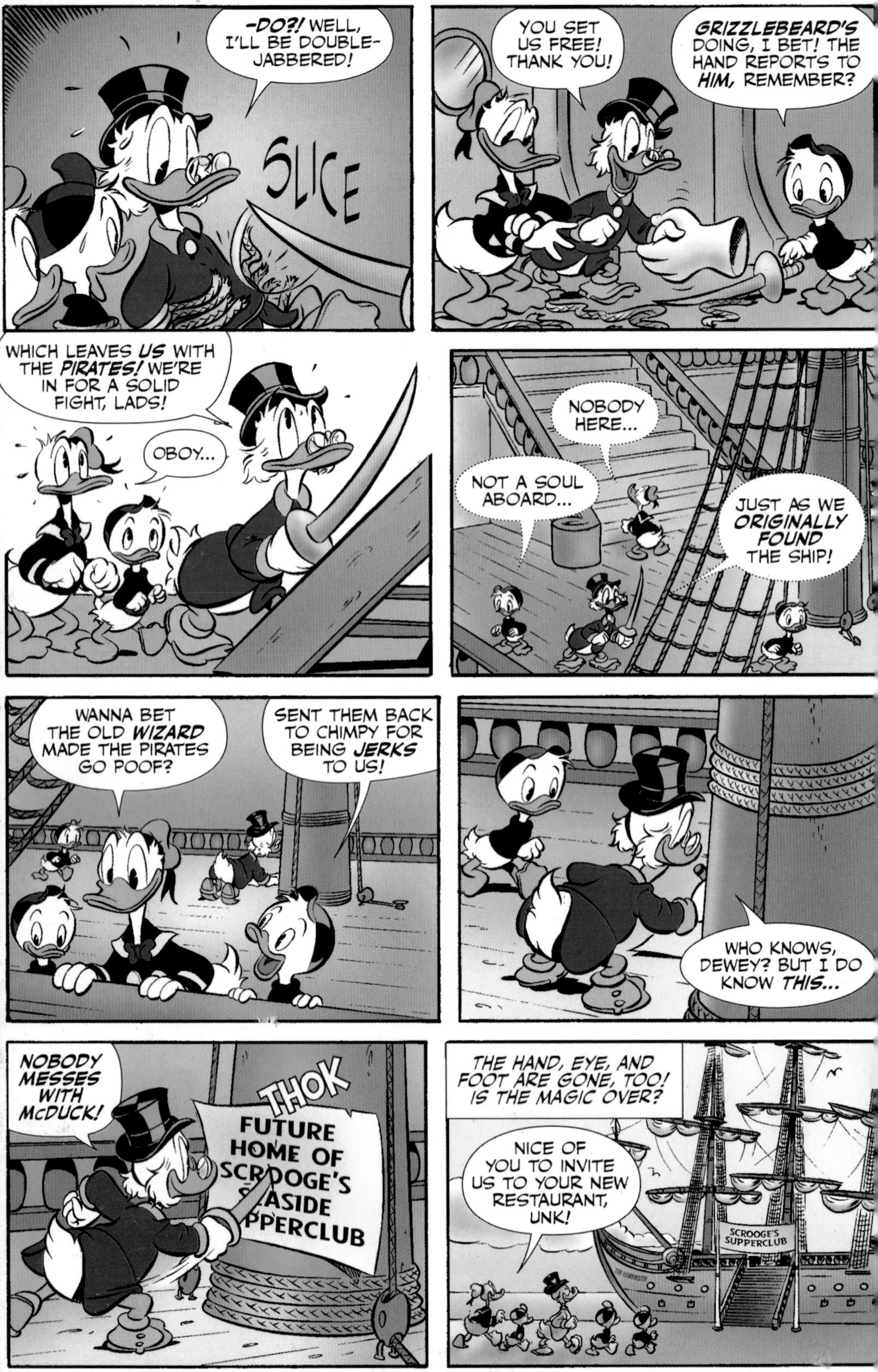
-DO?! WELL, I'LL BE DOUBLE-JABBERED!
SLICE
YOU SET US FREE! THANK YOU!
GRIZZLEBEARD'S DOING, I BET! THE HAND REPORTS TO HIM, REMEMBER?
WHICH LEAVES US WITH THE PIRATES! WE'RE IN FOR A SOLID FIGHT, LADS!
OBOY...
NOBODY HERE...
NOT A SOUL ABOARD...
JUST AS WE ORIGINALLY FOUND THE SHIP!
WANNA BET THE OLD WIZARD MADE THE PIRATES GO POOF?
SENT THEM BACK TO CHIMPY FOR BEING JERKS TO US!
WHO KNOWS, DEWEY? BUT I DO KNOW THIS...
NOBODY MESSES WITH McDUCK!
THOK
FUTURE HOME OF SCROOGE'S SEASIDE SUPPERCLUB
THE HAND, EYE, AND FOOT ARE GONE, TOO! IS THE MAGIC OVER?
NICE OF YOU TO INVITE US TO YOUR NEW RESTAURANT, UNK!
SCROOGE'S SUPPERCLUB

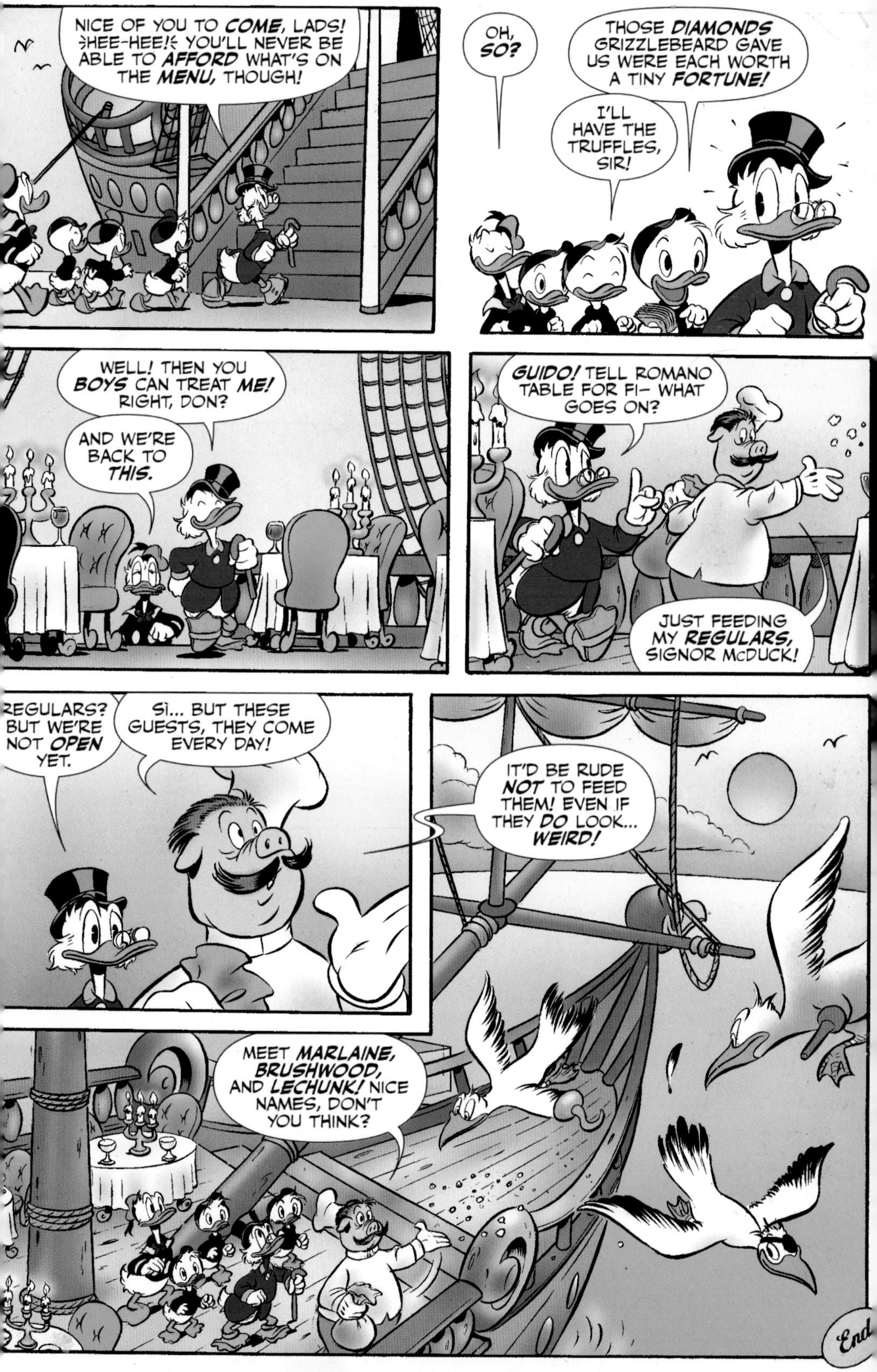
NICE OF YOU TO **COME**, LADS! HEE-HEE! YOU'LL NEVER BE ABLE TO **AFFORD** WHAT'S ON THE **MENU,** THOUGH!
OH, **SO?**
THOSE **DIAMONDS** GRIZZLEBEARD GAVE US WERE EACH WORTH A TINY **FORTUNE!**
I'LL HAVE THE TRUFFLES, SIR!
WELL! THEN YOU **BOYS** CAN TREAT **ME!** RIGHT, DON?
AND WE'RE BACK TO **THIS.**
GUIDO! TELL ROMANO TABLE FOR FI— WHAT GOES ON?
JUST FEEDING MY **REGULARS,** SIGNOR McDUCK!
REGULARS? BUT WE'RE NOT **OPEN** YET.
SÌ... BUT THESE GUESTS, THEY COME EVERY DAY!
IT'D BE RUDE **NOT** TO FEED THEM! EVEN IF THEY **DO** LOOK... **WEIRD!**
MEET **MARLAINE, BRUSHWOOD,** AND **LECHUNK!** NICE NAMES, DON'T YOU THINK?
End

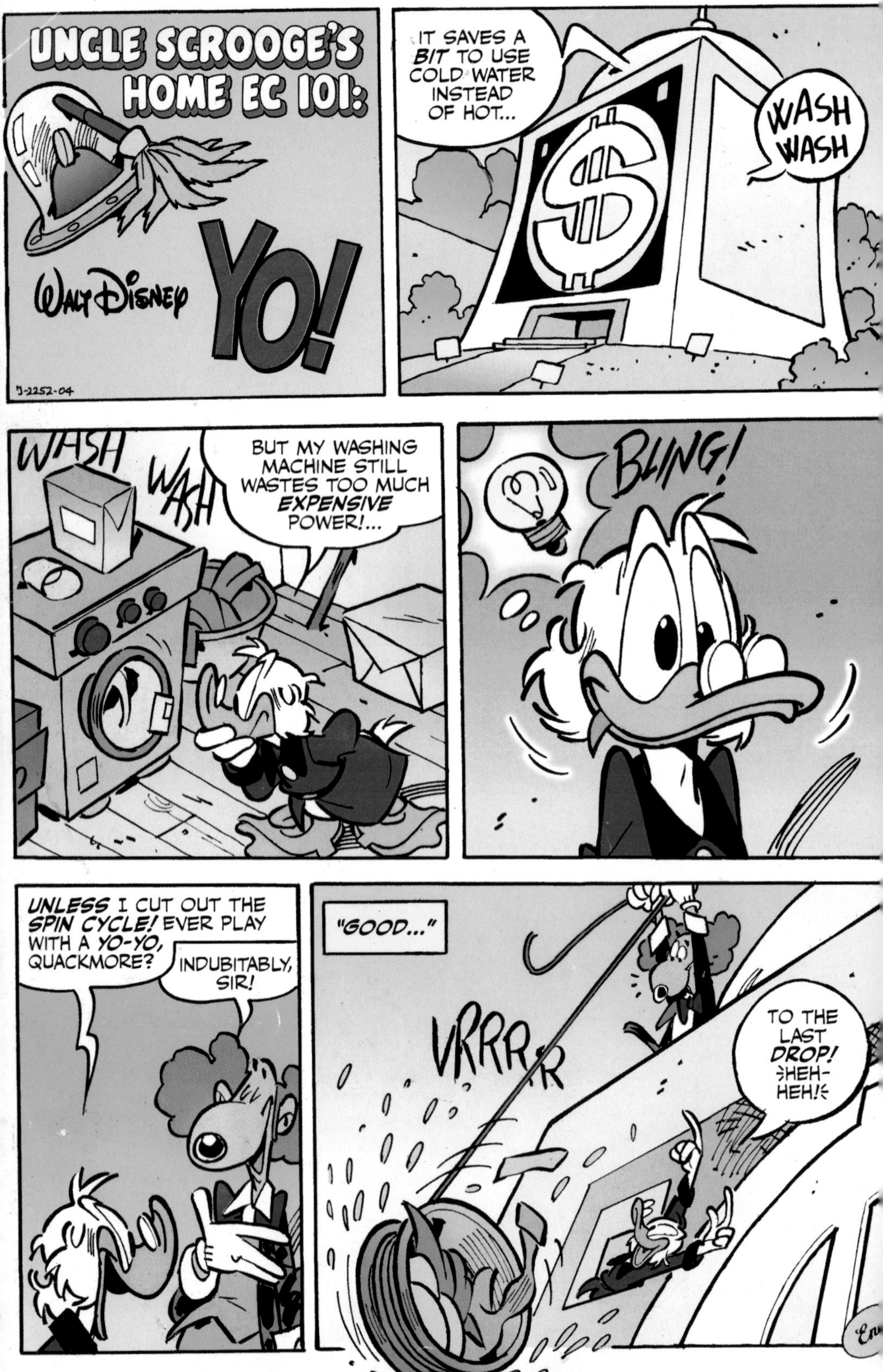

UNCLE SCROOGE'S HOME EC 101:
WALT DISNEY
YO!
J-2252-04
IT SAVES A BIT TO USE COLD WATER INSTEAD OF HOT...
WASH WASH
WASH
WASH
BUT MY WASHING MACHINE STILL WASTES TOO MUCH EXPENSIVE POWER!...
BLING!
UNLESS I CUT OUT THE SPIN CYCLE! EVER PLAY WITH A YO-YO, QUACKMORE?
INDUBITABLY, SIR!
"GOOD..."
VRRRR
TO THE LAST DROP! HEH-HEH!

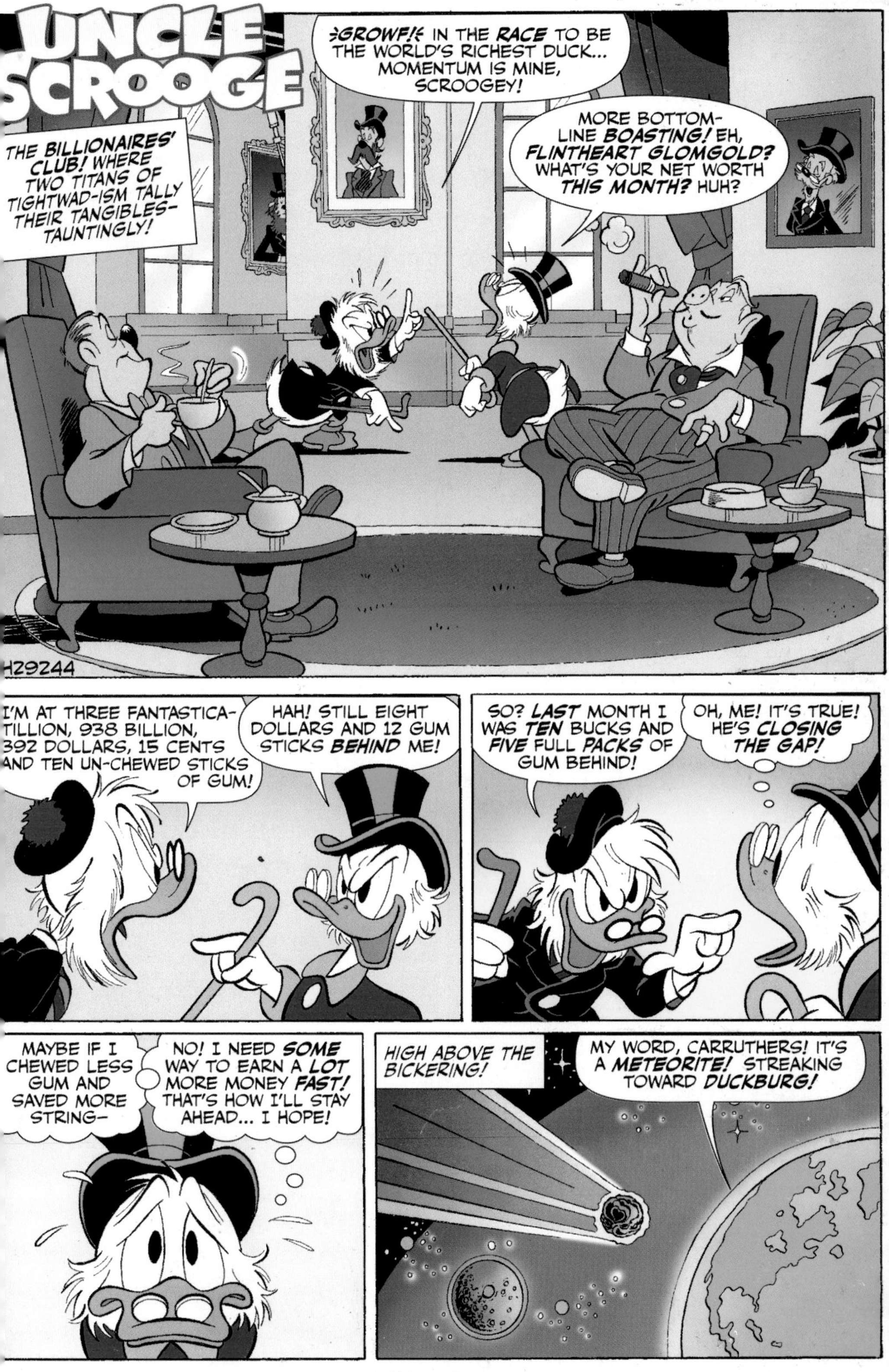
UNCLE SCROOGE
THE BILLIONAIRES' CLUB! WHERE TWO TITANS OF TIGHTWAD-ISM TALLY THEIR TANGIBLES- TAUNTINGLY!
⊰GROWF!⊱ IN THE RACE TO BE THE WORLD'S RICHEST DUCK... MOMENTUM IS MINE, SCROOGEY!
MORE BOTTOM-LINE BOASTING! EH, FLINTHEART GLOMGOLD? WHAT'S YOUR NET WORTH THIS MONTH? HUH?
H29244
I'M AT THREE FANTASTICA-TILLION, 938 BILLION, 392 DOLLARS, 15 CENTS AND TEN UN-CHEWED STICKS OF GUM!
HAH! STILL EIGHT DOLLARS AND 12 GUM STICKS BEHIND ME!
SO? LAST MONTH I WAS TEN BUCKS AND FIVE FULL PACKS OF GUM BEHIND!
OH, ME! IT'S TRUE! HE'S CLOSING THE GAP!
MAYBE IF I CHEWED LESS GUM AND SAVED MORE STRING-
NO! I NEED SOME WAY TO EARN A LOT MORE MONEY FAST! THAT'S HOW I'LL STAY AHEAD... I HOPE!
HIGH ABOVE THE BICKERING!
MY WORD, CARRUTHERS! IT'S A METEORITE! STREAKING TOWARD DUCKBURG!

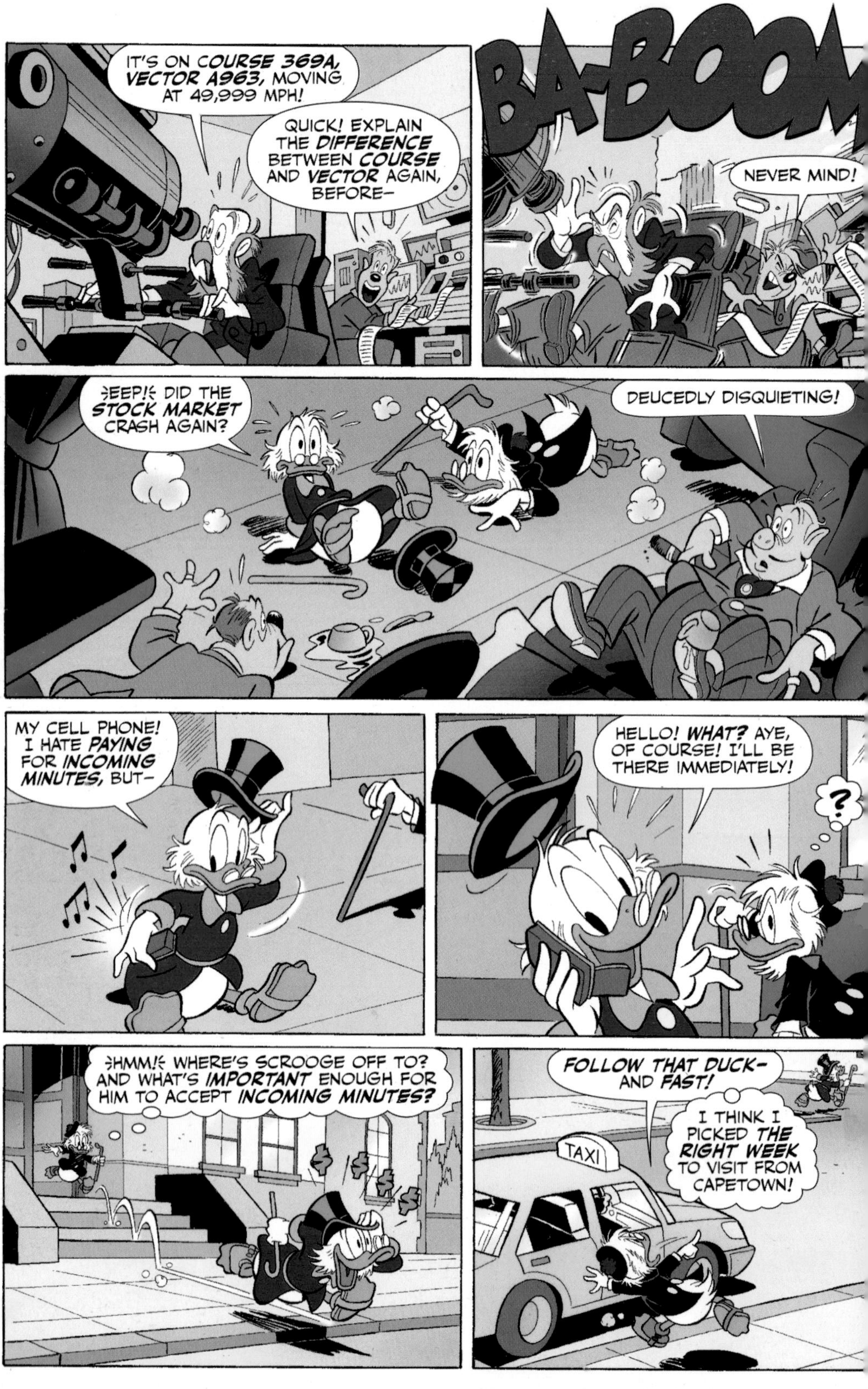

IT'S ON COURSE 369A, VECTOR A963, MOVING AT 49,999 MPH!
QUICK! EXPLAIN THE DIFFERENCE BETWEEN COURSE AND VECTOR AGAIN, BEFORE–
BA-BOOM
NEVER MIND!
EEP! DID THE STOCK MARKET CRASH AGAIN?
DEUCEDLY DISQUIETING!
MY CELL PHONE! I HATE PAYING FOR INCOMING MINUTES, BUT–
HELLO! WHAT? AYE, OF COURSE! I'LL BE THERE IMMEDIATELY!
?
HMM! WHERE'S SCROOGE OFF TO? AND WHAT'S IMPORTANT ENOUGH FOR HIM TO ACCEPT INCOMING MINUTES?
FOLLOW THAT DUCK– AND FAST!
I THINK I PICKED THE RIGHT WEEK TO VISIT FROM CAPETOWN!
TAXI

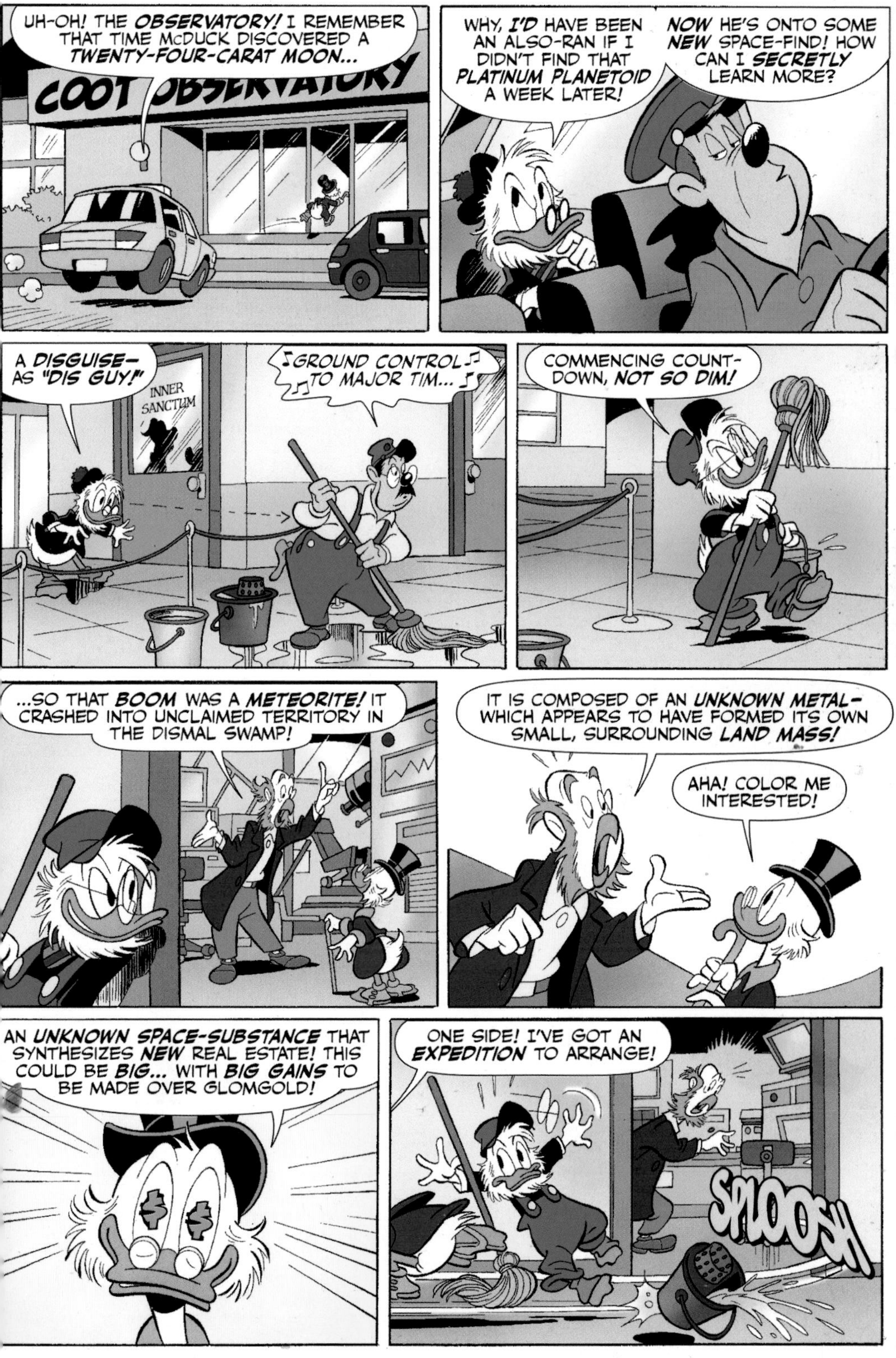

UH-OH! THE OBSERVATORY! I REMEMBER THAT TIME McDUCK DISCOVERED A TWENTY-FOUR-CARAT MOON...
COOT OBSERVATORY
WHY, I'D HAVE BEEN AN ALSO-RAN IF I DIDN'T FIND THAT PLATINUM PLANETOID A WEEK LATER!
NOW HE'S ONTO SOME NEW SPACE-FIND! HOW CAN I SECRETLY LEARN MORE?
A DISGUISE— AS "DIS GUY!"
INNER SANCTUM
GROUND CONTROL TO MAJOR TIM...
COMMENCING COUNT-DOWN, NOT SO DIM!
...SO THAT BOOM WAS A METEORITE! IT CRASHED INTO UNCLAIMED TERRITORY IN THE DISMAL SWAMP!
IT IS COMPOSED OF AN UNKNOWN METAL— WHICH APPEARS TO HAVE FORMED ITS OWN SMALL, SURROUNDING LAND MASS!
AHA! COLOR ME INTERESTED!
AN UNKNOWN SPACE-SUBSTANCE THAT SYNTHESIZES NEW REAL ESTATE! THIS COULD BE BIG... WITH BIG GAINS TO BE MADE OVER GLOMGOLD!
ONE SIDE! I'VE GOT AN EXPEDITION TO ARRANGE!
SPLOOSH

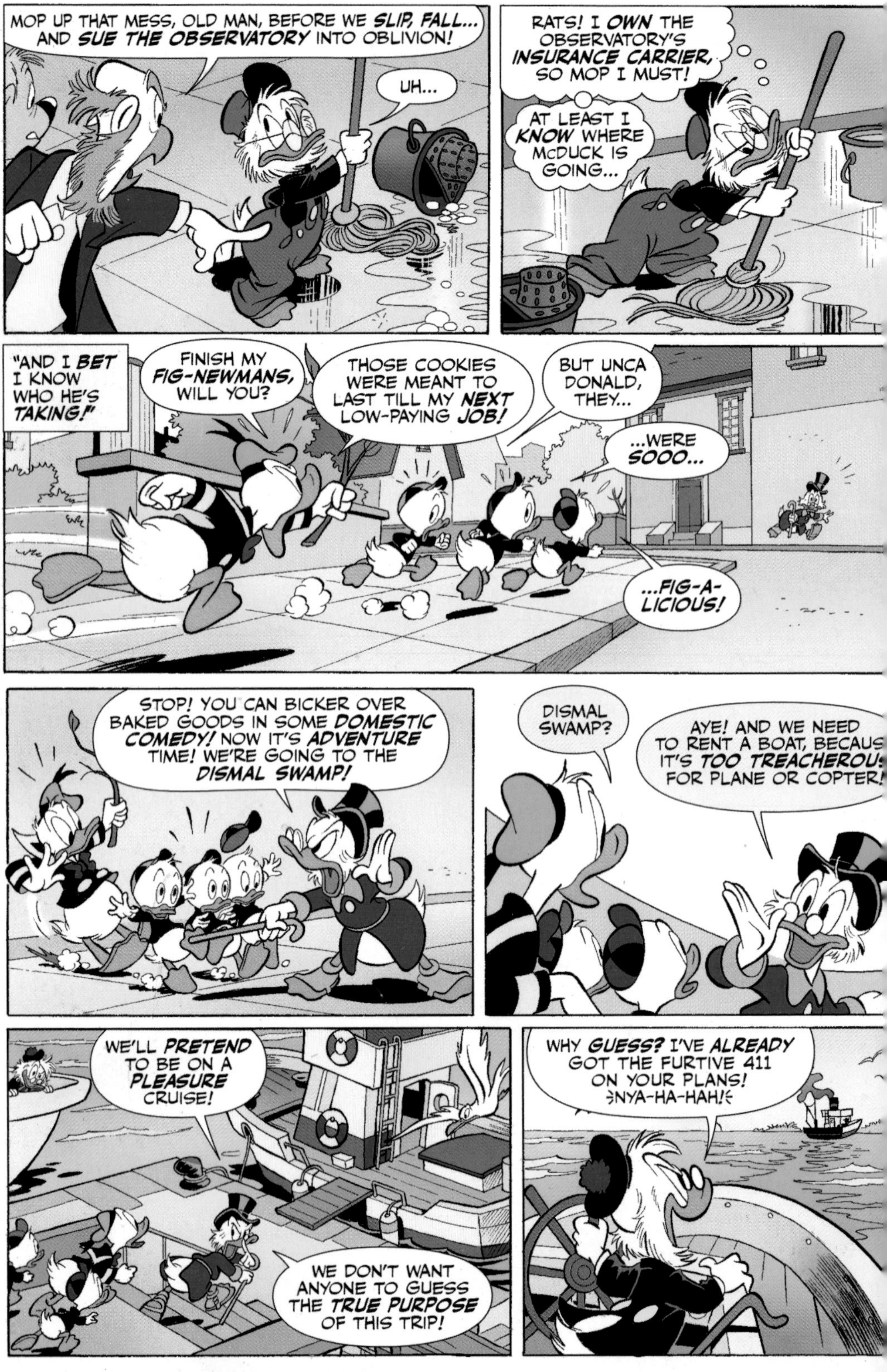

MOP UP THAT MESS, OLD MAN, BEFORE WE SLIP, FALL... AND SUE THE OBSERVATORY INTO OBLIVION!
UH...
RATS! I OWN THE OBSERVATORY'S INSURANCE CARRIER, SO MOP I MUST!
AT LEAST I KNOW WHERE McDUCK IS GOING...
"AND I BET I KNOW WHO HE'S TAKING!"
FINISH MY FIG-NEWMANS, WILL YOU?
THOSE COOKIES WERE MEANT TO LAST TILL MY NEXT LOW-PAYING JOB!
BUT UNCA DONALD, THEY...
...WERE SOOO...
...FIG-A-LICIOUS!
STOP! YOU CAN BICKER OVER BAKED GOODS IN SOME DOMESTIC COMEDY! NOW IT'S ADVENTURE TIME! WE'RE GOING TO THE DISMAL SWAMP!
DISMAL SWAMP?
AYE! AND WE NEED TO RENT A BOAT, BECAUS IT'S TOO TREACHEROU FOR PLANE OR COPTER!
WE'LL PRETEND TO BE ON A PLEASURE CRUISE!
WE DON'T WANT ANYONE TO GUESS THE TRUE PURPOSE OF THIS TRIP!
WHY GUESS? I'VE ALREADY GOT THE FURTIVE 411 ON YOUR PLANS!
NYA-HA-HAH!

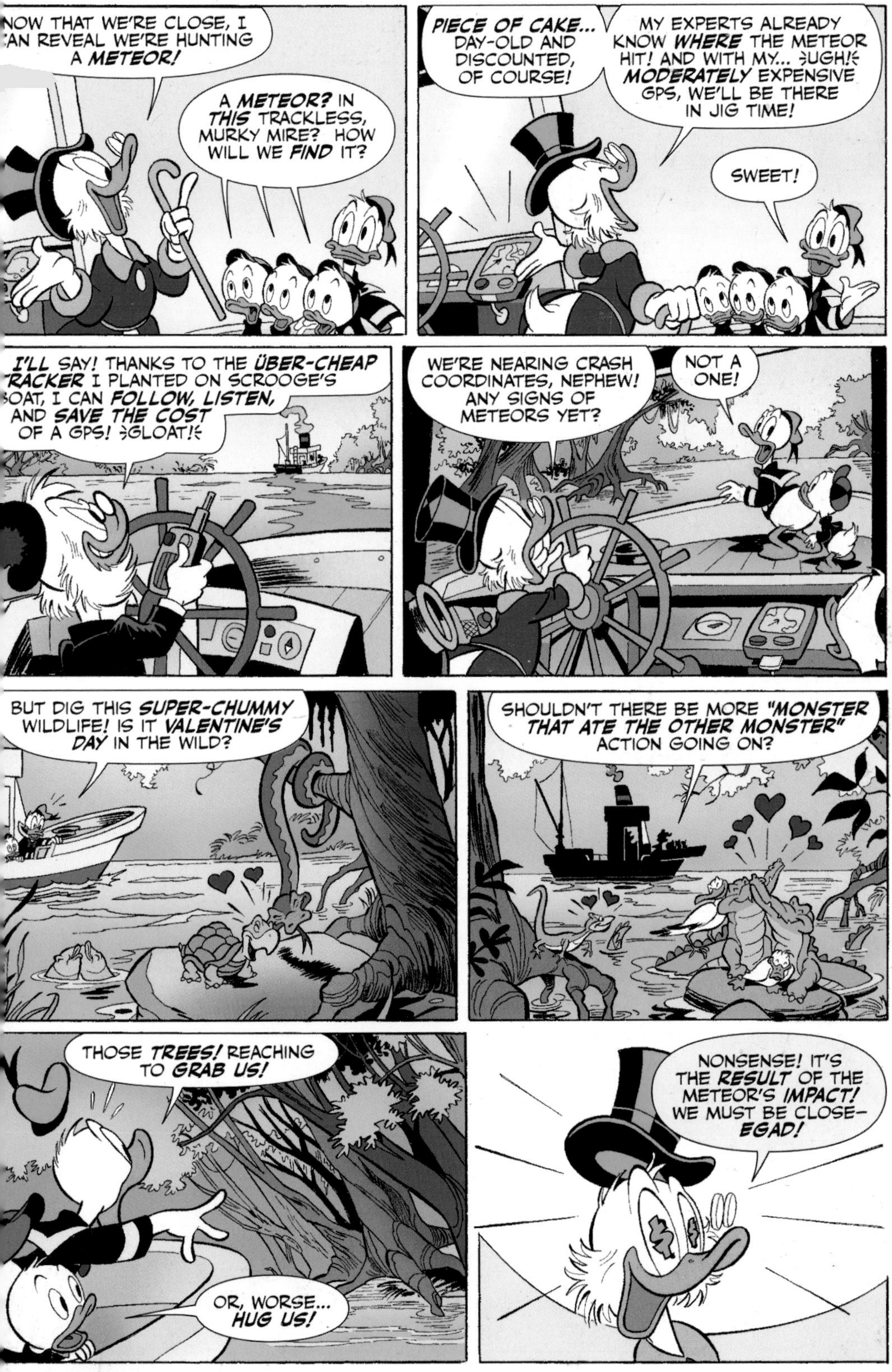
NOW THAT WE'RE CLOSE, I
CAN REVEAL WE'RE HUNTING A METEOR!
A METEOR? IN THIS TRACKLESS, MURKY MIRE? HOW WILL WE FIND IT?
PIECE OF CAKE... DAY-OLD AND DISCOUNTED, OF COURSE!
MY EXPERTS ALREADY KNOW WHERE THE METEOR HIT! AND WITH MY... UGH! MODERATELY EXPENSIVE GPS, WE'LL BE THERE IN JIG TIME!
SWEET!
I'LL SAY! THANKS TO THE ÜBER-CHEAP TRACKER I PLANTED ON SCROOGE'S BOAT, I CAN FOLLOW, LISTEN, AND SAVE THE COST OF A GPS! GLOAT!
WE'RE NEARING CRASH COORDINATES, NEPHEW! ANY SIGNS OF METEORS YET?
NOT A ONE!
BUT DIG THIS SUPER-CHUMMY WILDLIFE! IS IT VALENTINE'S DAY IN THE WILD?
SHOULDN'T THERE BE MORE "MONSTER THAT ATE THE OTHER MONSTER" ACTION GOING ON?
THOSE TREES! REACHING TO GRAB US!
OR, WORSE... HUG US!
NONSENSE! IT'S THE RESULT OF THE METEOR'S IMPACT! WE MUST BE CLOSE— EGAD!

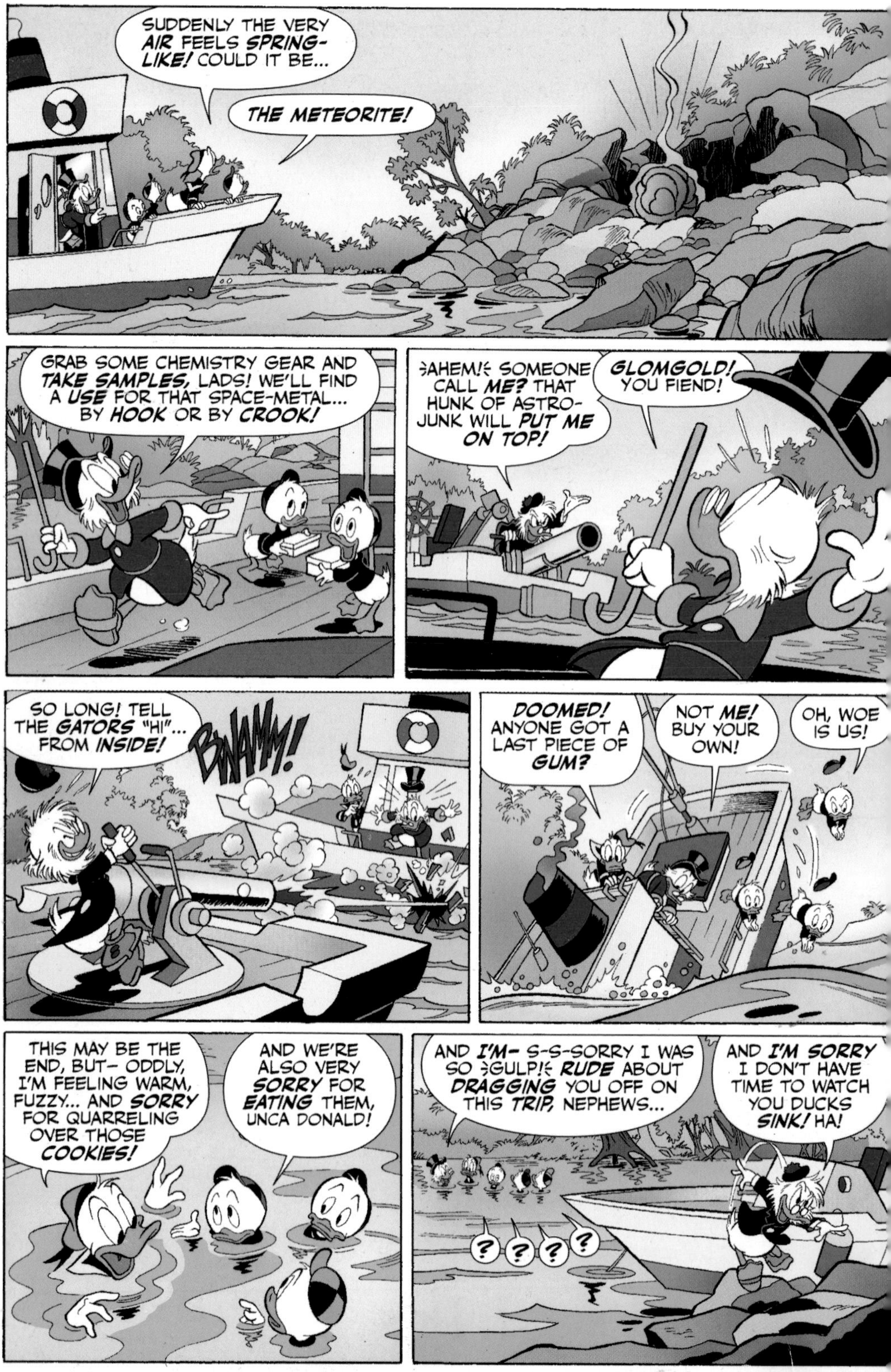
SUDDENLY THE VERY AIR FEELS SPRING-LIKE! COULD IT BE...
THE METEORITE!
GRAB SOME CHEMISTRY GEAR AND TAKE SAMPLES, LADS! WE'LL FIND A USE FOR THAT SPACE-METAL... BY HOOK OR BY CROOK!
AHEM! SOMEONE CALL ME? THAT HUNK OF ASTRO-JUNK WILL PUT ME ON TOP!
GLOMGOLD! YOU FIEND!
SO LONG! TELL THE GATORS "HI"... FROM INSIDE!
BWAMM!
DOOMED! ANYONE GOT A LAST PIECE OF GUM?
NOT ME! BUY YOUR OWN!
OH, WOE IS US!
THIS MAY BE THE END, BUT– ODDLY, I'M FEELING WARM, FUZZY... AND SORRY FOR QUARRELING OVER THOSE COOKIES!
AND WE'RE ALSO VERY SORRY FOR EATING THEM, UNCA DONALD!
AND I'M– S-S-SORRY I WAS SO GULP! RUDE ABOUT DRAGGING YOU OFF ON THIS TRIP, NEPHEWS...
AND I'M SORRY I DON'T HAVE TIME TO WATCH YOU DUCKS SINK! HA!
? ? ? ?

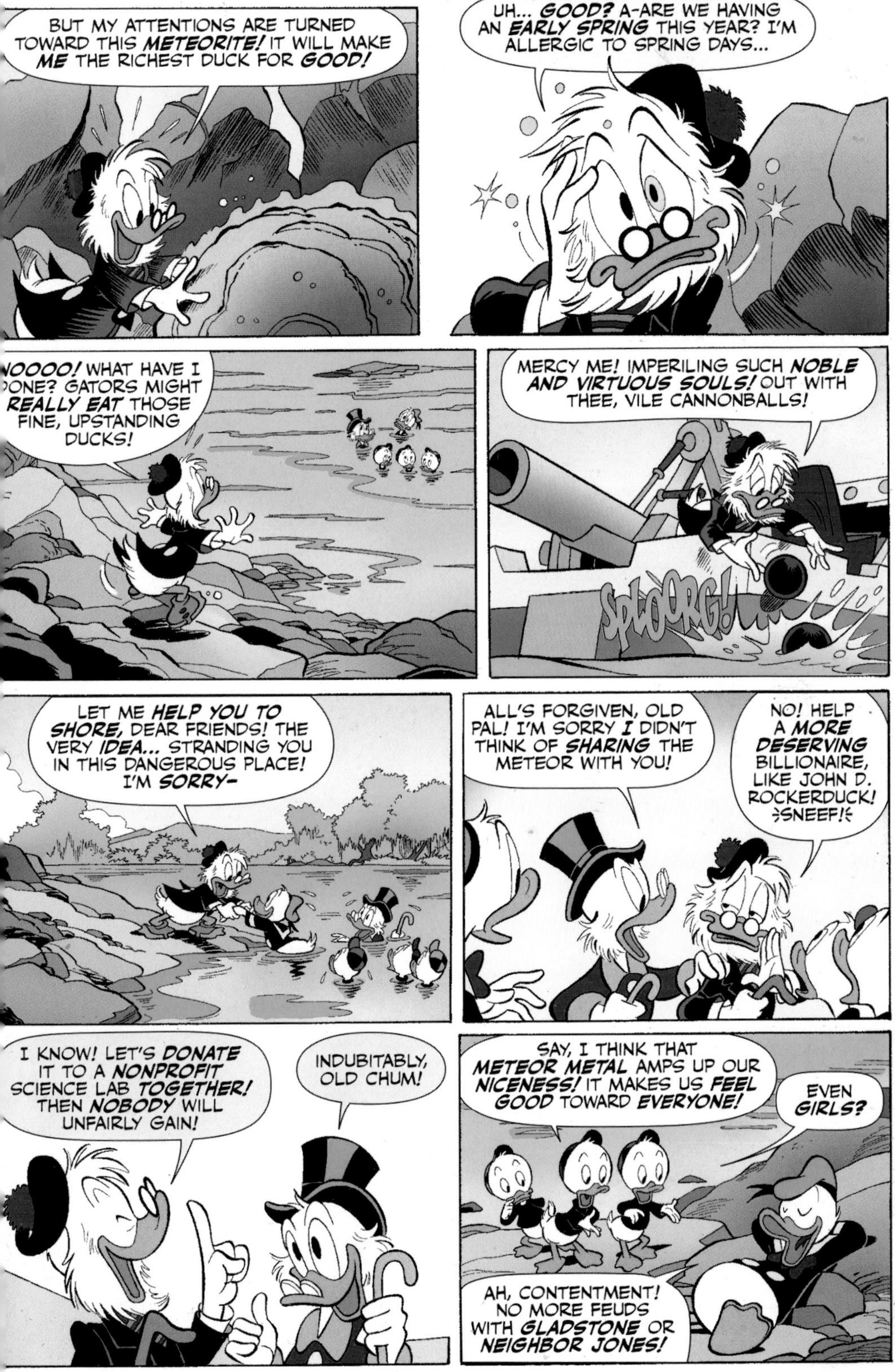

BUT MY ATTENTIONS ARE TURNED TOWARD THIS METEORITE! IT WILL MAKE ME THE RICHEST DUCK FOR GOOD!
UH... GOOD? A-ARE WE HAVING AN EARLY SPRING THIS YEAR? I'M ALLERGIC TO SPRING DAYS...
NOOOO! WHAT HAVE I DONE? GATORS MIGHT REALLY EAT THOSE FINE, UPSTANDING DUCKS!
MERCY ME! IMPERILING SUCH NOBLE AND VIRTUOUS SOULS! OUT WITH THEE, VILE CANNONBALLS!
SPLOORG!
LET ME HELP YOU TO SHORE, DEAR FRIENDS! THE VERY IDEA... STRANDING YOU IN THIS DANGEROUS PLACE! I'M SORRY-
ALL'S FORGIVEN, OLD PAL! I'M SORRY I DIDN'T THINK OF SHARING THE METEOR WITH YOU!
NO! HELP A MORE DESERVING BILLIONAIRE, LIKE JOHN D. ROCKERDUCK! SNEEF!
I KNOW! LET'S DONATE IT TO A NONPROFIT SCIENCE LAB TOGETHER! THEN NOBODY WILL UNFAIRLY GAIN!
INDUBITABLY, OLD CHUM!
SAY, I THINK THAT METEOR METAL AMPS UP OUR NICENESS! IT MAKES US FEEL GOOD TOWARD EVERYONE!
EVEN GIRLS?
AH, CONTENTMENT! NO MORE FEUDS WITH GLADSTONE OR NEIGHBOR JONES!

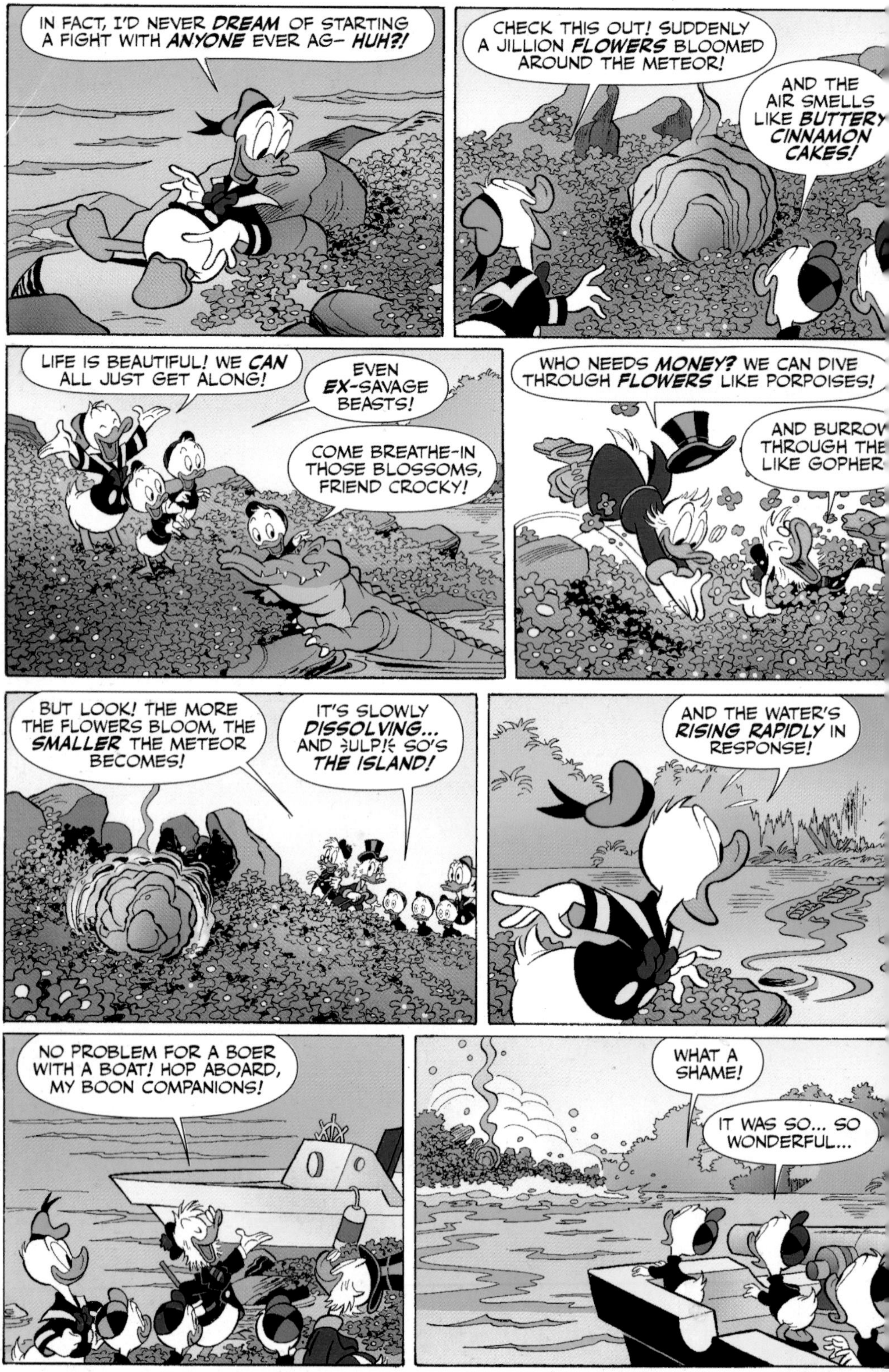

IN FACT, I'D NEVER DREAM OF STARTING A FIGHT WITH ANYONE EVER AG– HUH?!
CHECK THIS OUT! SUDDENLY A JILLION FLOWERS BLOOMED AROUND THE METEOR!
AND THE AIR SMELLS LIKE BUTTERY CINNAMON CAKES!
LIFE IS BEAUTIFUL! WE CAN ALL JUST GET ALONG!
EVEN EX-SAVAGE BEASTS!
COME BREATHE-IN THOSE BLOSSOMS, FRIEND CROCKY!
WHO NEEDS MONEY? WE CAN DIVE THROUGH FLOWERS LIKE PORPOISES!
AND BURROW THROUGH THE LIKE GOPHER
BUT LOOK! THE MORE THE FLOWERS BLOOM, THE SMALLER THE METEOR BECOMES!
IT'S SLOWLY DISSOLVING... AND GULP! SO'S THE ISLAND!
AND THE WATER'S RISING RAPIDLY IN RESPONSE!
NO PROBLEM FOR A BOER WITH A BOAT! HOP ABOARD, MY BOON COMPANIONS!
WHAT A SHAME!
IT WAS SO... SO WONDERFUL...

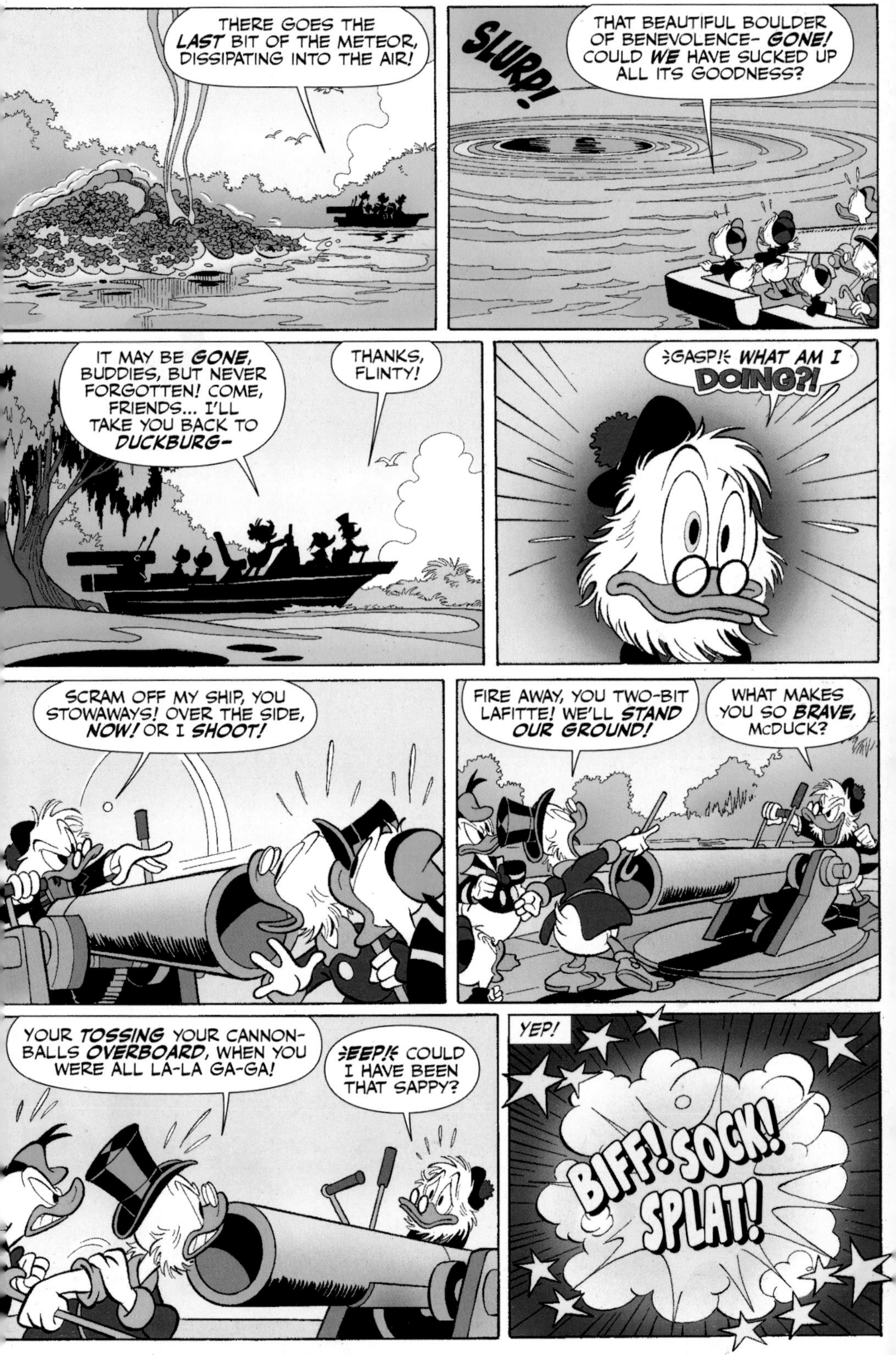
THERE GOES THE LAST BIT OF THE METEOR, DISSIPATING INTO THE AIR!
SLURP!
THAT BEAUTIFUL BOULDER OF BENEVOLENCE- GONE! COULD WE HAVE SUCKED UP ALL ITS GOODNESS?
IT MAY BE GONE, BUDDIES, BUT NEVER FORGOTTEN! COME, FRIENDS... I'LL TAKE YOU BACK TO DUCKBURG-
THANKS, FLINTY!
GASP! WHAT AM I DOING?!
SCRAM OFF MY SHIP, YOU STOWAWAYS! OVER THE SIDE, NOW! OR I SHOOT!
FIRE AWAY, YOU TWO-BIT LAFITTE! WE'LL STAND OUR GROUND!
WHAT MAKES YOU SO BRAVE, McDUCK?
YOUR TOSSING YOUR CANNON-BALLS OVERBOARD, WHEN YOU WERE ALL LA-LA GA-GA!
EEP! COULD I HAVE BEEN THAT SAPPY?
YEP!
BIFF! SOCK! SPLAT!

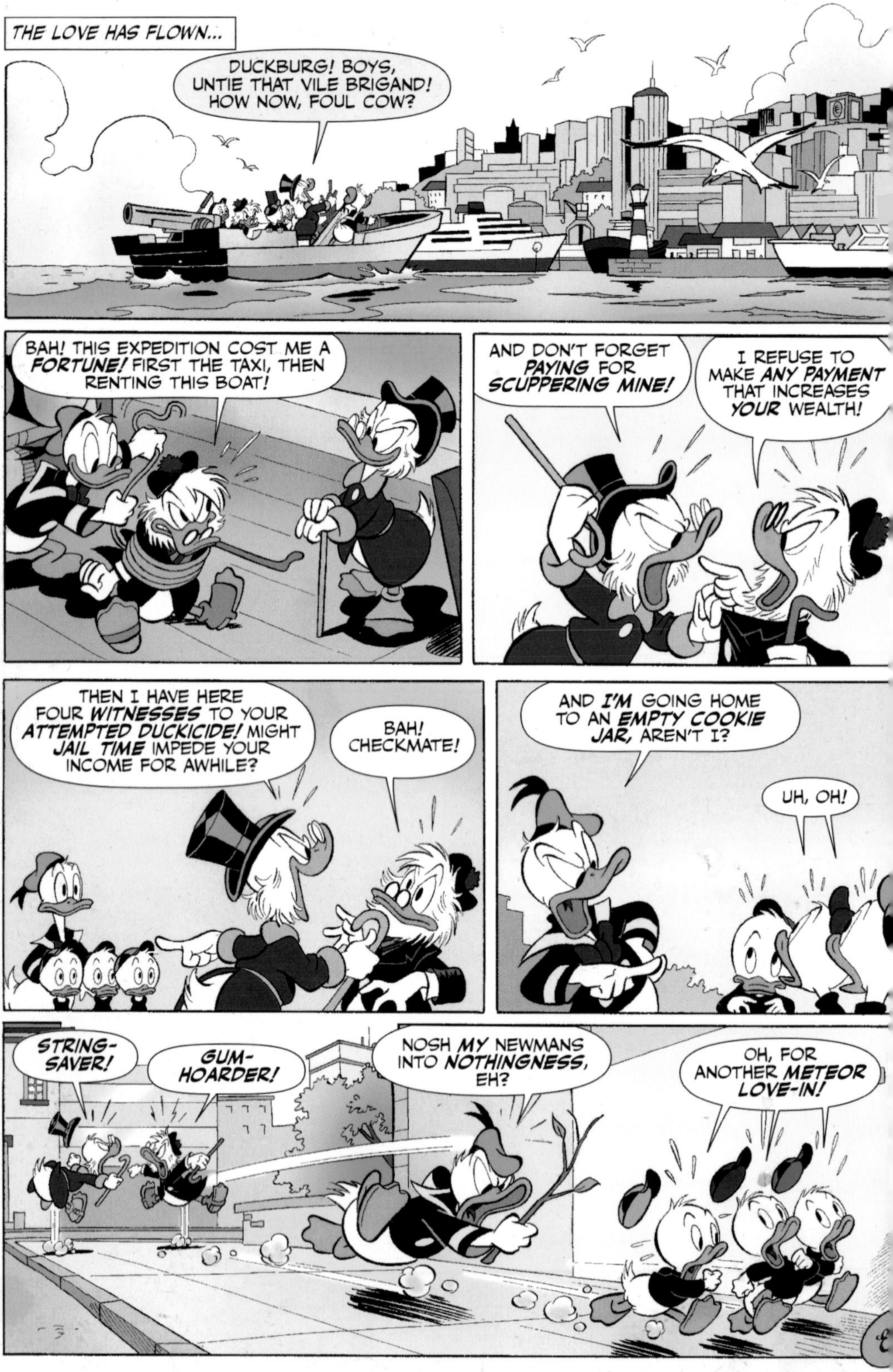
THE LOVE HAS FLOWN...
DUCKBURG! BOYS, UNTIE THAT VILE BRIGAND! HOW NOW, FOUL COW?
BAH! THIS EXPEDITION COST ME A FORTUNE! FIRST THE TAXI, THEN RENTING THIS BOAT!
AND DON'T FORGET PAYING FOR SCUPPERING MINE!
I REFUSE TO MAKE ANY PAYMENT THAT INCREASES YOUR WEALTH!
THEN I HAVE HERE FOUR WITNESSES TO YOUR ATTEMPTED DUCKICIDE! MIGHT JAIL TIME IMPEDE YOUR INCOME FOR AWHILE?
BAH! CHECKMATE!
AND I'M GOING HOME TO AN EMPTY COOKIE JAR, AREN'T I?
UH, OH!
STRING-SAVER!
GUM-HOARDER!
NOSH MY NEWMANS INTO NOTHINGNESS, EH?
OH, FOR ANOTHER METEOR LOVE-IN!

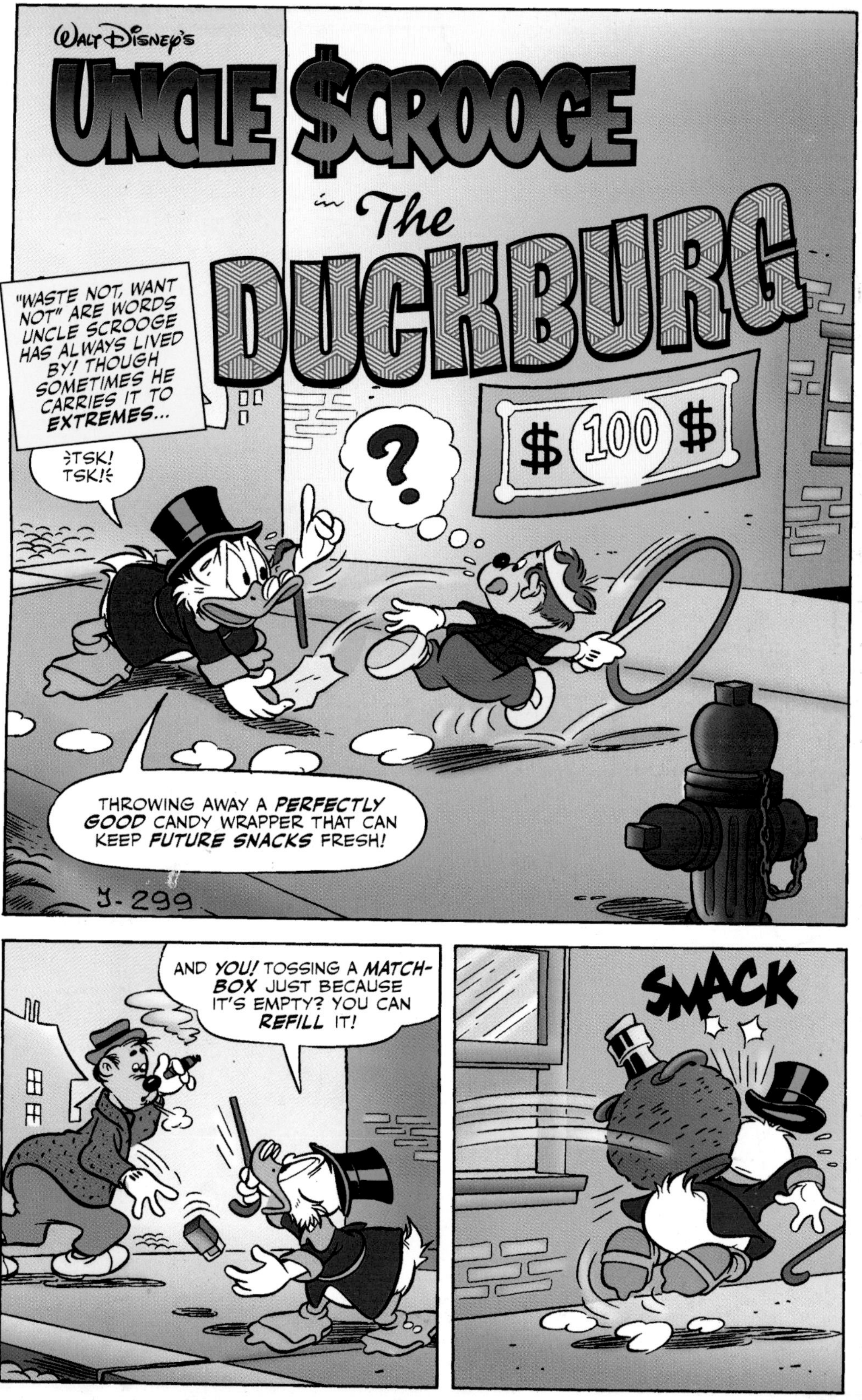
WALT DISNEY'S
UNCLE $CROOGE
in The DUCKBURG
"WASTE NOT, WANT NOT" ARE WORDS UNCLE SCROOGE HAS ALWAYS LIVED BY! THOUGH SOMETIMES HE CARRIES IT TO EXTREMES...
$ 100 $
TSK! TSK!
?
THROWING AWAY A PERFECTLY GOOD CANDY WRAPPER THAT CAN KEEP FUTURE SNACKS FRESH!
J-299
AND YOU! TOSSING A MATCHBOX JUST BECAUSE IT'S EMPTY? YOU CAN REFILL IT!
SMACK

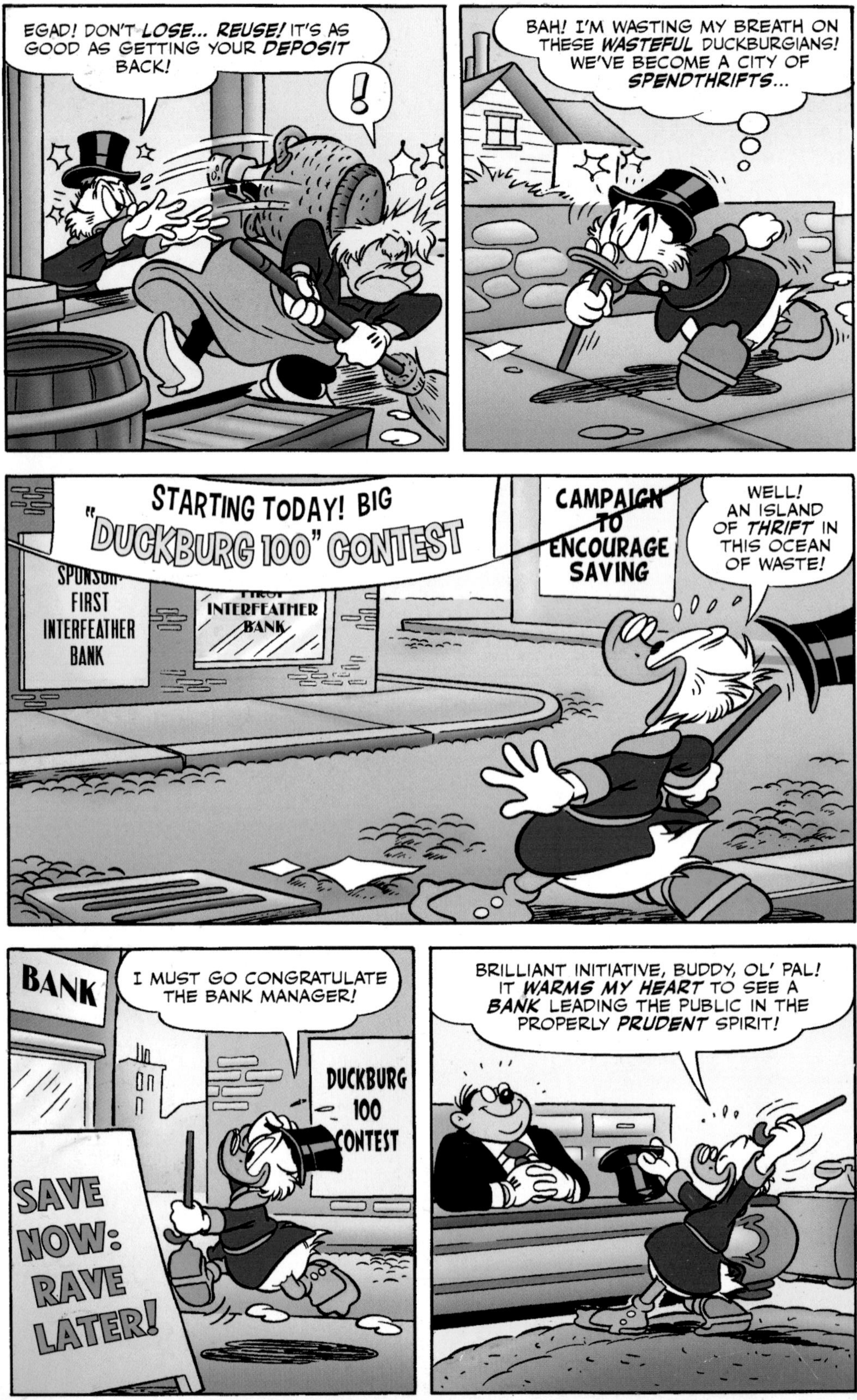
EGAD! DON'T LOSE... REUSE! IT'S AS GOOD AS GETTING YOUR DEPOSIT BACK!
!
BAH! I'M WASTING MY BREATH ON THESE WASTEFUL DUCKBURGIANS! WE'VE BECOME A CITY OF SPENDTHRIFTS...
STARTING TODAY! BIG "DUCKBURG 100" CONTEST
CAMPAIGN TO ENCOURAGE SAVING
FIRST INTERFEATHER BANK
INTERFEATHER BANK
WELL! AN ISLAND OF THRIFT IN THIS OCEAN OF WASTE!
BANK
I MUST GO CONGRATULATE THE BANK MANAGER!
DUCKBURG 100 CONTEST
SAVE NOW: RAVE LATER!
BRILLIANT INITIATIVE, BUDDY, OL' PAL! IT WARMS MY HEART TO SEE A BANK LEADING THE PUBLIC IN THE PROPERLY PRUDENT SPIRIT!

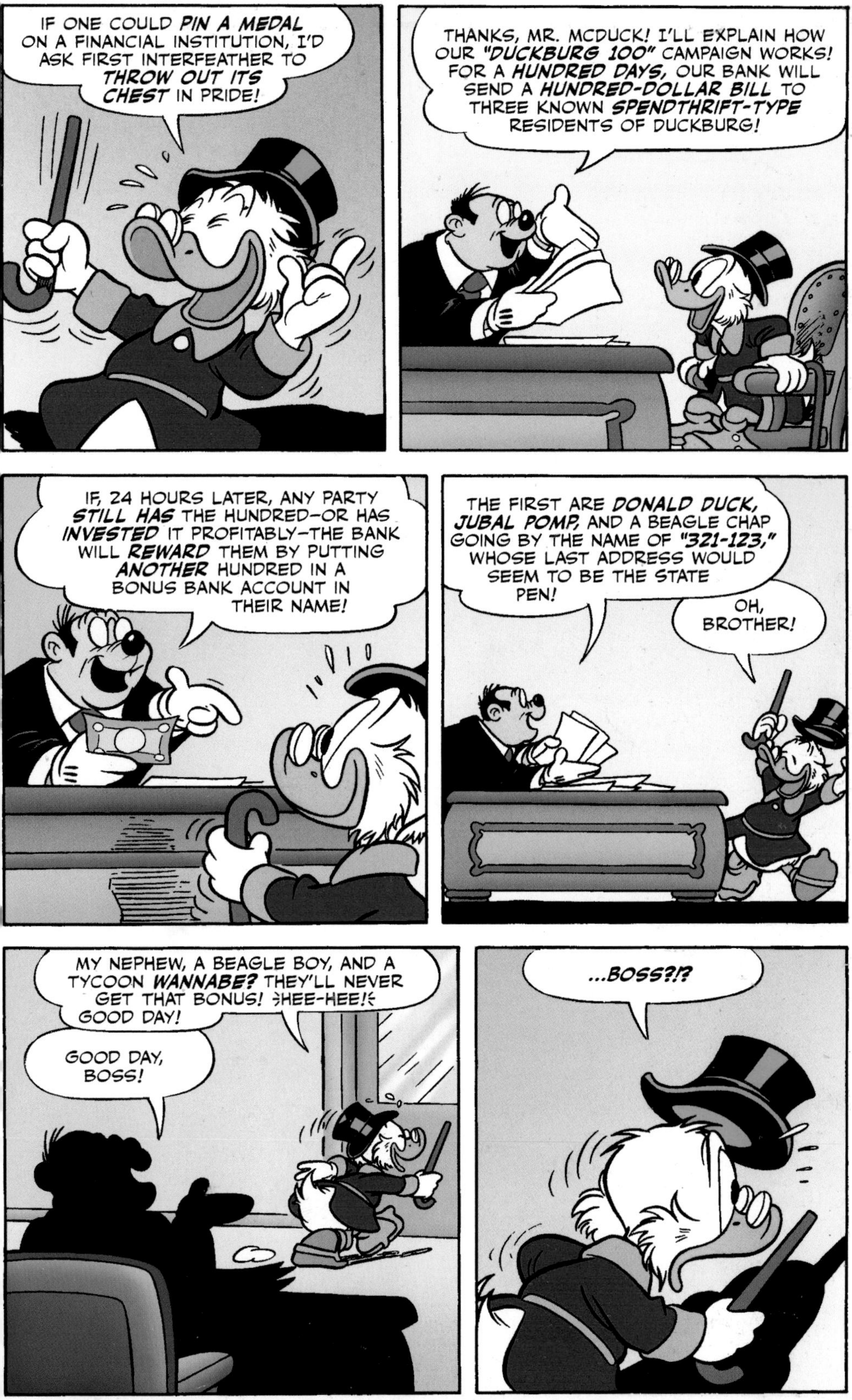
IF ONE COULD PIN A MEDAL ON A FINANCIAL INSTITUTION, I'D ASK FIRST INTERFEATHER TO THROW OUT ITS CHEST IN PRIDE!
THANKS, MR. MCDUCK! I'LL EXPLAIN HOW OUR "DUCKBURG 100" CAMPAIGN WORKS! FOR A HUNDRED DAYS, OUR BANK WILL SEND A HUNDRED-DOLLAR BILL TO THREE KNOWN SPENDTHRIFT-TYPE RESIDENTS OF DUCKBURG!
IF, 24 HOURS LATER, ANY PARTY STILL HAS THE HUNDRED—OR HAS INVESTED IT PROFITABLY—THE BANK WILL REWARD THEM BY PUTTING ANOTHER HUNDRED IN A BONUS BANK ACCOUNT IN THEIR NAME!
THE FIRST ARE DONALD DUCK, JUBAL POMP, AND A BEAGLE CHAP GOING BY THE NAME OF "321-123," WHOSE LAST ADDRESS WOULD SEEM TO BE THE STATE PEN!
OH, BROTHER!
MY NEPHEW, A BEAGLE BOY, AND A TYCOON WANNABE? THEY'LL NEVER GET THAT BONUS! HEE-HEE! GOOD DAY!
GOOD DAY, BOSS!
...BOSS?!?

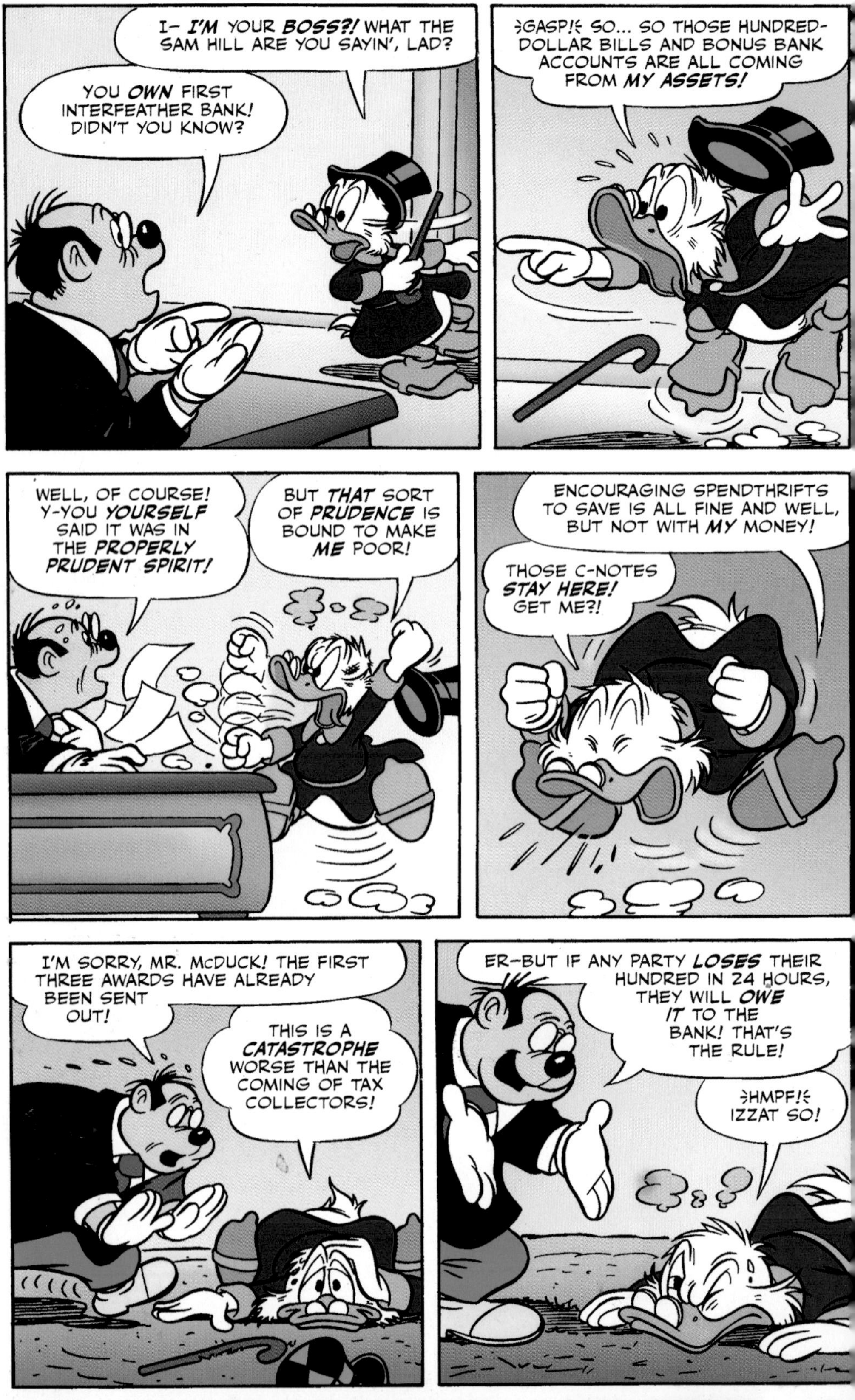
I– I'M YOUR BOSS?! WHAT THE SAM HILL ARE YOU SAYIN', LAD?
YOU OWN FIRST INTERFEATHER BANK! DIDN'T YOU KNOW?
GASP! SO... SO THOSE HUNDRED-DOLLAR BILLS AND BONUS BANK ACCOUNTS ARE ALL COMING FROM MY ASSETS!
WELL, OF COURSE! Y-YOU YOURSELF SAID IT WAS IN THE PROPERLY PRUDENT SPIRIT!
BUT THAT SORT OF PRUDENCE IS BOUND TO MAKE ME POOR!
ENCOURAGING SPENDTHRIFTS TO SAVE IS ALL FINE AND WELL, BUT NOT WITH MY MONEY!
THOSE C-NOTES STAY HERE! GET ME?!
I'M SORRY, MR. McDUCK! THE FIRST THREE AWARDS HAVE ALREADY BEEN SENT OUT!
THIS IS A CATASTROPHE WORSE THAN THE COMING OF TAX COLLECTORS!
ER–BUT IF ANY PARTY LOSES THEIR HUNDRED IN 24 HOURS, THEY WILL OWE IT TO THE BANK! THAT'S THE RULE!
HMPF! IZZAT SO!

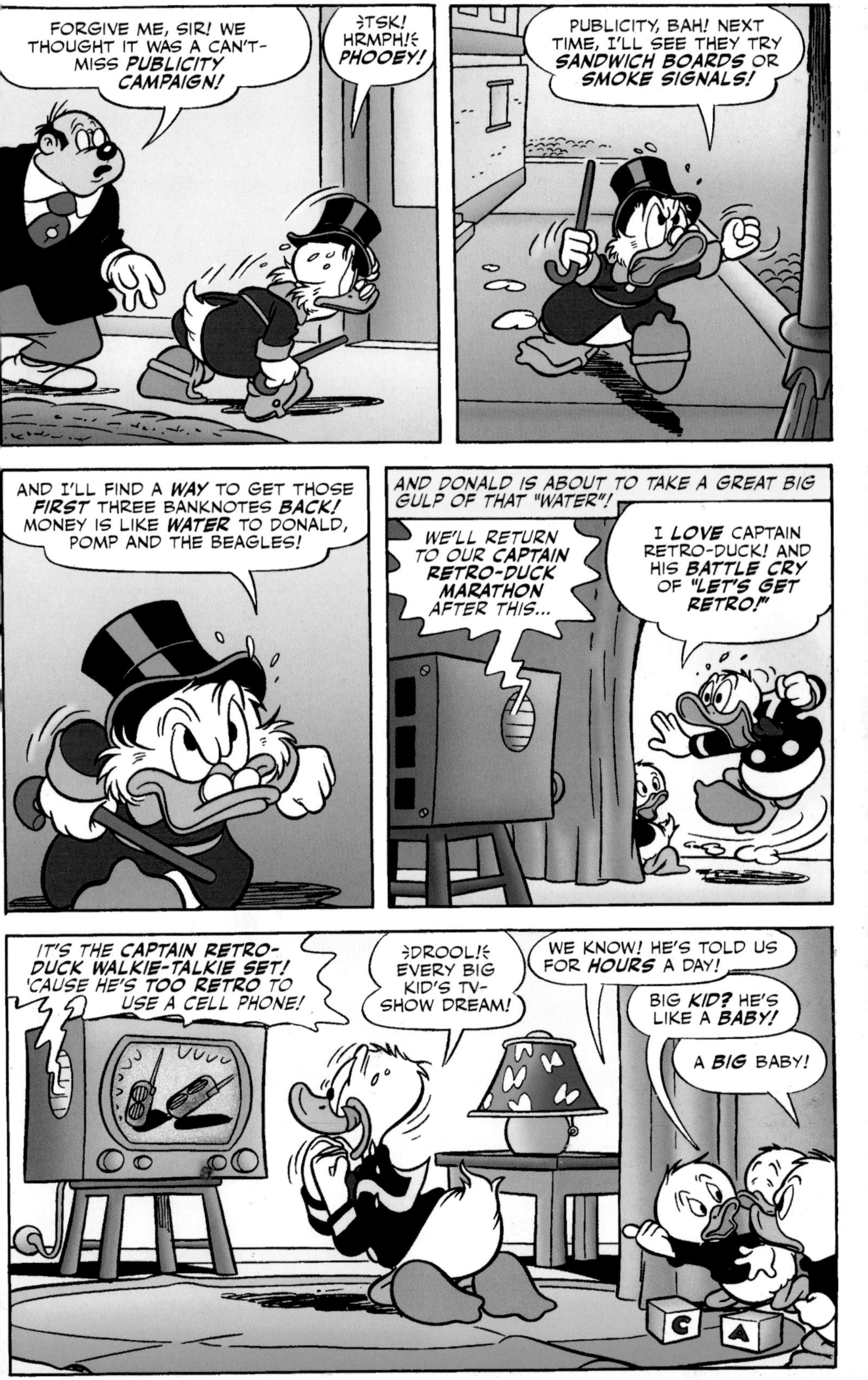
FORGIVE ME, SIR! WE THOUGHT IT WAS A CAN'T-MISS PUBLICITY CAMPAIGN!
TSK! HRMPH! PHOOEY!
PUBLICITY, BAH! NEXT TIME, I'LL SEE THEY TRY SANDWICH BOARDS OR SMOKE SIGNALS!
AND I'LL FIND A WAY TO GET THOSE FIRST THREE BANKNOTES BACK! MONEY IS LIKE WATER TO DONALD, POMP AND THE BEAGLES!
AND DONALD IS ABOUT TO TAKE A GREAT BIG GULP OF THAT "WATER"!
WE'LL RETURN TO OUR CAPTAIN RETRO-DUCK MARATHON AFTER THIS...
I LOVE CAPTAIN RETRO-DUCK! AND HIS BATTLE CRY OF "LET'S GET RETRO!"
IT'S THE CAPTAIN RETRO-DUCK WALKIE-TALKIE SET! 'CAUSE HE'S TOO RETRO TO USE A CELL PHONE!
DROOL! EVERY BIG KID'S TV-SHOW DREAM!
WE KNOW! HE'S TOLD US FOR HOURS A DAY!
BIG KID? HE'S LIKE A BABY!
A BIG BABY!
C A

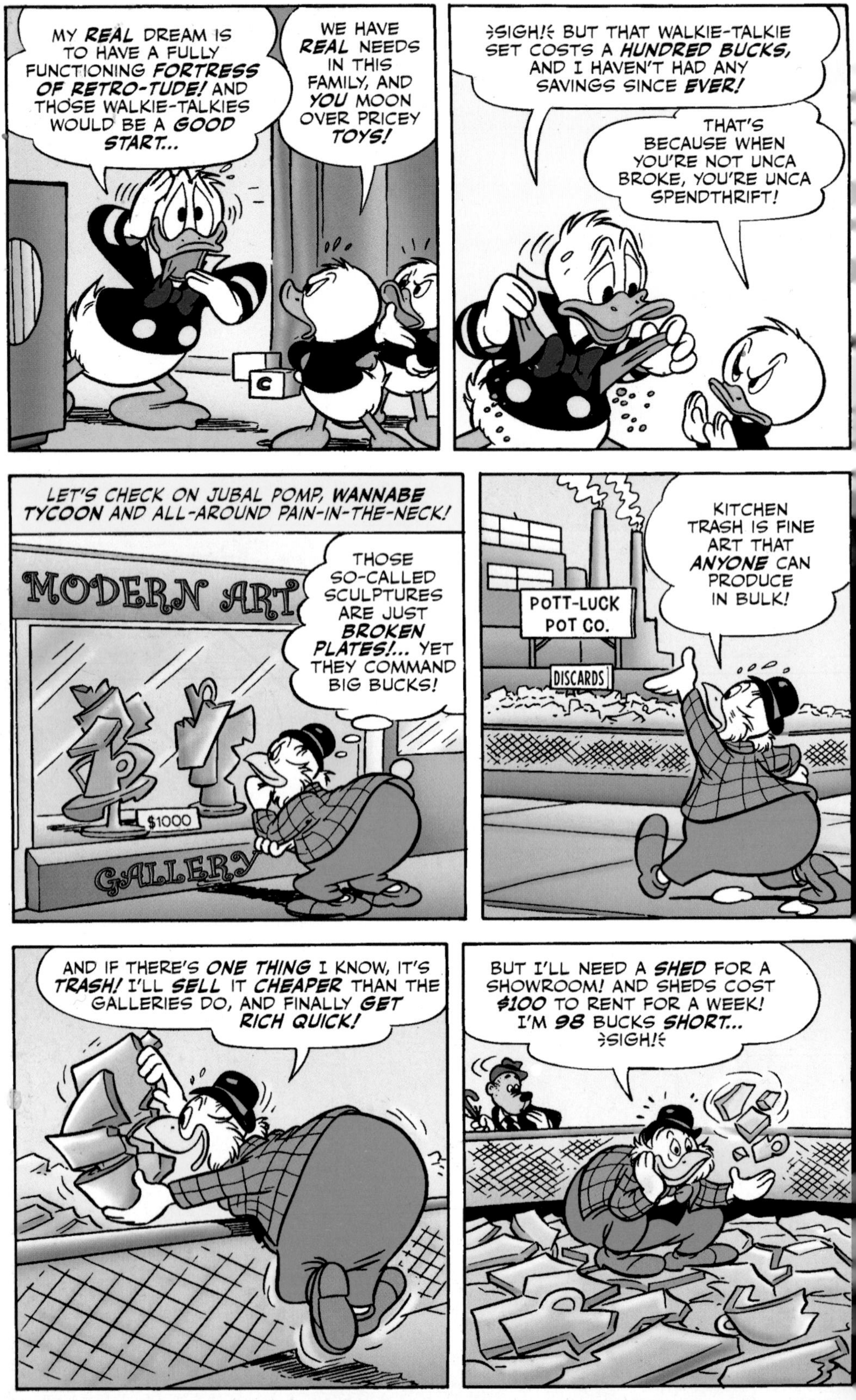
MY REAL DREAM IS TO HAVE A FULLY FUNCTIONING FORTRESS OF RETRO-TUDE! AND THOSE WALKIE-TALKIES WOULD BE A GOOD START...
WE HAVE REAL NEEDS IN THIS FAMILY, AND YOU MOON OVER PRICEY TOYS!
C
SIGH! BUT THAT WALKIE-TALKIE SET COSTS A HUNDRED BUCKS, AND I HAVEN'T HAD ANY SAVINGS SINCE EVER!
THAT'S BECAUSE WHEN YOU'RE NOT UNCA BROKE, YOU'RE UNCA SPENDTHRIFT!
LET'S CHECK ON JUBAL POMP, WANNABE TYCOON AND ALL-AROUND PAIN-IN-THE-NECK!
MODERN ART
THOSE SO-CALLED SCULPTURES ARE JUST BROKEN PLATES!... YET THEY COMMAND BIG BUCKS!
$1000
GALLERY
POTT-LUCK POT CO.
DISCARDS
KITCHEN TRASH IS FINE ART THAT ANYONE CAN PRODUCE IN BULK!
AND IF THERE'S ONE THING I KNOW, IT'S TRASH! I'LL SELL IT CHEAPER THAN THE GALLERIES DO, AND FINALLY GET RICH QUICK!
BUT I'LL NEED A SHED FOR A SHOWROOM! AND SHEDS COST $100 TO RENT FOR A WEEK! I'M 98 BUCKS SHORT... SIGH!

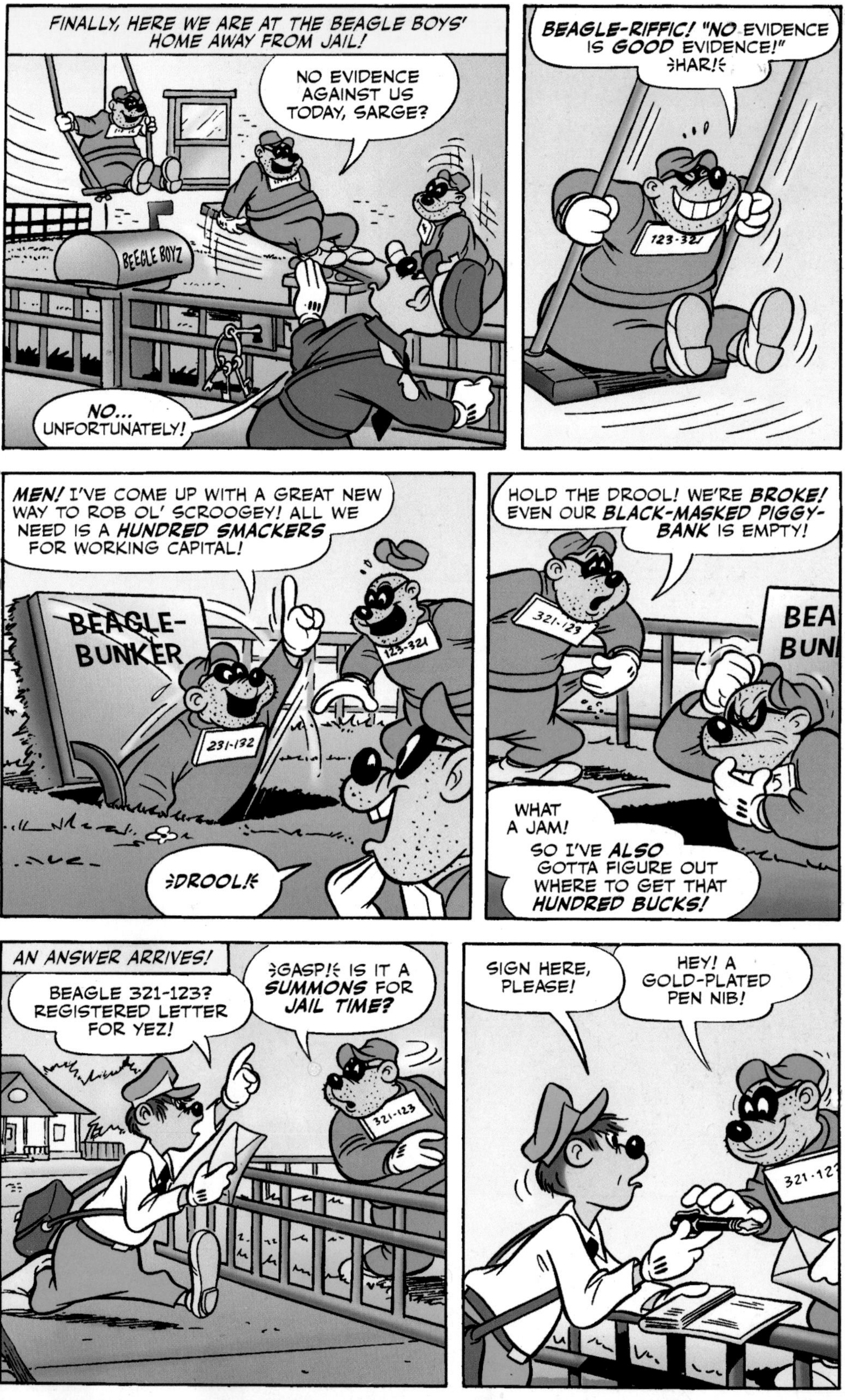
FINALLY, HERE WE ARE AT THE BEAGLE BOYS' HOME AWAY FROM JAIL!
NO EVIDENCE AGAINST US TODAY, SARGE?
NO... UNFORTUNATELY!
BEEGLE BOYZ
BEAGLE-RIFFIC! "NO EVIDENCE IS GOOD EVIDENCE!" HAR!
123-321
MEN! I'VE COME UP WITH A GREAT NEW WAY TO ROB OL' SCROOGEY! ALL WE NEED IS A HUNDRED SMACKERS FOR WORKING CAPITAL!
BEAGLE-BUNKER
123-321
231-132
DROOL!
HOLD THE DROOL! WE'RE BROKE! EVEN OUR BLACK-MASKED PIGGY-BANK IS EMPTY!
321-123
WHAT A JAM!
SO I'VE ALSO GOTTA FIGURE OUT WHERE TO GET THAT HUNDRED BUCKS!
AN ANSWER ARRIVES!
BEAGLE 321-123? REGISTERED LETTER FOR YEZ!
GASP! IS IT A SUMMONS FOR JAIL TIME?
321-123
SIGN HERE, PLEASE!
HEY! A GOLD-PLATED PEN NIB!

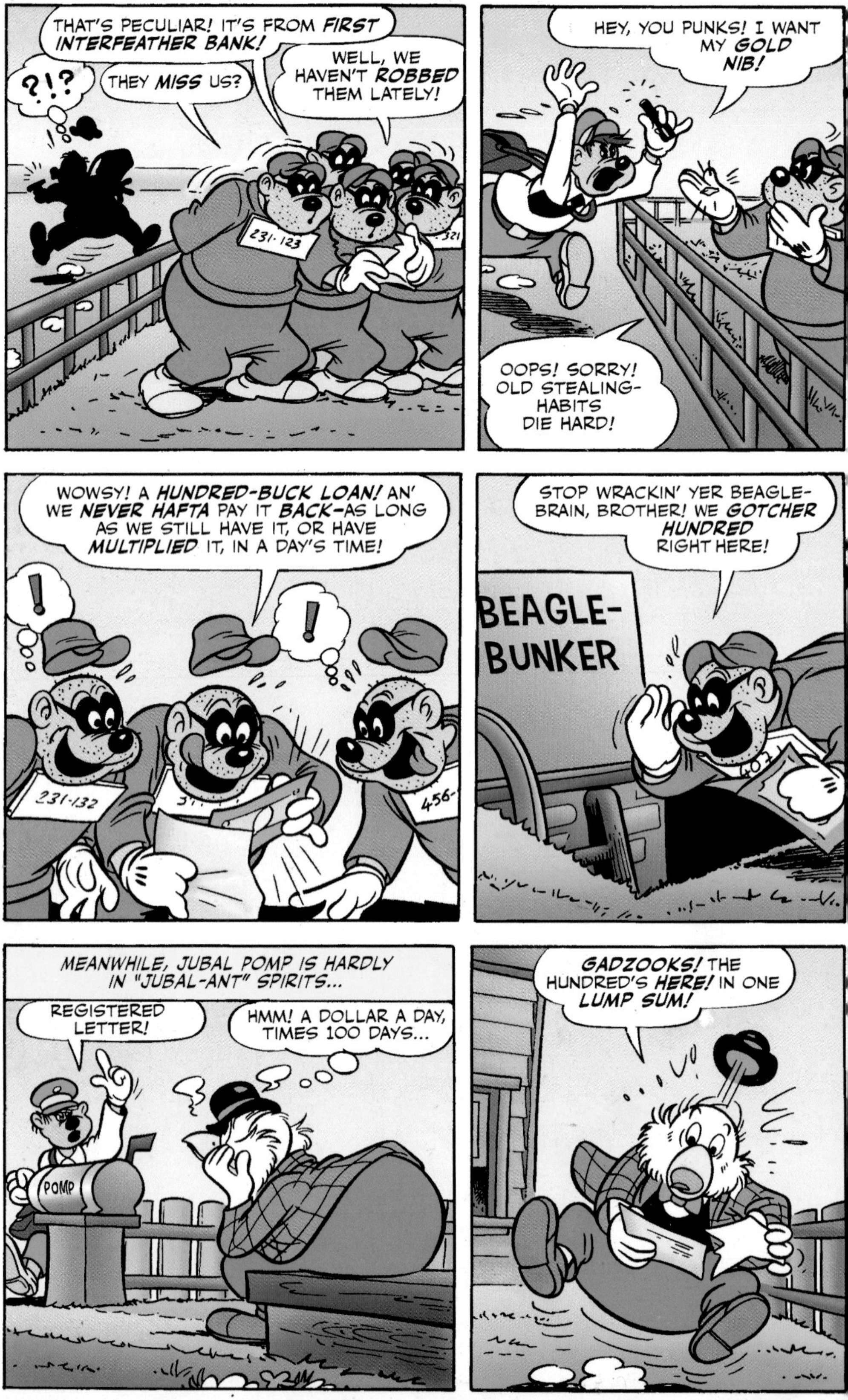
THAT'S PECULIAR! IT'S FROM FIRST INTERFEATHER BANK!
?!?
THEY MISS US?
WELL, WE HAVEN'T ROBBED THEM LATELY!
231-123
321
HEY, YOU PUNKS! I WANT MY GOLD NIB!
OOPS! SORRY! OLD STEALING-HABITS DIE HARD!
WOWSY! A HUNDRED-BUCK LOAN! AN' WE NEVER HAFTA PAY IT BACK—AS LONG AS WE STILL HAVE IT, OR HAVE MULTIPLIED IT, IN A DAY'S TIME!
231-132
STOP WRACKIN' YER BEAGLE-BRAIN, BROTHER! WE GOTCHER HUNDRED RIGHT HERE!
BEAGLE-BUNKER
MEANWHILE, JUBAL POMP IS HARDLY IN "JUBAL-ANT" SPIRITS...
REGISTERED LETTER!
HMM! A DOLLAR A DAY, TIMES 100 DAYS...
POMP
GADZOOKS! THE HUNDRED'S HERE! IN ONE LUMP SUM!

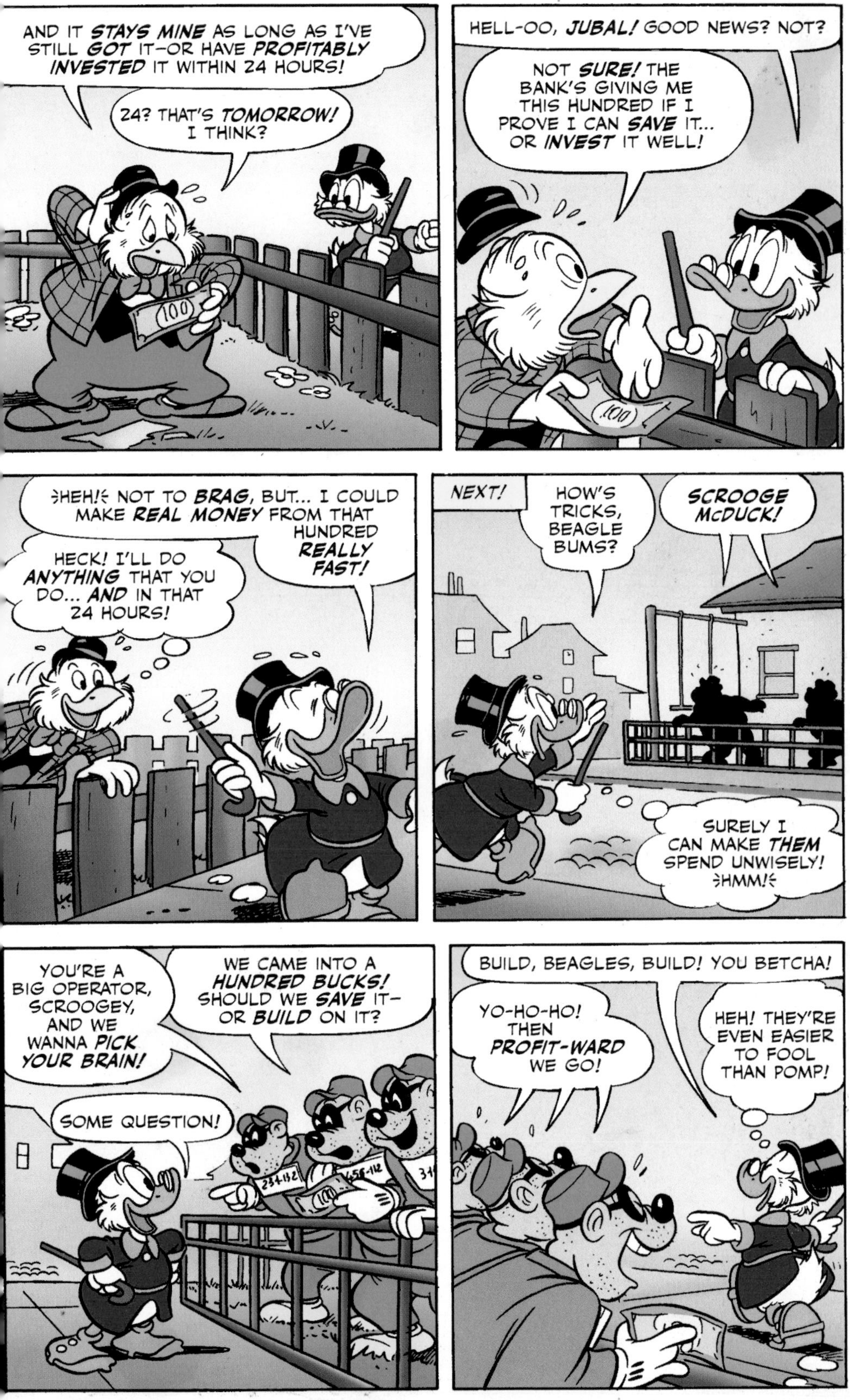
AND IT STAYS MINE AS LONG AS I'VE STILL GOT IT—OR HAVE PROFITABLY INVESTED IT WITHIN 24 HOURS!
24? THAT'S TOMORROW! I THINK?
HELL-OO, JUBAL! GOOD NEWS? NOT?
NOT SURE! THE BANK'S GIVING ME THIS HUNDRED IF I PROVE I CAN SAVE IT... OR INVEST IT WELL!
HEH! NOT TO BRAG, BUT... I COULD MAKE REAL MONEY FROM THAT HUNDRED REALLY FAST!
HECK! I'LL DO ANYTHING THAT YOU DO... AND IN THAT 24 HOURS!
NEXT!
HOW'S TRICKS, BEAGLE BUMS?
SCROOGE McDUCK!
SURELY I CAN MAKE THEM SPEND UNWISELY! HMM!
YOU'RE A BIG OPERATOR, SCROOGEY, AND WE WANNA PICK YOUR BRAIN!
WE CAME INTO A HUNDRED BUCKS! SHOULD WE SAVE IT—OR BUILD ON IT?
SOME QUESTION!
BUILD, BEAGLES, BUILD! YOU BETCHA!
YO-HO-HO! THEN PROFIT-WARD WE GO!
HEH! THEY'RE EVEN EASIER TO FOOL THAN POMP!

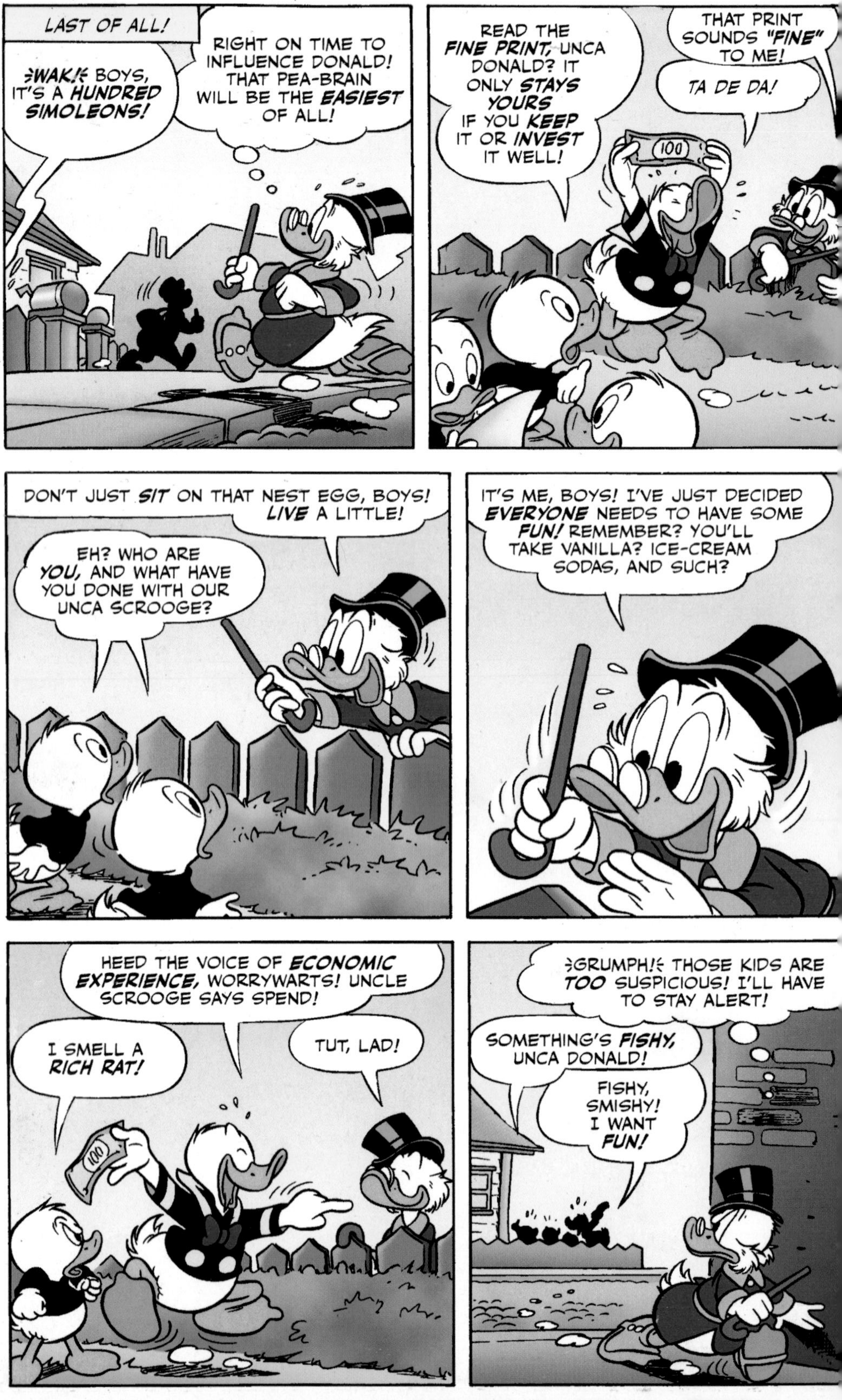
LAST OF ALL!
WAK! BOYS, IT'S A HUNDRED SIMOLEONS!
RIGHT ON TIME TO INFLUENCE DONALD! THAT PEA-BRAIN WILL BE THE EASIEST OF ALL!
READ THE FINE PRINT, UNCA DONALD? IT ONLY STAYS YOURS IF YOU KEEP IT OR INVEST IT WELL!
THAT PRINT SOUNDS "FINE" TO ME!
TA DE DA!
100
DON'T JUST SIT ON THAT NEST EGG, BOYS! LIVE A LITTLE!
EH? WHO ARE YOU, AND WHAT HAVE YOU DONE WITH OUR UNCA SCROOGE?
IT'S ME, BOYS! I'VE JUST DECIDED EVERYONE NEEDS TO HAVE SOME FUN! REMEMBER? YOU'LL TAKE VANILLA? ICE-CREAM SODAS, AND SUCH?
HEED THE VOICE OF ECONOMIC EXPERIENCE, WORRYWARTS! UNCLE SCROOGE SAYS SPEND!
I SMELL A RICH RAT!
TUT, LAD!
100
GRUMPH! THOSE KIDS ARE TOO SUSPICIOUS! I'LL HAVE TO STAY ALERT!
SOMETHING'S FISHY, UNCA DONALD!
FISHY, SMISHY! I WANT FUN!

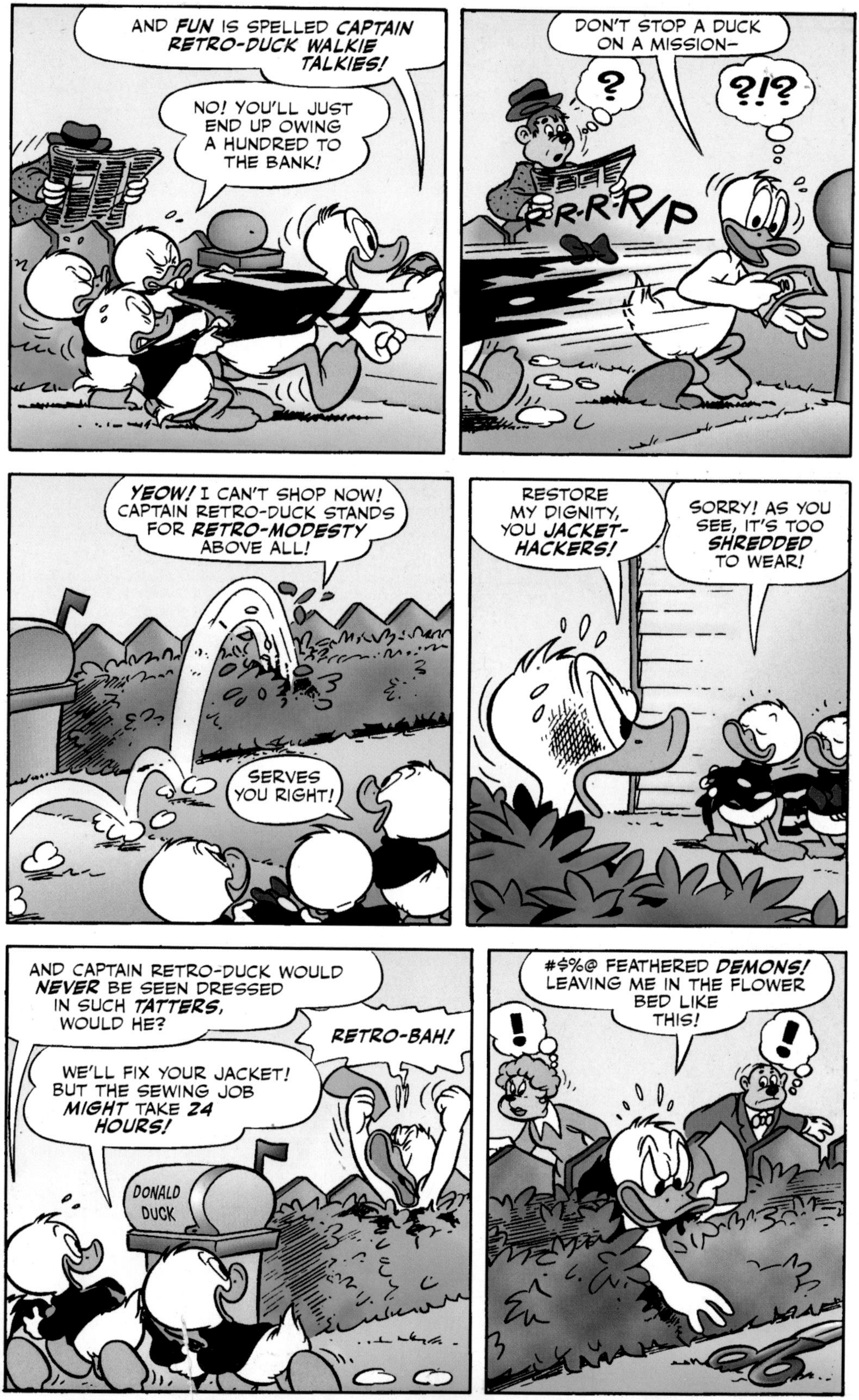
AND FUN IS SPELLED CAPTAIN RETRO-DUCK WALKIE TALKIES!
NO! YOU'LL JUST END UP OWING A HUNDRED TO THE BANK!
DON'T STOP A DUCK ON A MISSION–
?
?!?
R-R-R-R-R/P
YEOW! I CAN'T SHOP NOW! CAPTAIN RETRO-DUCK STANDS FOR RETRO-MODESTY ABOVE ALL!
SERVES YOU RIGHT!
RESTORE MY DIGNITY, YOU JACKET-HACKERS!
SORRY! AS YOU SEE, IT'S TOO SHREDDED TO WEAR!
AND CAPTAIN RETRO-DUCK WOULD NEVER BE SEEN DRESSED IN SUCH TATTERS, WOULD HE?
WE'LL FIX YOUR JACKET! BUT THE SEWING JOB MIGHT TAKE 24 HOURS!
RETRO-BAH!
DONALD DUCK
#$%@ FEATHERED DEMONS! LEAVING ME IN THE FLOWER BED LIKE THIS!
!
!

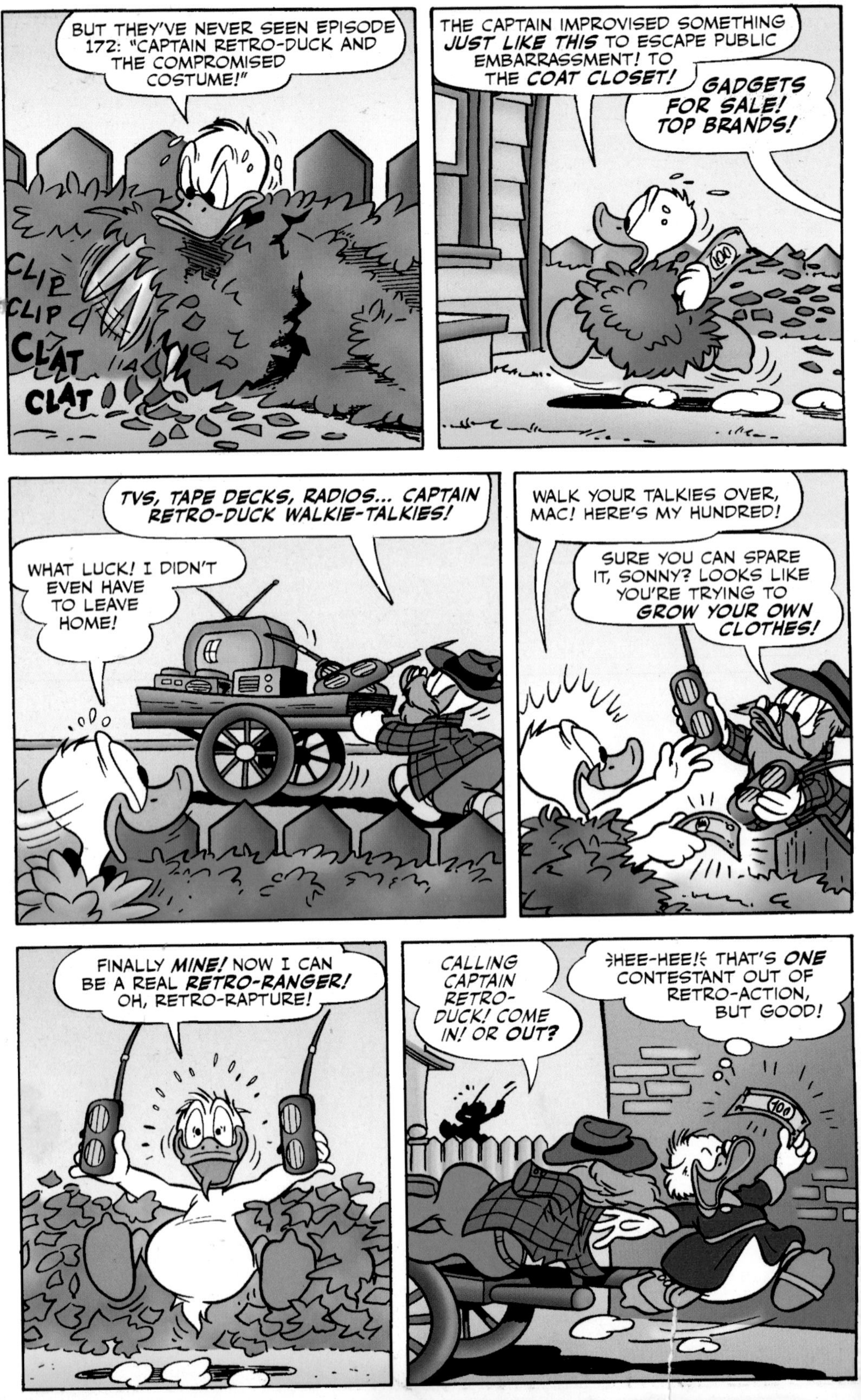
BUT THEY'VE NEVER SEEN EPISODE 172: "CAPTAIN RETRO-DUCK AND THE COMPROMISED COSTUME!"
CLIP
CLIP
CLAT
CLAT
THE CAPTAIN IMPROVISED SOMETHING JUST LIKE THIS TO ESCAPE PUBLIC EMBARRASSMENT! TO THE COAT CLOSET!
GADGETS FOR SALE! TOP BRANDS!
TVS, TAPE DECKS, RADIOS... CAPTAIN RETRO-DUCK WALKIE-TALKIES!
WHAT LUCK! I DIDN'T EVEN HAVE TO LEAVE HOME!
WALK YOUR TALKIES OVER, MAC! HERE'S MY HUNDRED!
SURE YOU CAN SPARE IT, SONNY? LOOKS LIKE YOU'RE TRYING TO GROW YOUR OWN CLOTHES!
FINALLY MINE! NOW I CAN BE A REAL RETRO-RANGER! OH, RETRO-RAPTURE!
CALLING CAPTAIN RETRO-DUCK! COME IN! OR OUT?
HEE-HEE! THAT'S ONE CONTESTANT OUT OF RETRO-ACTION, BUT GOOD!

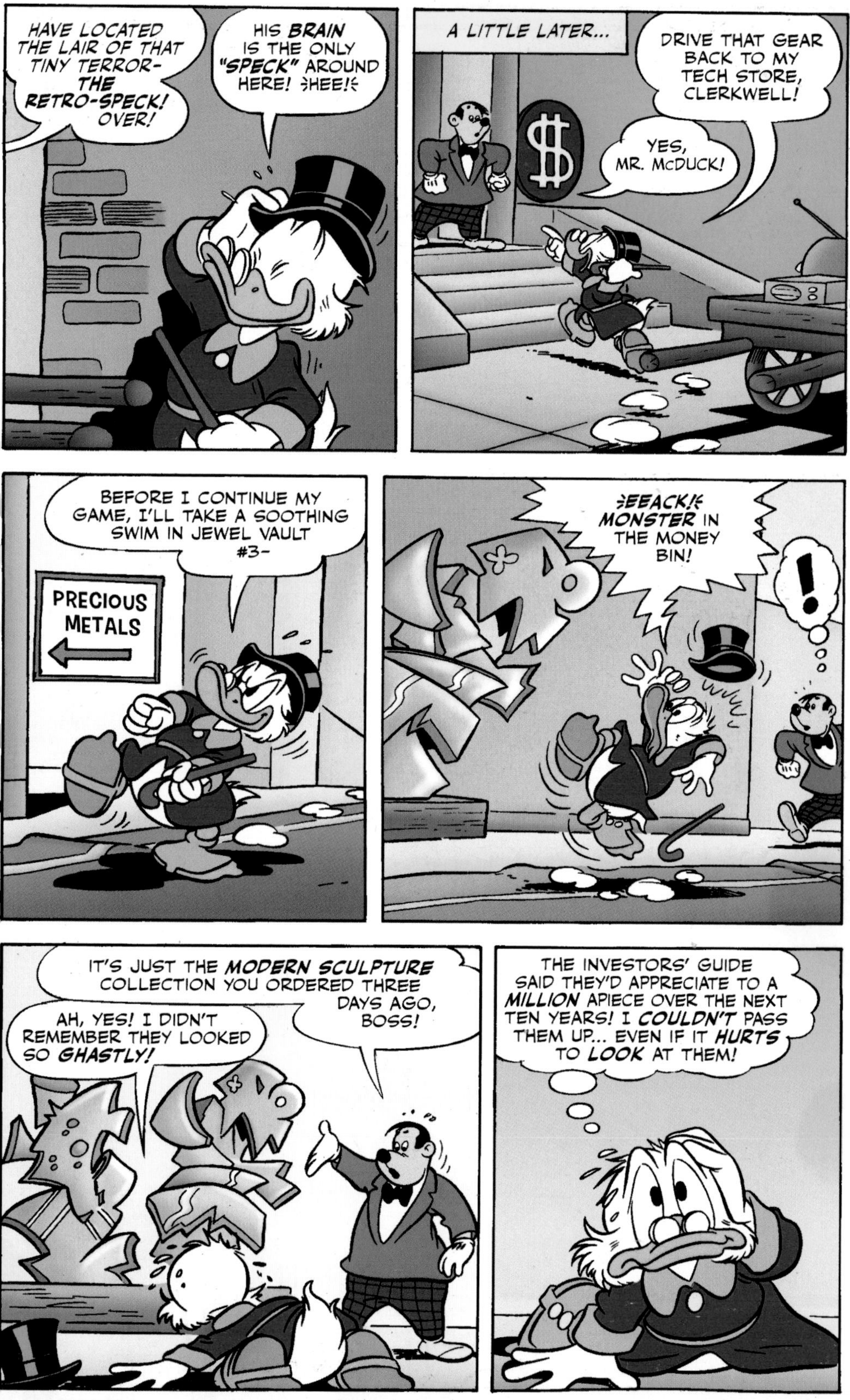
HAVE LOCATED THE LAIR OF THAT TINY TERROR- THE RETRO-SPECK! OVER!
HIS BRAIN IS THE ONLY "SPECK" AROUND HERE! HEE!
A LITTLE LATER...
DRIVE THAT GEAR BACK TO MY TECH STORE, CLERKWELL!
YES, MR. McDUCK!
BEFORE I CONTINUE MY GAME, I'LL TAKE A SOOTHING SWIM IN JEWEL VAULT #3-
PRECIOUS METALS
EEACK! MONSTER IN THE MONEY BIN!
!
IT'S JUST THE MODERN SCULPTURE COLLECTION YOU ORDERED THREE DAYS AGO, BOSS!
AH, YES! I DIDN'T REMEMBER THEY LOOKED SO GHASTLY!
THE INVESTORS' GUIDE SAID THEY'D APPRECIATE TO A MILLION APIECE OVER THE NEXT TEN YEARS! I COULDN'T PASS THEM UP... EVEN IF IT HURTS TO LOOK AT THEM!

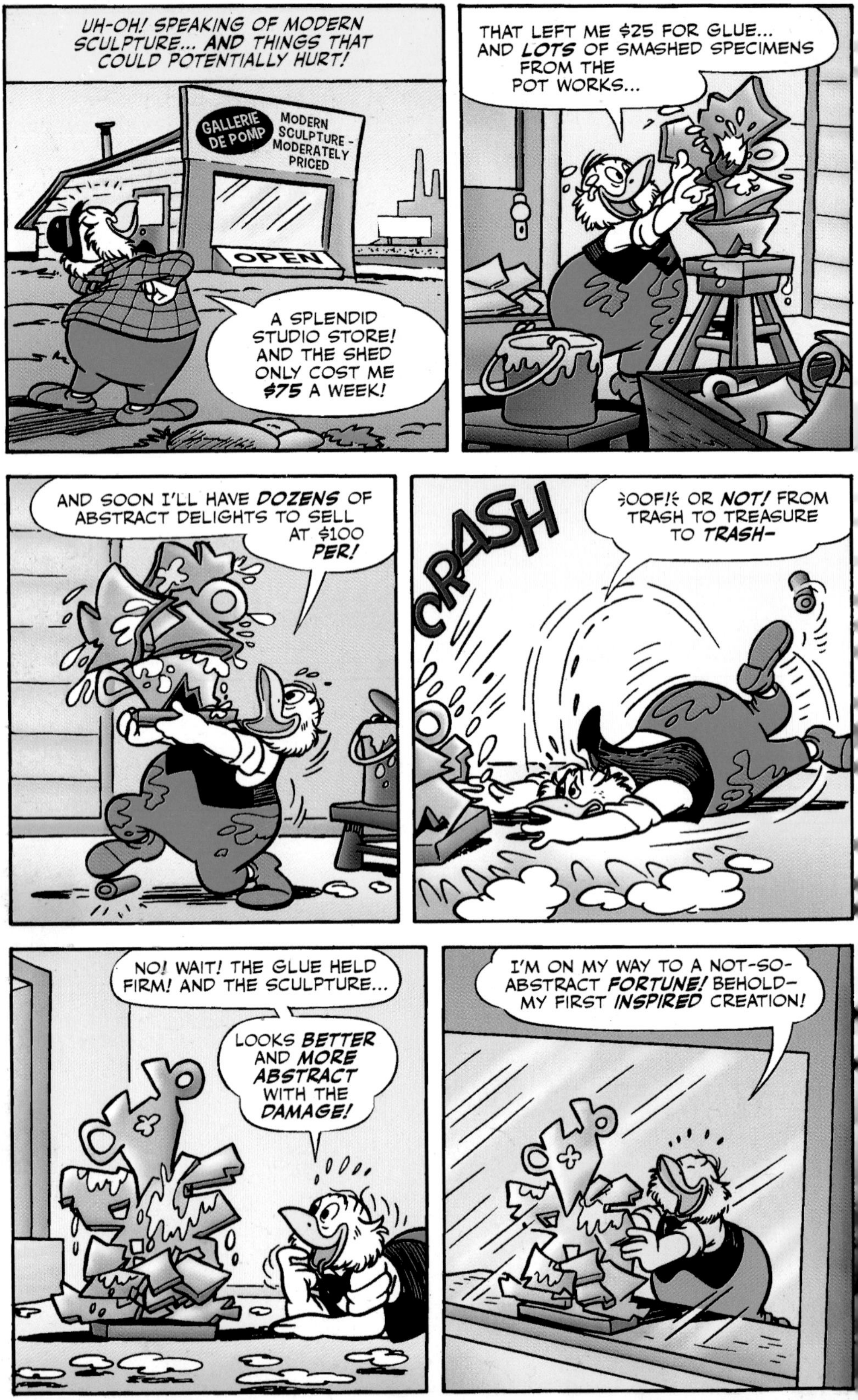
UH-OH! SPEAKING OF MODERN SCULPTURE... AND THINGS THAT COULD POTENTIALLY HURT!
GALLERIE DE POMP
MODERN SCULPTURE - MODERATELY PRICED
OPEN
A SPLENDID STUDIO STORE! AND THE SHED ONLY COST ME $75 A WEEK!
THAT LEFT ME $25 FOR GLUE... AND LOTS OF SMASHED SPECIMENS FROM THE POT WORKS...
AND SOON I'LL HAVE DOZENS OF ABSTRACT DELIGHTS TO SELL AT $100 PER!
CRASH
OOF! OR NOT! FROM TRASH TO TREASURE TO TRASH–
NO! WAIT! THE GLUE HELD FIRM! AND THE SCULPTURE...
LOOKS BETTER AND MORE ABSTRACT WITH THE DAMAGE!
I'M ON MY WAY TO A NOT-SO-ABSTRACT FORTUNE! BEHOLD– MY FIRST INSPIRED CREATION!

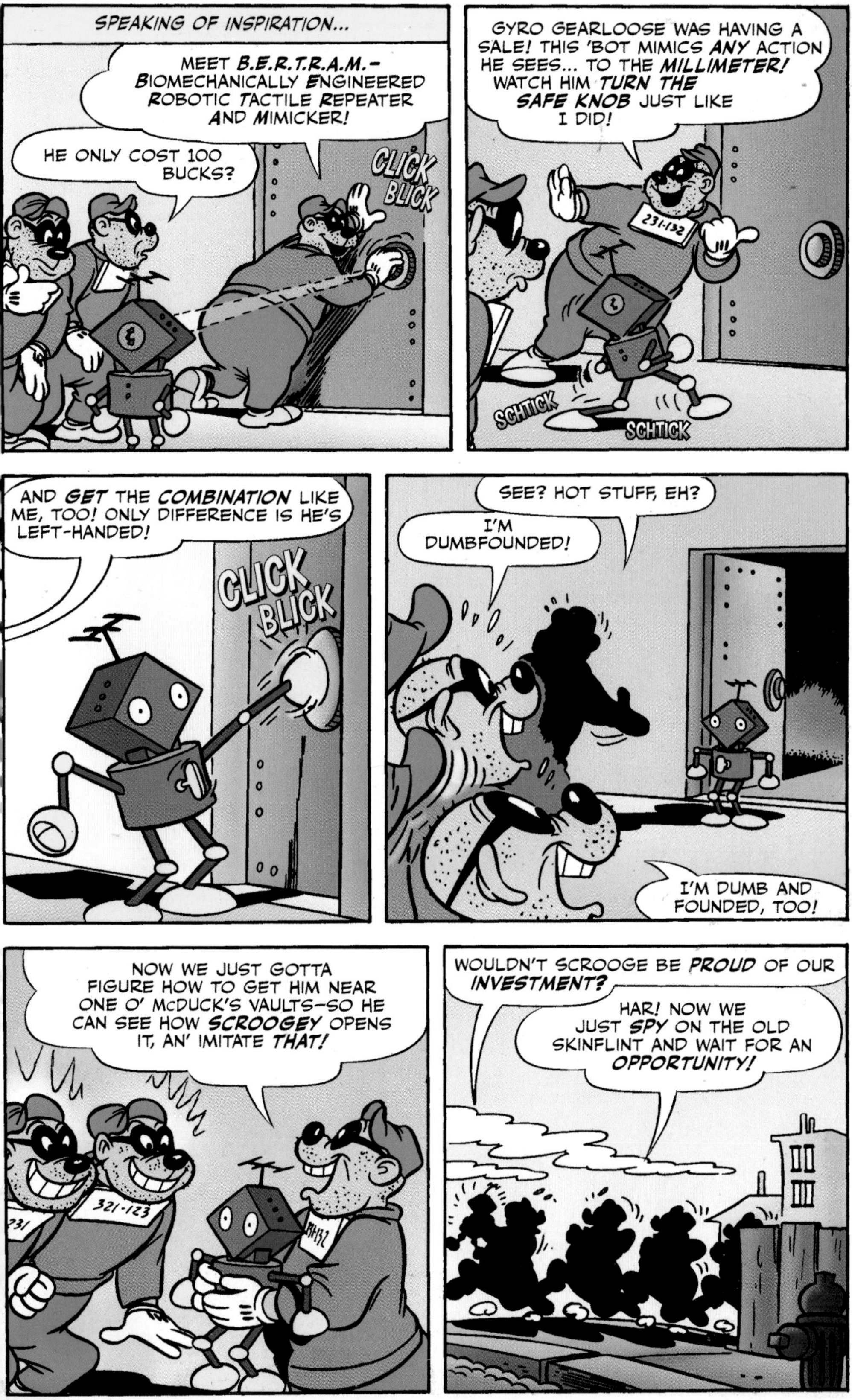
SPEAKING OF INSPIRATION...
MEET B.E.R.T.R.A.M.– BIOMECHANICALLY ENGINEERED ROBOTIC TACTILE REPEATER AND MIMICKER!
HE ONLY COST 100 BUCKS?
CLICK BLICK
GYRO GEARLOOSE WAS HAVING A SALE! THIS 'BOT MIMICS ANY ACTION HE SEES... TO THE MILLIMETER! WATCH HIM TURN THE SAFE KNOB JUST LIKE I DID!
231-132
SCHTICK
SCHTICK
AND GET THE COMBINATION LIKE ME, TOO! ONLY DIFFERENCE IS HE'S LEFT-HANDED!
CLICK BLICK
SEE? HOT STUFF, EH?
I'M DUMBFOUNDED!
I'M DUMB AND FOUNDED, TOO!
NOW WE JUST GOTTA FIGURE HOW TO GET HIM NEAR ONE O' McDUCK'S VAULTS—SO HE CAN SEE HOW SCROOGEY OPENS IT, AN' IMITATE THAT!
321-123
WOULDN'T SCROOGE BE PROUD OF OUR INVESTMENT?
HAR! NOW WE JUST SPY ON THE OLD SKINFLINT AND WAIT FOR AN OPPORTUNITY!

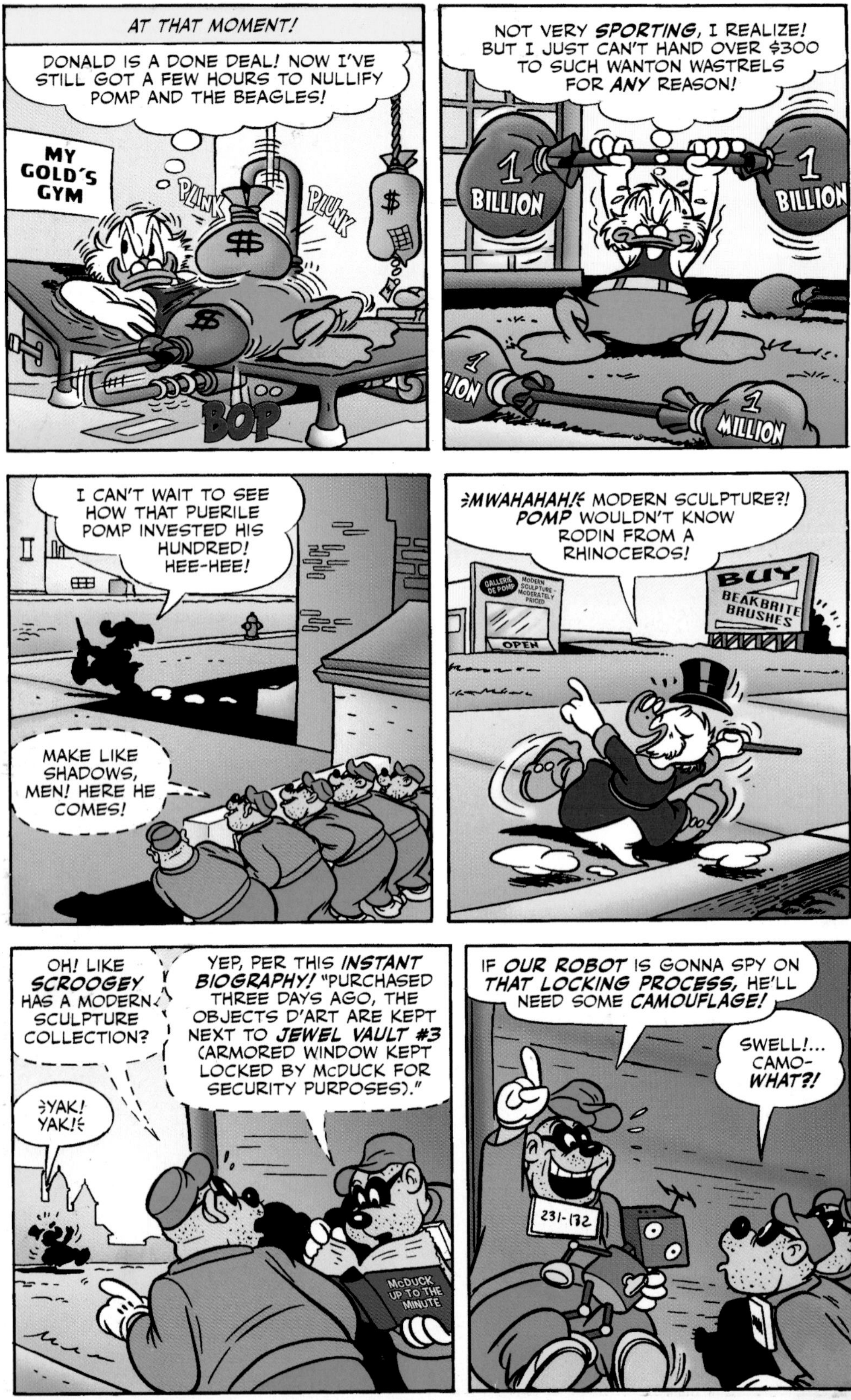
AT THAT MOMENT!
DONALD IS A DONE DEAL! NOW I'VE STILL GOT A FEW HOURS TO NULLIFY POMP AND THE BEAGLES!
MY GOLD'S GYM
PLINK
PLUNK
BOP
NOT VERY SPORTING, I REALIZE! BUT I JUST CAN'T HAND OVER $300 TO SUCH WANTON WASTRELS FOR ANY REASON!
1 BILLION
1 BILLION
1 MILLION
I CAN'T WAIT TO SEE HOW THAT PUERILE POMP INVESTED HIS HUNDRED! HEE-HEE!
MAKE LIKE SHADOWS, MEN! HERE HE COMES!
MWAHAHAH! MODERN SCULPTURE?! POMP WOULDN'T KNOW RODIN FROM A RHINOCEROS!
GALLERIE DE POMP
MODERN SCULPTURE- MODERATELY PRICED
OPEN
BUY BEAKBRITE BRUSHES
OH! LIKE SCROOGEY HAS A MODERN SCULPTURE COLLECTION?
YEP, PER THIS INSTANT BIOGRAPHY! "PURCHASED THREE DAYS AGO, THE OBJECTS D'ART ARE KEPT NEXT TO JEWEL VAULT #3 (ARMORED WINDOW KEPT LOCKED BY McDUCK FOR SECURITY PURPOSES)."
YAK! YAK!
McDUCK UP TO THE MINUTE
IF OUR ROBOT IS GONNA SPY ON THAT LOCKING PROCESS, HE'LL NEED SOME CAMOUFLAGE!
SWELL!... CAMO-WHAT?!
231-132

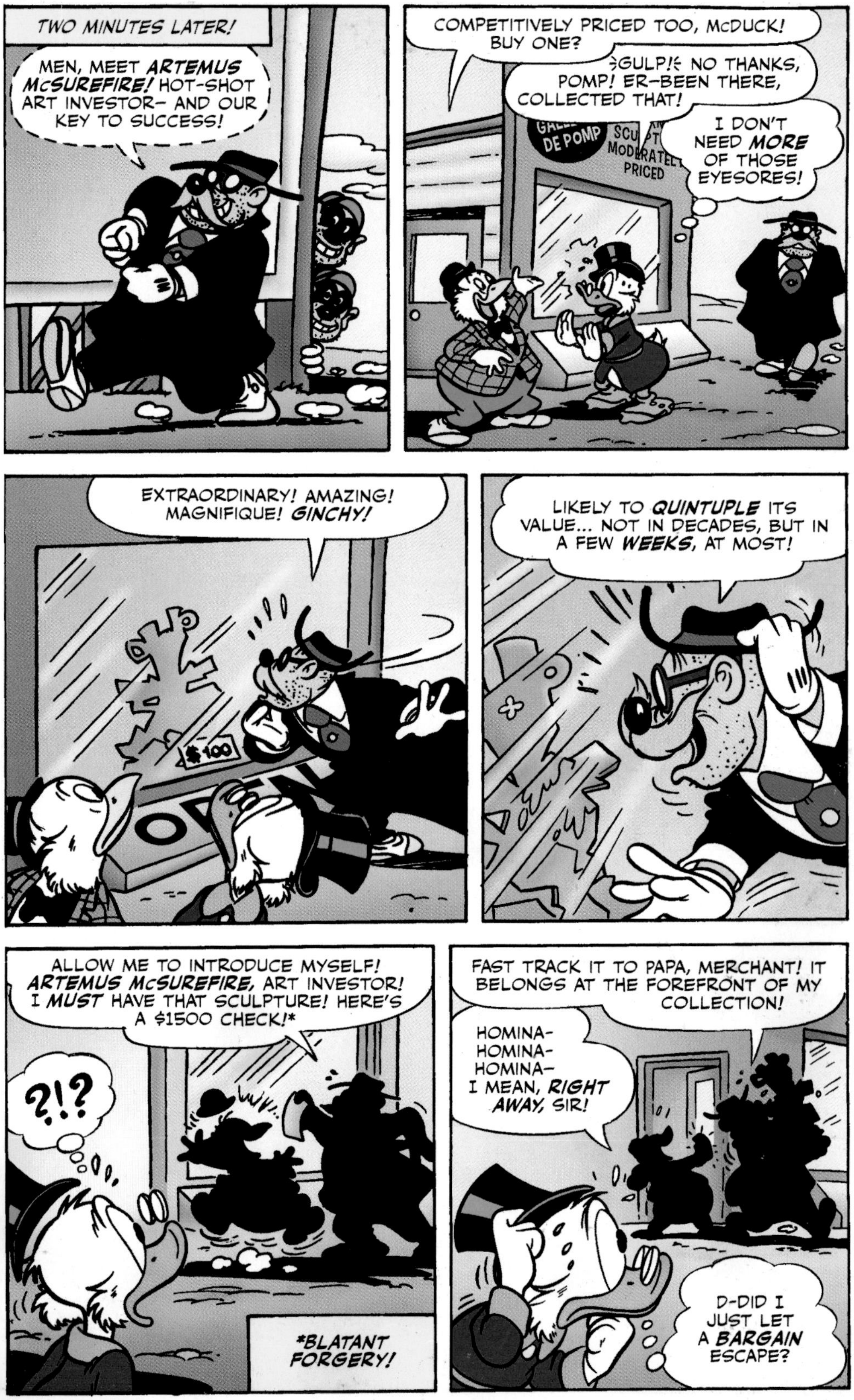

TWO MINUTES LATER!
MEN, MEET ARTEMUS McSUREFIRE! HOT-SHOT ART INVESTOR– AND OUR KEY TO SUCCESS!
COMPETITIVELY PRICED TOO, McDUCK! BUY ONE?
GULP! NO THANKS, POMP! ER–BEEN THERE, COLLECTED THAT!
I DON'T NEED MORE OF THOSE EYESORES!
DE POMP
MODERATELY PRICED
EXTRAORDINARY! AMAZING! MAGNIFIQUE! GINCHY!
$100
LIKELY TO QUINTUPLE ITS VALUE... NOT IN DECADES, BUT IN A FEW WEEKS, AT MOST!
ALLOW ME TO INTRODUCE MYSELF! ARTEMUS McSUREFIRE, ART INVESTOR! I MUST HAVE THAT SCULPTURE! HERE'S A $1500 CHECK!*
?!?
*BLATANT FORGERY!
FAST TRACK IT TO PAPA, MERCHANT! IT BELONGS AT THE FOREFRONT OF MY COLLECTION!
HOMINA- HOMINA- HOMINA- I MEAN, RIGHT AWAY, SIR!
D-DID I JUST LET A BARGAIN ESCAPE?

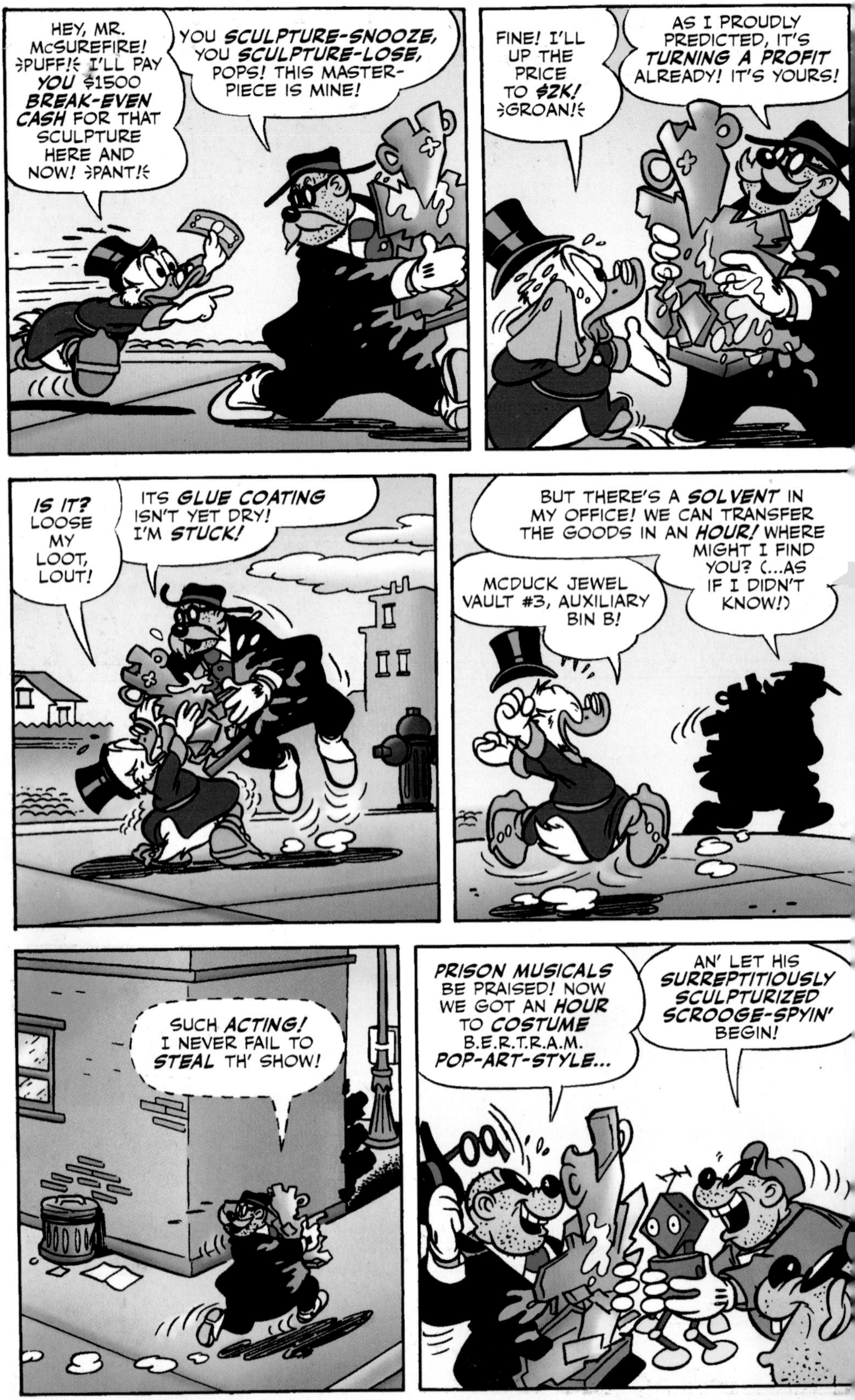
HEY, MR. McSUREFIRE! ≯PUFF!≮ I'LL PAY YOU $1500 BREAK-EVEN CASH FOR THAT SCULPTURE HERE AND NOW! ≯PANT!≮
YOU SCULPTURE-SNOOZE, YOU SCULPTURE-LOSE, POPS! THIS MASTER-PIECE IS MINE!
FINE! I'LL UP THE PRICE TO $2K! ≯GROAN!≮
AS I PROUDLY PREDICTED, IT'S TURNING A PROFIT ALREADY! IT'S YOURS!
IS IT? LOOSE MY LOOT, LOUT!
ITS GLUE COATING ISN'T YET DRY! I'M STUCK!
BUT THERE'S A SOLVENT IN MY OFFICE! WE CAN TRANSFER THE GOODS IN AN HOUR! WHERE MIGHT I FIND YOU? (...AS IF I DIDN'T KNOW!)
MCDUCK JEWEL VAULT #3, AUXILIARY BIN B!
SUCH ACTING! I NEVER FAIL TO STEAL TH' SHOW!
PRISON MUSICALS BE PRAISED! NOW WE GOT AN HOUR TO COSTUME B.E.R.T.R.A.M. POP-ART-STYLE...
AN' LET HIS SURREPTITIOUSLY SCULPTURIZED SCROOGE-SPYIN' BEGIN!

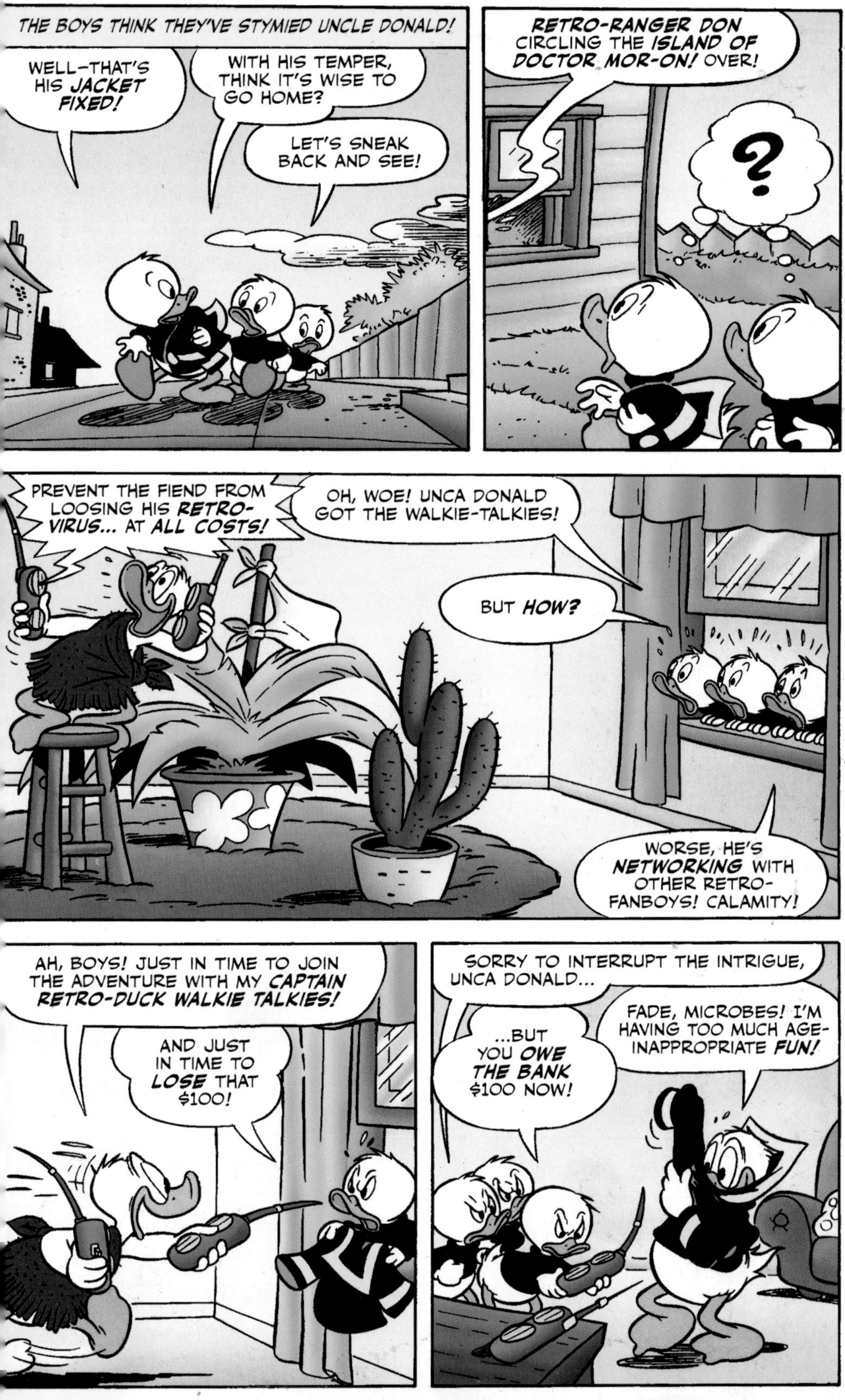

THE BOYS THINK THEY'VE STYMIED UNCLE DONALD!
WELL—THAT'S HIS JACKET FIXED!
WITH HIS TEMPER, THINK IT'S WISE TO GO HOME?
LET'S SNEAK BACK AND SEE!
RETRO-RANGER DON CIRCLING THE ISLAND OF DOCTOR MOR-ON! OVER!
?
PREVENT THE FIEND FROM LOOSING HIS RETRO-VIRUS... AT ALL COSTS!
OH, WOE! UNCA DONALD GOT THE WALKIE-TALKIES!
BUT HOW?
WORSE, HE'S NETWORKING WITH OTHER RETRO-FANBOYS! CALAMITY!
AH, BOYS! JUST IN TIME TO JOIN THE ADVENTURE WITH MY CAPTAIN RETRO-DUCK WALKIE TALKIES!
AND JUST IN TIME TO LOSE THAT $100!
SORRY TO INTERRUPT THE INTRIGUE, UNCA DONALD...
...BUT YOU OWE THE BANK $100 NOW!
FADE, MICROBES! I'M HAVING TOO MUCH AGE-INAPPROPRIATE FUN!

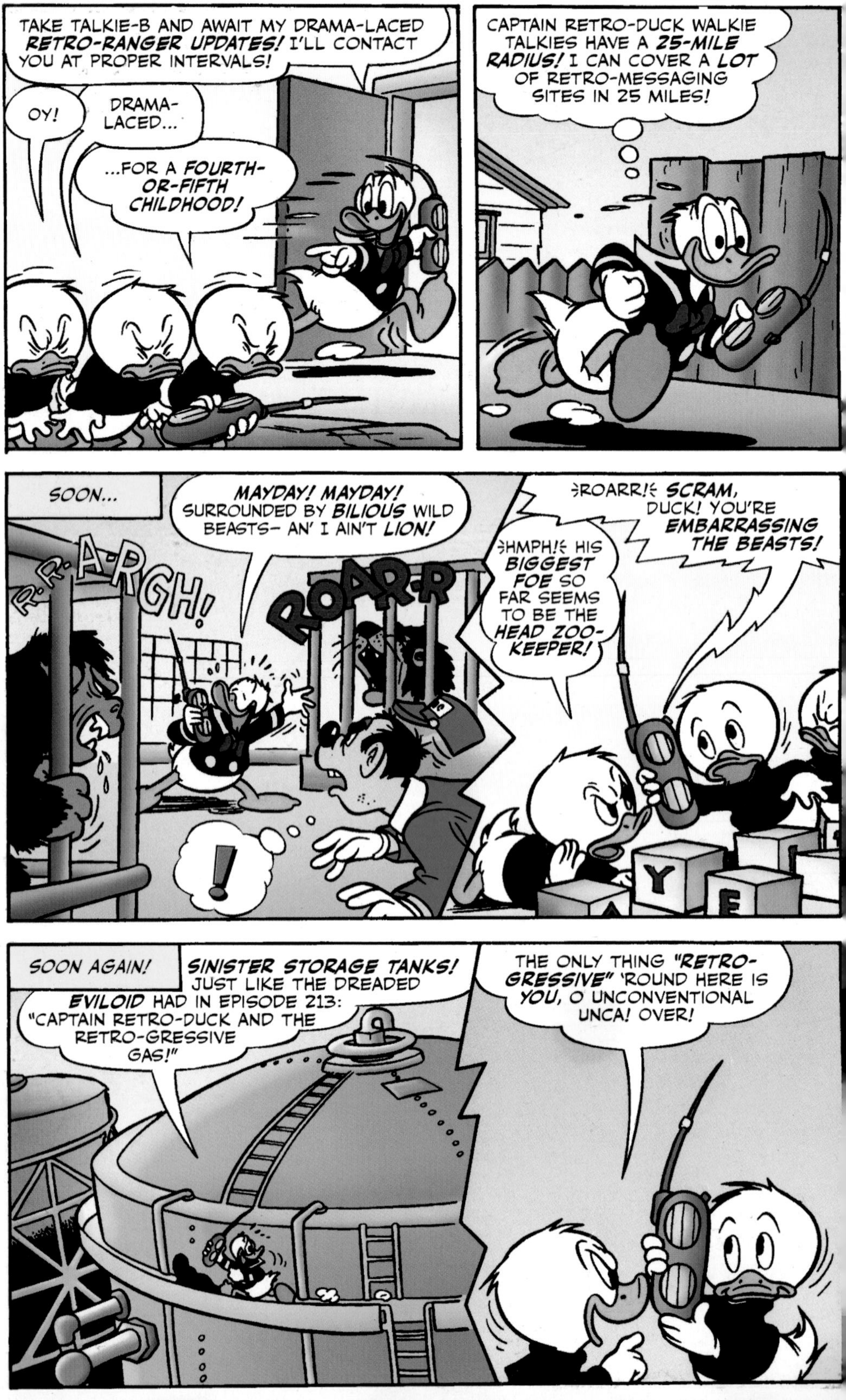
TAKE TALKIE-B AND AWAIT MY DRAMA-LACED RETRO-RANGER UPDATES! I'LL CONTACT YOU AT PROPER INTERVALS!
OY!
DRAMA-LACED...
...FOR A FOURTH-OR-FIFTH CHILDHOOD!
CAPTAIN RETRO-DUCK WALKIE TALKIES HAVE A 25-MILE RADIUS! I CAN COVER A LOT OF RETRO-MESSAGING SITES IN 25 MILES!
SOON...
R-R-A-ARGH!
MAYDAY! MAYDAY! SURROUNDED BY BILIOUS WILD BEASTS— AN' I AIN'T LION!
ROAR-R
!
ROARR! SCRAM, DUCK! YOU'RE EMBARRASSING THE BEASTS!
HMPH! HIS BIGGEST FOE SO FAR SEEMS TO BE THE HEAD ZOO-KEEPER!
SOON AGAIN!
SINISTER STORAGE TANKS! JUST LIKE THE DREADED EVILOID HAD IN EPISODE 213: "CAPTAIN RETRO-DUCK AND THE RETRO-GRESSIVE GAS!"
THE ONLY THING "RETRO-GRESSIVE" 'ROUND HERE IS YOU, O UNCONVENTIONAL UNCA! OVER!

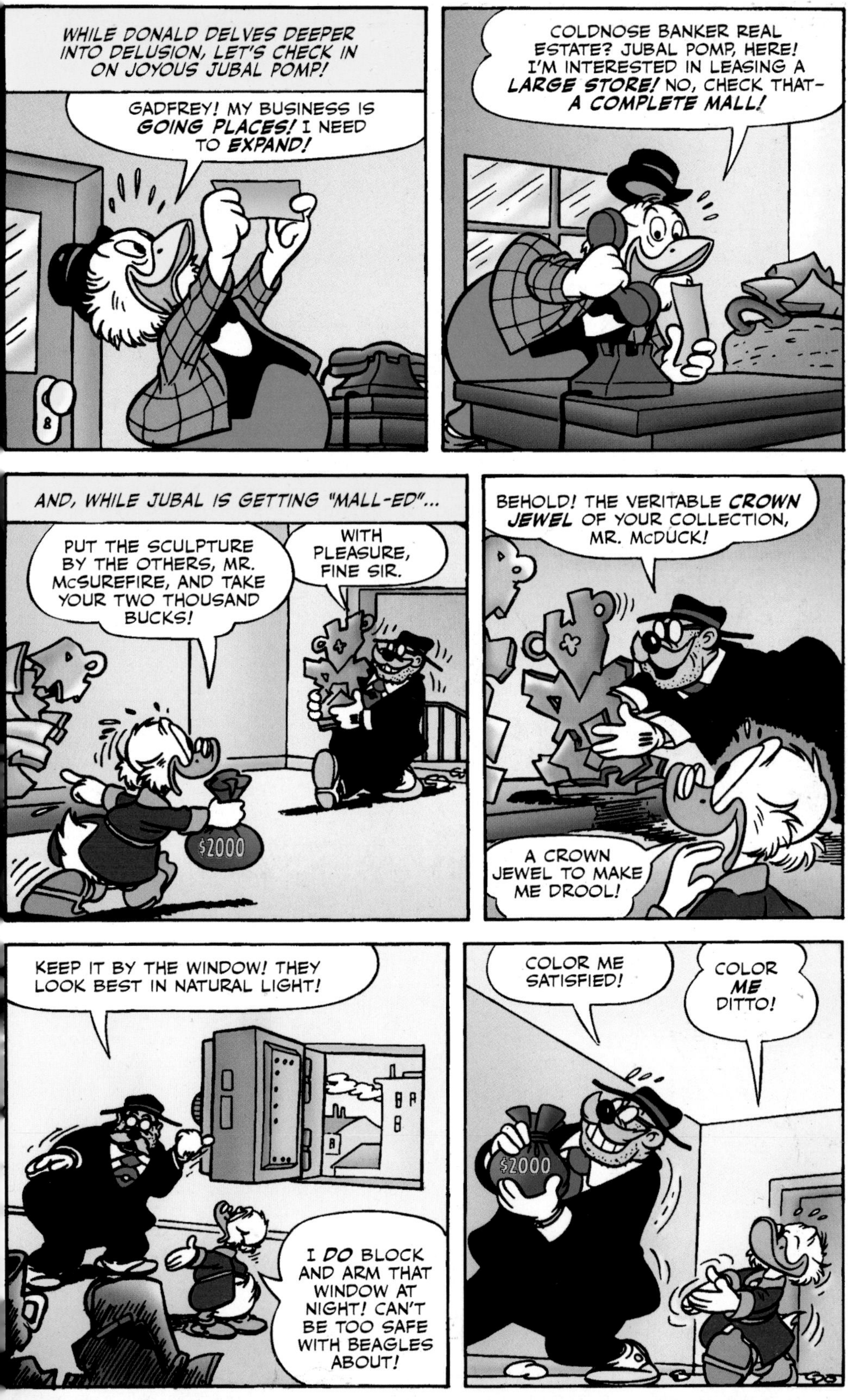
WHILE DONALD DELVES DEEPER INTO DELUSION, LET'S CHECK IN ON JOYOUS JUBAL POMP!
GADFREY! MY BUSINESS IS GOING PLACES! I NEED TO EXPAND!
COLDNOSE BANKER REAL ESTATE? JUBAL POMP, HERE! I'M INTERESTED IN LEASING A LARGE STORE! NO, CHECK THAT– A COMPLETE MALL!
AND, WHILE JUBAL IS GETTING "MALL-ED"...
PUT THE SCULPTURE BY THE OTHERS, MR. McSUREFIRE, AND TAKE YOUR TWO THOUSAND BUCKS!
WITH PLEASURE, FINE SIR.
$2000
BEHOLD! THE VERITABLE CROWN JEWEL OF YOUR COLLECTION, MR. McDUCK!
A CROWN JEWEL TO MAKE ME DROOL!
KEEP IT BY THE WINDOW! THEY LOOK BEST IN NATURAL LIGHT!
I DO BLOCK AND ARM THAT WINDOW AT NIGHT! CAN'T BE TOO SAFE WITH BEAGLES ABOUT!
COLOR ME SATISFIED!
COLOR ME DITTO!
$2000

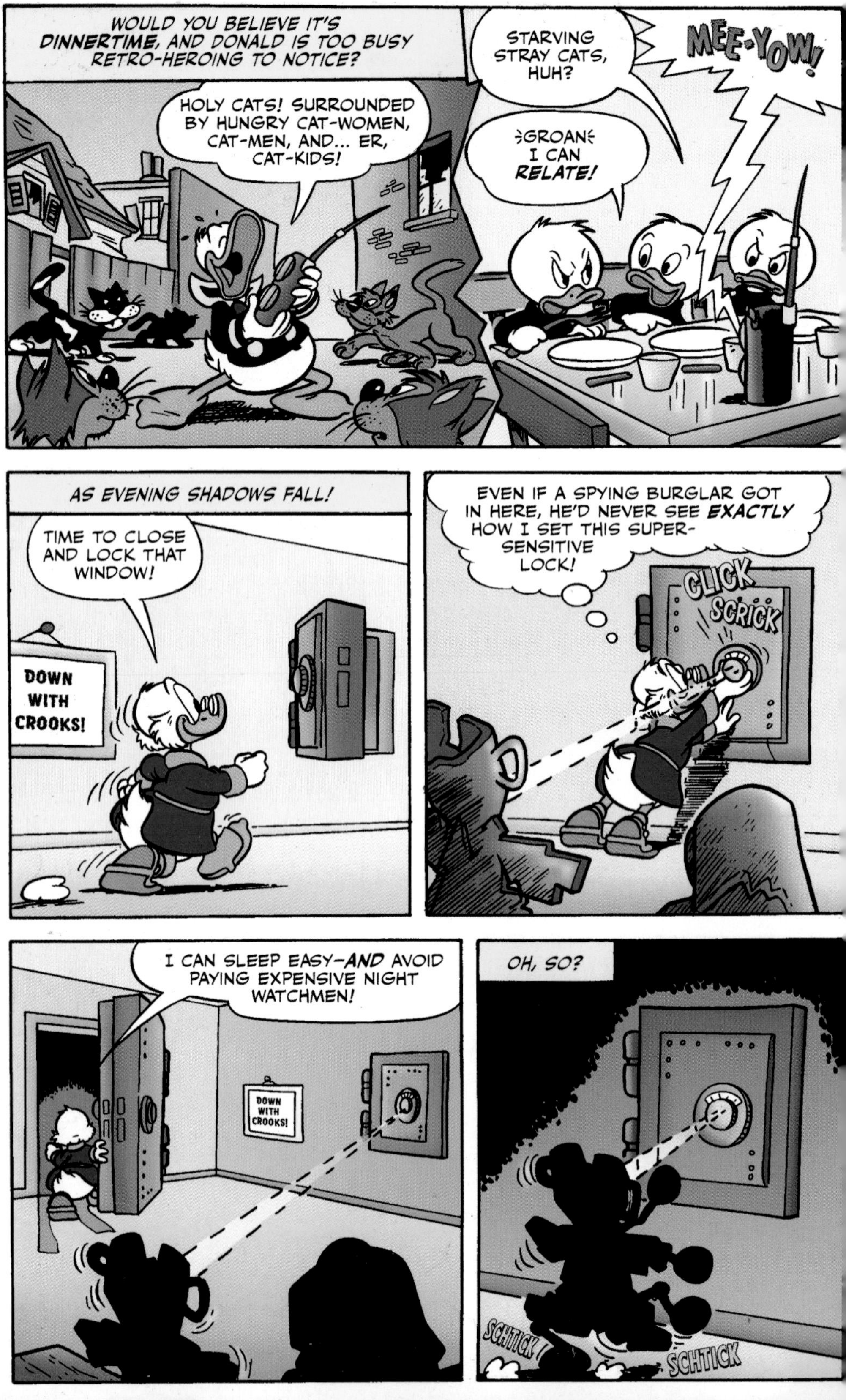
WOULD YOU BELIEVE IT'S DINNERTIME, AND DONALD IS TOO BUSY RETRO-HEROING TO NOTICE?
HOLY CATS! SURROUNDED BY HUNGRY CAT-WOMEN, CAT-MEN, AND... ER, CAT-KIDS!
STARVING STRAY CATS, HUH?
GROAN I CAN RELATE!
MEE-YOW!
AS EVENING SHADOWS FALL!
TIME TO CLOSE AND LOCK THAT WINDOW!
DOWN WITH CROOKS!
EVEN IF A SPYING BURGLAR GOT IN HERE, HE'D NEVER SEE EXACTLY HOW I SET THIS SUPER-SENSITIVE LOCK!
CLICK
SCRICK
I CAN SLEEP EASY—AND AVOID PAYING EXPENSIVE NIGHT WATCHMEN!
DOWN WITH CROOKS!
OH, SO?
SCHTICK
SCHTICK

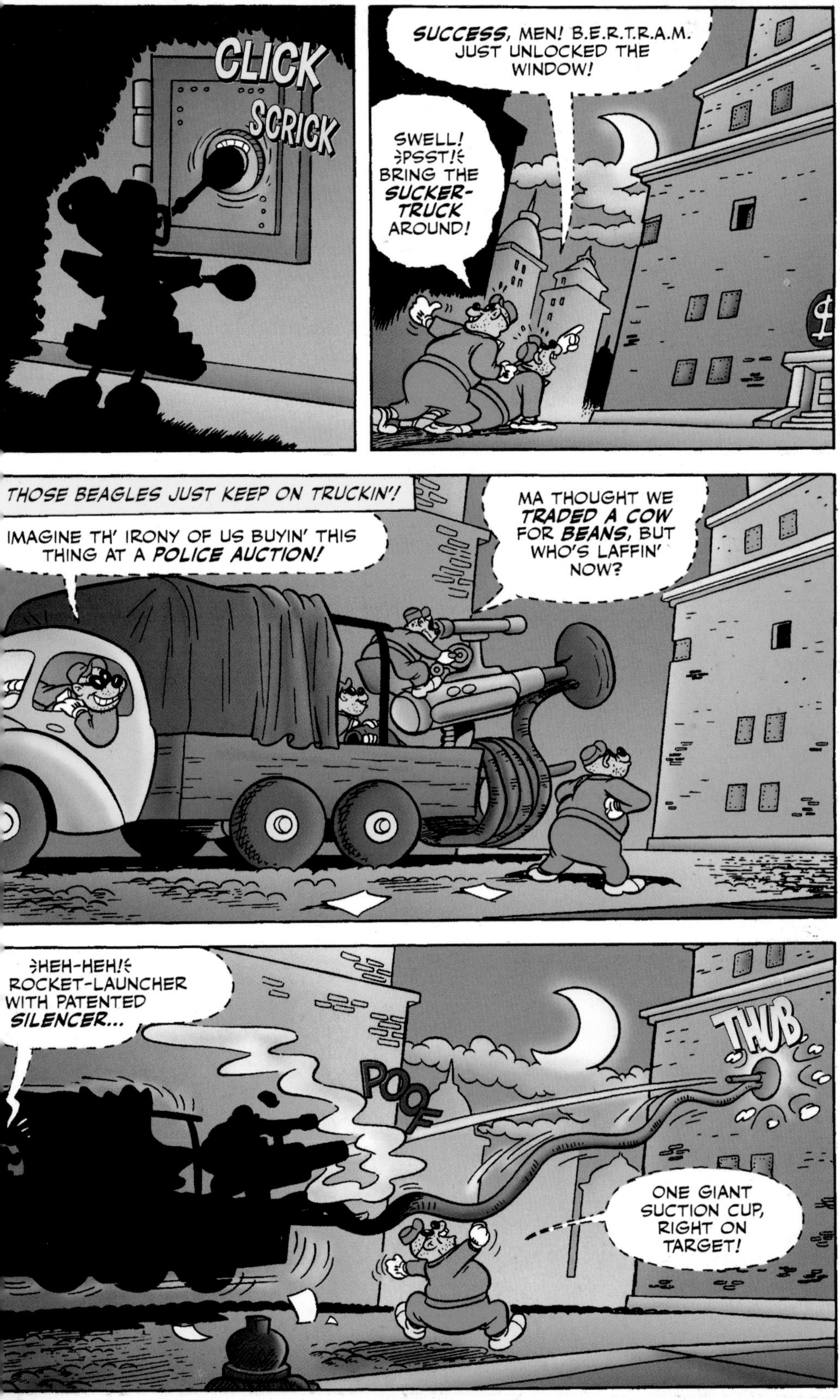
CLICK
SCRICK
SUCCESS, MEN! B.E.R.T.R.A.M. JUST UNLOCKED THE WINDOW!
SWELL! PSST! BRING THE SUCKER-TRUCK AROUND!
THOSE BEAGLES JUST KEEP ON TRUCKIN'!
IMAGINE TH' IRONY OF US BUYIN' THIS THING AT A POLICE AUCTION!
MA THOUGHT WE TRADED A COW FOR BEANS, BUT WHO'S LAFFIN' NOW?
HEH-HEH! ROCKET-LAUNCHER WITH PATENTED SILENCER...
POOF
THUB
ONE GIANT SUCTION CUP, RIGHT ON TARGET!

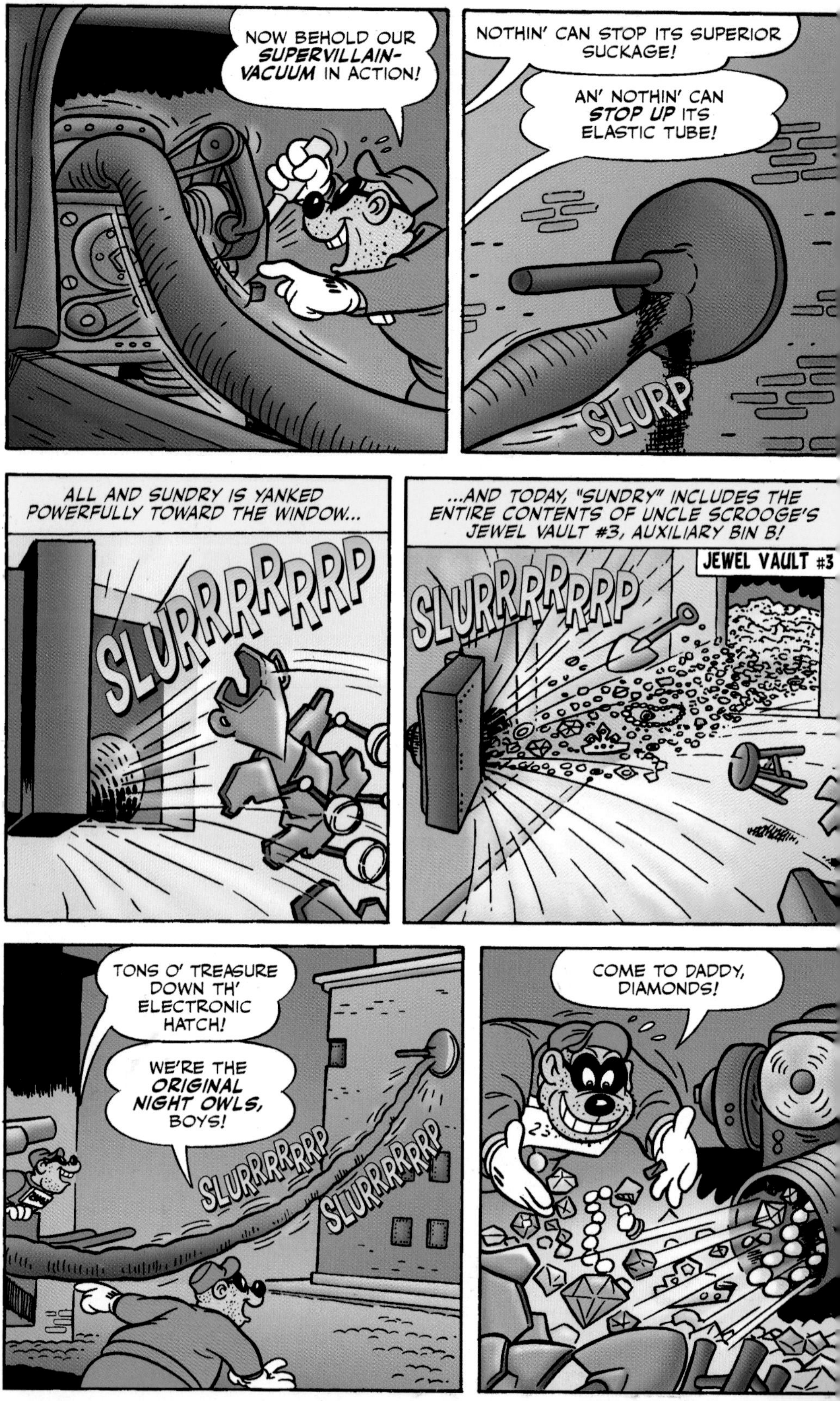

NOW BEHOLD OUR SUPERVILLAIN-VACUUM IN ACTION!
NOTHIN' CAN STOP ITS SUPERIOR SUCKAGE!
AN' NOTHIN' CAN STOP UP ITS ELASTIC TUBE!
SLURP
ALL AND SUNDRY IS YANKED POWERFULLY TOWARD THE WINDOW...
SLURRRRRRP
...AND TODAY, "SUNDRY" INCLUDES THE ENTIRE CONTENTS OF UNCLE SCROOGE'S JEWEL VAULT #3, AUXILIARY BIN B!
JEWEL VAULT #3
SLURRRRRRP
TONS O' TREASURE DOWN TH' ELECTRONIC HATCH!
WE'RE THE ORIGINAL NIGHT OWLS, BOYS!
SLURRRRRP
SLURRRRRRP
COME TO DADDY, DIAMONDS!

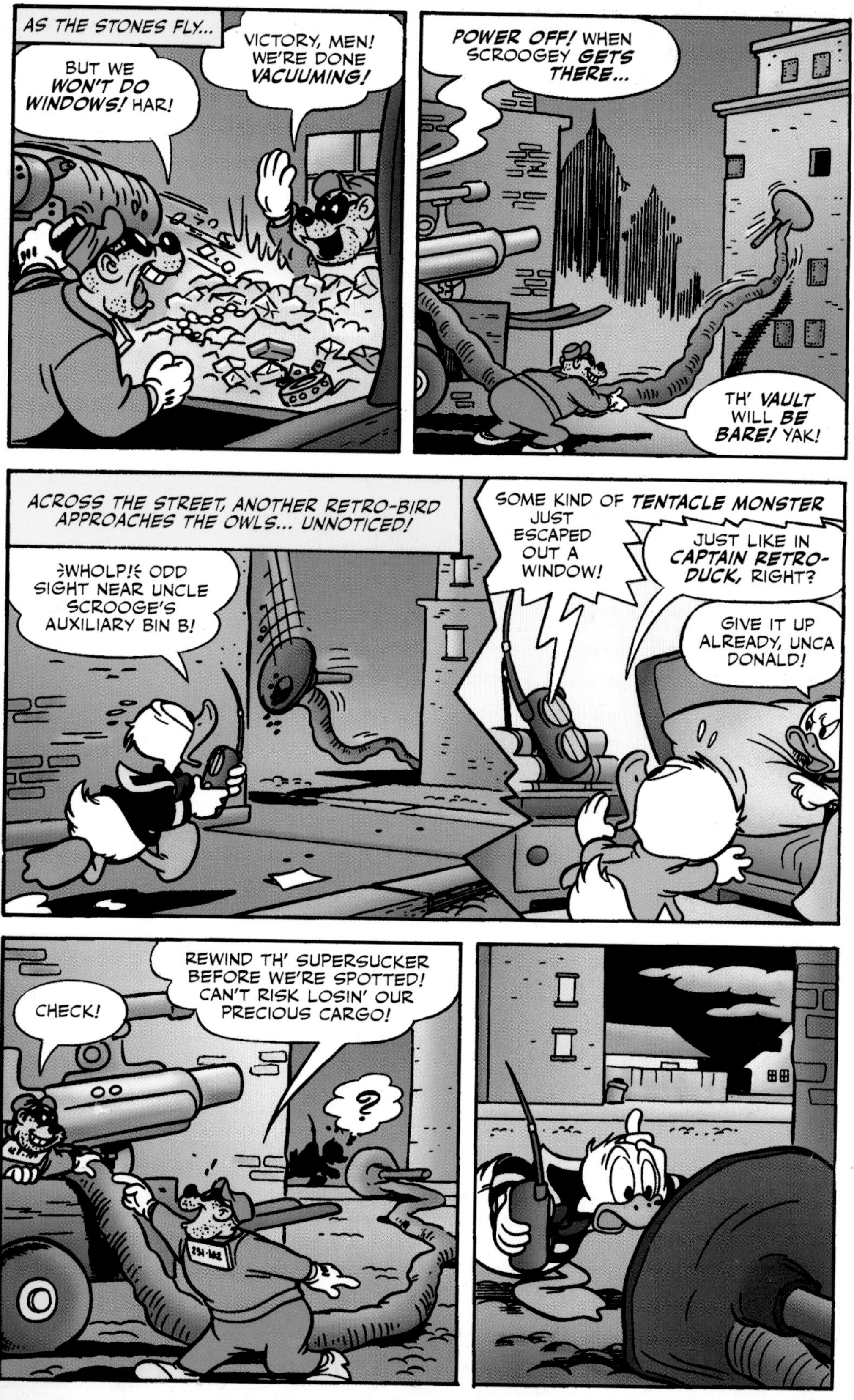
AS THE STONES FLY...
BUT WE WON'T DO WINDOWS! HAR!
VICTORY, MEN! WE'RE DONE VACUUMING!
POWER OFF! WHEN SCROOGEY GETS THERE...
TH' VAULT WILL BE BARE! YAK!
ACROSS THE STREET, ANOTHER RETRO-BIRD APPROACHES THE OWLS... UNNOTICED!
⋛WHOLP!⋚ ODD SIGHT NEAR UNCLE SCROOGE'S AUXILIARY BIN B!
SOME KIND OF TENTACLE MONSTER JUST ESCAPED OUT A WINDOW!
JUST LIKE IN CAPTAIN RETRO-DUCK, RIGHT?
GIVE IT UP ALREADY, UNCA DONALD!
CHECK!
REWIND TH' SUPERSUCKER BEFORE WE'RE SPOTTED! CAN'T RISK LOSIN' OUR PRECIOUS CARGO!
?

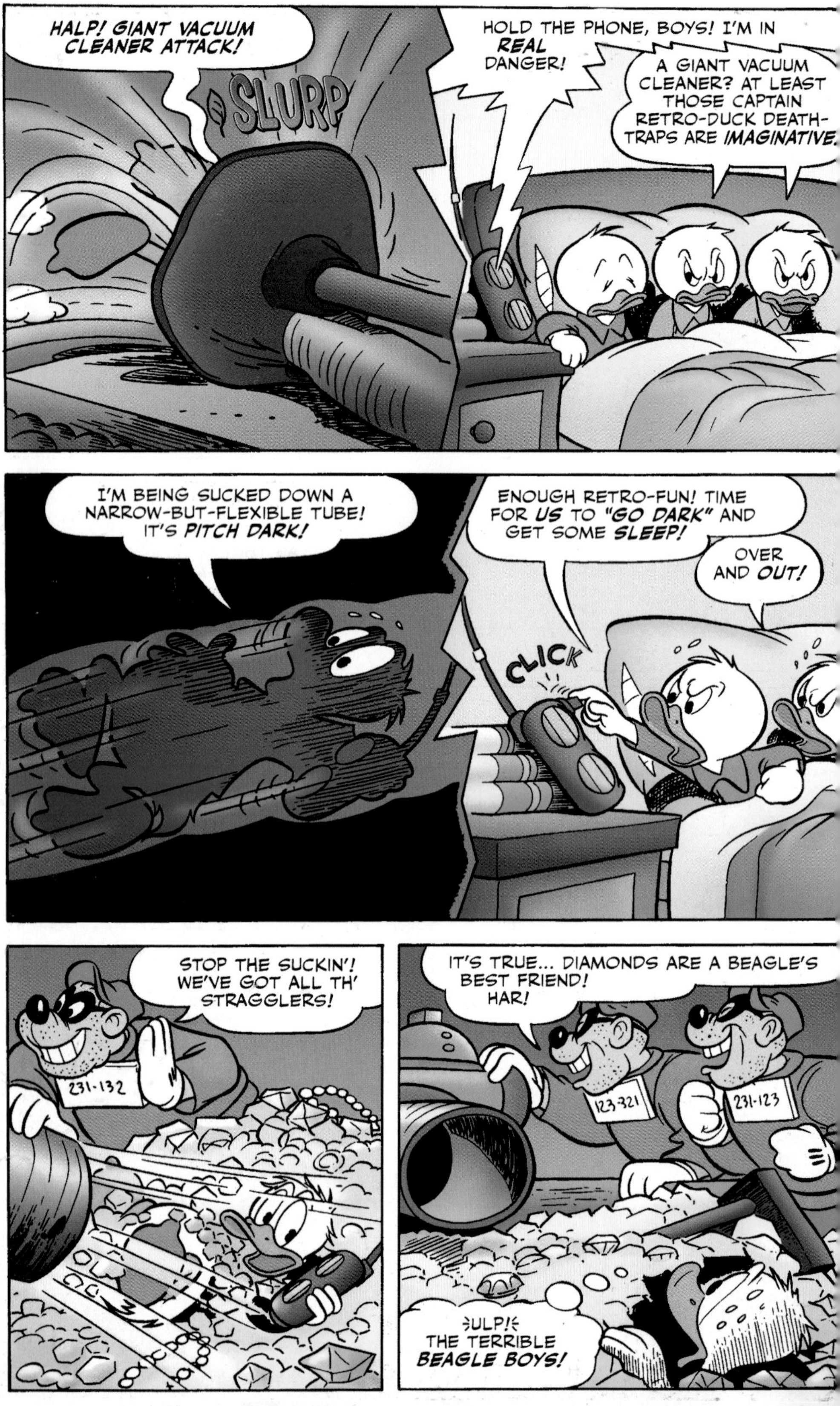
HALP! GIANT VACUUM CLEANER ATTACK!
SLURP
HOLD THE PHONE, BOYS! I'M IN REAL DANGER!
A GIANT VACUUM CLEANER? AT LEAST THOSE CAPTAIN RETRO-DUCK DEATH-TRAPS ARE IMAGINATIVE.
I'M BEING SUCKED DOWN A NARROW-BUT-FLEXIBLE TUBE! IT'S PITCH DARK!
ENOUGH RETRO-FUN! TIME FOR US TO "GO DARK" AND GET SOME SLEEP!
OVER AND OUT!
CLICK
STOP THE SUCKIN'! WE'VE GOT ALL TH' STRAGGLERS!
231-132
IT'S TRUE... DIAMONDS ARE A BEAGLE'S BEST FRIEND! HAR!
123-321
231-123
GULP! THE TERRIBLE BEAGLE BOYS!

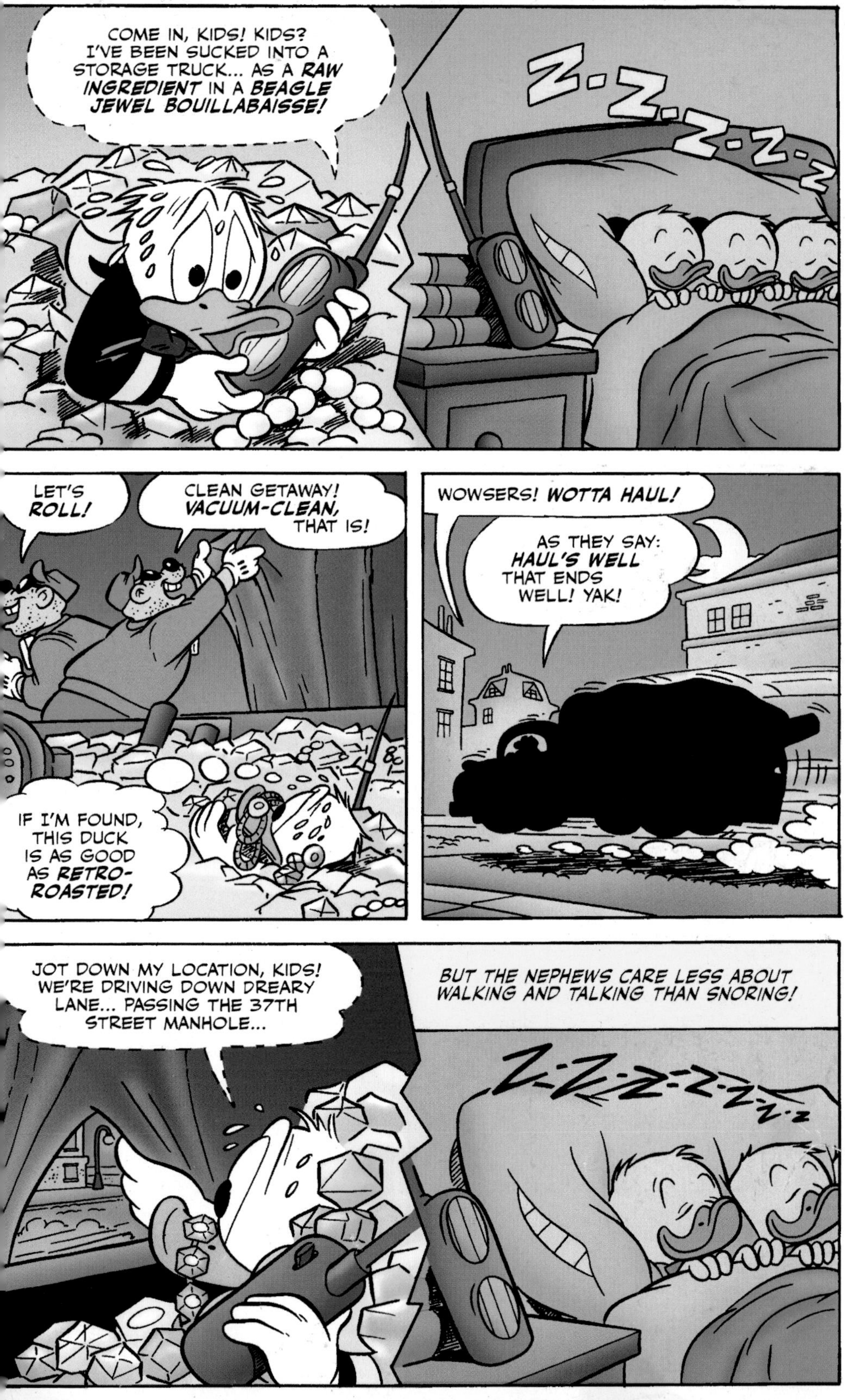
COME IN, KIDS! KIDS? I'VE BEEN SUCKED INTO A STORAGE TRUCK... AS A *RAW INGREDIENT* IN A *BEAGLE JEWEL BOUILLABAISSE!*
Z-Z-Z-Z-Z
LET'S *ROLL!*
CLEAN GETAWAY! *VACUUM-CLEAN,* THAT IS!
IF I'M FOUND, THIS DUCK IS AS GOOD AS *RETRO-ROASTED!*
WOWSERS! *WOTTA HAUL!*
AS THEY SAY: *HAUL'S WELL* THAT ENDS WELL! YAK!
JOT DOWN MY LOCATION, KIDS! WE'RE DRIVING DOWN DREARY LANE... PASSING THE 37TH STREET MANHOLE...
BUT THE NEPHEWS CARE LESS ABOUT WALKING AND TALKING THAN SNORING!
Z-Z-Z-Z-Z-Z-Z-Z

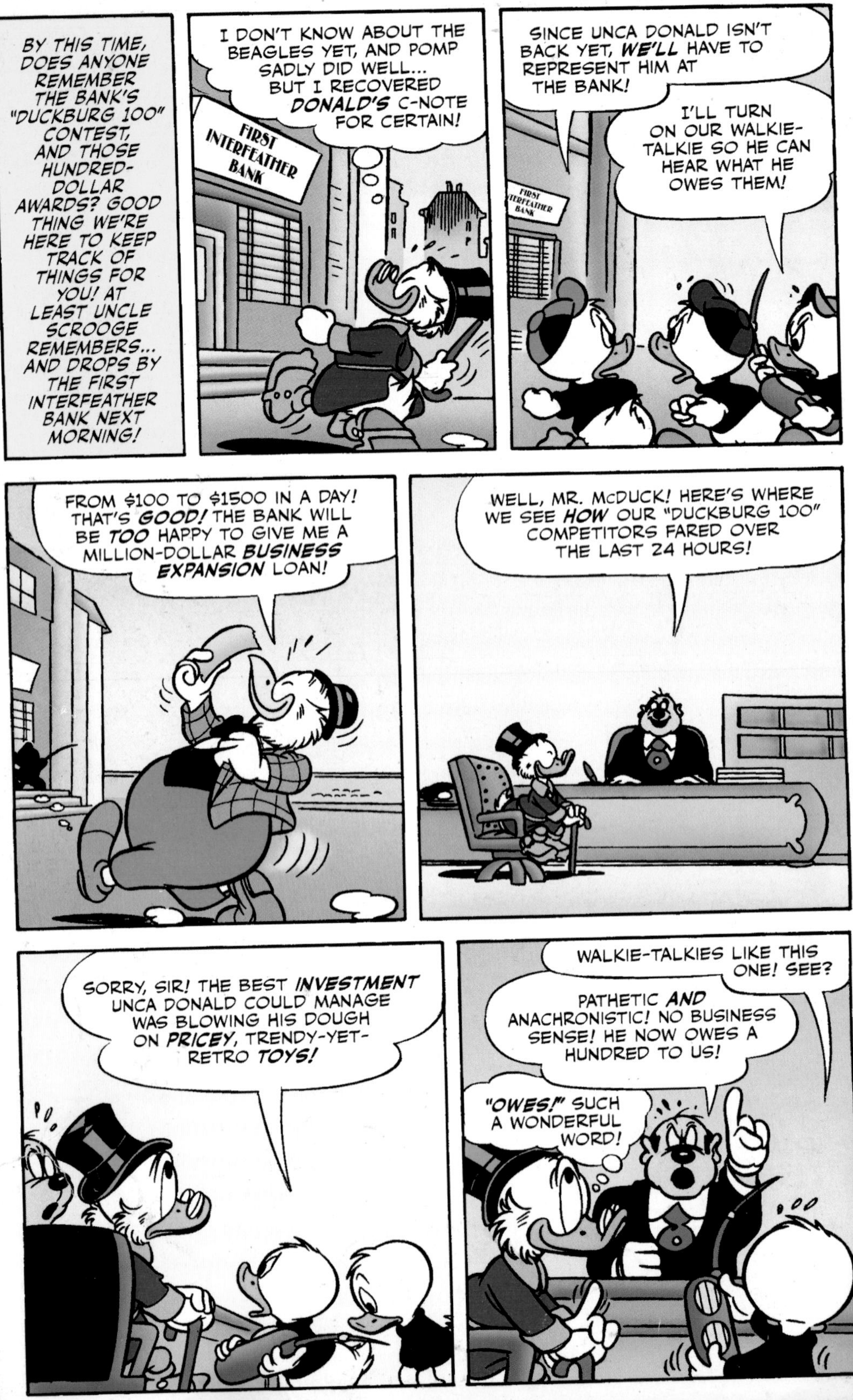
BY THIS TIME, DOES ANYONE REMEMBER THE BANK'S "DUCKBURG 100" CONTEST, AND THOSE HUNDRED-DOLLAR AWARDS? GOOD THING WE'RE HERE TO KEEP TRACK OF THINGS FOR YOU! AT LEAST UNCLE SCROOGE REMEMBERS... AND DROPS BY THE FIRST INTERFEATHER BANK NEXT MORNING!
I DON'T KNOW ABOUT THE BEAGLES YET, AND POMP SADLY DID WELL... BUT I RECOVERED DONALD'S C-NOTE FOR CERTAIN!
FIRST INTERFEATHER BANK
SINCE UNCA DONALD ISN'T BACK YET, WE'LL HAVE TO REPRESENT HIM AT THE BANK!
I'LL TURN ON OUR WALKIE-TALKIE SO HE CAN HEAR WHAT HE OWES THEM!
FIRST INTERFEATHER BANK
FROM $100 TO $1500 IN A DAY! THAT'S GOOD! THE BANK WILL BE TOO HAPPY TO GIVE ME A MILLION-DOLLAR BUSINESS EXPANSION LOAN!
WELL, MR. McDUCK! HERE'S WHERE WE SEE HOW OUR "DUCKBURG 100" COMPETITORS FARED OVER THE LAST 24 HOURS!
SORRY, SIR! THE BEST INVESTMENT UNCA DONALD COULD MANAGE WAS BLOWING HIS DOUGH ON PRICEY, TRENDY-YET-RETRO TOYS!
WALKIE-TALKIES LIKE THIS ONE! SEE?
PATHETIC AND ANACHRONISTIC! NO BUSINESS SENSE! HE NOW OWES A HUNDRED TO US!
"OWES!" SUCH A WONDERFUL WORD!

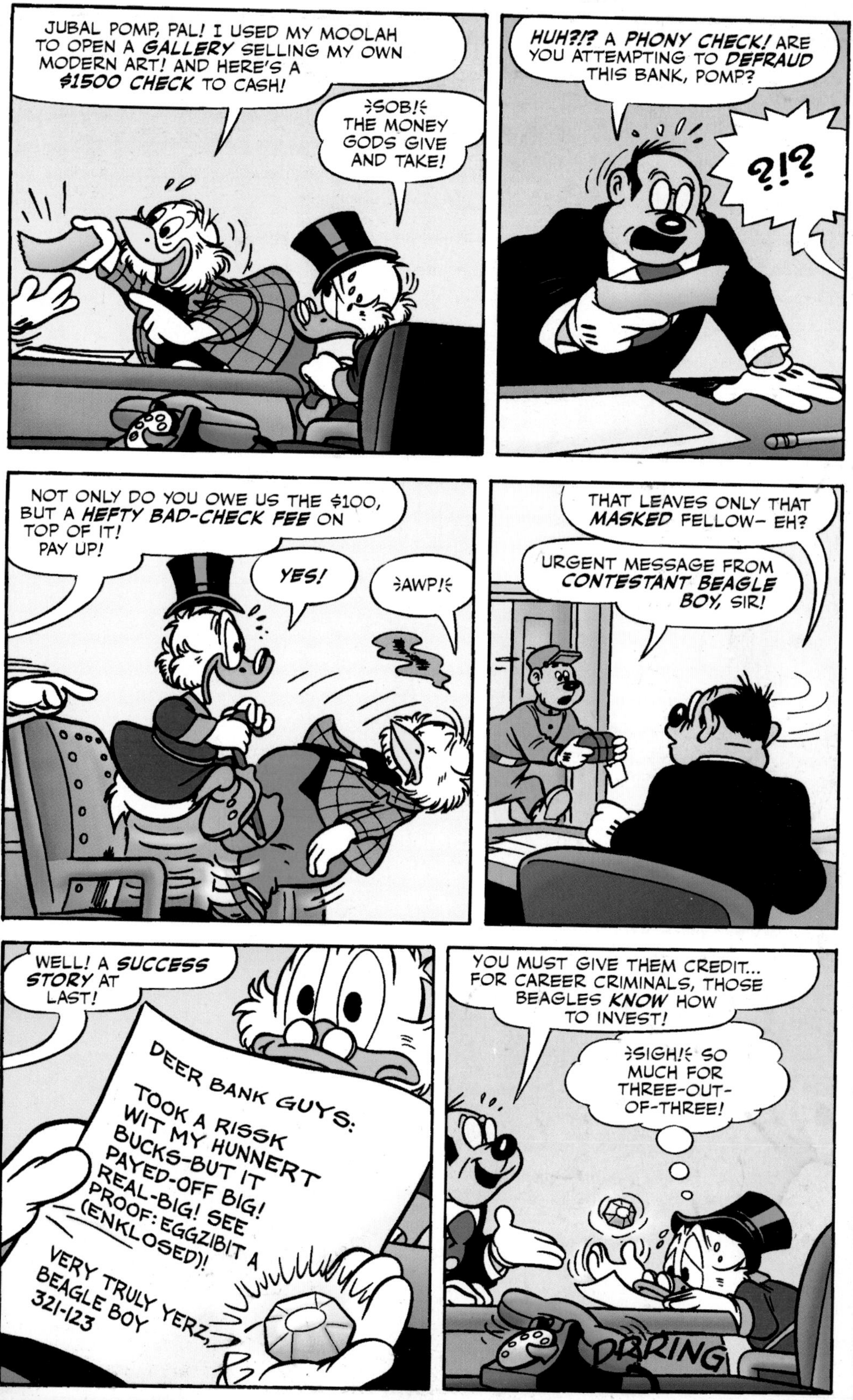
JUBAL POMP, PAL! I USED MY MOOLAH TO OPEN A GALLERY SELLING MY OWN MODERN ART! AND HERE'S A $1500 CHECK TO CASH!
SOB! THE MONEY GODS GIVE AND TAKE!
HUH?!? A PHONY CHECK! ARE YOU ATTEMPTING TO DEFRAUD THIS BANK, POMP?
?!?
NOT ONLY DO YOU OWE US THE $100, BUT A HEFTY BAD-CHECK FEE ON TOP OF IT! PAY UP!
YES!
AWP!
THAT LEAVES ONLY THAT MASKED FELLOW– EH?
URGENT MESSAGE FROM CONTESTANT BEAGLE BOY, SIR!
WELL! A SUCCESS STORY AT LAST!
DEER BANK GUYS:
TOOK A RISSK WIT MY HUNNERT BUCKS–BUT IT PAYED-OFF BIG! REAL-BIG! SEE PROOF: EGGZIBIT A (ENKLOSED)!
VERY TRULY YERZ, BEAGLE BOY 321-123
YOU MUST GIVE THEM CREDIT... FOR CAREER CRIMINALS, THOSE BEAGLES KNOW HOW TO INVEST!
SIGH! SO MUCH FOR THREE-OUT-OF-THREE!
DRRING

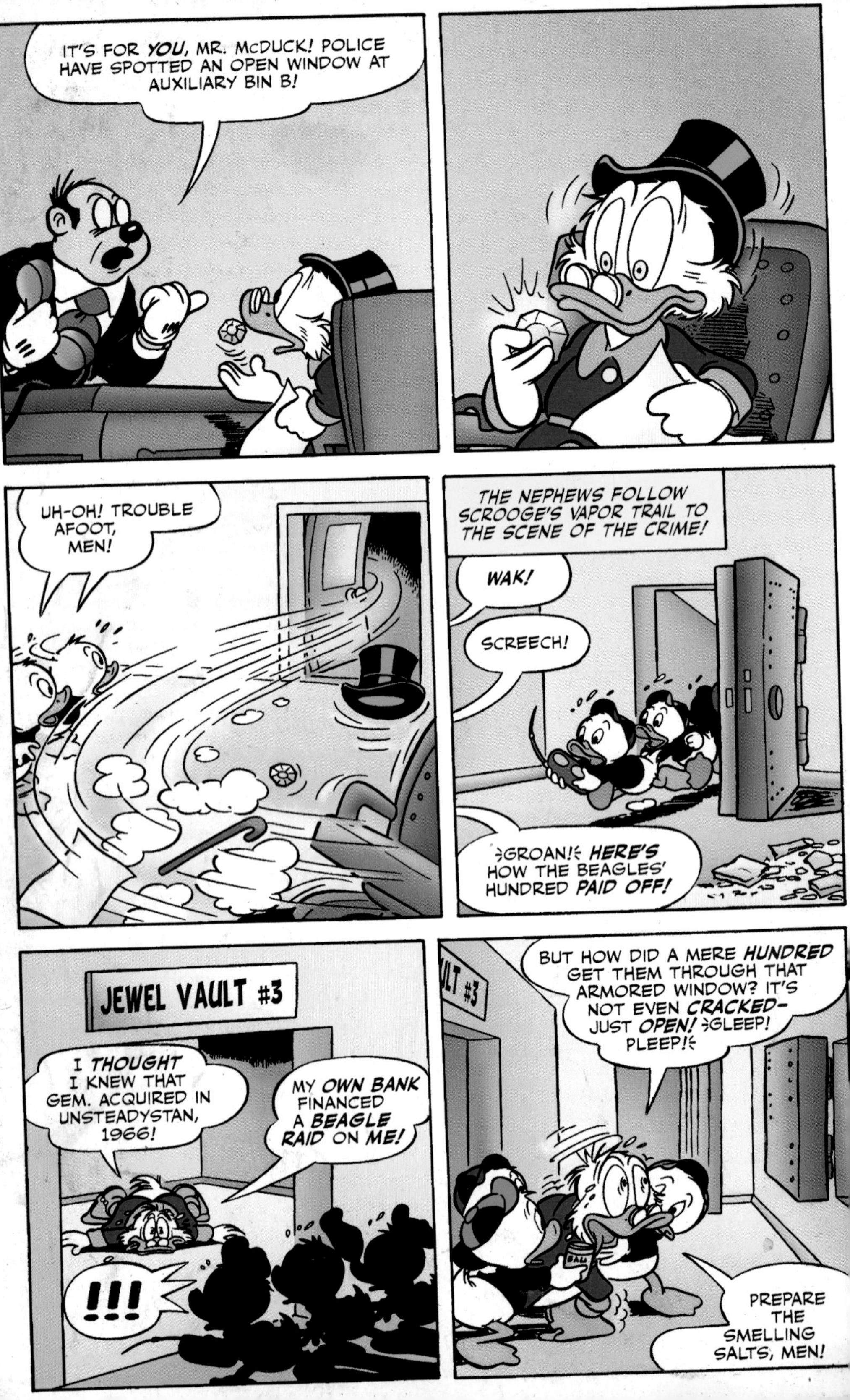
IT'S FOR YOU, MR. McDUCK! POLICE HAVE SPOTTED AN OPEN WINDOW AT AUXILIARY BIN B!
UH-OH! TROUBLE AFOOT, MEN!
THE NEPHEWS FOLLOW SCROOGE'S VAPOR TRAIL TO THE SCENE OF THE CRIME!
WAK!
SCREECH!
GROAN! HERE'S HOW THE BEAGLES' HUNDRED PAID OFF!
JEWEL VAULT #3
I THOUGHT I KNEW THAT GEM. ACQUIRED IN UNSTEADYSTAN, 1966!
MY OWN BANK FINANCED A BEAGLE RAID ON ME!
!!!
BUT HOW DID A MERE HUNDRED GET THEM THROUGH THAT ARMORED WINDOW? IT'S NOT EVEN CRACKED- JUST OPEN! GLEEP! PLEEP!
PREPARE THE SMELLING SALTS, MEN!